THE STRAY SPIRIT

LUTESONG BOOK ONE

R.K. ASHWICK

The Stray Spirit

Copyright © 2022 R.K. Ashwick

RK Ashwick Books

rkashwick.com

ISBN (Paperback): 979-8-9855819-1-1

ISBN (E-Book): 979-8-9855819-2-8

LCCN: 2022906466

First edition August 2022.

Edited by Kim Halstead

Cover art by Andrew Davis

Map & Illustrations by Lucia Vázquez de Prada

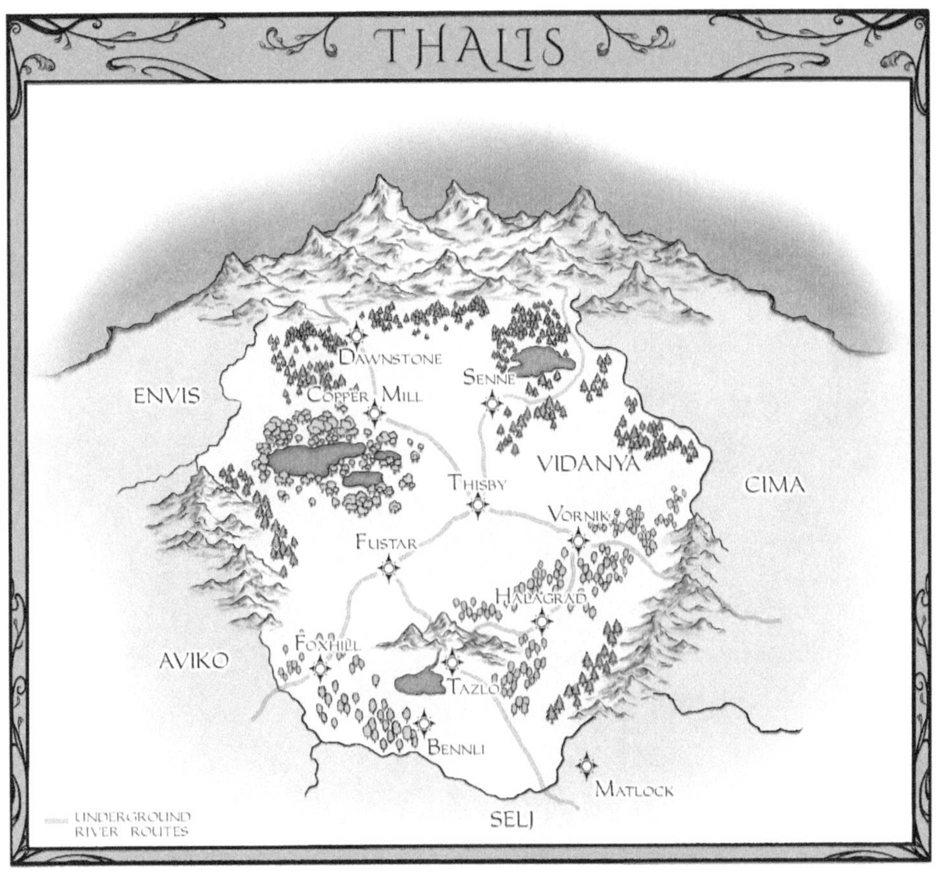

THALIS
ENVIS
DAWNSTONE
COPPER MILL
SENNE
VIDANYA
CIMA
THISBY
VORNIK
FUSTAR
HALAGRAD
FOXHILL
AVIKO
TAZLO
BENNLI
MATLOCK
SELJ
UNDERGROUND
RIVER ROUTES

CONTENTS

CHAPTER

ONE

As a bard, Emry was supposed to enjoy festivals.

And he did, most of the time. He loved the food, fried crisp and dripping with honey. The dancing, all bouncing lines and joyful circles. And above all, he loved the music—the warm echoes of a song in a packed tavern, filling the cracks in the crowd until nothing remained but the melody and the souls listening to it.

But his career had never hinged on such a song before, and so on this, the first night of Sada, he rushed up to the Red Rat tavern and knocked on the door. Heavy footsteps and a short, impatient huff answered from the other side.

"Set the flowers to the left," a stout voice said—distant, as if calling over a shoulder. "No, your *other* left, you—here, I'll just do it."

As the footsteps stomped away from the door, Emry wiped his sweaty palms on his waistcoat and took in the facade of the Red Rat. Like the rest of the plaza, the proud stone building before him shone with festival cheer: white flower garlands, gold banners, an elegant wreath of greenery on the door. But the tavern's exterior was nothing compared to the stage within, nor the crowds it would attract that night. Emry shifted the lute strapped to his back. He

1

couldn't care less about the decorations or drinks. It was the stage he needed.

Then the voice behind the door returned, shorter and gruffer. "There. Now don't touch it. And don't touch that. Actually—don't touch anything." The door finally swung open to reveal Tilla, the owner of the Red Rat, the bags under her eyes hanging as heavy as Sada banners.

"Tilla!" Emry smiled wide. "Happy Sada. I wanted to follow up on—"

Tilla rolled her eyes and began to close the door. "I don't have any openings."

"But"—Emry dropped his smile in a panic and leaned forward—"you said last week you'd have one for me."

Another huff, this one more impatient than the last. "That was before André stopped by with flowers and a pouch of twenty gold." She crossed her broad arms over her apron, where a little red rat was stitched into the corner. "What have you got?"

"I've got, um..." Emry patted his pockets, knowing full well he had two coppers and some lint if he were lucky. "I've got..."

"Happy Sada, Mr. Karic."

"Wait!"

The door slammed shut, and Emry slouched away from it. He enjoyed most festivals, he truly did.

Sada was no longer one of them.

"You don't know what you're missing!" a voice behind him shouted, its sharp edge not directed at him, but toward an inn down the street. "He's loads better than whatever two-bit musician you've got in your lineup tonight, I can promise you that!"

"Oh no." Emry's heart caught in his throat, and he turned to find a young woman with straight black hair and dark eyes staring down a neighboring innkeeper. He began a stiff speed-walk toward her immediately. "Oh no, oh no."

"And another thing!" Stef raised a finger. Emry picked up his pace. He knew he shouldn't have recruited her for this. What on earth was he thinking? "You wouldn't know good music if it slapped you on the—"

"Stef!" He forced another smile her way. "It's all right. We should go."

Her gaze lost none of its fervor as it swung round to him. "It's not all right—he promised you a spot!"

"I did no such thing!" the innkeeper said. Emry gritted his teeth. That was distinctly a lie, and all three of them knew it. But clearly, Sada wasn't the festival of keeping promises.

"We'll be going now. Happy Sada!" He rushed through the words before Stef could open her mouth, and carefully steered her to the edge of the mid-city plaza, away from the line of taverns and inns. "Stef, I appreciate the help, I really do, but I'm not trying to get blacklisted here—"

"Sorry, sorry," she grumbled, then gathered her skirts and sat on a crate of garlands. She peeked into the crate, plucked a white flower from its depths, and nestled it behind her ear. "S'not like that place was worth it, anyway. Their stage is small and their beer is awful."

Emry nodded along and sat on a crate opposite her. The sentiment was kind, but it didn't matter how small the stage was. It was a stage in mid-city Tazlo, on the first night of the new year's festival, in full view of the Guild. If he didn't book a spot tonight, after three years of effort...

"Emry? Stef?"

Emry craned his neck to find the source of the call. It was difficult at first, searching between the carriages, streamers, and gawking tourists—but before long, a man with orange curls and a deep blue Academy coat extricated himself from the crowd, breathing out apologies with every step.

"Excuse me—pardon me, so sorry—ah, there you are!" He stumbled up and grinned at his friends. "Any luck?"

Emry shook his head, and Stef gave an indistinct grumble.

The man deflated. "I'm sorry."

Emry's mood sank further. He was already disappointing himself today—he didn't need to disappoint his roommate, too. "It's fine, Marko."

"It's not fine—they promised you a spot!" Marko gestured to the taverns, his round glasses slipping down his nose.

"That's what I said!" Stef huffed and handed him another flower from the crate. "Here. Stole this just for you."

"Thanks, love." Marko kissed her on the cheek and twirled the flower stem between his fingers. Between his pensive frown and his long Academy coat, he looked every bit the thoughtful student. "And you're sure all of mid-city is booked?"

"All of it." Emry counted off the disappointments on his calloused fingers. "André's troupe bribed the Red Rat. The inn next door gave their stage to their cousin—"

"Who sounds like a dying cow," Stef muttered.

"*Stef.*"

"No, no. She's right." Marko nodded across the plaza. "What about the renovated alehouse? They're new, they need someone fresh on the stage."

Emry's ire flared. "They said..." He flexed the fingers he had been counting on, then set down his hand and sighed. "I don't want to talk about it."

Stef looked at Marko. "They don't want a northerner."

"They don't want a northerner!" Emry burst, launching out of his seat. "Can you believe that? As if they've ever been to Senne. As if they've ever seen any of the stages up there—!" Stef giggled, and he set his hands on his hips. "What?"

"Your accent." She tried and failed to swallow more giggles. "It comes out when you're angry."

His anger melted, and he twisted his mouth to keep from smiling. "Give me that." Before she could react, he plucked the flower out of her hair and stuck it into his own dark curls.

"Excuse you!" Stef slapped Emry's arm, then tugged on Marko's sleeve. "Marko, are you witnessing this thievery?"

But Marko wasn't paying attention to their petty squabble—he had twisted to look back out at the square, where two swirls of commotion had caught his eye.

The first was just ahead of them—a small huddle of musicians crowded around the stoop of the Red Rat, murmuring to each other and pointing. A rock settled in Emry's gut. That was André's troupe, down twenty gold and up one Sada opportunity.

The second bit of commotion was what the troupe was pointing to, what everyone else in the square was gawking at. It was the entire reason Emry needed that mid-city stage.

"Is that...?" Stef stood up, her hand still on Marko's arm. Marko nodded.

"Ella Sorman," he breathed. "That's her."

Emry rose to his feet to watch the woman descend from her carriage. Against the stark white Sada banners, she was a visual commotion in her own right. Her bright Avikan kaftan dragged along the cobblestones, and her brown fingers sparkled with gemstones. As she swept off toward the Lamb's Ear Inn—her performance space for all three nights of the festival—the golden pegs of her lute flashed in the sunset.

"How much do you think that cost?" Marko asked, almost whispering out of reverence. "All that gold?"

"I'm sure the Auric Guild covers it," Emry murmured. Gold was the music guild's symbol, after all—and as the oldest and brightest of its members, Ella Sorman surely merited a great deal of it.

As the woman of the hour disappeared into the inn, Emry swallowed. She would be one of many Guild members descending into Tazlo that night—and with their descent, every single musician in mid-city now had the chance to be noticed by them. Every bribing bard, every dying-cow lutenist.

Everyone except for Emry Karic.

"Come on, let's get out of here." Stef looped an arm around both boys' elbows and led them away, wrinkling her nose at the laughter spilling out of the Red Rat as they passed. "We'll figure something out."

THEY ESCAPED TO A TINY, tree-shaded overlook above the square, affording themselves an excellent view of both the crowds and the waterfall plunging the length of the city. Emry leaned against the railing and let the mist settle on his tawny, freckled skin. In mid-city's eagerness for Sada opulence, they had swathed even this spot in festival regalia: golden banners on the balustrade, white petals on the ground, flower garlands hanging from the tree.

The gaiety of the space only made his situation more depressing.

"I don't think I have a choice," he said as Marko leaned against the railing next to him. "I'll have to play at the Dancing Rabbit tonight."

"What, all the way up-city?" Stef toyed with one of the pennants, its embroidered sheaf of wheat twisting under her touch. It was the symbol of the goddess Hara, plastered all about the city to attract luck for the new year. Emry could almost feel the emblem laughing at him. "Isn't there anything farther down?"

Emry tensed. "The stages are all too close to the caves. I can't risk it."

Stef frowned at him. "Your family won't be in town, not on Sada."

"I can't risk it, Stef." Just the thought of it made his heart pound in his ears, until thinking of the remote, up-city stage almost soothed him. "There's nothing else to do. I'll go to Bron at the Dancing Rabbit and tell him I—"

The ground jolted underneath them, cutting off his words. Stef pitched forward with a yelp, and Emry grabbed her arm to steady her.

"You all right?" he called over the rumbling. She nodded, but he hardly registered it—for above him, the leaves in the tree were glowing white, as if they had trapped a patch of starlight. "What in Weir's name is this?"

"Don't worry, it'll be over soon!" Marko said as he helped Stef to the railing, and for a moment, the three of them froze there in wide, tense stances. Out in the street, passersby clutched at street lamps and each other for support. Streamers and garlands shivered and dropped from their perches. One such bloom dropped past Emry's nose, down to his boots—and withered before his eyes.

"What the—?" He turned to Marko, but before his friend could respond, everything stopped. The quake, the rumbling. Even the light in the tree winked out, as if it had never been there.

Once he was sure everything had settled, Emry slowly released his grip on the railing and shifted it to the lute strap crossing his chest. "Have you seen that before?" he asked, his eyes drifting up to the tree. Of the flowers that remained there, a scattering of them rattled in the breeze, as browned and shriveled as the one at his feet.

"'Course I have," Marko said, brushing flower petals off his sleeves with a casual shrug. "Saw it once before, when I first moved here. Did you not get surges in Senne?"

Marko wasn't the only one unshaken by the encounter. Stef was smoothing out her skirts, and out in the street, the passersby had resumed their normal flow. Their chatter was louder than before, but still casual, more curious than afraid.

"Surges?" Emry repeated. "*That's* what that was?"

"They're a southern thing," Stef said, her central accent clipping the words for emphasis. "Just harmless earthquakes, that's all they are. They pass by every five years or so. You've been in Tazlo for what, four years?"

"Three."

"Ah. Makes sense you haven't seen one, then." She picked a lingering petal out of Marko's hair and tossed it at Emry. "Hope another one doesn't hit while you're performing tonight. Wouldn't be fun trying to play through that, would it?"

Emry grimaced and shifted the lute on his back. *Fun* didn't sound quite right. *Bad luck* sounded more accurate, and far more in line with how his day was going.

"Well, I'm going to head to the Dancing Rabbit." He sighed and faced the steep road heading up-city. "You two enjoy yourselves down here, all right?"

They both took a step toward him.

"Down here?" Stef snorted. "We're coming with you."

"What?" He turned back with a frown. "Don't you want to catch one of the Guild members? Ella Sorman, or Karlson, or the Quartet—"

"Sure, we could catch one of them." Marko set an arm around Stef's shoulders. "But I hear it's good luck to spend the new year with a friend."

Emry cast a sheepish grin toward the cobblestones. He didn't deserve them; he truly didn't. "Thank you. But..." He took a steadying breath and toed the dried petals at his feet. The quake had ended, but his nerves hadn't yet settled. "If you don't mind, there's something I'd like to do first."

CHAPTER

TWO

"EMRY, are you sure there's a fane all the way out here?"

A playful *thwack* sounded behind Emry—Stef's hand against Marko's arm. "What, afraid the forest ghosts will get you?"

"*No.*"

Emry smiled, keeping his gaze forward into the darkening trees. "I'm sure we're almost there, Marko."

As they hiked farther away from the edge of the city, Emry took a deep breath, letting the scents of pine and soil wash out the festival perfume of pies and beer. Even after years of being away, it was still strange to him—if he were back in Senne, *this* was where the throngs of people would be. Not in the square, not in the taverns or the inns or the streets. The musicians would be wandering amongst the trees, offering gifts to the goddess Hara and her spirits with the hope they would be returned through the earth's bounty. Surely, at this very moment, his parents and sisters were looking at pines just like these. Perhaps they were singing the same songs he was about to perform.

Emry swallowed hard and kept walking. Thinking of his family wasn't going to help settle his nerves.

"Listen"—Marko cut into his thoughts with a warble—"I know

9

Bron said there was a fane in this area, but these things get torn down all the time. Maybe we should—"

Stef stopped. "Wait, is that it?"

Emry had to hold back a laugh. If Stef hadn't pointed it out, he would have walked right past it.

It was a small spit of a fane, little more than a wooden box on a tilted stake. Moss and cobwebs camouflaged the wood into the aspen grove behind it; Emry had to squint to keep its shape in focus.

"I'll just be a minute," he reassured Marko, then walked up to the fane. Long ago, someone in Tazlo must have built the little shrine in honor of the grove's spirit. They would have traded offerings here for love, or bounty, or luck...

Emry stooped to peer into the box, and found nothing but autumn leaves and dirt. Apparently, Tazlins had no need of spirits' gifts anymore.

"Anyone have any fruit?" he asked as he cleared away the leaves and cobwebs. It had been a while since he had visited a fane, but he had the sense to know this wasn't a respectful level of upkeep. "Fruit's the traditional offering, but spirits will take just about anything..." He turned to find Marko and Stef shaking their heads. "Fair enough."

He dug out a worn copper from his pocket, slotted it into the cubby, then stepped back to admire the grove. Even in the dying light, the stark white bark and yellow leaves of the aspen trees stood strong against the darkening pines. When he focused on the rustling branches and crisp breeze, he could almost forget about the Guild for a moment. About the surge, about his family, about Sada...

"So...does the spirit appear or something?" Marko ventured. Stef rolled her eyes. "What? My family doesn't do this sort of thing, not since the farm dried out. What does your town do?"

Stef scoffed. "Nothing. Spirits don't exist." As soon as the words left her lips, she clapped a hand to her mouth and looked to Emry. "I mean, um—not for us in Thisby! But in Senne, I'm sure it's... different..."

But the damage was already done. The charm of the grove winked away, leaving nothing but a bent coin, a silly wooden box, and the sounds of the city wafting in from beyond the pines.

"No," Emry said quickly, shoving his hands in his pockets. "Stef's right, they don't exist." Before either of them could make any feeble reassurances, he started back down the path and shot them a false grin. "Now, what say you to a few songs at the Dancing Rabbit? I think I owe you that much, at least."

TAZLO'S BUILDINGS shrank and withered on the vine as the trio plodded up the mountain. Here, the Sada decorations hung along crumbling eaves, the fabric worn by years of repeated use. For better or for worse, Emry's wardrobe looked more at home on these streets —his faded waistcoat and frayed coat were as tired as the banners and the people he walked by. He turned to make a comment on it, and found Marko and Stef in a whispering match.

"You tell him—"

"No, *you* tell him."

Emry frowned. "Listen, if I've got a stain on my shirt, please tell me now before I go on stage."

Marko raised his hands. "No, no stain!"

"It's nothing!" Stef cleared her throat. "He was just telling me about his day at work."

"At the library, you mean?" Emry looked to Marko, who began to fiddle with his glasses.

"Another boring day," he said quickly. "Just Academy students spilling brandy on the books, and all that." He gave a weak laugh and pointed to a building up ahead. "You want to go in?"

They had reached the Dancing Rabbit, a squat little tavern so far up-city that the air felt thinner. The tavern's regulars called the place well-loved; Emry called it a structural hazard. Its walls bowed, its ceiling sagged. The only things keeping the place together were a few rotting beams and a prayer.

But then its usual warm chatter wafted through the windows, and Emry relaxed. Perhaps it was a structural hazard, but the regulars weren't wrong. It *was* well-loved.

"Mr. Karic!" A bald man at the bar tossed a greasy towel over his shoulder and spread his burly arms wide in a welcoming gesture. "Finally, Sada can begin!"

A few of the regulars around him cheered and raised their mugs in agreement as Emry approached the barkeep, feeling a similar sort of ease that the grove had briefly provided. It was always reassuring to hear Bron's northern accent, even if years of living down south had rounded the edges. "Happy Sada, Bron."

"May Hara bring you luck." Bron's grin faltered as he offered Emry a beer. "I thought you said you were looking elsewhere tonight. Not abandoning me for mid-city after all?"

"How could I not play for you?" Emry accepted the beer. "Sada just wouldn't be the same."

It wasn't a total lie. This dead end of a stage was...comfortable. It was where he had met Marko and Stef, where he had gotten his first —and most reliable—Tazlo gig. Playing here for three years meant that Emry knew which songs bounced off the old beams above, which jokes rattled the windows with laughter. The faces looking at him over their mugs were ones he had made smile many times before.

Then a cold realization seeped into his bones. If he didn't break into mid-city this Sada, he could be playing at the Dancing Rabbit for years to come. Staying in up-city forever, never playing for the Guild.

Never making it back home.

"You can grace us whenever you like, Mr. Karic," Bron said, nodding to the empty corner that constituted a stage.

Another false smile crept onto Emry's face—it would become a permanent fixture, if this rotting festival didn't end soon—as he dragged a stool over to the corner. Cheers and whistles peppered the room as he settled in with his lute.

"Thank you!" He waved, winking to Marko and Stef at a table near the front. "What a welcome. I see Bron's hogwash has already made several of you delirious. Good start to Sada, good start."

A smattering of laughter made the rest of the room focus on him. He tried not to look any of them directly in the eyes.

"Who'd like to make a request for the first song of the festival?" he called. "Pick a bad song and you're cursed for the rest of the year. No pressure, though."

Emry forced himself to shed his anxiety as he played. The festival was still young, after all, bearing promises of joy and entertainment for both the singer and the audience—and so on the first night, very little expectation was thrown onto either party. Emry could joke in between songs, wander around the tables, make up a lyric based off how poorly Bron was dancing in the back of the bar. And in return, the tavern was free to sing as off-key as they liked, tapping their feet and pounding on tables. All Emry had to do was to play well, sing loud, and make sure his audience was excited to do it all over again the next evening.

At the end of the set, he collapsed into a chair at his friends' table while Marko shoved a beer his way.

"Bravo, as always." Marko pushed his shoulder and grinned. "Mid-city doesn't know what they're missing."

"Clearly, you didn't hear this stupid thing squeaking halfway through." Emry jerked his head toward his lute. That was another downside to three years of slogging in Tazlo—he had run out of money for repairs months ago.

"I didn't hear a thing," Stef reassured him. "If I didn't know better, I'd swear you trained at the Academy."

"Do I look like a student to you, Stef?" Emry took a sip of his beer. "Actually, don't answer that."

Stef lifted her own mug and muttered into it. "Cal certainly thought you did."

Emry choked on his beer.

"Stef!" Marko shot her a look, and Stef shot him one right back. Emry set down his mug, coughing. Whatever those looks meant, he didn't care for them to linger.

"Come on, what's going on with you two?" he managed through his spluttering.

"Nothing!" Marko blurted. "Um—do you want to come down to the square with us? We haven't seen the place all lit up yet."

It was a tempting thought, once Emry regained his breath and his friends' faces smoothed out. Marko wasn't talking about the street lamps, or the candles, or the oil lamps dotting every Tazlin window. Emry glanced at the white flower still in Stef's hair, now glowing blue in reaction to the tavern chatter around them. A rhythm bloom, Tazlo's unique Sada signature.

In daylight, it was difficult to tell the rhythm blooms apart from a simple white camellia. But in any kind of darkness, and with any kind of sound, they sparked. As the trio stepped out of the Dancing Rabbit and gazed down the mountain, they could already see the lines of pale garlands strung across the mid-city square, rippling with a gentle blue light as music tumbled out of every open door and window. Those dancing underneath absorbed the ethereal glow as they spun, their laughter and singing sending fireworks of turquoise up the strands in return. As the festival grew and the night deepened, the entire square glittered with the joy of a city seeking luck for the new year.

But while Marko and Stef linked arms and began their stroll into the blue light, Emry remained still. This was how Tazlo celebrated Sada, sure. But not how he once did.

"You go on ahead." He waved them along. "I'll meet you there."

As they disappeared, Emry shifted his lute on his back and veered once more down the dark forest path.

CHAPTER
THREE

ONE CHILLY WALK LATER, Emry found himself back in front of the fane. Nighttime now obscured the bright colors of the aspen grove, but had traded them for another color—the soft blue of several rhythm blooms, spared from Tazlo's Sada harvest. They pulsed gently in the middle of the grove, murmuring in response to the insects of the night and the last of the birdsong.

Emry picked his way into the ring of aspen trees, careful not to crush any of the rhythm blooms under his feet. He swung his lute around. Plucked a few strings to check the tuning. Looked up at the largest tree in the grove.

And felt very stupid.

"I—" he said aloud, then winced. His loud voice had no place here, but he felt the need to talk nonetheless. "I don't normally do this. Up north, you see, they…" He fidgeted. "Listen, I know you're not actually there, but—but I just really need the luck, all right? I, um…" He set his fingers into place on the strings. If he closed his eyes, he could almost pretend he was back in Senne. That his family stood behind him, waiting for him to start.

Alone now, he said, "I hope you like this, I guess."

He closed his eyes and began to sing.

When the gods begin to fight,
Through ground, rivers, trees, and light
Dance your way to Hara's shield
Follow her voice, she will not yield

To Shiro, who shakes and steals our souls
Or Weir, who turns our trees to coals
She will not yield, she will defeat
These gods, though this war will repeat

So dance your way to Hara's shield
Through cold and dark, she will not yield

Performing here was nothing like performing at the Dancing Rabbit, or anywhere else for that matter. He wasn't sure whether it was the springy moss under his feet, the gentle buffeting of the wind, or the lack of observers, but the music simply felt easier. His voice smoother, his lute less prone to its usual creaking and buzzing. It allowed him to shed his fear of mistakes, that tightly wound tension of waiting for a faulty sound, until singing there in the grove lifted him into weightlessness. Like his body hardly existed anymore, and the words floated up to the trees of their own accord. Even his hands melted away as they flitted across the lute, leaving nothing but the feeling of his voice in his head and the hum of the strings at his fingers.

When he finished the song and opened his eyes, he felt unsteady, as if his legs had forgotten how to walk. He shook his head in an attempt to ground himself.

But as he steadied and looked around, everything was just as it was before. No spirit appearing, no manifestation of luck. Just a man, standing in a forest, playing for a tree. Emry gave a small, humorless laugh at himself and turned back toward the path.

"Where are you going?" a voice asked. "I liked it."

Emry nearly sprang out of his skin.

"Who's there?" He whipped around. No one stood on the path. No one in the grove, either, save for him.

"Me. I'm here," the voice said again, bright and friendly.

Still no one around.

"That's rather unspecific." Emry's grip on his lute tightened. "Where are you, and what are you doing here?"

"What sort of question is that? I live here."

Slowly, he turned to the aspen tree. "This is a trick, right?" He leaned to look behind the trunk. "Whoever you are, you better show yourself—"

The gentle buzz of the insects around him abruptly went silent.

Then the ground jerked out from underneath his feet, sending him down into the moss. As he scrambled to his feet, the ground continued to shake, and he stumbled over to the tree for support. He dared one more peek around it. No one there.

As the quake intensified, the leaves of the tree and the surrounding grove began to glow white, like before. Emry squinted as the glow grew—being so surrounded by trees, the light was much stronger here than it had been at the mid-city terrace.

"Oh no..." There was the voice again. Through the rumbling, it sounded...rather young.

"It'll be okay!" Emry shouted, trying to glance up at the branches —perhaps there was a child who had climbed too high?—but the bright light forced him to close his eyes. "These surges are normal, apparently!"

A splintering crack jarred his ears, and the bark under his hands began to shift. Opening one eye against the glow, Emry watched as the smooth white bark of the aspen tree wrinkled and warped below his fingers. As it twisted, the surface blackened as if it were burning.

"No, it's not fine!" the voice shouted in a panic. "I'm not going to be able to hold on much longer. Can I borrow you?"

Emry staggered back from the trunk. "What do you mean, borrow me?" All around him, the brilliant light sent flashes of pain through his eyelids. "Listen, I can catch you if that's what you need!"

"Yes! Sort of!"

"What kind of answer is that—"

"Get ready!"

The trees all burst into a blinding glow. Emry yelled and in an instinctive flinch, threw his lute up in front of his face. As he raised his arms, something slammed into the lute, shoving the instrument into his chest and throwing him back onto the ground.

Then it all stopped. The quaking, the glow, the voice. The insects slowly resumed their evening song around him. Gasping for breath, Emry cracked his eyes open, expecting to see someone sitting on him.

But no one was there—just the lute.

"What is this?" the voice from the quake panted. As it spoke, the strings of the lute vibrated, and Emry realized the voice was floating up from the rose of the lute. "This isn't your body! This is...how did I get in here?"

"Shiro's hairy foot, what in the—?" Emry pushed the lute off of him and scrambled backward. "Are you inside my...and you were inside that..." He pointed at the tree, then stared at the instrument. This was a spirit. An actual, living spirit who—who...

His hand settled on his own chest, taut with the aftershock of fear. "I'm sorry, did you just try to *possess* me?"

"I didn't have a choice!" the spirit argued. "Look around you! That quake was about to push me out of my grove. I needed to attach to something new, or else—or else I'd die!"

Emry didn't have to look far to see what the spirit was talking about. In front of him, the once-pristine aspen tree was now bent and wrinkled, its surface entirely black. Shriveled leaves floated down from the dead branches, slowly burying the few rhythm blooms that had survived.

Emry swallowed and looked back at the instrument. "So you're... what, you're in my lute now?"

"Is that what this stupid thing is called?" the spirit asked. "Then yes. I'm not sure how, but I suppose I'm in it. Temporarily." They gave a frustrated sigh. "Now. If you don't mind, I'd like to take a look around. Could you walk around my tree with this thing, please?"

"What? No!" Emry scrambled to his feet, his heart in his throat. His most valuable possession, his only tool to secure any sort of future, was rotting *talking*— "Get out of my lute!"

"I can't," the spirit said, quieter this time. Their hard little breaths made the strings shiver. "It took all my energy to detach myself from my tree. Maybe in a few weeks, I could attach to another one—"

"A few *weeks*?" Emry grabbed at his hair. "Are you kidding me?"

"I don't know what kidding is. Is that like joking?"

"Yes!"

"Ah. Then no, I'm not kidding you."

Emry froze, his thoughts twisting into knots faster than he could unravel them. "But—so—if you're here...if you're *real*, then..."

He thought back to the coin he had left at the fane. No, not just that fane—all the fanes he had ever visited, all the groves he had ever sung at. Were those spirits real, too? Did they ever listen to his songs?

Did they ever pay attention to his pleas for luck?

"*Excuse* me!" the spirit pestered, interrupting his silent questions. "Can you show me around my grove now, please?"

Emry glared at the lute. He could never quite manage the same sharpness in his gaze that Stef bore so easily, but he did his best now. "You don't actually bestow luck, do you?" he snapped.

The spirit paused. "How on earth would I do that?"

A wave of anger, unexpected and unbridled, washed over him, and he stalked a circle around the lute, hands sunk into his curls.

"All the songs and the offerings. All the festivals and the stories and the ceremonies and the..." He gestured to the air. "They don't matter, do they? You don't give luck. You don't watch out for us on Hara's behalf. You just sit in a tree all day, don't you?" He stopped walking. "Can spirits do *anything* for humans?"

"Well, I"—the spirit spluttered—"I don't know how to give you luck, but—look, here!" A single rhythm bloom grew by the neck of the lute. "There you go, that's something. *Now* can you show me around?"

Emry stared at the single, insulting flower—then he strode over to the fane. "That's it. I'm taking back that coin I gave you."

"But—but it's not my fault I'm not lucky!" the spirit whined as he reached for the cubby. "And the coin is shiny. I like it. Please, leave it there? Please?"

Now that Emry could hear the voice more clearly, it was indeed young. More than a few years younger than him—though perhaps not as childlike as what he had pictured during the surge. A twinge of guilt surfaced, and he dropped his hand, his fingers brushing the edge of the fane. "Fine." Arms folded, he walked back into the grove. "You wanted to look at your tree or something?"

"Yes, please."

Emry picked up the lute, noting that it felt a bit heavier now, and circled around the dead tree while he wracked his brain for a solution to this new problem. Never mind mid-city versus up-city now—how in Shiro's name was he supposed to perform at all with a talking lute?

His gaze wandered to the surrounding trees. If this spirit was real, surely there were others. "So, this place..."

"Hold on." The spirit shushed him. "Oh, this is terrible—just look at the bark! This took so long to grow, too. It was the best tree in my grove."

"This forest, does it have any—"

"I don't think I can save it at all. How could something like this happen?"

Emry rushed through his words. "Are there any other spirits nearby?"

The spirit huffed. "There's one north of here. We talk through the roots sometimes. Though honestly, it's mostly me talking, they don't really answer. But I know they're there, I can feel it—"

Emry glanced up the path. "Would they know how to get you out of my lute?"

"Um...maybe?"

"All right. Are you done inspecting your grove?"

The spirit fell silent, as if it were giving the place one last, longing look. "I...suppose. But I *will* be back here soon."

Emry slung the lute onto his back and made for the path. "Agreed."

FOUR

THE ROAD farther up the mountain veered closer to the city before twisting away, giving Emry a moment to peek at what the Tazlins had thought of the latest quake. Any music up-city had stopped, leaving only the frenzied chatter of people taking to the streets to recount the event. Though he couldn't make out any specific stories, a few of them pointed to the forest and the blackened trees that now peppered his walk. One of the gossiper's gazes landed on him as they pointed.

"Hey! You all right?" they called. Emry stiffened.

"Fine, just fine!" He waved and hurried away until the path tucked him into the woods once more.

"Are we not going to talk to the other humans?" the spirit asked. Emry rubbed the growing ache in his forehead.

"We? No, *we* are not going to talk to the other humans right now."

They continued walking in silence, until Emry heard little muffled efforts coming from inside the lute, and the instrument shifted on his back. "Hey, don't break anything in there. This thing is barely useable as it is—"

"Sorry," the spirit grumbled. "I'm trying to get comfortable in this stupid not-tree of yours."

"Not-tree?"

"It feels like a tree, but it isn't. I don't like it."

"You're free to hop out any time."

"I told you, I can't—"

Emry sighed. "Yes, I'm aware."

"Why are you angry with me?" the spirit said. "It's not like I wanted to be in this lute."

"I didn't want it, either. All *I* wanted was a bit of luck," Emry snapped. "But clearly that was a mistake."

The instrument went quiet. "I'm sorry. I'd give you some luck if I knew how."

The young spirit did sound truly remorseful, and another pang of guilt softened Emry's tone as they walked. "As long as we're talking" —he hopped over a branch in the path—"why did that surge burn your tree? I thought these things were harmless."

"Surge?"

He waved at the canopy. "The quake and the glow and all."

"Oh, that." The spirit hesitated. "I'm not sure. Normally they're... the word you used. Harmless."

"But you said it was going to kill you."

"I don't know how to explain it to a human."

Emry rolled his eyes as he dipped under a low pine bough. "Try me."

"The surge is..." Another pause, as if the spirit was looking around for answers. "It's like it's made up of the same stuff I am. And my tree was trying to take it in, but it was too much, and it was shoving me out, and it was *rude!*" The spirit let out a breath and gathered themself. "So I had to jump to something else to survive. And now I'm in here."

"And you can't just"—Emry waved a hand—"float around or something until it's over?"

He could have sworn the lute bristled.

"Sure. *I'll* try floating, and *you* try not breathing!"

Emry held up his hands. "Sorry, I get it."

He hoped that would be the end of it, but the farther they walked, the more the spirit chattered, even as his eyes drooped and his feet ached.

"That tree *was* my favorite, you know," they said. "It even stored my rock collection. But if this other spirit knows how to get me back in sooner, I suppose I can jump into the tree to the south. Won't have quite the same view. Gets a lot of sapsuckers. Not as many flowers on that side, either, so I'll have to grow some—"

Emry grimaced as rocks poked through his threadbare shoes. "Please tell me we're almost there."

"Oh, wait—walk back a bit. You passed it."

"Hara take me."

Emry turned as he was bid and shuffled back until he spotted a dying glimmer—a single rhythm bloom, half-wilted in a tree's shadow. The only sound that drew out its light was the breeze that whispered through the grove.

The spirit didn't say anything for a while.

"So do I have to leave another coin or something to get them to answer our questions?" Emry craned his neck to search around the grove. "Play another song? Wish for more bad luck? Should I find another lute to—"

"They're not here," the spirit said.

"But you told me to walk here."

"I mean they're not *here*. They're gone."

"Oh." Emry's embarrassment intermingled with panic. "Well, maybe I'm not close enough for you to sense them. How about now?" He hopped off the path and walked in circles. "Anything?"

"No."

"How about over here?"

"No, I can't feel them." The spirit's voice quaked. "I don't think they made it through the surge."

"But..." Emry touched the nearest tree, running his fingers

against the dry, twisted bark. As he pulled his hand away, black soot streaked his fingertips. "I see."

The lute sank lower on Emry's back, and his stomach began to churn. He had only just discovered that spirits were alive.

And now he knew that spirits could die.

"I'm sorry you lost your friend," he mumbled.

"Me too."

They stood at the tree for a moment, Emry biting his lip. The folktales never said anything regarding spirit funerals. He supposed he would need to make something up.

Not that he wasn't used to making up melodies, but this was a little different.

"Did the spirit have a name?" he ventured.

"A name?"

"Sure. Might help to say their name and say something nice about them. That's what humans do, at least."

The lute shifted. "That sounds nice. To...Oak, I guess. You were a quiet spirit." They paused. "Was that good?"

"Very good." A thought surfaced as Emry picked his way back to the path. "Speaking of names—do you have one? I didn't ask before."

"I'm Aspen. What's your name?"

"Emry Karic."

"Hello, Emry. I think I'm supposed to say it's nice to meet you, but..." They trailed off, and Emry found his gaze dragged back to the dead tree. He got the sense that Aspen was looking at it, too.

"I don't understand," Aspen said. "I don't understand any of this. How could this happen to my grove? To theirs?"

"Whatever it was, you survived it," Emry tried to reassure them. "We'll get you back to your tree very soon, and you'll be just fine."

"But what about after that? What if it happens again?" The lute shifted again, as if Aspen were pacing back and forth. "I have to know what it was. How to protect my home. That was my strongest tree, you see. If another one of those surges comes along and I can't detach in time..."

Emry set his jaw as he glanced up at the moon, latticed by branches. "Let's get back to town first," he said. "Neither of us is going to get any answers standing here."

EMRY'S THOUGHTS swam in circles as he hurried back to the city. Marko and Stef would come looking for him if he didn't show his face in the square soon. If he sprinted home, hid the lute under his bed, buried it under every article of clothing he owned...but then how would he even pay rent this month? He could go into debt on an even cheaper lute—impossible—and squeak his way through a few more performances up-city. Mid-city was far out of the question at this point...

"So, the other humans in town," Aspen said as soon as the city lights blinked through the trees, "do they all have lutes?"

"No, they don't, and hush. I can't have them hearing you."

"Why?"

"Because—because..." Emry dropped his shoulders. There was no kind way to say this. "You're not supposed to exist, Aspen. Not just you. Spirits. Any spirit. You're not supposed to actually live in trees, or—or talk out of my only rotting source of income—"

"What do you mean, not exist?" The lute's strings vibrated angrily. "Addie's stories always talked about spirits. And you mentioned the stories yourself!"

"Wait, who's Addie?"

But the spirit kept going. "I thought humans knew I was there. You knew earlier that I was there! You gave me a coin and a song."

Emry's cheeks flushed. "I was being polite, in a sense. I didn't actually know you were there."

"Oh." Aspen paused. "Well...well, I did like the song. What was its name?"

Emry slipped into an alleyway, toeing the line of the up-city lantern light as people passed. "'Hara's Shield.' An old song from up north."

"That's lovely. No one's ever sung for me before, you know." The spirit's voice brightened. "Once I get back to my grove, will you do it again?"

Emry found himself regretting his plan to shove the lute under his bed. "Sure, of course. But in order to get back to your tree, you're going to have to be quiet around the other humans, all right?"

"Fine."

Emry glanced around, hand gripping the strap of his lute tightly. Though the music had resumed, groups of Tazlins still huddled together on the road, no longer reflecting back the joy of the festival in their voices or faces. He made a note of each huddle that dotted his path home, anyone who might notice that his lute now had a voice of its own. If he took a shortcut over the bridge and sprinted through a few side streets, he could get back to his crumbling little flat in—

"Emry!" someone called from downhill. Emry swore under his breath. Marko was puffing his way up the street toward him.

"Marko!" His voice went up an octave, and he cleared his throat. "You feel that surge—?"

"Where have you been?" Marko's chest heaved as they met in the street. "I've been looking all over for you!"

"Was, ah, just on my way to look for you," Emry said. "Wanted to see if you were—"

"Tilla wants you to play at the Red Rat."

CHAPTER

FIVE

EMRY STOPPED BREATHING.

"When?"

"Tonight. Now." Marko gestured downhill. "That idiot André got spooked by the surge, says it's bad luck to play after it, or something like that. Stranded the rest of his troupe just before they were about to go back on. If you don't get down there fast, Tilla's going to lose her whole crowd." When Emry gaped like a fish, Marko beamed and shook his shoulder. "Come on, this is what you were hoping for, right? The Red Rat! First night of Sada! Guild members everywhere!"

Emry tried to match his smile. "Yes—yes, absolutely! Thank you for finding me. I'll head over now. Meet you down there?"

"Wouldn't miss it! I just need to find Stef."

Emry set off at a terrified jog, barely having the wherewithal to avoid the spilled puddles of beer and wine trickling down the cobblestones. "Hara hates me. That's it, that's all there is to it."

"What's going on?" Aspen's voice perked up behind him.

"I need to perform tonight. With the lute." Emry wiped sweat off his brow. "Can this thing still even play?"

He staggered to a halt in a shadowed alleyway, tuned the strings

31

with shaky fingers, and plucked out the first few chords of "Hara's Shield." The lute still worked, at least—but something sounded different. He leaned closer to the instrument and tried the chords again, but the general clamor of the city cloaked the nuance he was straining to hear.

"Tickles a bit," Aspen muttered. This did nothing to help Emry's heart rate.

"Aspen, if I'm going to perform, you *have* to stay quiet."

"All right."

"I mean completely silent—"

"Fine! I said all right!"

If Emry's thoughts had been treading water earlier, they were drowning now. What if the possession made the lute sound worse? What if Aspen tried to sing along? Or sneezed? Did spirits sneeze?

His mind was still bouncing between catastrophizing and asking the difficult questions when his feet hit the stoop of the Red Rat for the second time that day. Standing stiffly in the doorway, Tilla grabbed his shoulder as soon as he was within reach.

"Finally! Where were you, the middle of the woods?" She shoved him into the tavern. "Get in there before my customers all leave to see that Sorman woman."

"Yeah, no pressure," Emry mumbled and pushed his way toward the stage.

The Red Rat tavern could have fit three Dancing Rabbits into its main room alone. Its long tables stretched underneath polished balconies, while soaring rafters above caught and swirled its patrons' laughter and drunk conversation. When mixed with music from its prized stage, nothing could compare to the experience—and if Emry was being honest, André's bribe of twenty gold was a little low to secure a place like this for Sada.

But he had to tear his eyes away from the beams above if he was going to actually navigate to the stage. Partygoers had dragged the tables about and piled themselves on top of them, passing mugs up to friends perched on the balcony railings. So many card games had been spread out on the floor that Emry lost at least five people money as he knocked over several decks on his way through.

"Took him long enough," a woman grumbled when he finally reached the stage. The *stage*—Weir's eyes, when had he last performed on a good one? One with working footlights, or boards that didn't look like they were going to break halfway through the set—

The annoyed woman cleared her throat. "You need to tune up?" she asked, her fingers tapping on her folded arms. Emry immediately recalled her face from watching André's troupe perform a week prior.

"No, already tuned." He stuck out his hand. "Shayna, right? I've heard you before. You have a beautiful voice."

"Peter said the same of you." She took his hand briefly and nodded to the fiddler behind her, who waved. "They said they heard you perform a few weeks back. For all our sakes, they better be right about you."

"Better be…" the drummer next to Peter murmured in agreement, unable to rip her eyes from someone in the crowd. Emry followed her gaze outward. A blond, sharp-jawed man close to the stage was leaning away from everyone else despite the packed house. As the man glanced back at the exit, a circular gold pin glinted on his vest, bright against his somber black waistcoat.

"Hara drag me to dust," Emry breathed and turned back to Shayna. "Is he from the Quartet or something?"

A predatory grin flashed across her face. "No. That's Damir Nedrov, Ella Sorman's manager."

Emry's heart pounded in his ears. "Are you sure?"

"Oh, it's him." The drummer leaned in as she spoke, eyes flitting back to the crowd every other second. "I went to Ella's performance earlier and saw him there with her. What do you think he's doing out of Ella's shadow?"

"Recruiting," Shayna said firmly. "He's got to be. They always look in Tazlo first, you know."

Emry swallowed. Yes, he knew that very well.

"That's how they found Karlson," Peter said, their enthusiasm grating on Emry's tightening nerves. "And June! And that other singer, what's his name—"

As Peter and the drummer tossed Guild names back and forth, Shayna turned to Emry. "We were talking about what songs to play before you arrived. The plan is 'Hara's Shield,' 'Cave River Folly,' and 'Spirit's Grove.'"

Emry's hands went cold at the title of the second song—his mother's favorite. He couldn't do it, not tonight. "I don't know 'Cave River Folly,'" he lied and grabbed at the first song that came to mind. "Could we do 'Vornik Reel' instead?"

"Oh, I like that one." Peter nodded eagerly. Shayna gave a conceding nod.

"Fine," she said. "'Hara's Shield,' 'Vornik Reel,' 'Spirit's Grove.' You'll take the harmony, and you'll get half of André's share at the end of the set." Her eyes glittered. "And you'd better not make a mistake in front of Damir."

Emry glanced back at the Auric Guild representative, who was quietly judging a drunk man behind him. He nodded, even as his palms began to sweat. "You got it."

As they all clambered up on stage, Emry waited to ascend last.

"What is all this?" Aspen whispered, their voice floating up at his shoulder. Emry jumped at the sound.

"I told you, I'm performing." He turned to the wall to hide his lips moving.

"Performing? You mean making music again? For all these people?"

"Yes, so you have to be *quiet*—"

The lute shifted. "If I'm going to keep quiet all the time, I want...I want reassurances!"

Emry watched the drummer nervously—he only had a second before he needed to follow her. "What reassurances?"

Aspen faltered. "I—I don't know, I just thought it was a good word to use."

Emry couldn't hang back on the steps any longer. "Fine, any reassurance you want, *after* this performance."

Whoops and whistles trailed his footsteps as he jogged up the stairs. He gave a humble nod to his borrowed audience and took what had once been André's seat. Far in the back, he could make out Marko's shoulders clearing a path for him and Stef in the crowd.

On stage, Shayna set to work recapturing their audience's attention. "Evening, everyone! Nothing like a good surge to shake up Sada, am I right?"

Shouts and the drunken pounding of feet floated up to the rafters. Up at the front, Damir rolled his eyes. He glanced at Emry, the newcomer onstage, then let his gaze slide off him.

Emry adjusted his hold on his lute—on his possessed, talking lute—and looked to Shayna for her cue.

By all accounts, "Hara's Shield" was a safe choice for a nervous troupe and an eager audience. Familiar, a little outdated, but bright and upbeat enough to ease the audience back into the performance. More importantly, it was quite a basic piece for a lutenist, and it let Emry ground himself while his hands rolled along with ease.

Andre's troupe wasn't bad by any means—though flat at times, Shayna knew how to parade about the stage to keep the tavern engaged. Peter made up for their shrill tones with their jaunty energy, and the drummer—Mila, if his memory served him right—bounced along with her beat. Emry found it easy to melt into the atmosphere they built and give it right back to the tavern, where the old balconies carried their sound to the very back of the crowd.

Emry almost didn't care that Damir still slouched against a column in boredom, or that Shayna's eager singing half-drowned out her bandmates. This was mid-city Sada, and the audience was happy. *His* audience was happy. If spirits truly couldn't bestow luck, then this would have to carry him through the next year.

"Thank you!" Shayna laughed as the crowd applauded. "And I

must say thank you to one Emry Karic, who was so kind to join us this evening."

She must have been satisfied with his performance, for she gave him a genuine smile as the audience cheered. In the back, Marko and Stef whistled loudly. Emry waved and shook his head with a sheepish grin. After a few more jokes, Shayna glanced back at the troupe. "Mr. Karic has picked a fun one for you all tonight," she said. "Apparently he and Peter aren't afraid of a bit of a challenge on the first night of Sada."

What was she talking about—? Emry froze. The reel. The stupid reel had a fiddle solo toward the beginning.

And a lute solo at the end.

"Let's see if Hara blesses their performance, shall we?" Shayna shot Damir a conspicuous look as she walked back from the edge of the stage. Behind her, Peter was fizzing with excitement—there would be nowhere to hide with a solo like this. The Guild would hear every bit of their ability.

Emry felt like he was going to die for all the same reasons.

He scrambled to sort out his thoughts as they sped through the first half of the song. For better or for worse, there was nothing he could do about his lute now. If he closed his eyes for his solo, he could pretend like he was performing back at the grove, where his fingers hadn't been wound so tight, where his breath hadn't been stolen away by the panic in his chest. He could pretend like no one was there, not even that man with the gold pin.

And so when it was time, when Shayna and Peter and Mila dropped off to give him the empty air of the stage to fill, he closed his eyes and jumped in.

But his lute had changed.

The shock of it was like missing the last step of a staircase. With every chord, he expected a creak or a buzz from the instrument— familiar flaws to mar the notes he worked so hard on. But something had swept away those blemishes and replaced them with depth. No, not just depth—a full and endless sort of reverberation that one could only hope for in concert halls.

As his shock faded, he dove eagerly into the sound, digging deeper as he improvised and twirled around the chords of the solo. He was almost light-headed at how easy, how good it felt to play like this. For a moment, there was nothing holding him back from showing off what he could do. No cheap instrument, no bribes, no rejections or insults or people singing over him. For a brief instant, the stage was truly his.

He opened his eyes at the end of the solo. The audience was whistling, the other troupe members beaming.

Damir Nedrov was standing straight and staring directly at him.

The last song passed in a blur, and Emry was vaguely aware of an encore or two before they finally staggered off stage. By the time they were done, he was half-convinced they had played straight through the second day of the festival.

"What in Weir's name have you been doing playing up-city all this time?" Shayna demanded over the din of the crowd, most of whom were trying to shuffle through the door and get a wink of sleep before repeating the Sada ritual tomorrow. "Who did you study under? You have to have trained classically—"

"I told you he was good!" Peter crowed behind her. "André couldn't have pulled that off, that's for sure."

"Emry!" Marko's hand shot up from over the crowd, and Emry gladly extricated himself from the troupe's focus to veer toward his friend.

But another hand grabbed his arm before he could surface.

"Emry, is it?"

He found himself face to face with Damir.

"Emry Karic." He stuck out his hand, hoping Damir wouldn't notice the shaking. The man's calculating gaze was no less intimidating up close. "Happy Sada."

"Damir Nedrov. Happy Sada," he grunted with a slanted Envis

accent, wrinkling his crooked nose as several careening fools stumbled past him. "Listen, I'd like to hear you play again."

"Me? And the others—?"

"No, just you. I heard the others earlier. They're not you." He slipped Emry a folded piece of paper. "Give this to Henri at the Lamb's Ear in two days. There'll be an opening for you and anyone in your own troupe before sunset."

"Sure. But—I don't actually have a troupe of my own, this was just a—"

"Play with Ella's troupe, then."

Emry blinked. "I'm sorry, what?"

Damir shrugged. "Ella likes to test out folks that way. Nowhere to hide. Cut the chaff from the, you know, whatever." He pulled out a pipe. "Now, if you'll excuse me..."

Before Emry could process what he said, Damir melted into the crowd.

"Hey!" Marko's hand on his shoulder dragged him back into the world. "Was that who I think it was? I saw the pin—"

"Yeah. It was—I, uh..." Emry stared at the piece of paper in his hand. Felt the weight of the lute on his back. "I'm going to head home, I think. Two sets in one night, you know?"

"Of course." Marko slid his arm around Stef's as they walked out. "But—you'll tell us all about that Guild person tomorrow, yeah?"

To Emry's relief, Shayna and the others hadn't caught Damir's quick exchange with him, and they were still scanning the crowd for the man when they handed Emry his coin purse. He left and rushed up-city to his flat in a delighted daze—Hara herself could have materialized before him and he wouldn't have noticed.

"All right." He set up the lute against the wall and perched on the edge of the bed, leaning forward toward the lute. "What *was* that, Aspen?"

"What was what?"

Emry smiled. "Come on, how did you do that? With the lute?"

"I didn't do anything." Aspen's voice bristled. "I stayed quiet, like you asked!"

"So you didn't change the lute, or—or use any sort of spirit magic?"

"No, of course not!"

Emry tapped his fingers on the bed, then picked up the lute and riffed a few random chords. The depth was still there. It was comical, that sort of sound coming from such a cheap make. Like a doll singing opera.

Despite his stinging fingers, he played a bit more, digging to figure out why it was different. It took him another half a melody to figure it out—the music felt like what he had heard when he was playing in Aspen's grove. Like the atmosphere there had concentrated itself into the wooden caverns of the instrument and poured out of the rose at his slightest touch.

"Are you angry?" Aspen asked after he stopped playing. "I thought the people liked your performance. I liked it, too, if that helps. If I did something wrong—"

Laughter bubbled up to Emry's lips. Disbelieving, exhaustion-addled laughter. "You did nothing wrong, Aspen. You..." He ran a hand through his hair and grinned at nothing. "I can't believe it."

"Believe what?"

The list for that was too long, so Emry waved off his own words and set the lute down again. "I believe it's time for reassurances, like you said."

Aspen brightened. "Oh, that's right. What can I ask for?"

Emry leaned forward, setting his elbows on his knees. "Anything. Name it."

"Well..." Their voice trailed off. "I'll be going back to my grove soon, you understand."

"Mm-hmm."

"But...until then, I need to learn how to keep it safe. Keep my home safe." Though the lute had no eyes, Emry could feel the spirit's gaze on him. "Could you help me with that? Help me learn, then take me home?"

Emry's smile faded. His enchanted lute wouldn't last forever, he knew that. As soon as Aspen was back in their tree, the instrument in front of him would return to normal, transforming like the cursed prince into a river fish at midnight.

He briefly considered saying no. He could say that he had no clue how to help—which was true—and beg the spirit to ask for something else, anything else...

But he was a Karic. He knew a little about wanting to go home.

"Of course," he said. "I'll help you."

SIX

DESPITE HIS EXHAUSTION, Emry's head buzzed from the moment he hit the pillow to the moment he got up. Aspen had said they would be strong enough to hop back into their tree in a few weeks—if he leveraged last night's success to perform as much as he could within that time, perhaps he could afford to order a new lute, one that sounded nearly as good as what he currently had. He'd still need a loan to secure a lute like that, of course, but if the Guild truly liked him, if they asked for more performances beyond Lamb's Ear, maybe even...

He let himself drift, just for a moment, to a fabricated future where he himself wore a gold pin. Once he had that, there would be no need to scrounge or go into debt. There would be no need to stay in Tazlo. He could head back home to Senne and—

"So when do humans normally wake up?"

Emry rubbed his eyes, grateful for the interruption. He was getting carried away with his thoughts. "When do spirits normally wake up?"

"I don't sleep."

"Of course you don't."

Emry rolled over and observed the room. The lute rested on the floor in its beat-up case, the lid open—it hadn't felt right closing it last night, not with Aspen in there. Damir's note lay on the chipped end table. Apart from that, the room was bare. Emry had sold the rug, as thin and grimy as it was, to a neighbor for last month's rent.

Yawning, he grabbed the folded paper from the table and rubbed his thumb over the seal, where the waxy details of the Auric Guild circle flashed gold in the morning sunlight. The smooth texture against his skin reminded him that last night hadn't been a dream—his lute was possessed, and he had caught the Guild's attention.

One out of two wasn't bad, he supposed.

As he took a deep breath and swung his legs over the side of the bed, a knock on the door made him jump.

"Emry, you up?" Marko's voice floated in. "Stef and I were going to get some breakfast."

Emry's stomach rumbled, but his promise to Aspen still hung in the air. "You go on ahead, Marko. I'm not quite recovered from yesterday."

As soon as Marko's footsteps faded down the hall, the lute vibrated. "May I come out for a bit?"

Emry frowned. "I thought you couldn't detach from the lute for weeks."

"Not detaching. Just projecting. I used to do it all the time when Addie was around."

"Um, sure." He set down Damir's paper. "You've mentioned her before. Who's Addie?"

Then a young wolf jumped onto the sheets. Emry shrieked and jolted away, rolling off the side of the bed and onto the floor.

"Addie was my friend." The wolf sat on the edge and looked down at Emry. "She was a farmer nearby, I think. She sat in my grove quite often."

Emry caught his breath on the floor amongst the dust bunnies, with Aspen the wolf tilting their head at him from above. When under close inspection like this, the spirit's projection didn't hold water. It was the lines that weren't quite right—they shivered and quaked, as if a stiff breeze would carry the wolf away. And when Aspen spoke, the wolf's jaw didn't move.

Emry couldn't decide if that was more or less terrifying.

"How'd you do that?" he spluttered.

"Do what?"

"Turn into—into that!"

"Oh." Aspen flicked their ears. "I don't know. I imagine myself like this, and here I am. Well, like I said, I'm still inside the lute. But I'm also here! Isn't it easier to talk to me this way?"

They grinned—an unsettling sight, with so many sharp teeth.

"I guess." Emry sat up slowly. "So, Addie. This friend of yours. When did you speak with her?"

"Oh, about fifty winters ago." The wolf yawned. "And I never spoke to her, really. Just projected into little animals to sit near her. She read things aloud, you know. Not the best way to learn the human way of speaking, but I think I'm doing all right, don't you?"

Aspen's tail wagged. Emry tilted his head. "How old are you, Aspen?"

"I've counted a hundred and twenty winters! I think. It's difficult, they all sort of blend together. How old are you?"

"Twenty-five...winters."

"Goodness, what a seedling." Aspen, who truly sounded no older than fifteen, panted down at him in a sort of laugh, then stretched and poked their nose at the window. "So, do you think anyone here knows what caused the surge?"

"You mean here in town?" Emry pushed himself to his feet. "I'm sure someone's got an idea."

To his surprise, Aspen's nose left an imprint on the window as they drew away. "Good. Then I'd like to...I'm not sure what the word is."

Emry wiped the imprint off the glass. "Investigate?"

"Ooh, that sounds very fancy." Aspen hopped off the bed and ran in a circle around the bare floor. "Yes, I want to *investigate.*"

"Whatever you'd like, Aspen." Emry stifled another yawn and

stretched his arms out above him. "But breakfast first, I think. Do spirits eat?"

"No."

Emry let out a relieved breath. "Good. I haven't got enough money for two pies."

～

BETWEEN THE BREAKFAST PIES, lunch pies, dinner pies, dessert pies, midnight snack pies, and traditional festival pies, bakers barely got a moment's rest during Sada. Back in Senne, Emry used to pride himself on the distinctly idiotic number of pies he could consume over the three days of the festival.

But they didn't make them the same in Tazlo, so today, he selected a sausage hand pie and hoped that the baker hadn't worked the crust into a tough oblivion.

"So, where do we start?" Aspen asked loudly. Emry nearly spit out his first bite.

"Aspen!"

Aspen dropped their voice to a stage whisper. "Sorry. Where do we start?"

In truth, he had no idea—but he wasn't about to admit that to the mythical creature on his back who could turn into a wolf at will, so instead, he frowned pensively as he tore off chunks of the hand pie.

"We go to someone who's awake," he said. "Someone who knows everything there is to know about the city."

～

AS HE HAD HOPED, Bron was indeed awake, humming in his baritone voice and sweeping inside the Dancing Rabbit. Emry rapped on the doorway to catch the man's attention. "How was the rest of the night, Bron?"

"Ah, Karic!" Bron waved a massive hand toward him, but the motion was tired. "Long night. Lost a few folks after the surge, but you can't really stop Sada, can you?"

"Certainly not." Emry flipped a chair up onto a table so Bron could sweep under it. "I actually wanted to ask you about that surge. What do you think caused it?"

Bron rubbed the back of his neck as he set aside the broom—it hadn't been doing much good anyway. "Ah, it's just Shiro trying to make trouble with Hara. It happens now and again, nothing to worry about."

Emry folded his arms. "Even though it killed some trees?"

"I've seen that before." Bron tapped his temple. "These eyes are older than they look, you know."

"When did it happen? Does it kill things often?"

"Saw it once, thirty, forty years ago." Bron looked him over. "Why do you ask so many questions? Worried about bad luck?" His eyes sparked. "You can't be, not after what I've been hearing about you from last night."

"Oh?" Emry smiled. "What lies have you heard?"

"Troubling ones," he said. "Ones that make me think you won't be playing at the Dancing Rabbit again."

Bron glanced sadly at the little performance space in the corner, and as much as Emry wanted the man to be right, he still felt an ache in his chest. "Don't say that." He mustered up a dismissive wave. "I'm sure I've got plenty of opportunities ahead of me to mess this up."

"Karic." Bron's face went very serious, and he placed a hand on Emry's shoulder. "Stop that. Must I remind you what happened the last time you said something like that? With Miss Cal?"

Suddenly Emry felt very small. "I—"

"There is no use cursing yourself. I don't want to see you like that again, not after last year." Bron let go of him. "Go. Make me proud."

Emry swallowed and tried to recompose himself. He still had an investigation to run, after all. "But I was going to ask, in the surges you've seen before—"

"I told you, it's nothing to worry about." Bron picked up the broom again. "I was scared too, first time I moved south and saw one. But I'm still here, aren't I?" He gestured to the street with a grin, then resumed sweeping. "Now go. Forget about them, and enjoy your Sada. You've got many things to celebrate."

The breakfast pie sat like a stone in Emry's stomach as he slouched downhill.

"Can I talk?" Aspen whispered.

Emry looked around. "Fine, fine. Here, we'll take the carriage roads."

They veered off toward the forest and entered a gentle, winding route down the mountain, one more forgiving for carriages and wagons. It was still early, and Emry only had to step off the road a few times to let some sleepy drivers pass. Once the road was empty, Aspen projected into the form of a crow, flitting from the lute to the branches above Emry's head. As they flew, their projection grew less wavering and a little more solid. If it wasn't for their chatter, they could have passed for a perfectly normal crow.

"I know a bit about what Bron said, about Shiro and Hara," Aspen said, keeping an easy pace with Emry from above. They swooped through the lower branches, their voice carrying easily in the morning breeze. "Addie's books talked about them sometimes. But I don't understand, why are they always fighting?"

"They're gods, gods always fight with each other." Emry kicked at a few crunchy leaves. "Hara against Weir, Shiro against Hara, Shiro against Weir. Mostly Shiro acting out, to be honest. There wouldn't be many stories if they didn't fight."

"I suppose so." Aspen dove and landed on the head of the lute. "Do you think it was Shiro, then?"

Emry dug up the other half of the breakfast he had stored in his pack and munched on it. Though cold and congealed, the pie at least gave him time to think. "If it's some sort of god," he mused through a mouthful, "why did I never see it in Senne? Why every five years? Don't tell Bron I said this, but..." He waved the last bit of crust. "I think there's a more natural explanation for this. Something more straightforward."

Aspen preened their feathers. "And who do we go to for that?"

Emry grinned—he finally had an answer for that one. "The most straightforward person I know."

UNLIKE EMRY AND MARKO, Stef spent most of her days down-city, selling cloth and enjoying the constant bustle of the plaza. Carriages crisscrossed in frenetic patterns at the flat base of the mountain, narrowly avoiding loud food stalls and louder Sada tourists.

Yet as urgently as the plaza moved, it all felt inconsequential in the shadow of the city's shining jewel: the Sumac nexus.

"I thought I could feel something like this through my roots, but..." Aspen, now a mouse in Emry's waistcoat pocket, poked their head out and locked their beady eyes on the nexus. "I never realized it was this *big*."

The Sumac nexus was the gaping mouth of a cave seated just behind the Tazlo Fall. Though the waterfall did its best to hide the cave behind rainbowed mist, it couldn't quite cover the yawning black hole that stretched four times as high as the nearest inn.

Despite its intimidating presence, the people of Tazlo held little fear of the towering darkness. Tourists, travelers, and merchants hurried in and out of the cave, eager to access the underground river route within. From there, river boats would whisk them off to any other nexus in the province of Vidanya and beyond. Though Emry gave the looming hole a wide berth, the cold mist that seeped out of it still made his skin prickle.

"Are we going in there?" Aspen's whiskers twitched in excitement. Emry shuddered and picked up his pace.

"No. And you'll have to hide in the lute again. We're almost to Stef's."

When Emry finally escaped into the store and tracked Stef down on the second level, he could hardly see her through the bolts of colorful, overpriced fabric piled up on her arms.

"Need any help?" he asked, holding his arms out.

"Emry! No, I'm fine." Stef glided easily down the steps without being able to see more than in inch in front of her. Behind her, Emry tripped on a bit of ribbon.

"Missed you at breakfast this morning," Stef continued, plopping the fabric on a table. "Tell me, are you famous yet?"

Emry set his shoulders back. "Yes, absolutely. Best friends with Ella Sorman and everything."

"I knew it." She began sorting through the bolts with nimble fingers. "What are you here for? If it's for a cloak, I'm afraid I've run out already. The caves have been freezing the past few days, apparently." She looked up quickly. "Oh, I'm sorry, I forgot you don't—"

"No worries." Emry held up a hand. "I actually wanted to ask you about the surge yesterday. Do you—?"

"Oh, not you, too." Stef groaned. "My customers haven't shut up about it, to be honest. The ones coming from Halagrad all say it's Weir trying to claim more territory."

As Stef turned away for a pair of shears, Aspen's head poked up out of Emry's pocket. Emry gently pushed them back down. "Really?"

"Yes, with all the glowing leaves." Stef waved dismissively at the air. "They look like stars, hence, Weir. But this couple from Bennli, they..." She cut a smooth line with the shears, then shook her head. "They keep talking about remnants."

The hair on the back of Emry's neck stood up. A few days ago, that word would have meant nothing. But now that there was a talking spirit mouse in his pocket... "Remnants? You mean the forest ghosts?"

As he repeated her words, an older woman near them reached for the nearest piece of wood—the end of the banister at the stairs.

"Hara give them peace," the woman muttered, then let go of the banister and tossed both of them a dirty look, as if mentioning remnants was going to make one manifest in the store. After the woman walked away, Stef rolled her eyes and returned to her work.

"Remnants, forest ghosts, whatever they're called," she said. "They were floating around the roads and spooking horses, according to the Bennli people. The remnants didn't last long, but their hackney driver nearly had a heart attack."

"Do you think they actually saw one?" As Emry spoke, Aspen's nose poked up again. Emry quickly buttoned his pocket shut, then smiled at Stef when she looked up.

"What, saw the thing that mums use to scare children into eating their vegetables?" Stef snorted. "No, it's a dumb superstition. They probably saw someone's scarf floating in the breeze, or a large spiderweb..."

Something plinked on the floor—Emry's button, its threads gnawed off. As Aspen wriggled their way out of the pocket and made to leap onto the fabric Stef was neatening, Emry buried a gasp, caught them mid-air, and stuffed them into his other waistcoat pocket.

"Or they just made up an exciting story for Sada," Stef continued, wholly unaware of the commotion. "Either way, remnants are as real as my will to care about them." As she set the fabric down, she gave Emry a crooked smile. "Why, you scared of them?"

"No." The word came out with more force than Emry intended. "I was just...wondering if they were related to the surges, is all."

Stef shrugged and pulled on the next bolt. "I've no clue—I'm as familiar with the surges as you are. Like I said, I don't think they happen up north. Thisby never got them."

Emry's pocket wriggled angrily—his investigation window was rapidly closing. "So you don't know what causes them?"

Her gaze narrowed. "No, I don't. Are you feeling well? Marko doesn't even get this spooked by the surges, and he hid from last week's thunderstorm." She paused. "Don't tell him I told you that."

Emry edged toward the shop door, angling the enraged pocket away from Stef. "Oh no, I'm not spooked. Just curious, is all."

Stef gave an unconvinced hum. "Well, if you do need anything else, Marko might know where to point you in the Academy library."

Emry winced. His desire to set foot in Cal's old haunt was almost as low as his desire to set foot in the caves. "I'll think about it. Thanks, Stef."

As soon as he was back on the street, Emry sighed and unbuttoned his pocket. "I'm sorry, I'm sorry—"

"That was *rude*!" Aspen squeaked instantly, their tiny eyes glaring up at him.

"I said I was sorry!"

"I know I can't give you luck, but that's no way to treat a spirit!"

Emry ducked back into the carriage routes as quickly as possible, keeping his voice low as the wagons passed. "I just didn't want Stef asking any questions. Once she starts, she won't stop."

"Fine." Aspen's mouse form gave the littlest huff. "But I refuse to be hidden when we go to Marko."

"Marko?" Emry repeated the name too loudly. The wagon driver tossed him a look, and Emry shuffled faster up the hill. "We're not going to Marko."

"But Stef said he can point to things," Aspen said. "Do you not like him? I thought you shared a nest with him."

Emry gave a begrudging smile at that. "I suppose we do, yes. But it's not Marko, it's, um…"

He looked down to find Aspen craning their tiny neck to stare up at him, and he reluctantly held out a palm to let them hop on. How to explain this to a spirit… "The Academy is—it's like the deep part of the forest."

"Oh." Aspen's whiskers twitched. "There's no paths?"

"No, it has hallways. Too many, actually."

"Is it mossy?" Aspen kneaded Emry's thumb pad with their tiny paws. "But it's so nice and springy, how could you not like moss?"

"No, not moss. It's more like—"

Aspen gasped. "Bears? Are there bears?"

Emry passed his free hand over his face. "Ghosts, Aspen! There are ghosts in the deep forest!"

"I see." Aspen tilted their head. "And...there are ghosts in the Academy?"

"Yes!" Emry faltered. "No. Not...not literally."

Aspen sat back on their haunches. "So what's in there?"

Emry dropped his shoulders in defeat—he couldn't even say a *person*. The student he had in mind wasn't there, and hadn't been there for a year.

And he had forgotten where he was going with the forest metaphor, anyway.

"Nothing," Emry sighed. "Come on. Twenty minutes in bear territory, then we're out."

CHAPTER

SEVEN

As the country's premier cross-province university, the Academy of Thalis insisted on using the same architecture in every city it claimed. As a result, its exaggerated features looked clumsy between Tazlo's narrow stone facades and delicate balconies. The library in particular squatted heavily at the edge of the academic plaza, with its wide wings and chunky, overstated brick. Even the elk statues in front looked a little overfed as Emry stared at them, shoving away the biting memories they dredged up.

"And you're sure you don't want to stay a mouse?" he asked with too much hope in his voice. They were both hidden in an alleyway across from the library, Aspen's mouse form sitting primly atop a stack of crates.

"Not if you're just going to trap me in your pocket again." Aspen pointed to a terrier trotting by. "What if I looked like that?"

"No dogs allowed in the library."

"What about that?"

Emry sighed. "No horses, either."

"Bird?"

"No."

"Elk?"

"No."

"But the statues—"

"Only humans, Aspen!" Emry pointed to the students scurrying in and out of the wide doors. "Only human shapes allowed in the library!"

"Oh." Aspen blinked. "Well, I can do that."

Emry stiffened, unsure if he should be unsettled or not. "You can?"

Aspen gave their whiskers one last preen. "One moment, please."

Emry kept a nervous eye on the street as an amorphous humanoid shape took form next to him. When he turned back around, he tilted his head. "Are you...Addie?"

"Yes!" Aspen grinned. "How did you know?"

It was clear that Aspen had spent a lot of time observing their old Tazlin friend, for they had spared no detail in their reconstruction. The mud on their boots and the dirt under their fingernails nodded to Addie's life as a farmer, but their bright green eyes and black braids looked as if they were sitting under a tree in dappled sunlight. In their oversized shawl, skirt, and head wrap, they didn't look a day over fifteen.

"Educated guess," Emry answered, then chewed his lip. "But I'm afraid you can't steal her look entirely. That's Addie's look, not yours."

"Oh." Aspen glanced out at the street. "Can I look like one of them, then?"

"No, you can't steal their faces, either."

Aspen stomped their foot. "Then how do you expect me to look like a human?"

Emry raised his arms. "I don't know! Try—all right, try looking like me. I give you permission."

"Exactly like you?"

"No, that'd be weird. Go younger."

"Why? I'm older than you."

"Not with that voice, you're not."

As Aspen pondered, they morphed. Their black pigtails shrank and lifted into a mass of dark curls. Freckles sprinkled their skin as it lightened into a tawny shade of brown. Emry noted that they borrowed Stef's skirt and vest, and stubbornly kept Addie's luminous green eyes.

"Better?" Aspen looked up at him. Emry folded his arms, ignoring the echoes of his siblings in the spirit's face.

"Does my hair actually look like that?"

"Yes."

"That's...unfortunate." He ran a hand through his own curls and tried to recall the last time he had cut his hair. "Can you hold that form for twenty minutes?"

Aspen was busy swishing their skirt to watch the movement. "Not sure what minutes are, but yes."

Emry rubbed his forehead. "Excellent."

As Emry had hoped, Marko was manning the front desk today, his glasses reflecting back the light streaming into the hall. But the dust-riddled beams added no joy to the arched ceilings, nor warmth to the cool marble floor. He wasn't sure how his roommate spent his entire day in here. "Hey, Marko, you free?"

Marko's head snapped up, and strangely, a look of terror flashed over his face.

"Emry! What are you doing here?" He jumped to his feet and glanced around.

"I'm...looking for a book." Emry took a small step back. "I thought the library was open to the public today."

"It is, but—"

"We're looking for books about surges," Aspen blurted from behind Emry. "Do you have any?"

Marko frowned, his gaze pinging between Emry and Aspen's faces. "Who's this?"

Emry thought fast. "Bron's relative from the north. Visited him this morning and got saddled with some babysitting."

Marko bit back a smile. "You? Babysitting?"

Emry set a hand to his chest. "Excuse me, I actually think I'd be very good at it—"

"Surge books, please!" Aspen set their hands on the front desk, their nails still speckled with bits of soil. "You're supposed to be good at pointing at them. Stef said so."

"Stef—?" Marko started. Emry quickly butted in in front of Aspen.

"We're looking for any books you have on the science of surges," he said. "Something that explains their causes."

"Well, um..." Marko wiped his palms on his jacket and looked around again. Emry followed his gaze, finding nothing but the normal traffic of students. "I'm afraid you'll be hard-pressed to find any books on surges. It's not exactly a legitimate field."

"There's a field in here?" Aspen wrinkled their nose. "I can't sense it."

"Field of science," Emry said quickly. "So, no one's researched it?"

"Oh, people have tried." Marko shrugged. "But there's hardly any lingering evidence to study, and most scientists only see the big ones once or twice in their lifetimes. Those who try are usually laughed off..."

A riffling sound distracted Marko, and they both looked over to find Aspen holding a book upside down, flapping the pages to hear them wobble. Marko adjusted his glasses and lowered his voice. "Bron *is* paying you to babysit, right?"

"It's more a favor I owe," Emry muttered, then gestured to Aspen. "Come on, time to go. No books for us here."

"None?" Aspen dropped the book. "None at all?"

Emry took a step toward the front door, already feeling lighter. "None at all, so let's go now—"

"What about Addie's books?"

Emry paused. "What, the folktales?"

"Oh, the archive has those." Marko jerked a thumb behind him. "Section D, back and to the right. But—"

"Thanks!" Aspen strode confidently toward Section F. To Emry's horror, their form began to flicker the farther they walked from the lute.

"Aspen, wait up!" Emry scrambled to grab their half-transparent shoulder, then waved back to Marko. "We'll just be a moment, thanks!"

Marko leaned over the desk as they speed-walked away. "But— but I didn't tell you—!"

Aspen slipped out of Emry's grasp and flickered once more.

"Oh, I'm sure I'll find it!" Emry jogged after the spirit until they had rounded a corner into a maze of bookshelves. "Aspen, keep close. I don't think it's a good idea for you to be too far from the lute."

Aspen smiled and held out a hand. "Well, if you let me carry it—"

"Absolutely not."

As Emry led them deeper into the stacks, they passed several Academy students, austere in their midnight-blue uniforms. Their straight-backed presence spiked Emry's nerves, and he kept his head down, furtively examining their faces to ensure he didn't know them. That they weren't one of her friends.

"Section D, Aspen," he murmured, tugging on the spirit's sleeve to ensure they followed him into the next maze of shelves.

One of the first books Emry found in this section—quickly pulled, in order to distract himself—was less than a delight to read, and even less so to read aloud to Aspen. It was a recent collection of spirit fables from the Bennli area, and it took on a dark tone within the first few pages.

"...And Shiro, being so angry at Hara and the spirits she created to preserve the forests, fought against them with all his strength, shaking the earth and burning the trees. Though her spirits fought back with their sun and storms, it was no use. Shiro's hand destroyed what Hara held dear, as cows and crops succumbed to his wrath. Remnants roamed the blackened fields, chasing the Altas away from their fanes until morning came again."

"Sounds like a surge to me," Aspen said, sitting atop a table in the corner. "Do you think that one really happened?"

Emry closed the book. "I hardly know."

Aspen toyed with a vase of dried flowers on the table beside them. At their touch, the petals bloomed back to life, then shriveled again in an eerie, breath-like pattern. "What would the field people say about it?"

"Field? The scientists, you mean?" Emry leaned back in his chair and rubbed his eyes. He was a bard, not a scholar. He was so far out of his depth that he could no longer see the shore. "Well, I'm not an Academy student, but I think researchers would, um...they would..."

Cal would, his words continued silently. Then, aloud: "They'd look for a primary source."

It took another round of searching and half a headache to find what he was musing on—a copy of a farmer's log, from forty years ago in Bennli. The time of the writing seemed to match the story, if Emry was doing his math right—and that was never a guarantee.

"Here we are." He waved the book around. "A primary source, or...you know, something like that." He cleared his throat and read aloud for Aspen, stumbling a little on the misspellings and shaky handwriting. "Quake around seven. Lasted several minutes. Southern crops dead when it passed, five cows dead...estimated loss of sixty gold in livestock..."

Emry stared at the log. Aspen stared at the storybook.

Then Aspen curled their knees up into their chest.

"Do you think Shiro really did it, then? Like the story said?" they asked, wide green eyes on Emry.

"Perhaps. Or"—Emry gestured with the logbook—"humans made up that story to communicate what they saw that day. To explain why their crops and cows died." He set it down alongside the storybook. "At the end of the day, it seems there's a bit of truth in both."

A bell tolled deeply through the library, echoing across the vast ceiling until its point of origin was utterly untraceable. On the far side of the section, a student scrambled to her feet and rushed out into the quad with her books, joining the fray of other young scholars being released into the sun. Though this part of the library boasted an excellent view of the bustling quad, Emry's stomach flipped looking at it.

"Where are they all going?" Aspen pressed their nose to the glass, watching the students buzz about like little navy bees.

"Lunch, mostly likely. The Academy gives everyone an hour." Emry's limbs grew heavy as he recalled waiting in that quad right as the bell tolled, watching for a particular face in the crowd. "Look, I'm going to put this logbook back, then we should go. I promised Marko I'd have lunch with him, and I've got to practice for that Lamb's Ear gig. We can investigate more tomorrow."

"Oh. Okay." Aspen kept their gaze on the quad. "Could you leave the lute here? I'd like to keep watching."

Emry hesitated. "You promise to stay here?"

"Of course."

"Promise promise?"

Aspen frowned. "What's a promise promise?"

"Never mind. Just stay here and don't creep anyone out." Emry grabbed the books and half jogged to the other section, his unease deepening as students filled the halls. Luckily, the library wasn't a very popular place for lunch, and the blue uniforms soon poured out like water in search of decent fare and some gossip with their friends. By the time he had reached the folktale section, his shoulders had relaxed again. Only a few more minutes, and he'd be out of the library, back in the street, and free of—

"Emry Karic?"

The voice sucked the air out of the room. He spun slowly on his heel, and even though he was expecting it, a violent emotional shock struck him square in the chest when he locked eyes with the speaker.

"Cal?"

EIGHT

THOUGH CALLIOPE BRESLIN stood several inches shorter than Emry, she managed to look down at him over her broad nose as if he were a dog shaking mud all over her boots.

"What are you doing here?" Icicles fell from her mouth as she spoke.

"I'm, um...putting this book back?" Emry held up the book.

Very smooth.

"I can see that." Her brown eyes flicked over him. "You don't work here, you're not a student, and you don't normally read. What are you doing here?"

Emry tried to step back, but his shoulder bumped into the shelf. "I'm allowed to be here, Cal." He turned to slide the book of fables back into its spot—it was the only way to keep himself from staring at her face. "What are...what are *you* doing here?"

But he couldn't hold an entire conversation looking at the shelf, so he took a ragged breath and turned back around. "I thought you said you had taken all the Tazlo classes," he continued, leaning against a nearby desk as if his heart wasn't threatening to bash its way out of his throat.

She looked the same as when she had left him a year ago—devastatingly put together in every way he wasn't. Polished boots, pressed skirt, Academy jacket. The gold and lace trim of the jacket only served to brighten the warm glow of her brown skin. The only trait of hers that roughly aligned with Emry was the freeness of her curls—though hers coiled tightly, while his flopped loose.

"I did take all the Tazlo classes." She shifted her weight. "I'm just attending a guest lecture. I'll be heading back to Vornik in two days."

"Oh. So soon?"

"Yes. I don't like to stay in one place, unlike some people."

Emry winced, and all the stupid, fanciful questions he had formulated in his head—how are you, what have you been studying, how have you liked Sada so far—dissipated with an acrid aftertaste. The sooner he was out of this room, the better.

"I'll get out of your way, then." He ducked toward the exit. "Sorry you had to see me."

But before he could escape her gaze, he collided with someone under the arch of the doorway. "Oh, excuse me—"

"Emry! I was looking for you," Aspen said brightly and handed him the lute. "I'm done watching the student humans. They all went other places. This building is big, like you said. Much bigger than my grove. How do they keep track of it all?"

Emry froze, his palms going cold. Aspen had changed. In the few minutes they'd been left alone, they had shrunk and replaced their height with nubby antlers. Claws stuck out of their fingertips, and—though Emry didn't want to look—he thought he saw a tail peeking out from behind them. "Aspen!"

"What? No one was around, and I thought it would be fun." Then Aspen peeked over Emry's shoulder. "Oops."

Emry didn't turn back around toward Cal. He didn't dare.

"Who," Cal said, after a long, tense silence, "is that?"

Emry reached behind Aspen and closed the door to the section. "Cal, I can explain—"

"So, what, you've joined a circus now?" She scoffed. "Did up-city not want you anymore? Better hope it's not a *traveling* circus—"

"What's a circus?" Aspen tilted their head at Emry. "Do you know her?"

"Ah, funny, too." Cal withheld no judgment in her voice as her eyes swept over the antlers. "I can't imagine you've been able to find much work in Tazlo these days. Sada's for singers, not jesters."

"Emry, what's she talking about?" Aspen asked. "Does she not like my look? Because I can change!"

Emry's eyes widened in fear. "No, no, please don't—"

But it was too late. Aspen's antlers and tails disappeared in a blink, and the spirit shook out their hands to rid themselves of the claws. Once done, they grinned proudly at Emry, then Cal. "There we go! All human again."

"Hara drag me to dust." Cal hurried a few steps back. "How did you do that?"

"I hardly know." Aspen scratched their head. "Comes with the territory, I suppose. Want to see me do something else?"

They morphed into a crow before her eyes. Cal shrieked; Emry locked the library door.

"It's all right!" He rushed in between them, arms raised. Aspen landed on his wrist and tilted their feathered head. "I'm sorry, Cal, Aspen's very friendly. Too friendly, actually—"

"Tell me what that thing is. Now," Cal demanded, one hand against the window, the other reaching for a heavy book.

"They're a spirit," Emry blurted. "They normally live in groves. This one fell into my lute."

Cal stared. "You expect me to believe that?"

"But it's true!" Aspen hopped up and down Emry's arm, each hop emphasizing their words. "Why does everyone think I'm not real?"

"Aspen, how about you go back into the lute for a second?" Emry said quickly. "Let me talk this through."

"Fine."

The crow disappeared, and the lute sank deeper into Emry's

hand. With his arms still raised, he set the lute down very slowly on the floor, then sat next to it. "Cal, I promise you're not hallucinating."

"I know that," she snapped—though Emry could see that theory winking out of her thoughts. "And—and this isn't some sort of sick joke? Some mirror trick?"

"Cal," he repeated, sharper this time. "You honestly think I would do something like that?"

Her gaze dipped down as she stepped away from the window. "No," she said. "You wouldn't."

"So, let's...let's entertain the hypothesis." Another one of Cal's words, foreign on his tongue. "That Aspen is a spirit, I mean."

"A spirit living inside your lute."

"Yes."

"All right. Well..."

Her gaze first landed on the lute, then on the book he had just put away. At a glance, she read the titles about folktales, gods, and spirits across the shelf. Squinted at the farmer's journal on the desk. Looked back to the lute between them.

Then she closed the curtains and sat down on the other side of the lute. "If I'm to entertain this hypothesis, I have questions."

"Of course."

She hesitated and shook her head. "No, I need my notebook first."

Emry suppressed a pained smile at the familiarity of her process. Grabbing a journal, tugging a pencil out of the tight black curls above her ear. Settling back down, spine straight, pencil poised. "So, if spirits are real..."

"We are, thank you," Aspen cut in. "There is no *if*."

Cal blinked at the instrument, then hesitantly directed her next question toward it. Emry's shoulders relaxed as she took her eyes off him. "And you normally live in trees?" she asked.

"Groves," Aspen corrected proudly. "I take care of far more than a single tree."

"So, you take care of nature?"

"I help it grow. All spirits do that. Have you not read any of the stories about us?"

Cal began to scribble in her journal. "If you live in trees, how can you also live in a lute?"

"It's a not-tree. That's what Emry and I talked about."

Cal looked up at Emry, who shrugged. She let out a small sigh and continued writing. "How did you get into the...not-tree?"

Aspen explained the previous night's surge and their search for answers—with some gently clarifying statements from Emry, who had never seen Cal write so fast before. When Aspen mentioned their journey to the dead spirit, she switched into an even more frantic shorthand.

"This is..." she mumbled. "There are more of you? Of course, there must be. But how many?" She addressed Aspen in the lute. "How many spirits are there?"

The spirit paused. "Not many. I could only sense about ten others through my roots."

"Where, in Tazlo? In Vidanya?"

"On this mountain."

"On this mountain alone?" Her hand made a motion to resume writing but twitched above the paper. A number of expressions flashed across her face before settling into disbelief. Emry leaned back. He never thought he'd see the day where she was overwhelmed by her own questions.

"I...I was going to ask..." She started to formulate a question, but footsteps echoed outside the locked door. The sound shook her out of her well of thoughts, and she shifted to pull out a pocket watch. "Hara take me—I'm sorry, I have to go."

"But, hold on!" Aspen said as she scrambled to her feet and tucked the pencil back into her hair. "You're not going to ask me any more questions?"

Emry grabbed the lute and stood up as well. "Aspen, she's very busy, I'm sure—"

The lute strings buzzed against his hand. "But what if she can help? You said you weren't an Academy student, but she is. What if she can figure out how to protect my grove?"

Emry looked everywhere but at Cal. Aspen was more right than they knew. If there was any student, any single mind at the Academy who could help them, it was her.

"She could. She absolutely could," he admitted. "But...it's up to her."

The answer came instantly. "Yes."

When Emry met her gaze with surprise, she scoffed. "What, you bring the largest discovery of the last century to the library inside your *lute*, and you expect me to..." She gestured vaguely as she stuffed her journal back in her book bag. "Listen, I don't have time today, but I can clear my calendar tomorrow. Are you free then?"

"Before sunset, yeah."

"Good." She strode over, unlocked the door, and yanked it open for them. "Don't come back to this section tomorrow. Go to section H at eight. There's an empty lecture hall in the back. No one will bother us there."

"Thank you!" Aspen said cheerily. Emry stopped in the doorway.

"Thanks, Cal," he fumbled. "I know you don't—"

"Go."

"Of course."

NINE

EMRY DROPPED his head and sped out of the section, not making eye contact with anyone until he blasted right past Marko on the front steps.

"Emry!" Marko grabbed his arm. "I've been waiting for you. Did you—?" One look at Emry's face made him sag. "I'm sorry, I'm so sorry, I should have said something earlier."

"It's okay."

"It isn't okay, I knew she was there and didn't tell you. I didn't want you to get upset, and look where that got you." Marko slumped. "Here, let's get something to eat. My treat. Oh, Stef is going to kill me..."

Marko was prepared to buy the entire cart for him by the time they reached it, but Emry declined everything except for a small chunk of ham thrown onto a slab of rye.

"I think she's going to be gone today or tomorrow, if that helps," Marko babbled as he ate, "so you won't have to see her again."

"Mm-hmm." Emry forced down the dry bread.

"Say, you performing anywhere tonight?"

"No, just practicing for tomorrow."

"Right." Marko nodded, then frowned. "Wait, what's tomorrow?"

Emry paused with the last piece of ham halfway to his mouth. He had never told Marko about Damir. "Oh, um—I'm going to be performing for Ella Sorman at the Lamb's Ear tomorrow. With her troupe."

Marko nearly dropped his own lunch. "You *what?*" he said. "Is this from talking to that man last night? You caught his attention?"

Emry let a grin slip back onto his face. "Guess so."

"That's incredible! That's—" Marko couldn't hug him *and* not get ham all over his waistcoat, so he settled for waving his arms at nothing. "We have to go out! We have to celebrate this!"

Emry laughed. "Not tonight, please. I've got to try to get some rest."

"Fine." Marko chomped on his rye and continued with his mouth full. "But after your performance tomorrow, we're going to do something fun, I promise."

Emry soon parted with Marko in the square and returned to his flat with every intention of practicing. If he recalled correctly, Ella traveled with a bagpiper, a drummer, a fiddler, a flautist, maybe even a cellist—they could perform anything, and he had to be prepared.

But when he sat on the bed and held the lute, nothing came. He got through half a scale before thoughts about tomorrow intruded, and after a few minutes, he lowered the instrument to stare numbly out the window. The view of the empty alleyway did nothing but let his thoughts churn.

"Um..." Aspen's voice rose from the lute. "Were you going to play?"

"Hm?" Emry sat up straighter, then flexed his hand and set down the lute. He couldn't get his fingers or his stomach to unclench themselves. "Maybe later. I can't right now."

A dog took shape on the bed. No, not quite a dog—just a smaller version of a wolf. Aspen sat patiently, their tail brushing against the blanket. "Are you nervous about playing tomorrow?"

"Yes. That's it."

The wolf kept staring. Emry avoided their piercing gaze.

"I shouldn't have asked that woman for help, should I?" Aspen asked.

Emry sighed. "No, that's not—"

"She was mean to you. I shouldn't have asked."

"Aspen, it was smart of you to ask. Really, if anyone can help you, it's Cal." Emry leaned back against the wall. "We just don't get along anymore."

Aspen tucked their paws under their body and looked up at him expectantly. It was a good thing the spirit had chosen puppy eyes for this, or else Emry might not have obliged. As it was, he dragged the threadbare covers over himself and propped up his pillow. If he was going to talk about this, he might as well be comfortable. "Aspen, how much do you know about girlfriends?"

"Only what was in Addie's stories." Aspen's tail wagged. "They're beautiful and smart, and they say things like 'I love you' and 'take that, foul beast' and 'I'm not going to kiss that river fish even if you paid me—'"

"Ah, so Addie read *The Prince's Curse*."

"Many times."

Emry nodded. "Then you know a little. But, I don't think there are any...*ex*-girlfriends in *The Prince's Curse*."

"No, there aren't—oh. I see." Aspen set their head down. "How long ago?"

"She broke up with me just before last Sada." Emry toyed with a thread hanging off the blanket. "We had been seeing each other for a year."

"Why did she break up with you?" Aspen sniffed his hand. "I don't know much about humans, but you seem like a perfectly good mate."

"Thank you, but..." Emry's throat tightened. Best skip over the details, so he couldn't dwell on them. "It was my fault. I messed it up, like I always do."

Aspen sat up. "You don't have to go tomorrow, you know. If you leave the lute at the library, I can talk with her myself."

"No, that's all right." Emry gave him a cracked smile. "I made you a promise, and I'm not going to just dump it on someone else. I'll go with you and help with what I can."

TEN

EMRY'S MOPING couldn't last forever, and he did manage to get in a few scales before sunset. But no amount of last-minute practice would make him significantly better in front of the likes of Ella Sorman, so he turned in early for a night of fitful sleep.

The next morning, he rummaged in his trunk for his cleanest waistcoat and cravat. Though he had accumulated several southern pieces over the years—more colors, less embroidery—the waistcoat he uncovered today still clung to the last of the northern flair in his wardrobe. It was dark green, as deep and cool as the forests around Senne. As he buttoned it up, his fingers passed over the gold vines embroidered at the edges, and he remembered with a pang that his mother had sewn them in.

"Well?" Emry shook off the ache and turned to Aspen. "How do I look?"

Aspen tilted their head. "You look the same to me. Is that good or bad?"

Emry let his shoulders drop. "It is what it is at this point." He fluffed his hair and turned to his satchel, which he desperately hoped had some sort of writing utensil and piece of paper in it.

Unlike Cal, he was terrible at writing things down, but he had to make a go of it if he was to be helpful today. "Aspen, you can't wear any antlers when we're in the library today. You have to look like a regular human."

"Are scales out of the question?"

"Definitely out. Very much out. Hara take me..." Emry mumbled and pulled a few scraps of paper from the bottom of the satchel—but they were already covered in a familiar, depressing scrawl.

Emry—

Don't leave Foxhill yet. Mum and Dad want to talk. Marley's been crying all day. Just stay where you are, we'll come to you.

Georgie

Emry swallowed hard and shoved the paper back down into the satchel. He had no time for this, not with everything else going on. "Breakfast time, Aspen. Into the lute you go."

Though a hint of sadness always tinged the last day of Sada, the streets this morning felt particularly gloomy. As Emry stood in line for a fruit dumpling—a small favorite of his, to steel himself for the day—he quickly discovered why.

"Did you hear about Foxhill?" a customer ahead of him stage-whispered to the baker. "Had a surge just like ours. Heard an entire field died. What *does* something like that?"

"Something must have gone wrong with their Sada." The baker shrugged. "Would you like one pie or two?"

"They saw remnants, too." Another customer jumped in, as if just waiting for someone to mention the quake. Emry saw them clutch a little wooden pendant at their neck and fought the silly urge to find a piece of wood himself. "They were flying all about, I heard. Foxhill almost canceled the rest of their festival."

"How devastating," the baker said flatly. "One pie or two?"

After being as polite as possible to the exhausted baker, Emry headed straight to section H of the library. Cal was right to call for such an early start—no other student would be awake at this hour, not after a festival night. When Emry reached the classroom, he slipped inside and locked the door behind him.

He had no reason to fear locking Cal out, for Cal was always the first in the room. Yet exactly when she had arrived, or if she had actually left the library the day before, was hard for him to determine. The books he had been using yesterday were stacked neatly on the lecturer's desk, now joined by several much taller piles. Journals, paper, quills, and a half-dead potted plant formed a small but sturdy fortress in front of Cal herself, who was carefully drawing a diagram that spanned several chalkboards. She didn't turn around to face them when they arrived.

"I can't believe I'm going to say this," she said as she drew, "but I found your initial approach to be the right one."

"I'm sorry?" Emry set the lute down on one desk and took the one next to it for himself, trying hard not to stare at the nostalgic smear of chalk highlighting her cheekbone.

"You were looking at actual accounts of surges, from journals and the like." She stepped back to appraise her drawing and wiped her face with her sleeve. "Though I found the folktales to be largely unnecessary, your other instinct was correct. My history books hardly said anything about surges in my research last night."

"Really?" Aspen asked, their human shape appearing atop the desk next to Emry. Today, their waistcoat and pants matched Emry's, even down to the gold embroidery.

"It's like what Marko said about the lack of science yesterday," Emry said. "If the surges are harmless every five years and kill a tree every forty, it might not make an important history book, but someone could write it down in a diary." He looked to Cal. "Right?"

Cal tilted her head. "What gave you the idea to look at primary sources?"

Heat rose in Emry's cheeks. "Well, I, um—"

Thankfully, Aspen cut in. "Why does everyone think forty

winters is a long time?" The spirit ran a hand through their hair in the same way Emry did. "It's not, not at all!"

"Really? How long do spirits live?" Cal reached for her notebook, leaving Emry to scramble before she descended into a tangential spiral of questions.

"Cal, what did you draw on the board?" he asked quickly.

"Oh, right." She remembered herself and strode over to the windows, her boots clicking on the weathered wood floor. "I thought I'd start by confirming what Bron and Stef said about surges only happening in the south. And it turns out, they were right."

As she drew a heavy curtain over the windows, the drawing on the chalkboards coalesced into something recognizable.

It was a map of Thalis, neatly divided into its five provinces. Vidanya, their province, stretched wide at the top, and a large, arcing line sliced the province across its lower third. Tazlo sat solidly below the line, just under the mountain range. In contrast, the dot marking Senne hovered far above the line. Emry shifted in his chair and focused on the southern region.

"What's that line across Vidanya?" he asked.

"What's Vidanya?" Aspen asked. Cal lit up.

"That's right, of course you wouldn't—" she started, then took a breath. "I'll explain it more later, but for now, Vidanya is the area in which we live. Tazlo is the city we're in. And this line is the upper limit of where all of the surges have historically happened."

"All of them?"

"All of the ones I've found so far in the journals."

"And what about the folktales?" Aspen leaned forward. Cal glanced back at them.

"I...may have checked a few of those, and they seem to line up as well," she muttered. "More than I thought they would."

Aspen hopped up to wander as Cal tapped circles on the map.

"I've also marked what places experienced surges this week," she said. Tazlo, Bennli, and Foxhill were all marked, alongside a few other smaller towns that surrounded them. "They're within the normal range, and from what I can tell from the past accounts, the surges should stop within about a week."

"So we just have a couple more days and we're fine?" Emry caught Aspen's look and raised his hands. "For the humans, I mean."

Cal set down her pointer. "Correct."

"What about the remnants?" Aspen's wandering brought them over to Cal's desk. "Are they normal?"

As they spoke, they casually ran a hand over the wilted potted plant. It burst into life in an instant, its leaves lifting, flowers blooming from dry buds. Even the tired soil in the pot seemed richer, darker, and Emry thought he caught a whiff of sunlight and rain.

Cal stared at it for a moment, her writing fingers twitching. "I am *going* to ask about that later, but—yes, I believe the remnants are normal." She glanced at the plant one more time before picking up a journal and reading its contents aloud.

Red Moon 852. Quake killed southern half of the apple orchard today. Ma went to check on the barn and came back screaming about ghosts. Marta and I can't go outside but we can see them out the window. They don't have faces and they float like the laundry out back. Went away by sunset but Ma still won't let us open the door. Made us say prayers to Hara instead, so they don't try to claim our bodies for themselves.

"They don't show up often in these accounts." Cal set aside the paper. "Only when the surges are strong enough to cause death."

Emry grimaced. "Confirms the myths, then."

Aspen's form wavered. "What do the myths say?"

"Did Addie's books not mention them?"

Aspen bit their lip. "She didn't like those stories. She skipped over those pages whenever they appeared."

To Emry's surprise, Cal was first to answer. "According to legend, remnants are the forest ghosts that appear after Hara's battles. Floating remnants of dead souls looking to reclaim a body." When she caught Emry's wide gaze, she rolled her eyes. "I did say I read some of the folktales, didn't I?"

But as she scoffed, Aspen's silhouette flickered, and Emry leapt to find a positive conclusion for the spirit. "So, it seems like all of this is perfectly ordinary, right?" he said, gesturing to the chalkboard. "All we have to do is figure out how Aspen can stay safe when the more deadly surges come around again."

But then Cal started chewing on the end of her pencil, dousing Emry's hopes. He knew that tell. It was the one habit of hers he didn't miss. "Cal, what's wrong?"

She hesitated, then grabbed a flimsy bit of newsprint and walked over to him. "Read this. Some tourist left it behind." She didn't meet his gaze, but now that she stood close to him, he could see the circles under her eyes, and he regretted not noticing them earlier. Whatever was bothering her, she must have discovered it the evening before.

He did as she asked and scanned the page. The newspaper itself was a simple gossip rag from Thisby, its words as cheap as the pulp it was printed on. But the article Cal had circled described, in rather embellished terms, a terrifying earthquake and the unsettling beauty of glowing trees.

"Sounds like Thisby had a surge," he said, not quite catching her concern. "Is that a problem?"

Cal went back to the chalkboard and circled Thisby. It was above the surge line, away from her other marks.

"Oh." Emry shifted in his chair. "Well—this can't be the only one, right? Surely some of the other accounts you read happened north of that line?"

Cal dropped the chalk back on the board. "None," she said quietly.

His mood sank as he regarded the stacks of books around her—at a glance, there must have been twenty, perhaps thirty of them, all bookmarked and dog-eared.

Aspen caught their reactions, and their form flickered again.

"But surely you haven't read everything yet," Emry jumped back in. "I could help, while you and Aspen talk."

Cal collected herself and nodded. "Yes, I suppose that works." She pretended to sound dispassionate about his offer, but was already flipping through her journal to a very long list of questions.

"Yes, thank you." Aspen fidgeted with a vine from the potted plant. As they twisted the stem, the flowers on the vine rapidly bloomed and closed. "I'd like to know if there are any stories about spirits fighting the surges."

Cal pulled a pencil out from behind her ear. "Well, I'd rather not put much stock in those sorts of stories, but if I could ask about your—"

Aspen glanced at her list. "Stories first, please."

Cal gave a tight-lipped smile and closed the journal. "Of course."

ELEVEN

EMRY SETTLED into a chair by the windows and built a stack of books to hide Cal and Aspen from view. But his little wall did no good—the books didn't block their conversation, and he found it impossible to ignore the cadence of Cal's voice as she read aloud to the spirit. It was so infuriatingly soft. How long had it been since he had heard that tone, or that voice at all, directed at him?

No use thinking about that. He slumped further in the chair and tried to focus on the words on the page.

Cal had started by giving him the journals she hadn't rifled through yet, and he was soon poring over tiny windows into past lives—statesmen writing down their puffed-up prose for posterity, farmers noting how well their crops did in the fall, merchants scribbling out records of handshake deals. Unfortunately for him, none of these windows featured quakes, glowing trees, or remnants.

Meanwhile, Cal and Aspen chattered happily beyond his wall of books.

"How many winters do you have?" Aspen asked.

"Winters? You mean how old I am? I'm twenty-five."

"Are all the students here twenty-five winters old?"

A pause. Emry imagined Cal smiling at the question and hated how well he could still picture it.

"No," she said. "I suppose I'm a little older, but the youngest aren't below eighteen."

"And they can read any book they want here?"

"Certainly—though some of the rare ones are reserved for the scholars."

Emry tossed the journal back onto the growing stack behind him and stood up to stretch.

"Giving up already?" Cal mumbled under her breath. Immediately, all the softness she had reserved for Aspen was gone.

"Well, you clearly weren't expecting me to be helpful anyway," Emry retorted, opening the curtain in an attempt to soak in some warmth from the sunlight. "I'm not finding anything in these stupid things."

"They're not stupid, they're incredibly rare and valuable glimpses into what life used to be like—" Cal rolled her eyes, reached for a storybook, and tossed it onto his pile. "Here, take one of those. Maybe you'll like that mindless drabble better."

"Cal, you said something about a scholar," Aspen said before Emry could respond with something unwise. "What is that? Is that like a student?"

Cal's face smoothed out as soon as she looked away from Emry.

"Not really," she explained gently. "I'm a student now, but I'm hoping to become an official Academy scholar within a few years."

Aspen frowned. "So...what exactly is it?"

The annoyed spark simmering in Emry's chest flared into words, fast and biting.

"It's someone who has all the knowledge in the world and chooses to do nothing with it," he snapped. "Someone who refuses to go out and actually use their talent. That's what an Academy scholar is."

Cal glared at him, and the temperature of the room dropped ten degrees. "Oh, and you're one to talk about people doing something with their lives, are you? Remind me how long you've been in Tazlo?"

Emry gritted his teeth, but held his ground. "At least I'm not locking myself up in libraries rather than—"

"Hey!" Aspen's voice jolted them like a thunderclap. "I'm sorry I asked! No one has to explain what a scholar actually is, all right?"

After a moment, Cal slid back into her chair, and Emry slouched down with the last book Cal had tossed his way. Somewhere beyond his stacks, Cal resumed reading aloud, though her tone was more strained than before.

The book in Emry's hands was a compilation of folktales from old groups, or fenns, that used to reign over Thalis. Compared to modern books, this prose plodded and languished, and though Emry thought he had a rough understanding of the fenn names of old— the Karics had descended from the Riu fenn, after all—these he hardly recognized. He read through names like Trava and Berg, without the faintest idea of where these people once lived on the map.

Though more mysterious in origin, the plot of these older folktales maintained the narrative thread of the newer ones. Hara, the maker goddess of humans and spirits, constantly defended her territory from Shiro, the maker god of the weather, and Weir, the maker god of the sky and stars. The gods fought, the gods blessed, humans laughed and cried and praised them. The usual.

Then one story from the Tera fenn made Emry sit up straight in his chair.

In the time of my great-grandmothers, Hara looked all around her world and declared it the finest.

"These rivers are my arms," she claimed. "These forests my eyes. See the spirits that move mountains, the humans that sing to me. None can make anything better than this."

When Shiro and Weir heard what she said, they shouted and hopped about in anger.

"How dare she claim the humans are better than my storms?" cried Shiro.

"How dare she say that the spirits are superior to my stars?" cried Weir.

Shiro began to stomp about the earth. In his fury, he hid her rivers under the mountains.

"Now no one can see what you've created!" said the god.

But when Hara refused to take back her words, he yelled and swept his shaking thunder across the entire world, trying to break apart what she had made.

"I shall help!" said Weir, and he threw his stars down upon her work. Hara fought through the blinding light, but could not keep the war from her little creations. The great battle destroyed many unlucky ones, spirits and animals and humans alike, until Hara emerged victorious. Wailing, Shiro and Weir retreated to the clouds and sky until the next great storm.

Emry looked up from the book. Damn himself, he'd have to talk to Cal again. He made his way over to the other side of the room, waiting until Cal had finished the story she was reading.

"Yes?" she asked sharply.

"Could you read this one?" He held out the book. She took it and scanned the page.

"Read it out loud, please?" Aspen asked. Cal cleared her throat and did as they requested, her frown deepening the further she read.

"I thought," Emry ventured, "that maybe it was talking about a surge. With all the stomping and the blinding—"

"Blinding light, yes." Cal swept over to the board. "It's not a *real* account, but if it refers to a real event, the Tera fenn would have been..." She lifted a piece of chalk, then set it down. "Hm. One moment."

Wiping chalk dust on her jacket, she strode out of the room, making sure to lock the door behind her. Emry and Aspen watched the door close.

"She reads very well," Aspen said.

"She does do a lot of it."

"I like it. It reminds me of Addie."

"That's nice."

Aspen lifted their eyebrows. "You know, if she's going to help us, you can't keep making her angry."

Emry drew a deep breath and nodded. "Fine."

They sat in an uncomfortable silence until Cal returned, reading and rereading the scrap of paper she carried.

"So where's the fenn?" Aspen asked. She didn't answer right away. Instead, she stood on her tiptoes to draw a mark toward the top of her map, near Dawnstone. It was far north of her other markings, almost at the edge of Thalis itself.

And very close to Senne.

"That doesn't make any sense." Aspen frowned. "When did this happen?"

"It's hard to estimate exactly when the story was first told, but..." Cal stepped back. "Up to five thousand years ago, according to one of my professors. The Tera fenn was rather small and fell to the Mulec fenn long ago. It's a wonder their elders' narratives survived."

"But the story itself." Aspen hugged their arms, their projection shrinking with the motion. "You mentioned humans dying, and something sweeping over the whole world. None of the other ones sounded so...bad."

Emry couldn't argue with their logic—the more he stared at the map, the more the story made him uncomfortable as well.

"Look at the spot." He nodded to the board. "Cal, if the points on your map suggest that whatever creates the surges comes from the far south, and the Tera fenn felt it that far north...this surge would have had to cover all of Vidanya to get there, wouldn't it?"

The one time he wanted Cal to correct him, she didn't. She just studied the map. "I think so, yes."

Aspen disappeared into the lute, and the plant on the desk withered.

"But how do I defend against something like that?" their voice half wailed from the rose. "I can't do anything against something that big!"

"There's no need to fear." Cal erased the Tera mark with a firm hand. "An ancient folktale doesn't constitute an actual real-life event, and even if it did, we have no evidence to suggest it would happen again."

"But what about the surge in Thisby?" Aspen whined through the lute strings. Cal raised her hands.

"We have *little* evidence to suggest it would happen again. Practically nothing," she said, glancing furtively at Emry for support.

"Cal's right," Emry fumbled. "Practically nothing."

The lute fell silent for a moment. "Then how do we find the other ancient stories?"

"Pardon?"

"To make sure there aren't any more like it. Where do we find those?"

"Surely the library...?" Emry started, but Cal shook her head.

"Apart from that book"—she nodded to the Tera narrative—"very few transcriptions exist of narratives from that long ago." Then her nose wrinkled at a thought. "I suppose you could go to an Alta, if you really wanted to. I believe there's one at the fane outside of Vornik..."

"What's an Alta?"

Cal pressed her lips into a line as she neatened the books in front of her. "Outdated oral storytellers, mostly. They maintain fanes, perform ceremonies, pass down folktales. That sort of thing."

Aspen reappeared then, standing between them and the door. "So, when can we go to the Alta in Vornik?"

Both humans in the room suddenly found themselves backpedaling.

"I haven't got the time. I have to attend my lectures at some point—"

"No, we can't go all the way to Vornik!" Emry looked between Aspen and Cal. "We'll find someone in town, right, Cal?"

Aspen's expression crumpled. "I thought you said you were going to help me survive all this."

"I am," Emry babbled, "but I can't leave Tazlo right now—"

Cal nodded fervently alongside him. "Besides, there has to be better evidence than some old tales from an *Alta,* surely—"

Aspen's face darkened further, and before Emry could stop them, they picked up the lute, pulled the strap over their shoulder, and crossed their arms. "Fine. If you don't take me to the fane, I...I won't answer any questions about my spirit powers!"

They pointed, and the potted plant burst back to life. Cal barely held in a gasp. Emry almost laughed.

"You can't do that," she stammered. "This is the biggest discovery of the last—the last *forever*! I have to know—"

"And you"—Aspen turned their wild gaze on Emry—"I'll—I'll do something to the lute!"

Emry's blood froze.

"You wouldn't." He tried to take in a breath and failed. "You can't—I'm playing at the Lamb's Ear tonight, you know that!"

"The Lamb's Ear?" Cal's gaze whipped to him. "Really?"

Emry raised a hand to his chest, as if that would get his lungs working again. "Yes, really. Ella Sorman's manager asked me to play. I have to have the lute!"

Cal leaned back, and of all things, smiled at him. His breathing stuttered again. "Emry, that's...Weir's eyes, you're playing for the *Guild* tonight?"

"Not if I don't have the lute!"

Cal snapped her attention over to Aspen. "Give him the lute," she ordered. "We'll go to Vornik tomorrow, after the festival's over."

"All of us?" Aspen held up the instrument, green eyes flashing.

"Yes, fine, I'll go, please just..." Emry reached for the lute. As soon as Aspen gave it back, he half collapsed into a chair, hand at his forehead. He barely heard the others speaking.

"...very rude of you, Aspen, you have *no* idea what it means..."

"Rude of you to leave me to die...wasn't actually going to break the lute or anything..."

"Are we done here?" Emry forced out.

"Yes," Cal said. He didn't look at either of them—just slung the lute on his back and strode toward the door. The instrument slid down his back as Aspen disappeared into it.

"What time?" Cal called out. His hand paused on the door handle.

"I'm sorry?"

"What time is your performance at the Lamb's Ear?"

"Early, before sunset. Why?"

"I'd, um..." Her usual confidence faltered, her eyes looking everywhere but his face. "I'd like to be there. If that's acceptable to you."

His grip on the handle tightened, and all the brief progress he had made in calming down his heart was lost. "Yes," he said, before his better judgment could grab the reins. "Of course."

"Best of luck, Emry."

He nodded and slipped out into the stacks.

CHAPTER
TWELVE

ASPEN HAD the good sense not to speak again until they were back in Emry's flat, a peeling cluster of rooms all of twelve paces wide and ten paces long. As Emry stormed in, his mind replaying the last half hour in fits and starts, the place couldn't have felt more claustrophobic.

"I'm sorry," Aspen blurted. "I won't do it again, I'm sorry—"

Emry slammed the door shut. "Whatever. You got what you wanted, didn't you?"

As he dropped the lute on a wobbly chair and paced about the kitchen, Aspen took shape on the table, their human form small and wavering.

"I was just—I was scared, all right?" They hugged their knees up against their chest. "I don't like this. I don't like being in the lute and not in my tree, and no one wanted to go to Vornik to figure it all out, and I was scared." They looked up at Emry. "I didn't mean to scare you, too."

Emry met their gaze and stopped pacing—his anger couldn't quite stand up to the sight of a mythical being shivering on his kitchen table. The stories said that spirits could summon sunlight, call storms, move mountains.

They didn't say anything about their fears.

So he let out a long, slow breath and settled onto the chair next to Aspen. "It'll be okay," he said. "We'll both be okay."

They sat in silence for a while.

"Is Vornik a bad place?" Aspen asked.

"Hm?"

"You didn't want to go. Is Vornik really so bad?"

Emry fidgeted as he thought back to the letter sitting at the bottom of his satchel. "No. Vornik itself is fine. It's more—I just haven't left Tazlo in a long time, and..." He shook his head and picked up the lute. It was a silly fear—there was no risk of anyone finding him. Cal never traveled by river. "As long as we take the carriages, Vornik will be fine. Now, how many pieces do you think I can practice before sunset?"

THE ENTRANCE to Lamb's Ear Inn swarmed with tourists, but Henri the innkeeper waved Emry inside as soon as he saw his sealed note.

"Ah, yes, yes," he said. "Damir told me you were coming. Leave your lute by the other instruments. And your friend got you a table."

"Oh, Marko's already here?" Emry's spirits lifted. Henri's bushy eyebrows knit together as he gestured toward one end of the room.

"No, that woman over there. The Academy student."

He peeked around the corner. Cal was perched at a table not far from the stage, sipping wine and leafing through a pocket-sized notebook.

Henri strode off, leaving Emry gulping in the doorway. He was ready—or as ready as he could be—to perform in front of Ella Sorman that night.

He was not ready to perform in front of his ex-girlfriend.

His emotions, mixed with every step, hardly left him time to appreciate the ridiculous splendor of the Lamb's Ear. The inn wasn't a place he could afford to frequent, even on a non-festival day, and the decor made sure to rub it in his face at every turn. Being from the province of Selj, Henri insisted on covering every open space with rich fabric, plush pillows, and warm candlelight. And if the textural feast wasn't sufficient for his customers, the actual feast surely would be—Emry had to wind around all manner of steaming dishes and imported wine on his way to the stage.

All in all, it was little wonder that the most prominent member of the Auric Guild chose to perform in this space for Sada.

"Can't I sit with you and Cal?" Aspen asked, their voice muffled in the case, as Emry set the lute down by the other instruments.

"Not tonight," he whispered. "But we'll be performing soon, with some people who sound much better than me. You'll like them, I promise."

"Oh, I doubt they can sound better than you," Aspen said. Emry half smiled and patted the case before turning toward Cal. Whether she realized it or not, she glowed in the candlelight from the table, her curly hair forming a wide, soft halo around her face. Emry straightened his waistcoat and walked over to her.

"Hey, Cal."

"Hello." Cal tucked away the little notebook as he sat across from her. "How are you feeling?"

"Good. Ready, I think," he fumbled. "I had a small chat with our... new acquaintance."

"How much did you tell them?"

"I said we're fine as long as we stick to the carriage routes."

She pursed her lips, fingers tapping the stem of her wineglass. "You're still going to Vornik?"

"I already told them I would."

"I see."

A shadow of disappointment and something else passed over her face. Emry bristled at the former. "Listen, I realize it will be painful to continue dealing with my presence, but they'll be traveling in *my* lute, you can't just take them away—"

"Of course not, that's not what I meant."

"What, then?"

When she met his gaze, her eyes shone. "Is this really what gets you out of Tazlo, after all this time? A coerced promise to a—a being you hardly know?"

If she had punched him, it would have hurt less. "You're right," he said quietly. "I'm sorry, I have nothing to say for myself. I'll try to keep the Vornik trip as short as possible."

"That would be best." She turned away and drank her wine.

Luckily for Emry, help arrived in the form of two friendly faces at the entrance by the bar.

"Emry!" Marko and Stef waved—then instantly froze when they saw his companion.

"Stay there, I'm getting a drink!" Emry called back and stood up. "Cal, do you, um, want anything—"

"No, thank you."

He nodded and hurried off to his friends, who—much to the chagrin of the other bar patrons—hadn't moved from their spot.

"Emry?" Stef immediately felt his forehead with the back of her hand. "Are you feeling okay?"

"I'm fine, really—"

Marko grabbed his arm. "She's not staying for your performance, is she?"

"Quick, get him something to drink," Stef said, pushing Marko away. "What's happening? Why is she here?"

Emry rubbed the back of his neck. "I—ah, ran into her in the square and happened to mention I was playing. She asked if she could attend, and I said yes."

Stef's eyes narrowed at the half truth. "If you're sure you're okay with this..."

Marko came back with two drinks—wine for Stef, a small beer for Emry. "You'll be on stage soon, can't have too much. Though"—

he glanced over at Cal—"maybe I should've bought you something a bit stronger."

"Mr. Karic!" Henri waved at Emry from his place near the stage. Emry handed his untouched drink back to Marko.

"Go sit with Cal and drink it for me. I'm afraid my time is up."

As Stef wrinkled her nose, Marko took her arm. "Let's be polite," he reminded her gently.

"Yes, yes, I know."

Ella's troupe members, all legends in their own right, had gathered by the stage to tune their instruments. As if the golden pegs, strings, and keys flashing around their fingers weren't intimidating enough, all five of them turned to look at Emry in disdain as Henri approached with him in tow.

"My good friends, I believe Damir already told you about Mr. Karic." Even Henri seemed uncomfortable under their scrutiny—after shoving Emry forward, he scurried back to the bar.

"Yeah, Damir told us." The bagpiper at the head of the group didn't extend her hand to him. "You play and you sing?"

He froze briefly. Oh gods, he was talking to Ella Sorman's group. He was talking with them, then he was going to play *alongside* them —he steadied himself and cleared his throat. "Yes, I do."

"Get your lute and tune up." She continued speaking as he opened the case. "You'll lead three songs. 'The Long Road,' 'Woman at the Fane,' and 'Hara's Shield.'"

Emry heard the tiniest of whisper-cheers come from the lute at the mention of the last song.

"Three songs, then you're off the stage. No encores and no talking to Ella unless she approaches you. Understood?"

"Understood." Emry nodded. The bagpiper turned around and resumed her conversation with the rest of the troupe, leaving him to tune.

"...Charity case..." He could barely hear them over the growing noise of the crowd. "Damir's going soft..."

Emry dared one glance at the audience in time to see Ella Sorman and Damir Nedrov take their reserved seats near the front of the stage. Damir was already slouching again, and though Ella's patterned kaftan gave off the appearance of gaiety, her dark eyes remained serious. If he was one note off that night, she'd hear it.

But Sada had one last gift to give, for just as he finished tuning, the Lamb's Ear began to douse its lanterns.

It was yet another sign of extravagance that the inn could afford rhythm blooms both inside and out—after all, the flowers were expensive to maintain outside of their natural habitat, and it was difficult enough wrestling them into garlands for the partygoers outside. But the Lamb's Ear had spared no expense this year and hung large trailing pots of the blooms from the beams above. The audience's vocal wonder at the hanging garden only increased its beauty, as bursts of blue mimicked their laughter and delight.

Emry took a deep breath in time with the soft lights. He could be a nervous mess later, after this was all over. He was playing before Ella with her own troupe. If he didn't have at least a little bit of fun tonight, it would be a waste of a perfectly good night.

When it was time, he ascended to the stage behind the Guild members and took the center stool.

"We'll take your cue," the bagpiper said. Emry swung his lute around and looked out at the crowd, all shadow and soft blue.

"Evening, everyone! Happy last night of Sada!"

Marko gave an obnoxiously loud cheer. The audience laughed, and so did Emry.

"Someone either had very good luck this year, or can't be done with Sada soon enough." He flashed a grin at the crowd. "But I think you deserve some music regardless, right?"

Performing with Ella's troupe was leagues away from performing with André's troupe. To start, there was no need for prancing or wooing the crowd—their talent drew in the audience on its own merit. Not a single note was flat, not a rhythm disjointed. They played as if they were a single person behind Emry, not five, and in a duet like that, Damir wasn't wrong—there was no place for him to hide.

So he didn't. He focused on their sound and matched them beat for beat like it was a dance, and when it was time to breathe between songs, he took those precious moments to joke with the audience and the band —for this wasn't a concert hall, after all; this was Sada, and Hara enjoyed laughter just as much as song. By the end, he had poured so much effort into those three pieces that he felt like he was going to collapse.

But as they descended the stage, he couldn't stop smiling. That was what he had wanted. *That* was what he had wanted when he had left home—the music swirling, the perfect band, the audience matching his energy. The way nothing else mattered when he was on stage.

Nothing except perhaps Ella Sorman's opinion of his playing.

"Not bad at all." The bagpiper clapped him on the shoulder, a gesture that nearly sent him to the floor. "Emry, was it? Thanks for playing with us."

All around him, the other troupe members nodded and gave similar compliments. Emry worked hard to return their level of cool, understated enthusiasm as he picked up his lute case with trembling fingers. "Thank you. Happy Sada, and best of luck traveling out of the city tomorrow, yeah?"

They chuckled and waved as he walked off, certain his lungs had forgotten how to work until he reached his friends' table.

"Marko," he gasped as he flopped into a chair. "Marko, they said they liked me—"

"Of course they did, you buffoon!" Marko shook his arm, his grin wild. "Congratulations!"

Stef squeezed his shoulder and pushed a drink his way. "Amazing. You did great up there, you really did."

Emry's focus shifted to Cal, who was failing to hide a beaming smile behind her hand.

"Incredible," she finally said, half laughing. The rhythm blooms caught the sound and sent it rippling across the room. "To finally see you in front of Ella, I…" She tried to compose herself and shook her head. "Thank you for letting me watch. Really, it was spectacular."

Emry tried to form some sort of response, something that kept him from gaping like a fool at her smile—gods, how long had it been since he had seen it?—but was saved the effort, for Ella Sorman and Damir were making their way over to their table. Though his legs wobbled, he forced himself to stand and give half a bow. "Ms. Sorman, Damir, thank you for the opportunity, this was—"

The towering woman, taller than him even without the braids piled atop her head, looked him up and down once. "Impressive," she said, then swept off. Emry's heart stopped.

"Thank you!" he tried, but she was already swallowed up in the crowd, effortlessly ignoring the adoring fans around her. Damir stepped in and pulled out his pipe.

"Yeah, Ella wants to see you again," he said. "You got a calling card or anything?"

"Calling card?" Emry repeated. The closest thing to a calling card in up-city Tazlo was a debtor's note, and he wasn't even going to be in Tazlo after tomorrow. "I'm actually going to be in Vornik starting tomorrow—"

"You are?" Marko frowned at him. Damir was unfazed.

"Ah, we'll be there soon. Council business and such. Where will you be staying?"

"Um." His mind blanked. His plan to find a cheap Vornik inn at random was already backfiring. He couldn't make up a name, could he—?

"Here." Cal's hand shot past him, holding a card out to Damir. "He'll be staying here."

The card had Emry's name scribbled over her Academy address. He turned in time to see her tuck a pencil back behind her ear.

"Thanks." Damir pocketed the card. "We'll be there in a few days, maybe a week. Will you still be in Vornik then?"

"Yes, you can contact him there," Cal answered for him.

"We'll be in touch. Happy Sada." And off he went, puffing on the pipe. The whole table went silent for a moment—then they all stared at Cal.

Emry finally got the words out. "Cal, you can't be serious. You can't possibly want me to stay with you."

"Are you at all aware of how expensive Vornik is?" she retorted, but didn't meet his gaze as she grabbed her coat and fiddled with the buttons. "Especially if you're staying for more than a few days?"

"I'll find my own way. I have no intention of bothering you—"

"Do you want a place to stay or not?"

Emry stopped himself. "I do."

"Then meet me at the carriages by eight tomorrow. Any later than that, and you can catch your own ride to Vornik."

Emry nodded. "Eight, got it."

"Good. Well"—she looked back at Marko and Stef—"it was nice seeing you two again. Have a lovely rest of your Sada."

A few uncertain goodbyes later, she turned on her heel and strode out of the inn. Emry immediately grabbed his beer.

"Emry." Marko watched him chug it down. "Are you sure about this?"

"No." He slammed down the mug. "I need to go pack."

THIRTEEN

Aspen almost blew their cover five times that morning.

"We're going to Vornik, we're going to Vornik!"

"I know, I know. Shush, we're going downstairs."

Marko was waiting for Emry at the door when he emerged with an overstuffed satchel and lute in hand. He held out a little pack wrapped in paper and string. "Stef and I got you some food for the road. Listen, now that you've slept on it—are you *really* sure about all this? I mean, you haven't even said why you're going—"

"I'm really sure, and I'll tell you later." Emry took the pack and stowed it in his satchel. "We're taking a carriage, it's only a day to Vornik, and I'll return as soon as I can. I'll be okay."

Marko adjusted his glasses. "With Cal, though?"

Emry nodded, displaying more confidence than he felt. "I wouldn't know where to start, but...let's just say I owe you a full explanation when I'm back."

Marko hesitated, then opened the door for him. "All right, then. Safe travels."

"Thanks for the food, and tell Stef I said so." He walked through the door, then felt a surge of warmth and turned. "And thanks for everything. I really don't know what I've done to deserve a friend like you."

Marko smiled. "Go impress the hell out of the Guild, Emry."

As Emry slipped into the flow of hungover tourists leaving Tazlo, he tried to sort out the unreasonable giddiness that kept bubbling over his apprehension. At first, he told himself that it was because of Ella Sorman yesterday—a completely fair response, given the circumstances. She *had* told him he was impressive.

But he knew that underneath, it was because of Cal, so he did what he could to temper himself. He would not bother her while he stayed with her, that would be certain. He would restrict himself to simple hellos. Polite remarks. Comments about the weather. Perhaps comments about the weather leading to a casual conversation over lunch—no, no. Absolutely not.

He took care to avoid the crowds surrounding the Sumac nexus —lines of bleary-eyed people waiting for the underground rivers to sweep them away. Those unwilling to dirty their cloaks on a little cave mud instead filled the carriage stop, forcing Emry to navigate a wealthier but equally bleary-eyed mob when he arrived there.

As expected, Cal was already inside the inn, nursing something dark and bitter. Like the other customers, she looked tired and regretful—though whether she regretted letting him stay with her, or the early hour she had selected to depart, he wasn't sure.

"Don't suppose I can buy you another one of those before we head out?" He nodded to the mug.

"No, I'm all right." She waved a hand and went about gathering her belongings, slipping a folded bit of newspaper into the pages of a book. "I've learned about two more cities experiencing surges this week."

"Which ones?"

"Fustar in the west, and Matlock, over the border in Selj." She pushed away her mug and strode outside, leaving Emry to follow behind.

"Anything particularly bad?"

"Not beyond the damage we've already seen. Fields, groves, that sort of thing."

"Oh, no need to sound too torn up about it," Aspen grumbled from inside the case. Emry gently bumped the lute with his palm.

"Apologies, Aspen," Cal said discreetly, then glanced at Emry's hand. "Where's your luggage?"

"Um, here?" He gestured to his lumpy satchel. She rolled her eyes and passed her immaculate suitcase over to the carriage driver. Emry began digging in his pockets for his passage fare—which, of course, had spiked for post-festival travel.

"At the risk of being annoying," he said to Cal as he handed the coins to the driver, "I have to thank you again for helping me—"

"Please don't mention it." She focused hard on adjusting her sleeve. "It was entirely selfish. I merely wanted to get more time with our new acquaintance, nothing more. Now, if you'll excuse me, I need to study on the way there."

His previous excitement deflated. "Right, of course."

She ducked into the carriage quickly, and when he settled into the seat across from her, she was already hiding her face with a book.

"Emry, can I sit next to Cal?" Aspen asked from inside the lute.

"Um, sure." Emry glanced at her, and she gave the smallest of nods. He shifted onto the seat next to her just before another passenger opened the door.

"And this stops at Karlovy before connecting to Halagrad, yes?" a warbling voice asked the carriage driver. "Good, thank you."

A well-bundled woman smelling of outdated perfume clambered into the carriage, taking up the opposite seat with herself, five hat boxes, and a little white terrier. She took one look at Emry and his wrinkled traveling cloak, gave a sniff, and turned her gaze to the window.

As the carriage jolted into movement, Emry closed his eyes. He hoped that a bit of sleep would whisk him through most of the ride to Halagrad and the connecting trip to Vornik, if only to keep his mind off of what he was doing.

Aspen, however, held no such hopes.

"Cal," they whispered after five minutes of bored silence, "what are you reading?"

Emry glanced over at the old woman, who was still looking out the window, then pointedly nudged the lute, hushed it, and closed his eyes again. One minute later—

"I wish I could read," Aspen muttered. Emry quickly elbowed the lute again.

"*Shush.*"

The old woman peeked over at this. Cal cleared her throat and looked not at the lute, but directly at Emry.

"I'd be happy to teach you how to read," she said, a mischievous glint in her eye. Emry felt the old woman's judging eyebrow lift at this.

"Thanks, Cal." He glared. She smirked and turned back to her book.

Ten silent minutes passed, and Emry was finally drifting off to sleep, when—

"Oh! You have a dog, too?"

This was the old woman, pointing an arthritic finger at the space between Cal and Emry.

"No?" Emry looked down and slumped. Aspen, now a dark brown terrier, thumped their tail excitedly against the seat. The woman's white terrier began to bark.

"Ms. Breslin, please control your dog." Emry lifted Aspen and placed them on Cal's lap, right in front of her book. She shot a glare at him.

"Apologies, ma'am," she mumbled to the woman, then tried to lift her book free—but Aspen had already curled up on it.

"Not at all! I love little doggies." The woman leaned toward Cal.

"Please tell me, what is its name and breed? My little Ringlet came from a breeder in Bennli..."

Emry smiled to himself and curled up in the corner as the woman jabbered all the way to the Karlovy stop. As soon as the old woman disembarked with a yipping Ringlet in tow, Cal pushed Aspen off her lap and reopened her book with an annoyed snap. "Get off my seat, Mr. Karic."

"With pleasure."

Leaving the lute next to her, Emry stretched out on the free seat across from her and tossed his cape over himself like a blanket. According to the carriage driver, Halagrad was still a few hours away —plenty of time to sleep away the gnawing anxiety that grew worse the farther they rolled away from Tazlo.

FOURTEEN

An hour later, Emry woke to the sound of horses squealing and wheels creaking to a stop.

"What's going on?" He sat up and immediately clutched the seat —the carriage shook as if it were rolling over a bed of rocks.

"It'll be over soon!" The driver's panicked voice floated in from outside. Across from Emry, Cal had one hand pressed to the wall and the other steadying the lute case. As she looked out the window, white light from the glowing forest reflected back in her eyes.

"It's a surge," she said. "Aspen, get in the lute. We'll be safe in here until it's over."

After the spirit's terrier form disappeared, glowing white particles began to float past the window, drifting north.

"Is this a part of the surge?" Emry leaned closer to the glass. As he watched, the tiny particles built up, tumbling more quickly, until they resembled a violent snow. The faster the particles moved, the more the forest pulsed with light.

"Not from anything I've seen before." Cal squinted. "Perhaps it's visible streams of the surge's energy. Hold on, let me write this down..."

As she rummaged through her satchel, a particle phased through the wooden door and floated into the carriage. Emry blinked. "Cal?"

"I just need to find my notebook. If these streams indicate a more intense surge—"

More particles slipped through the wood. "Cal, I don't think we're safe here."

"What do you mean? Of course, we—" She looked up and stared at the pinpricks of light wobbling past his knees. "Oh."

Emry grabbed the lute case and tossed his cloak over it. A useless gesture—if the energy traveled through wood, surely it could travel through cloth—but it made him feel better in the moment.

"What's happening?" Aspen's voice bounced from the jostled lute. "I don't feel so good."

"Stay inside, Aspen." His grip tightened on the case's handle. "Where do we go?"

"Let me look around." Cal ducked outside.

"Hey!" the driver shouted at her. "I said, it'll be over soon!"

Cal ignored him and darted off. After she left the window's line of sight, Emry sat back and grimaced against a sudden wave of dizziness.

"Aspen"—he reached out to the wall to steady himself—"you still there?"

"Still here," they said, their voice hollow.

A knock sounded on the door. Cal's face was back in view, blurry through the thick glass. "Out!" she was shouting. "Come out, I've found something!"

As soon as Emry entered the snow-like surge, his head swam, and he leaned back against the carriage wheel.

"Over there." Cal pointed. He squinted to see her target—the ruins of an old stone cottage, sitting off the path in a mossy clearing. The white, shimmering air filtered around the stone walls like beams of sunlight, leaving clear patches behind the stone where the energy couldn't reach. "I think we can hide behind the walls and get out of the surge there—"

Behind them, the horses snorted and held their heads high, hooves stamping the ground. The driver made an attempt to calm them, but they ignored him and struggled forward.

"Get back inside!" The driver waved frantically to them. Emry looked to the particles swirling inside the carriage, then the stone ruins. His vision tilted sideways.

"We have to hide," he said, staggering a little. "The horses must feel like this, too—"

"Like what?" Cal grabbed his arm.

He struggled to keep her face in focus. "What do you mean? Don't you feel it?"

The carriage driver cried out as the horses bolted forward.

"No, wait!" Cal shouted, but there was no stopping them. As the carriage jolted down the road, the lute began to vibrate on Emry's back.

"Can we get to the ruins now, please?" Aspen's voice broke.

"Follow me." Cal plunged into the undergrowth at the side of the road. Emry stumbled as he followed—something was pinpricking his limbs, though he saw no thorns in the brush. He glanced down at his arms and blinked hard. Were those stars floating in front of his eyes, or glowing under the skin of his wrist?

"Come on!" Cal was already behind the stone, gesturing for him to move forward. He half ran, half stumbled until he could grab the next tree for stability.

"I don't know how long I can hold on," Aspen said, their voice barely a whisper. The glowing bark under Emry's fingers began to twist.

"Almost there." Emry staggered back. "Almost there—"

Taking one shaky breath, he pitched himself away from the tree and collapsed into the shadow of the ruins.

The world felt calmer behind the stone shield. Though the ground still shook, nothing shimmered or floated through the air. The pinpricks in his limbs subsided, and as soon as his vision steadied, he checked his arm. Nothing glowed.

Several held breaths later, the earth fell still again. The streams of white disappeared, and birdsong returned to the branches above them. Emry closed his eyes and let his cheek rest on the cool soil. "Aspen?"

"I'm here," the spirit said through their own heavy breaths. "I'm lucky you found this spot. One more moment and I would've had to let go."

Emry heard Cal's boots crunch in the leaves by his head, and he opened one eye. "How about you, Cal? You all right?"

"Just fine." She knelt down next to him. "What did you feel?"

Emry pushed himself to his knees. "Dizzy, mostly." He rested his palm against his forehead and winced. "Did you really not feel any of that?"

"No, thank goodness." She plucked a leaf from his hair, then pulled him to his feet. "I wonder why."

"Emry's not alone," Aspen said. "Look at the trees."

They did so. All around them, mangled, black trunks and withered leaves randomly dotted the landscape. Desiccated branches hung limp next to perfectly green ones.

"Some of them were affected, some of them weren't," Aspen continued. "I don't know why, but—Emry must be like one of the unlucky trees."

"Love that, thank you," Emry mumbled. Next to him, Cal leaned forward to inspect the landscape.

"What's that?"

Emry followed her gaze over the mossy wall.

He didn't see them at first—they were barely visible in the sunlight, like spiderwebs floating in the breeze. But when his eyes did focus on them, it was difficult to look away. Two concentrations of silvery mist twisted in the air, sliding up against tree trunks, then melting off. Occasionally, they would form a tendril in the shape of a wing or a claw, dragging it along the earth before morphing back into a shapeless form. As they stretched in a slow desperation over the ground, the moss and foliage beneath them shriveled and darkened.

"Remnants?" Emry whispered. As he spoke, one of the claw shapes reached lazily in their direction. He shivered and touched the wooden lute on instinct.

"I don't like them." Aspen started quiet, then grew more insistent. "I don't like them at all. We need to leave."

"Everything's fine, Aspen." Cal set a hesitant hand on the lute. "They don't seem to be doing anything—"

A squirrel skittered down one of the dead trees toward the nearest remnant, its tail dusted with charcoal. It regarded the floating mist with a tilt of its head, then turned to hop off—but the remnant was too quick. It dove straight into the creature, the mist siphoning into its fur in a blink. The squirrel flashed white once, then fell unmoving into the leaves.

Cal swallowed and took the lute from Emry. "Yes, good idea. Time to leave."

CHAPTER

FIFTEEN

AFTER A PANICKED JOG away from the remnants, it took them several hours of walking to reach the edge of Halagrad. Though still slightly woozy, Emry kept a sharp eye out for their runaway carriage.

"I'm going to find him and get our money back," he muttered.

Cal looked him over.

"Not in that state, you aren't."

"Then *I'll* get our money back."

"You'll do no such thing, Aspen." Cal adjusted her satchel hanging off her shoulder. "Let's just focus on getting our luggage and finding another service to Vornik."

But Halagrad was in far too much of a tizzy for Cal's plan to work. Between neighbors gathering to gossip, markets scrambling to close up shop, and a few people looking as unsteady as Emry had felt, the streets—and carriage services—had dissolved into chaos.

"Sorry, miss," the hackney owner shouted over the mess, "but we've canceled our connecting trip. No one wants to drive in this weather. You're best off finding a place to stay before they fill up!"

All around them, people were cramming themselves into any available building. Though no one in the city knew quite what had

109

happened, they did know one thing—Halagrad's buildings of brick and stone hadn't let in a single particle of the surge.

"There's got to be someone—" Cal started, but the owner had already walked away. She rubbed her eyes and turned back to Emry. "Come on, let's try somewhere else."

"This was the last service. We've asked around at all the others."

She gave a tired gesture to the city at large. "Then we'll ask for rooms, I suppose."

They restarted their circuit around the town. Once again, they were left in the street.

"We're full up, but I can give you a spot in the stables for cheap," the last innkeeper said. "It's all I have left."

"No, thank you." Cal's shoulders slumped. After all the walking and retreading of steps, her feet dragged. "We'll find another way out of here."

They stood on the sidewalk, looking out at the town that held nothing for them.

"Are there any other towns within walking distance?" Emry asked, though his aching feet already protested the words.

"Not unless you want to walk ten miles." Cal chewed her lip as she thought. Emry scrambled for another idea. There was one option they hadn't explored yet, and he couldn't risk it popping into her head.

"What if we got a horse somehow?"

"That would be easier. But if the carriages aren't going, no one's going to let their horse out of the city walls, either." Then she frowned and looked at him. Emry cursed inwardly. "There is...one other way out."

"No." His throat went tight. "You know I can't do that."

His face must have betrayed his panic, for she pulled him into a side street and set a hand on his arm. "I don't think we have a choice. The nexus might be the only open place left."

"Cal, please—"

"What's happening?" Aspen appeared next to Cal in their human form—weak and transparent, but still there. "What's our way out?"

Emry found a crate to sit on and tried to catch his breath, but it was as if he was in the surge all over again. "It's the river routes," he forced out. "I can't be seen there."

"Why, did you make someone angry?" Aspen gasped. "Are there bears there, too?"

"No bears, Aspen." Cal sat on the crate across from Emry. Aspen did the same. "Emry, it'll be one boat ride, and we're very far from Senne. Keep your hood up, stay behind me, and we'll be in Vornik by evening with no one the wiser. But we cannot stay here."

As she glanced nervously at the darkening streets, Aspen's post-surge form flickered in the slight breeze. She was right—they couldn't stay here. Emry passed a hand over his face and forced himself to take a deep breath.

"If—*if*—the boats haven't stopped because of the surge," he said, "then we can take one out of here. But never again, you understand?"

"Understood." Cal reached forward and touched his hand. "And thank you."

She set off in the direction of Halagrad's nexus. Emry shook out the tingling in his hand and followed.

UNLIKE THE GAPING maw of Tazlo's nexus, the Halagrad nexus camouflaged itself into the verdant foothills curling around the city. From the path, all Emry could see was a narrow black eye embedded into the mountain, letting a raging river pass through into the deep. At the head of the path, a wooden sign blared at them in paint that had been recently refreshed:

KARIC SUB-RIVER SERVICE
Your Access to the Sumac Routes and Beyond
Operating 7 Days a Week, 8-8

Please Dress Warmly!

"What's it say?" Aspen said, taking their place as a fluffy mouse on Emry's shoulder. Emry's stomach churned.

"Nothing," he said, and pressed forward.

Halagrad had built a walkway leading into the nexus only a few yards above the river, leaving the water's constant spray to nip at their boots as they hurried into the tunnel.

"Emry"—Cal's voice echoed about the stone walls—"really, think—what's the worst that could happen?"

"Capsizing in the rapids is pretty bad," he mumbled. "A stalactite falling on you could be worse, though that doesn't actually happen—"

"You know what I meant."

Emry pulled his hood up over his head and shifted to walk behind Cal. "Let's just get in there."

The lantern-dotted tunnel boasted a modest number of passengers as it descended into the caverns. Though faster than carriages, the narrow river boats allowed little room for luxury items—nor did the damp, frigid caves give off any sense of sophistication. As a result, those who did pass by in the tunnel were mostly merchants, medics, or plain ordinary folk. It was part of the reason Emry had once loved the river routes.

As the tunnel gradually opened into a large, dusky chamber, Aspen's whiskers twitched in excitement. "So, this is what's underneath the roots! Can we stop to see, please?" they whispered, their little eyes locked on the curtain stalactites that framed the pathway. The lanterns here tossed sharp shadows up the towering stones, and Emry felt an echo of the same awe he had experienced when admiring the stalactites as a boy.

But today, he kept walking past them. "You'll see plenty more of those down by the river, Aspen—"

"Oh, my flowers grow here, too!" Aspen cried, and their feathery mouse weight disappeared from Emry's shoulder. A brown terrier now hopped about his feet, trying to balance on their back two paws as if to better see the ceiling. Emry looked up to what their black nose pointed at.

"Hush—and I'm sorry, but they're not flowers," he whispered and stopped to pick up Aspen as a few other passengers shot him looks. "They're glow-worms. I see the resemblance, though."

Up at the top of the cavern, far beyond where the lanterns could throw their light, glimmers of green pricked the darkness like stars. They pulsed dimly in time to the footsteps of the passersby below.

"Fascinating." Cal's low voice next to him made him jump. "I've read about these, but to actually see them in person...you know, they're brighter than I expected."

Emry couldn't help it.

"Maybe if someone wasn't afraid of getting their expensive cloak dirty, they wouldn't be so surprised."

Cal glared at him. "At least carriages won't tip me into a freezing river at a moment's notice."

Aspen wiggled in Emry's arms. "Are these not-flowers in every cave?" they asked. Emry turned away from Cal's glare to regard the twinkling lights.

"They're all over Vidanya, but they only light up like this a few times a year. Sada season is one of them."

The murmur of the passengers in the tunnel picked up as more people wandered in—no doubt other stranded visitors having the same idea as Cal. Emry fiddled with his hood. "Come on, let's keep going."

The tunnel narrowed again until it finally spilled them into the dock area—a massive cavern cradling a black, mirror-smooth lake. The vast space allowed for a bifurcated dock, with sleek, narrow passenger boats to the left, and larger merchant boats to the right. People on both sides all waited and toiled under the supervision of massive stalactites dripping from the vaulted ceiling. Most kept their voices low, as if loud noise would break one of the stone needles and shatter the lake like glass.

Up ahead, the portly man emerging from the boathouse held no such fear.

"Silver per person for Vornik, two silvers for Thisby!" he shouted gaily into the chill void. "Don't forget to sign the logbook as you pay."

Much like the boat runners inspecting their transports, the boathouse manager swung about in a traveling cloak embroidered with trees, flowers, and sheafs of wheat—friendly Hara symbols, to ward off Shiro's capricious floods. Emry glanced at the man's face and gave a small sigh of relief—he didn't recognize him.

He hung back for a moment, his insides tumbling even as his heart lit up at the sight of the boats. How could he feel so immensely uncomfortable in a place that had once felt like a second home? Even the cold cavern air stung his throat in what felt like a form of punishment.

"So…" Cal's hesitant tug on his sleeve broke him away from watching the familiar routine of the runners at the boats. "How exactly does one navigate these?"

Emry reluctantly stepped out of the flow of passengers from the tunnel and set terrier Aspen on the ground. "It's nothing to worry about. Get in line, and when you get to the manager, say you're going to Vornik—but make sure they're taking the blue route, not the red one." He dug around in his purse and handed her two coins. "Here's my silver, and another one to buy yourself a second cloak. The blue route only gets colder as you go, and that thing isn't going to do you any good down here."

Cal rolled her eyes and took the coins as he gestured to her typical southern cloak—heavy on the color, light on actual function. "Do you want a second one as well?"

"No, I'll be fine. Oh, and"—he touched her arm as she turned to join the line—"don't write my name in the logbook, just yours."

"Of course." Cal nodded and headed toward the manager.

"Can I ride in the boat?" Aspen whispered, keeping close to Emry's heels.

"Only if you stay in your dog form, and you can't talk in front of the runner." As Aspen brushed against his foot, he noticed their terrier shape was much more solid than their human form earlier. "You feeling better after the surge?"

"Oh, yes." Aspen's ears perked up at him before they sniffed the ground. "Thank you for asking."

The discomfort of being inside the caves again made it difficult for Emry to stand still, and before he realized what he was doing, his feet had led him over to the boats. His gaze roved over the transports automatically—no damage across the hulls, no cracks in the frame, no rot that he could see. If he had a lantern, though, he could step closer and check more thoroughly…

"What are you looking at?" Aspen asked. Emry shook his head and stepped away from the boats.

"Force of habit. Just making sure they're all safe."

"Are you afraid of the boats like Cal?"

Emry snorted. "Seeing as I was practically raised in them, no."

One of Aspen's ears flopped. "I thought humans grew up in houses?"

"Ah." Emry let himself smile at that. "What I meant was—I used to be a cave runner, is all."

"Oh." Aspen sniffed at the wood around his feet, then looked up. "Emry, a fane!"

They scurried off toward the end of the docks without warning.

"Wait!" Emry scrambled to follow. He feared the spirit's enthusiasm would carry them straight over the edge and into the water—but the terrier skidded to a stop in front of a small cubby. It wasn't unlike Aspen's fane in build, but much better taken care of, likely by the boathouse manager. Though buckled from the higher humidity of the caves, the cubby boasted a decent number of coins, flowers, and pinecones.

"Can we put something in for the spirit?" Aspen's tail wagged.

"All right." Emry rummaged around for a copper and placed it in the cubby, where it clinked against the other offerings. "Is there actually a spirit here? Can you feel it?"

"Well, I can't connect with the ground here quite as well, but..." Aspen sat on all fours, lowered their head, and closed their eyes.

After a moment, the shadow of a large fish slid under the surface of the water.

"Yes! Hello!" Aspen jumped up, ears perked—but the fish slipped away just as quickly. "Oh. Okay, then."

"I'm sorry, Aspen."

"No, I should've expected it," they said, though their drooping tail betrayed their disappointment. "Spirits don't...talk like humans do. I'll miss that, once I'm back in my grove."

If there was no sight so heartbreaking as a sad dog, there certainly wasn't one like a sad spirit dog.

"I'll come visit you," Emry offered. "We can still talk."

"Oh, could you, please?" Aspen's tail was back in action. "That would be lovely—"

"Excuse me, sir," a cheerful voice said behind Emry, "a reminder that you'll have to keep your dog in your lap at all times when you're on the boat."

"Apologies." Emry only half turned to the voice—it was the manager. He touched his hood to make sure it was still up, then gestured to Aspen. "Won't be a problem at all. Come on up, Aspen."

But Aspen jumped into his arms a little too eagerly, and the hood slipped down. The manager squinted. "Do I know you?"

Emry didn't dare meet his gaze. "No, I don't believe so—"

"Wait. Are you a Karic?"

Emry froze. "Um...no?"

But it was no use—the man's face had split into a grin, and he was clapping him on the shoulder with a calloused hand. "Emry Karic! By Hara, do you look just like your father."

Emry desperately fought the urge to jump straight into the water. Behind the man's shoulder, standing by an open boat, Cal stood in shock.

"Your father passed through here a few weeks ago for inspections," the manager continued blithely. "Gods, you even have the same eyes and everything. I'll have to tell him you passed through, too!"

"Oh, that's not necessary, they don't want to know—"

"Of course, they would! Last they mentioned, you were somewhere near Foxhill. But you finally came back!" He squeezed Emry's shoulder. "You get on the boat over there, the runner'll be out in a second."

The man winked and retreated, leaving Emry to walk over in a daze.

"Emry, I'm so sorry." Cal rushed up to meet him. "I didn't know —to think he would actually recognize you..." She took a gentle hold of his wrist. Each of her fingers was ice cold, but it barely registered.

"That," he said, his voice shaking, "*that* was the worst thing that could have happened."

"Let's get you on the boat." She started to step in.

"Right foot," he blurted without thinking.

"What?"

"Step in with your right foot. Left foot's bad luck."

He had half a mind to laugh at himself. What use was luck to him now?

CHAPTER

SIXTEEN

Emry followed Cal into the boat, holding too tightly to Aspen's dog form as he sat. The only benefit to his heart beating so fast was that it drowned out the thoughts rattling his mind—though Cal was doing her best to break through both.

"Listen, the news about you being in Halagrad isn't going to get to them right away. Who knows, you could be back in Tazlo before they even find out you were here."

But even as she reassured him, a question lingered behind her eyes.

"Please don't start," Emry mumbled.

"I won't, I won't." Cal drew back. Paused. "But have you really not written to them at all? Not once all this time?"

"Why would I?" he burst, his words skittering across the lake. Aspen, and several others at the dock, gave a start. "Does it look like I've accomplished anything with my life?"

Thankfully, their runner ambled up at that moment, saving them from the heavy air of Emry's long-standing habit of disappointing people.

"Vornik, yeah?" The beefy woman trundled into the boat, looking

121

impervious to the cold in her layers. "Should be a couple hours. Keep those cloaks handy—this route gets colder as you go."

It was fortunate that the first stretch of the Vornik route was one of the most beautiful in southern Vidanya, or else Emry might have chosen to throw himself overboard and swim the rest of the way just to stop his mind from whirring. Stalactites and lumpy stone pillars gave way to a score of sinkholes, all curtained in vines and glittering sunbeams. Aspen tapped a paw on one low-hanging vine as they passed through the pools of light, and flowers rippled up the foliage.

Then the temporary warmth of the sunbeams disappeared, leaving only water, cold air, and lantern light for the second half of the passage. Cal's shivering quickly grew in frequency, until Emry could no longer avoid her. Without a word, he unclasped his own traveling cloak and draped it over her legs.

"No, no, I'm fine," she said, but her words came out through chattering teeth.

"I insist," he murmured, then set to work adjusting her other cloak until she was as insulated as possible. "Better?"

He had wrapped her so thoroughly that she couldn't grab his hand, though he could see her arm make an attempt. "I really am sorry—"

"I'm sorry, too." Aspen wriggled in Emry's arms. "It was all my fault, I messed up your hiding—"

The cave runner frowned and looked over her shoulder at the third voice. Emry shushed them both and sat back.

"I'd rather not talk about it," he said, and they floated the rest of the way in silence. By the time they reached the Vornik docks and made their way up to the surface, he had grown so used to the quiet of the caves that the jumbled noise of the city jarred his ears.

"The Academy is a short walk from here!" Cal had to shout as they ascended through the Vornik nexus—a massive sinkhole in the center of the city, wrestled into navigability by carved spiral staircases. Those walking up pressed themselves to the stone wall to allow descending passengers through. "Keep close to me, the central square is usually busy. Aspen, you might want to stay in the lute."

The spirit grumbled and disappeared as they reached the top of the stairs, and Emry was immediately glad Cal had asked them to stow away.

Unlike Tazlo and Halagrad, the city of Vornik had no mountains to vie with for space, and as a result, its roads sprawled and stretched. The crowds, too, expanded to fill the space until Emry could hardly take a step without bumping shoulders with someone else.

Today, the noisy crowd clustered around a stately, if old-fashioned, pillared building at the southern edge of the central square. A smattering of green-coated soldiers kept the group from ascending the stairs to the building, where a woman also clothed in forest green attempted to address the shouting audience.

"Councilman Hasek has heard your concerns!" Her voice carried poorly over the din. "We are very confident that these surges will be over in several days!"

"Is he going to send soldiers to fight the remnants?" one man called out.

"We are, ah, still working on that, but they are no reason to panic—"

"Those aren't the stories coming from Bennli!"

Cal shook her head at the hubbub and took Emry's arm to better navigate him through the square. "We can go visit the Alta tomorrow morning," she said as they left the plaza behind and slipped into quieter streets, ones lined with pale stone townhouses, tiny gardens, and delicately wrought street lamps. The closer they got to the Academy, the younger the faces around them looked. "For today, I can get you into my dorm in Esther Hall, but you're going to have to stay away from the windows overnight, so the proctors don't see you. I'll get you food from the dining hall, and I'll check the mail every day for word from the Guild."

"Can I come out now?" Aspen asked.

"As a human, yes."

Aspen the human appeared and kept an easy stride with them, matching Emry's clothing and cloak. To Emry's relief, their flickering from the surge had subsided.

"After we see the Alta," Aspen said, "are we going to play music for that man again? Damir?"

Emry fought down a mixed wave of elation and anxiety. "Hopefully, yes. But not today."

"And why do we want this man to like us?"

"He's a part of the Auric Guild."

"Ah." Aspen nodded sagely. "And the Aurics gild what, exactly?"

Cal bit back a laugh. "The Auric Guild is a group of highly talented musicians working for the Vidanya Council," she said. "Quite a small group, too. There are, what, twenty of them?"

"Fifteen, at the moment," Emry said. Aspen frowned.

"So, what do they do if they don't gild things?"

"Perform, mostly." Emry nudged Aspen. "But there are some rumors about what they did back in wartime."

Aspen's eyes went wide. "What did they do?"

"Some say"—he leaned in dramatically—"they were spies."

Aspen gasped. "Spies?"

"Yes." Emry grinned. "Secret messengers, diplomats, that sort of thing. All paid by the Council to do their bidding."

"Oh, please." Cal snorted. "Can you imagine anyone from the Quartet being a spy? They've hardly got a rational brain cell between the four of them. Just last month, the cellist almost broke her hand starting a bar fight over major chords."

Emry held up his hands. "I'm not saying anyone in the Quartet was ever a spy, but—surely the Guild could have done *something* fun during the Thalis peace accord."

"Yes, I believe they got drunk," Cal said, a ghost of a smile crossing her lips. "In reality, the Thalis Councils have been at peace for years. Nowadays, the Guild doesn't actually do much other than perform at state events, and in cities that have any sort of grievance against the Council. Usually helps clear the air."

"And they play in Tazlo for Sada," Emry added.

"And they get drunk," Aspen said with confidence. "Emry, do you also want to get drunk?"

Emry shook his head as Cal laughed. "No, I'm not interested in that part."

"Then why do you want to join the Guild?"

Cal's smile faded, and Emry's temporary joy from old rumors vanished, replaced by the echoes of the boathouse manager's words. "I have to," he said quietly. "It's the only way I can go home."

SEVENTEEN

Esther Hall stood proudly as the tallest and most ostentatious residence hall on the Academy's Vornik campus. Unlike the other residences, which were shoved unceremoniously behind administrative buildings, this one lounged in the middle of ornate gardens and swirling pathways. As they stepped inside, the signature Academy brick transitioned into dark wood paneling, stretching into candlelit study and dining halls. Emry caught a glimpse of one such hall before the door closed—it looked ready for a formal dinner, all stark white cloth and gleaming flatware.

"This is certainly an upgrade from the Tazlo apartments," he whispered to Cal as he followed her up the stairs. The Tazlo residences, though certainly nice, had to cram all their rooms up against a mountainside, leaving little space for the rich and stifling airs that now surrounded them.

"I suppose so," Cal said dismissively. Behind her, Aspen ran a finger along the polished railing, then tugged on Emry's sleeve.

"This is very different from where you live."

Emry gave them a flat look. "Thank you for noticing, Aspen."

He soon learned why Esther Hall was so tall—the residences had two floors, with a parlor downstairs and what Emry assumed was Cal's room at the upper end of a spiral staircase. The parlor's sofas and tea tables were clearly designed for socializing, but had been shoved aside for something else—a heavy desk, dragged and positioned right next to the hearth. If he had to guess from the scratched floor and the tread marks going from the door to the desk, Cal had moved it herself to allow for efficient studying as soon as she entered the room.

"You'll stay on the sofa"—Cal pointed into the parlor, then up the stairs—"and the washroom is up here. I'll have to cancel the maid service while you're here. Can't have them seeing you…"

As she climbed the stairs, a thought struck Emry. "Cal, is it going to be…weird for anyone else that I'm here?"

She paused on the steps. "Well, like I said, I can't have the proctors noticing you're here—"

"No, I mean, are you…" He gestured inarticulately. "You know, seeing anyone?"

"Oh." She tucked a curl behind her hear. "No, I'm not. Now, if you'll excuse me, I need to unpack."

A foolish spark flared up in his chest, and he stamped it out just as quickly.

"Can I go up there, too?" Aspen called. "I want to see what a washroom is!" They grabbed the lute and ran up the stairs behind her without waiting for an answer. Emry set down his satchel and sat gingerly on the sofa. As he suspected, the unyielding cushions had been built for brief stays over tea or cards—not for sleeping. But the back pain was preferable to whatever price the Vornik inns charged, so he fluffed up the decorative pillows as best he could and dug around in his satchel for a snack.

His fingers brushed a few scraps of paper, and his heart sank.

"What does that thing do?" Aspen's voice echoed down the staircase.

"I'll show you later," Cal said as she came back down, holding a stack of blankets and pillows. "I realize the sofa isn't very comfortable, but if it's only for a week or so…"

He blinked at the pile of soft fabric—a surprisingly kind gesture, from someone who had every right to make him sleep on the floor. "It'll be great, thank you."

But her hands stayed on the blankets when he reached for them, and he looked up to find her searching his face. "Are you sure you don't want to talk about the boathouse?"

Emry's heart dropped even further. Just a pity gesture, then. "I'm sure."

She gave a stiff nod, then released the blankets and made for the door.

"I'm going to the dining hall. Yes, Aspen, you can come along. Emry, would you like anything?"

He couldn't meet her gaze this time. "No, I'm not hungry."

"What's in the dining hall?" Aspen opened the door.

"Food, mostly. Hopefully some tea."

"Then maybe you can explain to me what food tastes like…"

Their conversation faded down the hall, leaving Emry alone.

The problem with silence in an unfamiliar room, in an unfamiliar city, was that nothing could drown out his thoughts. The boathouse manager's words, Cal's words, the fear and the disappointment—it all looped in his head in loud, jarring snippets he couldn't push away. He looked around, but there was nothing familiar to distract or reassure him—not even his lute, which was now traveling down to the dining hall with his ex-girlfriend.

He set down the blankets and wandered over to the window, which afforded him a view of the gardens behind the building. His thoughts swung out of their previous loop and into a different, yet no less painful, rut. If he had gone to Vornik with Cal when she had asked him to last year…if he hadn't chained himself to the hope of catching the Guild's eye in Tazlo…would he have been out walking along those garden paths with Cal right now? Would he be staying in her room, rather than on the sofa in the corner?

He knew he shouldn't. He was usually good at resisting. But after several untethered minutes, he decided to swim down further, and reached into his satchel for the half-torn, grease-stained scraps of paper that he couldn't bring himself to throw out.

Emry—

Don't leave Foxhill yet. Mum and Dad want to talk—

He had already read that one. He tossed it aside and unfolded the next letter. It was the oldest one he had saved, and its age showed through the smudged writing and tattered corners. It was dated from over three years ago, but he could still make out his older sister's bold handwriting.

Dearest dumb brother,

Come on, you've been gone for three weeks. Don't you think it's time to come home now? As stubborn as they can be, I promise that Mum and Dad didn't mean what they said. Just come home and talk it through with them. Marley's getting worried. I might even start missing you in a few days. And bring that lute back—I promised a friend I'd let them borrow it for Sada.

Stop being a dumb-dumb,
Georgie

He flipped to the next one, unable to help himself.

Dear Emry,

No, they haven't exactly admitted that they were wrong to give you an ultimatum like that. They think that by throwing themselves into early Sada preparations, they can ignore the problem and what they said to you. But I promise, Marley and I aren't letting them forget it. We can't have you miss Sada.

If it entices you to come home at all, Nana's bringing some pies over tomorrow to taste-test and wants to hear what you've been practicing. And I mean "hear" metaphorically, since her other ear is well and truly gone—but still. Please come home.

Take care of yourself,
Georgie

The next one was dated two weeks later.

Emry,

Took me a while to figure out where you were staying in Foxhill, once my letter to Thisby got returned. Don't worry, I haven't told Mum or Dad. But—listen, Mum broke down at dinner yesterday. Then Dad did. It should go without saying that Marley did, too.

After all my efforts, it was Nana who did it. At the end of dinner, she said she'd save a pie for you, and there they went. They still haven't told her how long you've been gone.

They're not going to make you join the family business, or expect you to join the Guild before you show your face, or any of the stupid stuff they said months ago. They just want you back. If you take the green river route when you get this letter, you can still make it back with a few days to spare.

Love,
Georgie

The last one was littered with redirecting stamps and forwarding addresses. By the time it had reached him three years ago, it looked nearly as crumpled as it did now. He didn't need to read it—the words had hammered themselves into his heart long ago.

He smoothed out the creases and opened the letter anyway.

I can't believe you left. How could you? They were going to apologize, they had completely forgiven you. How are Mum and Dad supposed to break the news to Nana? What in Shiro's name am I going to tell your baby sister? That her brother didn't even want to consider coming home? That he was afraid of owning up to his mistakes, his stupid ideas?

I don't know if this letter is ever going to get to you. But after all this, you better come back home with one of those stupid gold pins, or not at all.

EIGHTEEN

Emry woke to a dull headache and a hand shaking his shoulder.

"Come on, you have to eat before we go." Cal's face shifted into focus, a bittersweet sight after his restless dreams of letters and pins. "I want to catch the carriage to the fane in thirty minutes."

He pushed himself to sit up, then winced and grabbed his neck. The blankets and pillows had helped, but not enough. "I'm not hungry," he muttered.

"Eat it anyway," Cal said. "You didn't have supper, and I don't recall seeing you eat lunch yesterday, either."

Aspen sat cross-legged on the coffee table across from him. "Yes, you should eat. I'm interested to know what that tastes like." They pointed at the tray of food Cal had placed next to them. It overflowed with tea, cheese, bread, and something that actually did wake up Emry's stomach—a fruit dumpling. He glanced at Cal, who graciously pretended not to notice him go for that first.

But she had unfortunately been serious about wanting to leave for the carriage, and so Emry got to work stuffing pastry into his face, washing up, and describing the taste of plum filling to Aspen all at the same time.

"Are you sure you're not able to eat anything?" he asked Aspen as he shrugged on his jacket, which was so beaten at this point that he assumed the very walls of Esther Hall were judging him for wearing it. "Because you're really missing out."

"Well, there's no need to rub it in."

As soon as Emry was ready, they followed Cal out of the hall and into the sunny quad.

"The fane is less than an hour outside Vornik," Cal explained as they walked. "We'll take the carriage first, then it's apparently a bit of a walk into the forest—"

"Cal!" A tall, ginger-haired student rushed across the grass and nearly tackled her with a hug. "I heard about Halagrad—you weren't traveling there when the surge hit, were you? Are you all right?"

Cal smiled and returned the hug. "I'm fine, Marie, thank you."

"Oh, good." Marie let out a breath. "Didn't know if you were going to come back half glowing or something—"

Cal's smile dropped. "Glowing?"

But Marie had broken off as soon as she saw Emry and Aspen. "Who are they?"

Cal grimaced for the briefest moment, then replaced it with a polite smile as she gestured. "This is Emry and Aspen. Emry and Aspen, Marie."

Marie's eyes went wide. "Emry?" She grabbed Cal's arm and made a great show of turning her around so they faced away from him. "Ex-boyfriend Emry?" she continued in a scathing stage whisper. Emry winced.

"Yes."

"The one who refused to leave Tazlo?"

"Yes, Marie."

Marie glanced back at them. "Well, what in Shiro's name is he doing here? You aren't back together—"

"No. It's a long story, I'll tell you about it later." Cal took a large step away from Marie and turned back around. "This way to the carriages."

Marie tossed Emry a look of severe judgment as they parted ways, leaving Cal to lead them to the outer gates of the campus.

"Sorry about her," Cal mumbled as soon as Marie was out of earshot. "I...may have disparaged your name a bit upon coming to Vornik."

Emry swallowed and held up a hand. "Completely within your right."

Their walk swept them right into the fray of the central square again—though today, the activity was centered on the sinkhole rather than the Council building. When Cal saw what had drawn everyone's gaze, she gasped and reflexively grabbed Emry's arm. On his other side, Aspen did the same.

"What happened to them?" they asked. Emry's mouth fell open.

"I—I hardly know."

Ahead of them, passengers stumbled out of the black hole of the Vornik nexus, crying and calling for help. The luckier ones looked like Emry did back in Halagrad—unsteady, queasy, a little worse for wear. The others clutched at their arms or legs, and through their clawing grasp, their limbs glowed a fierce white. They were the ones screaming in pain and falling onto the cobblestones. Medics pushed through the crowd to catch them, but judging by the panicked looks on their faces, their medical books said nothing about these sorts of injuries.

"Remnants?" one of them called. The woman helping the injured up out of the nexus shook her head.

"The surge itself, coming through the blue route," she shouted back. Based off her cloak, she looked to be the boathouse manager. "There was nowhere to hide—"

"How many more are there?" the medic asked.

"Three more boats, plus others who were at the docks. It's going to take a while to get them up the stairs..."

As more medics rushed down into the nexus, Aspen's hands shook, and Emry took the initiative to guide them away from the chaos.

"I don't like this," Aspen warbled. "Not at all—"

"It was just a strong surge," Cal said firmly, or tried to. "This could still be over in a few days."

"But humans didn't get hurt like this in the other stories! Not except for the old one!"

"I told you, we can't rely on that single story—"

Aspen pointed back to the square. "Then why are people getting hurt?"

Cal didn't have a good answer for that, and so they walked in silence until the rush of the nexus was far behind them.

Though they arrived at the carriage stop already exhausted, Cal's mood was about to get worse.

"What is this...?" She squinted at a leaflet posted up near the stop. Down the road, Emry could see a green-jacketed Council aide posting more of them. He glanced over Cal's shoulder to read it aloud for Aspen.

"The Forsgren Quartet, performing at the...Trellis?" He looked to Cal.

"It's an outdoor performance space in west Vornik." She tore down the leaflet and stared at it. "Do they seriously think they can distract the public at a time like this?"

"Who?"

"The Council, that's who!" She crumpled up the paper and began gesturing with the malformed ball. "How—how imbecilic and completely predictable. Of course, they're not going to restrict travel or start research on the surges or, Hara forbid, actually *communicate* to the public—no, they're just going to have a couple of bards perform and hope that cheers everyone up!"

Her tirade continued until they were in the carriage, when Emry thought it best for everyone within a thirty-foot range that he try to redirect her energy.

"Cal"—he cleared his throat—"I believe you were going to ask Aspen some questions?"

"I—" She stopped, looked at Aspen as if they hadn't been sitting there the whole time, then lit up like a beacon. "Yes, I was. I'm taking you to the Alta's fane, which means—I finally get to ask my questions!"

Aspen brightened as well. "Yes, all right."

She dug into her pack for her journal, took out her trusty pencil from behind her ear, and wiggled in her seat. Emry leaned back, feeling an unexpected twinge at seeing this side of her again. How many times had he listened to her ramble about her lectures, or attended her practice presentations, or simply basked in her excitement while she spoke of topics and theories beyond his comprehension?

Not enough times, if he was being honest.

"First," Cal said, pencil poised, "what exactly can spirits do?"

Aspen frowned. "What do you mean?"

"What are your powers?" she said. "I know you can make things bloom and grow, revitalize plants, that sort of thing. You can reach out to other spirits, and you can project animal forms. But what else can you do?"

Aspen shrugged. "Nothing. That's it."

Cal's pencil hesitated over the paper. "That's it?" she repeated. "What about moving mountains, calling storms? All the powers from the stories?"

Emry half smiled. "You mean from those old folktales you don't like?"

Cal ignored him.

"Well," Aspen backtracked, "maybe if I were older, and attached to my grove again..." They looked at the lute on Emry's lap. "Perhaps I could try some of those things. But I'm afraid I can't do any of that now."

"Oh." Cal nodded, and jotted down a few reluctant notes. "So, you're stronger in your grove?"

"I think so. I do miss my grove." Aspen set their chin on their hand as they watched her write. "I like it a lot. I worked hard on the flowers and the trees and the moss. I think you'd like it, too. Emry saw my home, but you didn't." They turned to Emry. "Do you ever miss home?"

He blinked—he wasn't at all prepared for that question. "Um."

"See, Cal said that you—"

"Aspen!" Cal hissed.

"Oh, right." Aspen sat back. Emry looked out the window. Clearly, they had spoken while he slept the night before. Part of him didn't mind—it spared him from having to repeat the shameful details himself.

The other part of him wished Aspen didn't have to know about his failures.

But on the other side of the carriage, Aspen was unruffled by the knowledge. "Well, if you get to ask questions, so do I, and I think it's my turn." They wiggled in their seat just like Cal had, then smiled up at her. "How long have you been reading at the Academy?"

Cal closed her notebook. "Reading? You mean studying?"

"Yes."

"Five years."

"Five winters?" Aspen leaned forward. "Are all the students there that long?"

Emry smirked at the trees passing by. It seemed Aspen knew how to needle them both.

Cal faltered. "Ah, not exactly. Some only need two years for their degrees. But there's a lot I'd like to study, so I'm continuing on."

"What have you studied?"

"Well, this quarter I'm attending lectures on astronomy, litera-ture, Vidanya history..." She began counting on her fingers. "Then last year I studied calculus, a bit of physics, and marine biology. The year before that..."

She continued the list, leaving only one part out. Emry sat up.

She had spilled his secrets last night, but not hers. He shouldn't say anything, he really shouldn't—but he couldn't help himself.

"You forgot one," he said.

She looked at him sharply. "No, I didn't."

"Yes, you did."

"Tell me!" Aspen copied Emry's pose, sitting up straight. "I don't like secrets, they're no fun. I like to know things. And I'm answering all *your* questions truthily."

"Truthfully."

"Truthfully," Aspen repeated. "Please?"

Cal twisted the pencil in her fingers. "Political science," she said. "I went into the Academy thinking I was going to study politics and join the Council."

"But you were just yelling at the Council."

"Yes, because they are, by and large, idiotic and inane and useless."

Emry folded his arms. "They'd be less idiotic and inane and useless if you had graduated and joined them like you said you would." She glared at him, but he didn't back down. "If you had stuck around after that election, you could be helping them right now—"

"No, I'd be waist-deep in that political muck, watching people die as Council members shoot off nothing but hot air and stupid ideas." She crossed her arms. "I'd be just as useless as them."

Something in Emry's chest clenched. "Calliope Breslin, I refuse to believe that. Don't you dare say that you're useless, because you're not and you know it."

The intensity in his voice took both Cal and Aspen aback, and they stared at him as the carriage rolled to a stop.

"We're here," the driver called. "Walk down that path to the fane. Should get you there in about twenty minutes."

"Thank you," Cal responded, then composed herself and landed one last frigid gaze on Emry. "You're in no position to judge my choices."

NINETEEN

CAL LEAPT out of the carriage and marched down the overgrown path into the forest, Emry and Aspen trailing behind her.

"Aren't you going to apologize?" Aspen asked, padding close to Emry's legs. They had taken their wolf form once the carriage was out of sight.

"Not when I'm right," Emry said. Aspen's ears flicked.

"Humans are interesting," they mumbled, and picked up their pace to trot ahead, sniffing along the leaves and brush until they came across a stream. Ears perked up, they hopped down the bank and began splashing about in the water.

"Hello?" they called. "Hello, spirit?"

Emry veered off the path to follow them, and found that the bank was littered with several rhythm blooms, their petals all closed in the bright sunlight. Up ahead, Cal reluctantly doubled back to observe.

"There's a spirit in the stream?" Emry asked as Aspen alternated between sniffing the air and splashing. "What's it connected to?"

"Oh, could be anything. A tree by the stream, plants in the water. If I were connected to a tree myself, I could sort out exactly where…" After another round of splashing and calling, they sighed. "I don't think they're going to appear. Do you think it's because they don't have a fane? Every spirit should have a fane."

They trotted out of the water, shook themselves off, and nosed around in the undergrowth. Before long, they returned with a fragile ring of bark in their mouth and wedged it onto a forked sapling by the stream. Cal slid down the banks in time to watch the sapling grow to Emry's waist, while vines snaked up its trunk to secure the hollow branch to its post. Flower buds dotted the vines as they spread, releasing a sweet, relaxing scent into the air.

"Do you think they'll like it?" Aspen sat next to their creation, panting heavily. After the effort of growing the fane, their wolf form had shrunk significantly.

"Absolutely," Emry said, and dropped a copper into the mossy cubby. Cal reached over and dropped one in as well.

"I'm sure they'll come visit you on our way back," she reassured Aspen. "Once they've had a chance to admire it."

"I hope so!" The spirit's tail wagged, and they bounded forward along the path.

THE DEER TRAIL continued farther into the forest, at times getting so overgrown that they nearly lost the thread of the path. And other than the gathering clouds and the birds chirping above, no one else joined them on their walk in either direction.

"Is this a large fane?" Aspen asked from the lute. Soon after building the water spirit's fane, they had mumbled something about conserving their energy and practically flopped into the case. "I thought there might be more visitors."

"Technically, it's one of the largest in southern Vidanya," Cal said. "But people hardly visit fanes anymore."

"Because they don't think we exist."

"Because..." Cal paused. "Because spirits are lovely, but people go to fanes for problems that spirits can't fix—like money, and health, and love. Flowers aren't going to fix those problems."

"Not true," Emry said. "You can sell some flowers for money, turn others into medicine, and give the pretty ones to those you love. See, flowers have just fixed all your problems. Aspen might as well be a hero."

Aspen giggled. Cal rolled her eyes, but she bit back a smile as she turned away.

A few minutes later, the first signs of the fane popped into view from between the trees.

"Wow…" Aspen reappeared at Emry's shoulder in human form. "Is this really it?"

The deer trail ended at a worn stone archway framing a massive cedar tree. The archway itself was riddled with holes that held all of the fane's offerings—a smattering of old fruit, coins, and flowers, along with yellowed slips of paper where visitors had written wishes or requests. Behind the archway, stone benches ringed the base of the tree. Emry imagined that in full sunlight, the warmed stone seats would be quite pleasant.

"I'll make the offering for this one," Aspen said, and picked up a dried leaf. It crackled and flattened in their palm, the fierce red of autumn returning to it in full force. They took the newly perfect leaf and placed it carefully into an open cubby.

"Very nice, Aspen," Cal murmured, but she was already looking beyond the offerings to the rest of the fane. Farther behind the tree, a long pavilion stretched out under its shade, flanked on three sides by intricately carved stone markers. Though large enough for festivals and events, today the pavilion housed a single person—a hunched old lady sweeping leaves off the stone floor with her broom, whistling as she went.

"Do you think I should go rebuild that other fane?" Aspen turned. "I had no idea they could be big like this—"

"No, no, the one you built is fine as it is," Emry reassured them before they could bolt off. "Not everyone needs a fane this ostentatious."

"*I* want a fane this ostentatious."

"All right, then. We'll build one for you when you get back." He nudged Aspen. "Don't you want to hear what the Alta has to say about the stories?"

This seemed to convince Aspen for the time being, and they wandered over to the cedar tree as Emry waved at the old woman.

"Excuse me," he said. "Do you know where we might be able to find the Alta for this fane?"

The woman stopped whistling and turned toward them. Her face soured immediately, and she jabbed a gnarled finger at several papers nailed clumsily to the front pavilion post.

"How many times do I have to—look, if you want to book a wedding here, you'll need to either write to the address on the sign or learn how to read. I've got nothing to do with that rotting schedule."

Emry and Cal looked at each other in mild panic. Aspen snorted behind them.

"No, no, that's not—"

"Not what we're here for, at all—"

"Then if you're here to pray, you're welcome to it." She caught sight of the lute on Emry's back and narrowed her eyes. "And if you're going to play, I sure hope you're good at it."

"We're not here to do either." Emry rushed through his words. "We're looking for the Alta to ask them for stories about surges, so if you'd please direct us to them, we'd very much appreciate it."

The woman stiffened. "Stories about the surges?" she repeated, fiddling with the broom. "Well. You're the first ones to ask for those. Ah...come in, then." She gestured to the pavilion, empty save for a few cushions lined up along the back. Cal looked around.

"Wait—where's the Alta?" she asked. The woman leaned the broom against the post and massaged her wrists.

"You're looking at her," she said. "Brinna, Alta of the Cedar Fane.

Now sit, sit. I haven't got all day—well, I do, but my back is acting up, and I can't kneel for too long."

As the woman turned, Emry finally caught it—the sheaf of wheat embroidered on the back of her shawl. Though Altas told stories of every god, they often decorated themselves in the symbols of Hara, much like the cave runners. Mildly offending Shiro or Weir was a small price to pay if it meant Hara would make their fane prosper. It comforted Emry to see such a traditional embroidered display so far south.

He stepped forward, then turned back to Aspen, who had placed a hand on the cedar tree and was frowning up at the branches. "Aspen, you coming?"

"Mm-hmm." The spirit reluctantly backed away from the tree and joined them under the pavilion. Together, they took up all the faded cushions the place had to offer and sat in a semicircle on the cold, dusty floor. Off in the distance, thunder rumbled low.

"So." Brinna kneeled on her cushion, knees cracking. "Which surge stories are you interested in? There are plenty from Vornik— though judging by that accent, boy, you don't seem to be from here. You from Dawnstone?"

"Close. I'm from Senne." Emry shifted. "But that's actually what we wanted to talk about. We'd like to know if you have stories about bigger surges. Ones going beyond Halagrad, perhaps to Thisby. Or even Dawnstone."

Brinna tapped her knees, eyes unfocused in thought. "Surges going that far," she mumbled. "Well, I'd need to recall where the fenns lived at the time..."

Cal restrained a sigh. "It's possible there aren't any," she said quickly, preparing to stand again. "If you can't think of one, we'll be on our way—"

Emry pointed to the satchel at her side. "Cal, did you bring the book?"

"Hm?"

"The one from the Tazlo library, with the Tera story."

Cal hesitated, then dug into her bag and handed it to him. Emry hid a smile—always prepared, even when she didn't want to be. He opened the book to the scarlet ribbon Cal had tucked into the pages and offered it to Brinna. "Does this story sound familiar at all?"

Brinna took the book and mumbled over the first few words. "In the time of my great-grandmothers, Hara looked all around her world and declared it the finest..."

The wrinkles on her forehead deepened, and Emry's hope sparked. If she truly didn't remember any other stories like this one, perhaps it was a load of nothing, like Cal thought. Thisby was simply unfortunate this time around, as were the poor people from the Vornik nexus. This would be over in a few days, and everything would go back to normal—

"I see. You're looking for stories about the white wave," Brinna said quietly, and set the book down between them. No one wanted to pick it back up.

"You've heard of this before, then?" Emry asked, his hope doused. Brinna nodded.

"The late Alta, she...passed down these stories close to the end of her life. During a storm, of course. Stories like these can only be told during storms."

Outside the pavilion, rain began to patter on the leaves and archway, slowly darkening the stone into a sullen gray. Brinna pressed her lips into a line and settled back on her heels. "It seems I am given no excuse. I will start with the first one I remember."

CHAPTER

TWENTY

With Brinna's consent, Cal took notes while the Alta spoke, marking her hand-drawn map as Brinna mentioned the fenns that first told the stories. Cal didn't seem to put much energy into her notes for the first story, nor the second. And when the third ended, she tucked her journal back into her bag, assuming—or perhaps hoping—the tales of Shiro and Hara and Weir had run their course.

Brinna eyed her motion. "Already tired of my voice, girl?"

"No, ma'am—"

"I don't blame you. It's not as nice as it used to be." She scratched at her throat. "But you asked for the stories, not me."

"You have more of them?"

Brinna raised an eyebrow. "Did I say I was finished?"

Cal reopened her journal and resumed taking notes, and before long, her marks sprawled from Bennli all the way up to the northernmost mountain range of Thalis. As the stories continued and the paper darkened, Emry nervously drummed his fingers on the floor.

But Aspen was first to vocalize the growing fear.

"This truly happened?" They stood and paced behind Emry and Cal as Brinna paused for a sip of water. "This was actually real?"

147

Their voice shook, and their form briefly guttered. Brinna squinted at them.

"I wouldn't assume that, Aspen," Cal jumped in. "These stories were from thousands of years ago. I can't imagine they're accurate to what the fenns may have witnessed at the time, if they witnessed anything at all."

Brinna gave a sharp, humorless bark of a laugh. "I can assure you that is not the case," she said, her eyes flaring. "In order to tell these stories, I had to repeat them back dozens, hundreds of times before the late Alta was satisfied. If you go to the Great Pine Fane in Thisby, or the Fir River Fane in Copper Mill, they'll tell you the exact same tales I just told you."

Cal stiffened. "But surely some of the past Altas embellished them along the way, or changed them for dramatic effect—"

Brinna's expression sharpened as she leaned forward. "We don't tell these stories on a whim, or simply to entertain. Before your precious books, this is all our ancestors had of their history. All *your* ancestors had of their history. And though their successors may not believe me, I will not betray their words, not as long as I live."

They stared at each other until Cal broke.

"Apologies." She looked down. "I did not intend to insult you or the late Altas."

Brinna surveyed Cal's Academy uniform, then shifted on her heels. "I suppose I should have expected it," she muttered. "But you listened well enough. You are forgiven."

As Brinna resumed sipping water, Emry bit his lip, a doubt of his own forming in his mind—but the Alta must have seen it on his face, for she motioned toward him and gave a grunt while she drank.

"Alta, if..."

"Please, boy, call me Brinna. My title is for ceremonies."

"Brinna, if the Altas shared the stories between the fenns...isn't it possible that this was just one story from the south that made its way to the north?" Emry glanced at Aspen, who hadn't stopped pacing during the argument. "The white wave may never have actually reached that far in reality."

"I don't think so." It was Cal who responded this time, her finger tracing the marks in her notebook. "You see, the Mulec fenn and the Berg fenn have the same stories, with the same descriptions—but they developed in isolation, on opposite sides of the province. They never could have met to share their story, could they?" She looked to Brinna for confirmation. To Emry's dismay, the Alta nodded.

"Fenns did often meet at Sada to exchange their stories, but you're right. Not all of them would have seen each other. And even when they did share their knowledge, the same narrative integrity applied."

Emry tilted his head. "They met at Sada?"

"Of course, they did. Sada used to be much bigger than what it is today, even from what you may have experienced in Senne. Over half the fenns met with their neighbors in the underground river routes, to sing and exchange stories. If they came across a fane in their journey, they were required to eat a meal and sing again, to please the spirit." She stroked her lower lip in thought. "Oh, the northern fenns had this one song they loved. How did it go…"

She hummed a few bars in her scratchy voice, and it was Aspen who recognized it instantly. "'Hara's Shield,'" they said. "That's Emry's song."

Emry smiled at them. "That's kind of you, but it's not my song, Aspen. I didn't write it."

"Ah, but it *is* your song." Brinna's eyes glittered. "Didn't you say you were from Senne? The Riu folk up in the north were the first ones to sing 'Hara's Shield.' Go on, play it for us. Shiro knows no one needs to hear me sing it."

At first, Emry was afraid he'd have to compete with the rain to be heard. But the roof of the pavilion caught his sound easily enough, and he settled against one of the stone tablets with his lute in hand.

When the gods begin to fight,

Through ground, rivers, trees, and light
Dance your way to Hara's shield
Follow her voice, she will not yield

To Shiro, who shakes and steals our souls
   Or Weir, who turns our trees to coals
   She will not yield, she will defeat
   These gods, though this war will repeat

So dance your way to Hara's shield
   Through cold and dark, she will not yield

Normally, the dancing tune lifted moods—but this time, its jaunty verses about shaking and trees turning into coal took on a different tone, one much more suited to the rain around them.

"*You* did this." Aspen began kicking at Emry's foot, little rabbit kicks that he barely felt. "You sang the song about surges, and that brought the surge to my grove—"

"No, it didn't!" Emry held up his hands. "It wasn't my fault!"

"Oh, I know it wasn't!" Aspen spun away after kicking one last time. "I just wanted to blame something for the end of the world!"

Cal shifted in her seat. "Aspen, we haven't explored all the possibilities yet."

"What other possibilities are there?" Aspen gestured out to the trees. "Your ancestors saw it happen. They sang about it. They *warned* you about it. And now both spirits and humans are dying, and we're just—just sitting here!"

Cal stood up, her eyes sparking. "I agree that the chances of this being a small event are slim, but if we're going to try to spread this warning, we need to look more deeply into this—"

"How much more?"

"Aspen." Cal folded her arms. "This sort of research takes years—I can't just fit it into a matter of days."

Aspen's form wavered again, and Brinna rubbed her eyes. Before she could start asking questions, Emry stood up and set a firm hand on the spirit's shoulder. "Brinna's been very generous sharing all her stories with us. I think we should head back and let her rest before we look more into this."

Aspen shrugged out of Emry's grip. "Fine."

As they made to leave, a haggard woman under a torn umbrella trudged up toward the fane, looking as grim as they felt. Brinna pushed herself to her feet with a creak.

"Come back tomorrow." She waved the trio off. "We can look more deeply then, if you like."

"Thank you, Alta." Cal gave a stiff half bow and led Emry and Aspen out into the spitting rain. The woman with the umbrella slotted a pinecone offering into the arch, then plodded toward Brinna.

"Good afternoon, Alta."

"Ah, Vesta." Brinna reached out toward her. All the sharpness she had used to greet Emry and Cal was gone. "I was wondering when you might stop by."

Vesta sank onto the cushion that Cal had been sitting on. "Yes, I'm afraid it's gotten worse…"

Emry continued past the archway, but Aspen stopped at the cedar tree and looked up.

"Aspen?" Emry lowered his voice. "Is there a spirit here, too?"

"I think so. One at the stream, and one in this tree…" Aspen placed a hand on the bark again. As Emry and Cal waited for them, the wind caught the conversation going on under the pavilion.

"Your son again?" Brinna murmured.

"Yes. Mr. Novak refuses to send for another medic, and I can't pay for one myself, not after the surge struck my garden…"

"But the neighbors you mentioned—"

Vesta crumpled further. "Just lost a cow to the surge, too. I couldn't possibly ask them."

"Well, I'm sure if we pray to the spirit…"

Out of the corner of his eye, Emry saw Cal frown, but he held his tongue until Aspen stepped away from the tree and they left the fane behind. "Cal, do you know anything about that?"

"Unfortunately, yes. Mr. Novak is the mayor of Racine, a town north of here. Everyone knows he's going to run for Council next year."

"And let me guess, he's useless?"

Cal gave a grim smile. "How on earth could you tell?"

Emry found himself waiting for a comment or question from Aspen, but nothing came—not even when they passed by the stream and the fane they had made. As the road came into view, he gently nudged the lute case.

"You've been awfully quiet back there," he said. "What are you doing?"

"I'm sleeping."

"Don't give me that. Spirits don't sleep, you told me that yourself."

"Fine." Aspen appeared as a mouse on Emry's shoulder. "I'm... frustrated."

"Okay."

"The spirit wouldn't talk to me," they said. "I could feel it living there in the tree, and I tried asking them questions—but they didn't say a single thing back. They just...gave me an annoyed feeling. Sort of like Oak, back in Tazlo."

"Perhaps they didn't want to be bothered," Cal offered.

"But I was asking them important things!" Aspen's volume no longer matched their tiny form. "Like—like how they protect their tree, and if they ever talk to the people who visit, and what remnants really are! Why wouldn't they answer me?"

"I wish I knew, Aspen." Emry said, trying to keep his voice confident—but next to him, Cal had taken out her pencil and begun to chew on it. "I'm sure you can try again tomorrow."

TWENTY-ONE

THEY ARRIVED at Esther Hall in time to sneak a late dinner up to Cal's rooms, then spent the rest of the day in their separate corners—Cal studying at her desk, Emry quietly strumming on the sofa, and Aspen hanging absently from the staircase. Emry had hoped that some of the pall of Brinna's stories would dissipate by the following morning, but when Cal ducked out for breakfast, she returned in an even darker mood than before.

"What is it?" he asked—but she shook her head, tugged surreptitiously on his sleeve, and headed up the stairs. She passed by Aspen, who was kneeling at the coffee table and practicing drawing shapes with a pencil.

"Cal, how am I doing?" They held up the paper—their newest row of circles was actually fairly decent. "Do you think you could teach me to write soon?"

"It would be my honor, Aspen. We can start after we visit Brinna today." She squeezed their shoulder and hurried up the stairs, Emry following closely behind.

Seeing her room at the top of the stairs unnerved him in a way that he should've expected, but hadn't thought of. It looked almost identical to her old room in Tazlo—hardly a book out of place on the desk, no dust to be seen. The only adornments on the wall were little reminders of home—postcards, letters, an indiscernible drawing from a cousin in Fustar. With the exception of some new plants, even the layout of the decor matched what he recalled from a year ago.

When she closed the door behind them, he stood in the middle of the room and found it hard to swallow.

"So, what is it?" he repeated. Cal reached into her pocket and handed him a folded scrap of newspaper.

"There was a surge in Jay's Bridge yesterday. It's farther north than Thisby, up near Copper Mill."

"That would be the farthest north so far, right?"

Cal nodded, and Emry scanned the paper. The report described a scene identical to what they had witnessed at the Vornik nexus the day before. Glowing injuries, mystified medics, general panic.

Just below the report, another article ran quotes from the Forsgren Quartet and other members of the Guild—all stiffly worded, state-prescribed phrases telling their adoring fans not to worry. That this would all be over soon.

"Ridiculous," Emry muttered, but chose not to elaborate in front of Cal, lest she go down another rabbit hole. He handed back the paper. "Why don't you want to tell Aspen?"

Cal folded the article over and over as she spoke. "They seemed so out of sorts yesterday, I don't want to make them worry more. But..."

The folded square of paper was as small as it could get in her hands.

"But?"

She looked up at him. "When we go to Brinna, we should...see if the stories describe how the fenns survived. Just to be safe."

Emry's stomach clenched. He didn't realize how much he had been depending on Cal's skepticism until now. It had been easy to push away the worry when someone else near him had doubted so fiercely.

He swallowed down the anxiety and nodded, keeping up a calm front. "Of course."

Brinna already looked weary when they returned to the fane that morning.

"I would say it's good to see you again, but given the circumstances..." She sighed and dragged over her cushion. "What would you like to hear about today?"

Cal already had her tools out and ready. Journal laid before her, pencil in hand, a backup pencil stuck behind her ear. "If it's not too much trouble, I'd like to hear the same stories again. Map out the themes first, see how much lines up with what we're seeing today..."

"Is that one going to join us?" Brinna nodded to Aspen, who was sitting cross-legged in front of the cedar tree, craning their neck to look up at the branches.

"Maybe later," Emry said, taking a spot next to Cal. "They're just...very into praying. They'll join us once they're done."

Brinna knelt down and massaged the back of her neck. "Very well. If you recall the Trava fenn's experience..."

Cal's paper map soon wasn't enough to track the information, and before long, they were pacing around a makeshift facsimile laid out across the stone floor. Sticks formed a rough outline of Vidanya's borders, gating in leaves, stones, and dried flower petals.

"Remind me what the petals are again?" Emry said, meandering clockwise. Cal twisted the necklace at her throat as she wandered counterclockwise.

"Dying trees, spirits leaving their groves."

"Which we've seen." Emry glanced at Brinna. "Um—well, the trees, at least. And the rocks?"

"Remnants."

"Also seen. The leaves?"

"Humans, injured or dead."

"Regrettably, seen," Brinna finished. Emry squinted down at the last marker left—a few acorn shells scattered in the south. He toed them with his boot.

"For the, uh, acorns," he said, "you keep mentioning broken earth. Land swelling like waves in a storm, Weir's starlight cracking up through the ground...do you think they're still talking about the earthquakes?"

His shoulder bumped into Cal's as their paths met. He murmured an apology and made to sidestep her, but to his surprise, she remained there, arms touching, eyes fixed on the map.

"No, the wording is too specific across the narratives," she said. "But no one's seen swelling or cracking land this week, as far as I can tell. It's the one inconsistency between the stories and what we're seeing today."

"And is that good or bad?"

"Both." Cal chewed on her pencil. "If we never see broken earth, perhaps there will be no wave. But if I try to present this information to a body like the Council with such an inconsistency, it will weaken my argument."

"Even with everything else?"

"If there's any sort of way to ignore the apocalypse at their doorstep, they'll take it," Cal muttered. As she surveyed the floor in a dark cloud of thought, she leaned almost imperceptibly into Emry's arm. "Even if we do figure out how the fenns survived the last wave..."

Emry was almost afraid to speak, lest he chase her off. "You had a thought on that?"

"Yes." She shook herself out of her cloud and started pacing again, shifting away from Emry's side. He gathered himself and continued in the opposite direction. "Yes, I had a thought on that. From your song, actually."

"Not my song," he mumbled. "But what about it?"

"It's 'Hara's Shield' and the mention of Hara's voice, specifically. Almost every single fenn in the far north uses the same wording as the song when they talk about the wave. The verse about cold and dark, in particular."

"Well, that's death, obviously." Emry shrugged. Both women glared at him. "Or—or not?"

Cal tapped her pencil against her palm. "Think about the song lyrics. How she will not yield, how the song tells you to seek out her shield—"

Emry grinned at her from across the map. "Sing it for me? I can't recall."

She shook her head, a small smile twisting across her face. "It could also be a place of protection, a way the northern fenns survived the wave. And the voice is what leads us there."

Brinna scratched her chin. "What kind of protection, though?"

"What we used," Aspen said. They were standing at the edge of the pavilion, their head tilted. "Back in the forest, after the surge struck and the carriage ran away."

Brinna stood up. "You were caught in one of the surges this week?"

"Yes, near Hala..." Aspen looked to Cal. "Hala..."

"Halagrad," Cal finished for them. "We hid in the ruins of an old house. The surge's energy couldn't pierce the stone."

They all looked around at the same time, at the stone tablets that walled in the pavilion at the south, east, and west sides. That conveniently didn't hold an inch of space between them.

"Emry," Cal said, "are any of the northern fanes built like this?"

"No, not at all." Emry gave half a laugh. "I always thought the south was weird for building them like this."

"Then the north must have had something else like it to protect them." Cal flipped through her journal. "What sort of stone structures can you recall from living up there?"

Emry shot her a look. "Ah, yes, let me draw from my experience as an expert on ancient northern Vidanyan architecture." Cal gave him a flat look, and he raised his arms. "I don't know! There was an old stone mill that got knocked down when I was ten?"

As he anticipated, this line of inquiry led to nothing but frustration. Brinna was the first to give up, cracking her back and shuffling off with a sigh.

"I'm making tea. Tell me if you magically recall an ancient stone tower in Senne," she grumbled. "Or you could play something on that lute again. Shiro knows I don't get many good musicians out here in the woods…"

As Emry pulled out the lute, grateful for the break in the interrogation, Brinna muddled around with a tiny fire pit she had clearly made for herself back behind the pavilion. When she caught Cal glancing at her work, she shrugged. "What? As much as I enjoy talking, it wears on the throat after a while."

"I'm not arguing," Cal said quickly—but another question danced at her lips. Retreated. Came back again. "Brinna…why are you an Alta?"

Brinna gave a short laugh. "What, do I tell our stories that badly?"

"It's not that. It's…it's just that there are so few Altas left. If I'm not mistaken, you're the only one even near the city. Why did you choose to be one?"

Emry riffed quietly on nothing at all as Brinna shuffled back in with her cup of tea, the steam masking a flash of pain in her gaze. "Needed something to do after my wife passed," she said, trying to keep her tone brusque. "Figured I'd be good at it. I was praying at this fane twice a week, I had already memorized half the stories from the late Alta…" She shook her head. "And when all the other devout have left, trees make for good company."

"That's true." Aspen nodded, then jerked a thumb back at the cedar tree. "Except for that one."

Brinna frowned. "Why is that?"

"Well, they still won't say anything to me, for one—"

Emry messed up a chord, loudly. "Brinna," he said, making a show of adjusting the pegs on the lute while throwing a pointed look Aspen's way, "do you have any favorite stories?"

"Of course." Brinna was still eyeing Aspen with some confusion. "I'm rather fond of your Riu fenn, myself. Any fenn that claims half their blood is ice water certainly doesn't fool around when it comes to their tales."

Emry smirked. Most folk in Senne still liked to claim that, Georgie included.

"I know this boy is from the watery north, but"—Brinna turned to Cal—"your accent sounds much closer to home."

"Yes, I'm from Etris," Cal said as she adjusted a stick lining the map. "My mother says we're descended from the Zora fenn."

"Of course, you are." Brinna slurped her tea. Cal's frown sharpened.

"What's that supposed to mean?"

"Were you born at dawn, day, or dusk?"

"Dawn."

Brinna smiled into her tea. "Ah, so brilliant *and* proud."

Emry laughed. Cal glared at him.

"What about Tazlo?" Aspen jumped in. "What are the stories about them?"

Brinna tapped thoughtfully on the side of her mug. "Tazlo's more difficult. It was a contested land for a very long time. Stoll had it, then Berg, later the Canica...it's a changing place. That's the most I can really tell you."

"Oh." Aspen's excitement faded, and slowly, all their eyes fell back on the map.

"Do you think anyone else out there is connecting the dots?" Cal finally asked, to no one in particular. "Is anyone else seeing where we might be headed?"

"There must be," Emry answered out of reflex, but his reassurance sounded hollow, even to himself. When the haggard mother Vesta made another appearance at the path, they took it as their cue to leave.

"Coming back tomorrow?" Brinna stood at the edge of the pavilion to see them off.

"I'm afraid I can't," Cal said. "I've been absent too long from my lectures. I'll need to attend a few of them before my professors wonder where I've been. But perhaps the day after?"

Brinna nodded, then switched her focus to Vesta. The circles under the poor woman's eyes had grown since they'd last seen her.

"Time to pray?" Brinna asked. Vesta nodded, and they retreated back under the pavilion.

TWENTY-TWO

THE NEXT MORNING, Cal was up before Emry could wrestle himself out of his morning stupor. He had to shake himself awake to catch the flurry of words she was spouting as she prepared to leave.

"I've got lectures all day, then a few errands to run after," she said, bag and shawl already in hand. "Will you two be all right alone? I don't have a spare key, so I'll need to meet you back here to let you in." She paused. "Assuming you don't want to be locked in here all day, of course."

"No, no, s'fine." The words ran slow and thick on his sleepy tongue. "Aspen and I will get some fresh air or something."

"Yes, please!" Aspen jogged up to him. They were, of course, as awake and bright-eyed as Cal, leaving Emry no choice but to splash some water on his face and catch up to their energy level.

"Where are we going first for the fresh air?" Aspen bounced once they were outside in the sunlight. They had shifted their clothing into something akin to the Academy uniform, though Emry spotted a few flowers peeking out of the pockets.

"Looks like there are some gardens around here." He yawned. "I thought we'd walk through those."

As he had hoped, the gardens were just what they both needed. Aspen spent their time eagerly explaining what was growing well—and fixing what wasn't. They focused on the flowers in particular, ensuring that each one bloomed in perfect color. And the more the flowers flourished, the more their scent woke Emry up. He had to laugh as they left the frantically growing trellises behind—he wished he could see the face of the gardener who next entered there.

"Would be nice if the whole place was like that," Aspen said as they gestured to the open lawn of the Esther Hall quad. "I don't understand all this plain grass. Where's the moss? Where are the flowers? If this were my grove, I'd start by—"

"Emry!" someone called, and they turned to find Marie striding toward them.

"Hello," Emry said uncertainly. "Marie?"

"Yes." She flicked her ponytail off her shoulder. "Do you know where Cal is?"

"She went off to a lecture, said she'll be gone all day. Why?"

Marie pursed her lips and turned away, as if his words had tasted sour. "Nothing, just wanted to follow up on her note." She began to prance off, then paused. "So, you really dated Cal for a year?"

"Um—yes?"

"And what are you doing here?"

There was no good way to explain that he was researching the pending apocalypse with a forest spirit. "Visiting...someone else."

She folded her arms. "Did you ever get into that guild, or whatever was so important to you back in Tazlo?" Judgment oozed out of her voice. Emry set his jaw.

"Still working on it."

"Hm." She gave him another scathing once-over before turning. "Cal can and will do better than you. Don't get in her way."

"*Hey!*" Aspen launched at Marie. Emry shot out his arm to block them. "You apologize right now, that was very rude—"

"Don't bother, Aspen. Come along." Emry dragged the spirit away until they were outside the Academy gates.

"Why'd you hold me back?" Aspen gestured back to the quad. "She was threatening you! She said terrible things!"

"Trust me, I've been hit with worse." Emry let go of their arm. "Don't worry about me, it's not worth a run-in with the proctors."

"You're my friend." Aspen huffed and straightened their Academy jacket. "Of course, I'm going to worry about you."

This took Emry back. "Um—thank you." He cleared his throat and looked around him. "Now, how about we explore this city properly, yeah?"

In Emry's view, any true exploration of a city involved trying all the different foods it had to offer, so he counted out what he thought he could afford for the day and frittered it away on all the little treats he could find—fried cheese from one stall, dumplings from another. Tempting little skewers from a place farther south, crammed with cinnamon-dusted pastry, followed by a cider that hit so sharply on the back of his tongue that he almost spat it out.

"Ooh, don't explain to me what that one tasted like." Aspen made a face. "I don't think I want to know."

Emry was washing away the taste of the cider with another skewer when they reached the central square around midday. To his relief, no injured passengers were crawling out of the nexus today, but the gathering mob at the front of the Council building had doubled. All around them, posters blared out more feeble distractions, and Emry took one down to read it out for Aspen. Karlson at the Tilted Cap, the Forsgren Quartet at the Trellis again—even Ella Sorman was now involved, playing at the Sumac Hall.

"We can assure you, the surges will be gone very soon!" Another Council spokesman, taller and more booming than the representative the day before, was out on the steps trying to quell the crowd.

"But what about the injured? Or the people who died yesterday?" a woman cut in. "Has the Council called in more doctors?"

"We have several arriving via the emergency river route today," the spokesman said with a confident nod.

"Have the soldiers trained in guarding against remnants?"

His confidence faltered. "Ah—I'll need to, um, check with our sergeant—"

The crowd piled onto the spokesman's hesitation, and soon he retreated back into the building. Some tried to follow, but the soldiers at the base of the stairs remained resolute.

"I get it," Aspen mumbled as they crossed the square to explore the eastern side of the city.

"Get what?"

"Them." Aspen nodded back to the crowd. "I'm afraid for my grove. They're afraid for theirs. And no one knows what to do about it."

The spirit kicked a pebble down the cobblestones. Emry searched around for something to boost their mood again.

"Oh, look!" He jogged forward. "Bet you haven't seen one of these before, have you?"

A stone fountain burbled happily ahead of them. All elaborate carvings and floating flower petals, the sculpture was the most humble part of the upscale eastern shopping district. Emry handed Aspen a copper—sure to be an insult to the fountain, but it was his last coin for the day—and gestured to the sparkling water.

"Go on, throw it in and make a wish."

Aspen looked at the coin, then at him. "Is it a fane?"

"Ah, no. But I see why you'd think that." He grinned. "It's just a fun human thing. You make a wish—silently, or else it won't come true—then toss the coin into the water."

"All right." Aspen closed their eyes, threw in the coin, then opened one eye. "Aren't you going to throw one in?"

"Oh, no. I've spent enough money today."

"Then why'd you let me throw one in?" Aspen leapt to grab the coin back, but Emry caught them and laughed.

"No, no, your wish will turn into a curse if you take it back!" He squeezed their shoulder. "Besides, you've never done it before. It was worth it."

Worth it for a moment—after that, Aspen latched on to any

other sparkling thing they could see in the street. "Can I throw a coin in that?"

"That's a lantern."

"How about that?"

"Can't throw a coin at a lady's dress, Aspen."

Aspen picked up a broken glass bottle, its sharp edges shimmering white. "How about this?"

Emry grimaced and carefully took the bottle from their hands. "Let's not return to Cal wounded, shall we?"

They continued exploring until the sun set, then doubled back to the Academy on sore feet. Or at least, Emry did—while he winced and hobbled, Aspen bounced happily along the curb in bare feet, no worse for wear. It took Emry a moment to realize there was a rhythm, if a vague one, to their steps. "What are you doing?"

Aspen hopped from one foot to the other. "Dancing."

"Ah." Emry held out a hand. "You know who should teach you some human dances?"

The spirit took his hand and flitted around him in a circle, blissfully uncaring of the looks from other passersby. "You?"

Emry laughed. "No, I'm the last person you'd want." They switched hands. "Cal should teach you."

"Just like how she'll teach me to write?" Aspen looked up at him, green eyes wide. "Is she as good at dancing as she is writing?"

For a breath, Emry recalled swirling dresses and murmuring dance halls. Candlelight and soft hands warding off Tazlo's winter chill. Cal's smile as she spun around him, making sure their shoulders brushed just so as she passed.

Then Aspen circled round him again, and he shook his head free of the memory. "Yes, I daresay she is."

Aspen slowed down and furrowed their brow, as if Emry's thoughts had transferred to them in the dance. "If you had made a wish from the fountain," they asked, "would you have wished for Cal to be your mate again?"

Emry stumbled. "That's a, uh, very direct question, Aspen."

"I don't see the point in asking indirect questions."

"Um…" He ran his free hand through his hair. "No. No, that's not going to happen."

"Why not? Has she found another mate?"

"No, she said she wasn't seeing anyone."

Aspen shrugged. "So…why not?"

"Didn't she tell you about why we broke up in the first place?"

Aspen reluctantly let go of his hand. "Yes. She wanted to go to Vornik, and you stayed in Tazlo. For the Guild, she said." Emry grimaced. He was positive she had used stronger language than that to explain it. "But that was a long time ago—"

"Doesn't matter. Nothing's changed." He gave a humorless laugh and gestured at himself. "I'm still the same stupid, failed musician I was a year ago, and she was right to leave me behind."

They walked silently through the Academy gates, then Aspen stopped, their hands in little fists. "I can't fight you like I tried with Marie," they said, "but you're being mean to yourself, and you need to apologize."

Emry stopped, opened his mouth, then closed it. "I—"

"Emry?" Cal's voice shot across the quad, edged with urgency. "Emry Karic?"

He whipped around. "Cal?"

She was searching wildly around the entrance of Esther Hall, holding something in her hand. As soon as he waved her down, she grabbed her skirts and sprinted toward him.

"What's wrong?" He rushed to meet her, searching her face for any hint of the news—another surge? More injured from the river routes?

But when they met in the middle, she was out of breath and beaming.

"This came in for you." She handed over what she had been clutching so tightly—a small envelope addressed to him. He ripped it open, stared at the sturdy card it held, and laughed out of disbelief.

"What is it?" Cal bounced on her heels, already perfectly aware of what it was. Aspen caught up behind Emry and peered over his shoulder.

"Please read it out loud," they begged. Emry opened his mouth, but only laughter came out, floating like bubbles from his lungs.

"I can't do it, you read it—"

Cal grabbed the card. "Ms. Sorman requests the honor of—oh Hara, *Emry*—of Mr. Karic's presence at the Sumac Hall for the purposes of Guild entry examination..." Cal broke out into laughter along with him. "Three days? They want you to play for the Guild in three days?"

He grinned so hard he thought his jaw might break. "Gods, I've got to practice."

Cal squealed and wrapped her arms around his waist. "Emry, this is incredible! I can't believe it—I mean, I can, of course I can! But —oh, you know what I mean."

"Thank you, Cal." He returned the hug, a little dizzy at the feeling of her head against his shoulder, her hair tickling his chin. As he steadied himself, two more arms snaked around both of them.

"I'm very happy for you." Aspen smiled up at him. Emry reached over and ruffled their hair.

When Cal let go of him, she plucked a thread off his waistcoat and looked him up and down. "I've got to get you something new to wear. I'm not letting you perform for the Guild in this clothing. Marie would know which one of the stupid boys in my lectures has the best fashion sense—perhaps you could borrow something..."

A blush crept across Emry's face the more she analyzed his appearance. "That would be great, but—I really should go write to Marko about this. He'll kill me if I don't tell him."

"Yes, absolutely." Cal turned and led the charge back to Esther Hall—but not before tossing him a smile that nearly made him trip over his own feet. "But don't think you're getting out of the clothing bit. I *will* find something for you."

TWENTY-THREE

Dear Marko,

Made it to Vornik fine. Playing for the Guild soon. May want to make a wish at a fane for me—or have Stef do it. I think this might be it.

Staying with Cal hasn't been bad. She hasn't kicked me out so far, at least. Between the free room and food, I might be able to make next month's rent without selling my soul or something. I'm not sure how I'm going to repay her for all this, to be honest.

I'll be back in Tazlo soon. If another surge hits there, get behind a stone wall and stay put. Tell the others the same, will you?

Stay safe,
Emry

CAL SENT off the letter for him before starting Aspen's foray into literacy—and to Emry's delight and alarm, the spirit was reciting the entire alphabet by the time Cal turned in for the night.

"You need anything?" she asked Emry, one foot already on the steps. Next to her, Aspen was dangling from the ironwork, muttering letters under their breath.

"No, spirit teacher." Emry settled into the sofa with his lute. "I'll be practicing for a bit longer."

As she retired for the night, he sat back and began to practice— quietly, so as not to alert the neighbors or interrupt Aspen. He'd surely be playing alone before other Guild members at the Hall, so he mentally sifted through the soloist pieces he knew. Something as virtuosic as he could manage, of course. If he had the money for new sheet music—no, no. Best not try to learn something new with so little time to prepare...

He didn't notice it until a few pieces in, when he happened to look up at the spiral staircase. A pair of delicate slippers had settled on the top step, as if a certain someone was trying to listen in on his practice. He smiled to himself and switched to "Tree and the Stream"—Cal's old favorite—and the slippers pulled back out of sight.

THEIR WALK to the fane the next morning looked entirely different than it had two days ago. The rain had washed the air until it sparkled, leaving plenty of open space for bright sunbeams and the last of the falling leaves to play with one another. Aspen soaked all of it up, and there was no walking pace the two humans could set that was fast enough for them.

"Can I please run ahead?" they begged, their wolf form a blur twisting around their legs. The tongue lolling out of their mouth gave Emry an idea.

"Want to test how far you can get from the lute?"

"Yes! Yes yes yes—"

He picked up a stick and threw it as far as he could. "Fetch!"

Aspen yelped and tore after it.

"Emry, I don't think it's very dignified for spirits to be playing fetch," Cal admonished, but laughed as Aspen zoomed into the undergrowth, a puff of leaves trailing in their wake.

"They don't seem to care." Emry shrugged, then waved to Aspen as they reappeared with the stick in tow. Twenty yards out, their form flickered severely, and Emry gave a sharp wave. He wasn't keen to find out what would happen to Aspen if they strayed too far from the lute. "That's far enough. Come on back!"

"All right!" Aspen trotted back, the stick in their mouth sprouting new leaves and little green branches. As they grew closer, their shape solidified again.

"So, which Guild members do you think will be at your exam?" Cal asked as she watched Aspen's bouncing gait. "I do hope Karlson is there. I've seen him perform. You two have a similar style."

Emry shook his head. "That's very generous of you, but I caught his set at last year's Sada, and he's loads better than me."

"I disagree. You two have the same sort of—oh, what is it…" Cal lit up. "Showmanship! That's the word."

"Showmanship?"

"Yes. You're not like Ella or the Quartet. They're…above the audience, if that makes sense. You and Karlson aren't." Her eyes glittered. "You talk to the audience like you're friends, you make them comfortable. It's easier to have fun when you're on stage." She turned away and trailed her hand along a low-hanging branch. "At least—that's what I think."

For all his supposed on-stage chatter, Emry couldn't come up with a single word in response. He just stood there, ears burning and heart sputtering, as Cal bent down and held out her hand to Aspen's wolf form. "May I see that stick?" Aspen dropped it into her hand, and she smiled as she marveled at all the new growth. "Fascinating…" she murmured, and though Emry was sure he should be admiring the literal magic Aspen had cast on the branch, he chose to admire her instead. How the light struck her hair, her cheeks, reflected back in her eyes. How soft her gaze was when she said things like *friend* and *comfortable*.

He was entertaining the absurd idea that he could perhaps ask to take her arm for the rest of the walk when the ground began to shake.

"Hara take us." Cal dropped the stick and grabbed at her skirt. "If we run, do you think we can make it to the fane in time?"

But the leaves above them were already glowing, and a white light gathered over the horizon.

"Come to the stream!" Aspen bolted off into the water, past the fane they had built the other day.

"Water isn't going to protect us, Aspen—"

"I'm not talking about the water!" they said, then shouted at the stream. "You have to help us! Please!"

Emry and Cal skidded to a halt along the banks just as a fawn appeared in front of Aspen. Despite the quaking earth, their spindly legs stood as rigid as stone in the stream.

"Is that the water spirit?" Cal looked to Aspen, but neither creature responded to her. The deer nodded first to Aspen, then to the humans, before disappearing with a flicker.

"Get together!" Aspen backtracked out of the water. "The spirit says we have to get together—"

Emry threw one arm around Cal and reached toward Aspen, who rushed over and curled in against them just as a wave of white particles hurtled through the trees. Emry closed his eyes, angled his body to cover the others, and waited for the energy to strike them.

But the impact never came, and the searing light that flashed through his eyelids faded. Not daring to move from his spot, he opened one eye, then the other.

The poisonous white energy of the surge streaked over their little huddle, as if it were washing over a dome far above their heads. Outside the shield, plants shriveled and died—but the rhythm blooms at Emry's feet did little more than rustle.

"Cal, open your eyes." He squeezed her shoulder. She did as he asked and, after looking around them in wonder, slid away from him to approach the wall of the dome. He followed her nervously, Aspen not far behind.

"The other spirit is doing this?" she asked, leaning close to the shimmering wall.

"I think so."

"But it must take so much energy, don't you think?"

Emry's heartbeat spiked as she reached out toward it. "Please don't get too—"

Then the ground gave a jolt, and Cal pitched forward. Emry leapt and reeled her back in—but as he did, his left hand slipped out of the barrier. A small shock of pain, like a bee sting, pricked his fingers as soon as they touched the particles outside. He whipped his hand back with a wince.

"Rotting hell," he muttered, holding his wrist and shaking out his fingers. "Cal, you all right?"

Cal watched his hand in horror. "What happened?"

"It's fine, it's fine. Just a sting." He yanked his sleeve over his hand. It was already numb up to the knuckles, and he could see a dull white glow through the thin fabric.

"Are you sure?" Cal reached for his hand, but he hid it behind his back.

"Yes."

Before she could persist, the quaking died down, and the dome around them slipped away. All around them, blackened trees cut crisp silhouettes against the sunny day—but the water spirit's grove remained intact.

"Thank you, thank you, thank you!" Aspen entered the stream, dipped their nose into the water, then bounded over to the fane. The flowers along the vines there bloomed tenfold. To supplement the offering, Cal pulled several apples out of her pack and stuffed all of them into the fane. "I don't think that's quite enough for saving our lives"—she stepped back—"but that's what I have."

"Oh, I'm sure they're not picky," Aspen said.

Emry trailed behind Cal and Aspen for the rest of the walk.

Oddly, their near brush with death had only given his companions more energy.

"Do you think I could do that, too?" Aspen babbled, their tail wagging. "If I can practice making those shields, I could go back and protect my grove, like they did—"

"Shields." Cal was walking and writing at the same time. "Do you think Hara's Shield was a *spirit* shield? Did people gather at fanes up north for their protection? Perhaps I could tell my family to find a fane in Etris, just to be safe..."

As their chatter continued, Emry tried to stretch out his hand—but his fingers creaked and stung. He pulled back his sleeve to see white lines throbbing from his finger pads to his knuckles, and sucked in a breath.

"Emry?" Aspen called out. The fane was in sight, and they had shifted into their human form.

Emry yanked off his cravat, wrapped it around his hand, and stuffed his hands into his pockets. Surely, the light would fade away. It had to. "Coming."

TWENTY-FOUR

Wʜᴇɴ ᴛʜᴇʏ ʀᴇᴀᴄʜᴇᴅ ᴛʜᴇ ꜰᴀɴᴇ, they found Brinna and Vesta huddling inside the pavilion. Thankfully, neither the humans nor the cedar tree before them looked any worse for wear.

"Brinna, are you all right?" Cal asked as soon as they approached. "Did the surge hit here, too?"

"We're right as rain, thank you very much." Brinna waved off the question. "Not a single bit of it made it past the stones."

"Another one of Hara's many blessings." Vesta beamed, clutching Brinna's arm. "Alta, our prayers two days ago—the spirit must have taken them to Hara herself. They must have."

Brinna's eyebrows rose. "Did they?"

"A medic showed up at my doorstep this morning. I hardly know how or where from, but they're tending to my son this very moment." Vesta laughed. "Can you believe it?"

Brinna smiled—a new sight for Emry. "That's wonderful, Vesta. Thank you for telling me. Hara must indeed have heard you."

As Brinna continued talking, Emry glanced at Cal, who was suddenly very busy leafing through her journal. "I had no idea goddesses could contact medics directly," he mused. "How convenient."

Cal avoided his gaze as she spoke. "I'm not one for gossip, of course, but I heard that Marie's father is a good friend of Mr. Novak, and *he* caught wind of a grave rumor that could impact the man's run next year. Something about, oh, I'm not sure"—she waved a hand—"denying medical care to his constituents to pocket the local budget money for himself." Cal pulled out her pencil and twirled it in her fingers. "But it's a good thing that rumor is clearly false, isn't it?"

Emry grinned. "Clearly."

"Now." Brinna shuffled out to them with her broom as Vesta retreated down the hill. "How in Shiro's name did you three get through the surge unharmed? We're not going to pretend there are any convenient ruins along the path to this place."

"A spirit protected us!" Aspen grinned and threw their arms out wide. "You should have seen it, they created this big dome, and it shielded us, and it was amazing!"

Brinna frowned. "A spirit?" She looked to Cal and Emry, and saw they weren't smiling. "You're serious?"

"Trust me, I didn't think that I'd be one to say this, or one to break this to an Alta, but"—Cal cleared her throat—"spirits are real."

Aspen looked up at Cal. "Can I tell her that I'm a spirit now?"

"Ah, I believe you just did."

Brinna stared at them for a moment. Then her face darkened. "Now, I can't take such claims lightly. You're telling me that this"— she gestured at Aspen—"this little one, can do what's in all the stories? Summon the sun? Call the rain? Make the flowers bloom at their—"

Aspen waved at the ground. Flowers opened all around their feet, pushing up through autumn leaves. Brinna took a staggered step back. "You..." Her knuckles went white as she clutched the broom. "But that would mean—all this time, I've been telling spirit stories to an actual spirit?" Her gaze snapped to the humans. "And you didn't rotting *warn* me?"

"But I liked hearing them!" Aspen smiled. "I've heard some before, of course. But it's not like there's an Alta at my grove or anything."

"Your grove," Brinna repeated. "Then how are you—"

"Here?" Aspen gestured to Emry's lute. "I'm living in that for now."

Brinna looked from the lute to the cedar tree. "And is there truly a...?"

"Yes!" Aspen's enthusiasm waned. "But I can't get them to talk to me."

"Incredible." Brinna stared at the tree, fingers dancing across her lower lip—then she gathered herself up with a brusque laugh at herself. "Well. I—I am an Alta. I really shouldn't be surprised, should I?"

Cal smiled. "We won't tell anyone."

"Thank you." Brinna gave a curt nod, then muttered as she trudged back to the pavilion. "Shiro's beard, the one day I didn't bring any tea with me..."

Emry pointed to the path. "I can go get some, if that will help—"

"No, no, just give me a moment to catch up." She pinched the bridge of her nose and sighed. "You...spirit child. You mentioned a shield of some kind?"

"Yes, they did." Cal opened her journal and hurried to follow Brinna back to the map, which had survived their time away with only a few rocks out of place. "I think it might be the answer to Hara's Shield. Perhaps people went to the northern fanes and asked the spirits to protect them during the wave?"

Something about that didn't sit right with Emry. "But only the fenns in the north talked about Hara's Shield," he said as he followed the women. "And clearly, spirits in the south can create shields, too. Why isn't the story about Hara's Shield everywhere?"

Aspen nodded. "And Emry's song—"

"Not my song—"

"And Emry's song talks about the cold and dark." Aspen frowned. "The spirit's shield was nothing like that. It was nice and bright."

"Hm." Brinna regarded the silent cedar tree once more, then turned to Emry as he set down his lute case with his good hand. "You going to play again for us today?"

"Not today," Emry said quickly. As much as he was willing it away, the pain in his other hand hadn't yet subsided. "My apologies."

Cal's eyes narrowed at Emry, but Aspen remained oblivious, tapping their chin in an absentminded pattern. "It doesn't matter if the spirits' shields are Hara's shields or not," they said. "Even if we find a safe place for humans and animals, the spirits will still need to protect their groves. Our groves," they added quickly. "We've got to warn them, too."

They ran over to the cedar tree, placed a hand on it, and closed their eyes.

"They can truly communicate with the spirit like that?" Brinna murmured as they watched Aspen. Cal flipped through a few pages in her journal.

"Aspen thinks so, yes." She kneeled down and traced a handwritten note with her finger. "Brinna, I wanted to ask you about the one story you told from the Berg fenn, the one that mentioned—"

Then all around the fane, the wind picked up, swirling fallen leaves into spirals. At the tree, Aspen stumbled backward as if shoved, and their face twisted in anger in a way Emry had never seen before.

"No, you have to listen to me!" they shouted. "You can reach out to the other spirits, I know you can. If you could just tell them this wave is coming—"

A new voice rumbled over the wind like thunder, so much so that Emry looked up at the rapidly gathering clouds above—until he realized the cedar tree shook to its cadence.

"I will tell them nothing," the voice boomed. "Spirits are meant to sleep, to shepherd their grove in silence. Nothing more."

"What?" Aspen stood their ground. "No, that can't be true—"

"But you have woken me." The thunder curled with anger. "I cannot sleep like I used to, nor can the spirit in the water. You have cursed us like you have done yourself, you wandering stray."

Aspen's hands balled into fists. "Wandering? I'm not a—I'm not going to stay like this, you know! I'm going to go back to my grove one day!"

"Then go." The command rolled out like a wave, and with it, a vast elk shape stepped out of the tree. Emry craned his neck to see its antlers, which phased through the upper branches of the cedar tree without disturbing a single needle. "Burden me no more with your human chatter."

Aspen widened their stance. "No! You're going to help me! You're going to help *them*!"

Thorns crawled about their feet as they shifted into wolf form, growing larger and larger until their shape danced like flame—but even with all their effort, the wolf's shoulder hardly reached the upper haunches of the elk's legs.

"Hey!" Emry rushed out of the pavilion and skidded to a halt between the two massive creatures, holding out his hands toward them. "Enough of this. Stand down, both of you!"

As his arms moved, the cloth from his injured hand fell away, revealing white threads pulsing all the way up to his wrist.

"Emry?" Aspen's voice and shape shrunk. "What's wrong with your hand?"

"Nothing," he started—but it was too late. Aspen was next to him in human form, Brinna and Cal catching up from behind. The spirit grabbed his hand, and he flinched away with a curse.

"You said it was just a sting." Cal took hold of his arm more carefully, her grip stopping at his forearm. "How well can you move it?"

He tried to bend one finger. The pain made him gasp.

"Okay, okay, it's all right." Cal guided him to a stone seat by the giant elk's hooves. Her hands trembled as she pulled back his sleeve, revealing the glow slipping further into the veins at his wrist. "It's— it's going to be fine, Em."

Emry swallowed. Hara drag him to dust, why did she have to pull out that nickname now?

"Cal, the Guild in two days," he breathed, panic flooding him. "If I can't—"

"We'll take you to a medic."

"If I can't play—"

"You *will* play."

Aspen looked up at the spirit elk, their eyes welling. "How do I help him? Tell me, there must be a way!"

The elk remained stubborn. "It is not my place—"

The sound of straw thwacking wood cut them off. Everyone

turned to find Brinna hitting the trunk of the cedar tree with her broom.

"Not your place?" she spat. "Not your *place*? Do you know what you are? Do you know why people leave you offerings, you selfish, ungrateful oaf?"

The clouds stopped gathering. The wind died down. The elk stared and blinked at her.

"I'll tell you why!" Brinna continued. "They want you to help them! Not that you've ever done *that* before in what I can only imagine has been a very long life of absolutely nothing. But you have a chance to fix that now, you great antlered dolt!"

The elk reared their head back in a haughty pose. "What do you expect me to do, woman?"

"You will call me Alta, and I expect you to help!" she shouted. "Talk to the other spirits! Heal that man's hand! I don't clean your rotting fane every day for nothing!"

As they watched, the older spirit shrank, until they were the size of a normal elk. They wandered over to the archway, sniffed at all the offerings. Looked at Emry's hand.

"Well," they said. Now that the facade of thunder was gone, their voice sounded normal. Not quite male, not quite female—and certainly not rolling across the ground. "It seems as if your human is...what do your stories say?" The spirit looked to Brinna. "Unlucky?"

Brinna set down her broom. "The humans affected by the surges are said to be...yes, unlucky. Cursed, ill-fated. Whatever phrase you like."

"Yes, like one of the unlucky trees out there." Aspen pointed to one of the twisted, blackened trees in the distance—a victim of the last surge.

"I feel better already," Emry said flatly. Cal took his good hand and squeezed it.

"I think it's just an unscientific way of saying that you're more susceptible to this...spirit energy than others. Right?" She looked to the elk, who strode up to Emry on graceful, silent limbs and lowered their nose to his hand. Their ears flicked back, and a growl tumbled in their throat.

"Yes. Your body is not fighting off the energy that is trying to bond to your hand."

Emry's stomach lurched. "But—it'll stop trying eventually, right?"

The elk snorted. "Not before you lose the hand."

Cal's grip tightened, and it took everything in Emry not to vomit.

"What do we do?" Aspen demanded.

"Find another living entity for the energy to bond with. A plant will work best."

Aspen scrambled around and pulled up a branch. Like the fetch stick, it immediately bloomed to life as they placed it on Emry's lap. "Why a plant?"

"It will not do to use an animal or a human. You will have merely shifted the problem."

"But won't it kill the plant?"

"I'm fine with that," Emry mumbled. Both spirits shot him a look.

"Close your eyes," the elk said. "Can you sense the energy?"

"Um..." He dug around mentally, wincing at how much the pain intensified when he focused on it. But there it was—a creeping feeling, like something was crawling under the skin of his palm. As it tried to burrow deeper, intermittent stings shot up his wrist. "Yes, I can sense it."

"Force it out into the branch."

"How?"

"I cannot tell you how."

"Try breathing," Aspen advised to his right. After gingerly placing his hand on the branch, he did so. As he breathed in, he visualized the energy leaving through his fingertips and traveling into the branch. As he breathed out, he pushed.

The energy reacted instantly—digging in deep, scrabbling for purchase as Emry tried to push it out. He took another ragged breath and tried again, and again. It had to come out, he had to have his hand back, he *had* to—

A flash of white light flared against his eyelids, and a final shock of pain sent him reeling back. As he opened his eyes with a gasp, the light jumped from his hand to the branch, then dissipated in a silver mist.

"You did it!" Cal leaned against his shoulder to look at his arm. "Can you move it now?"

He lifted his hand. Except for a slight tremble, he could now flex his fingers without any stiffness or pain. He let out a deep sigh of relief and half collapsed against her without thinking. "It's fine."

To his surprise, Cal held him upright, while Aspen poked at the branch. "And the plant's fine, too?"

"The plant is enough to draw the energy out, but not enough to sustain it." The elk spirit stepped back, looking more than a little proud of themself.

"But why does the energy want to bond?" Aspen asked. The older spirit tilted their head.

"Why do you and I need to bond to a grove?"

"To survive, of course." Aspen looked down, then frowned. "The remnants must be the same, right? Those ghosts that follow death."

"Ah, those." The spirit bowed their head. "They are...leftovers from the surges. Half-formed bundles of spirit energy looking to become what we are, to bond somewhere to survive. Their attempts only serve death." Their great head swung round to survey the forest. "Consider yourself lucky you have not seen any today. They will try to bond with you, if given the chance."

Emry shuddered, and Cal wrapped her arm around his. "I think we should get you back home."

He nodded. Now that the fear had sunk out of him, he was left with nothing but relief, exhaustion, and lingering tremors in his hand. Cal helped him to his feet, then turned to Brinna.

"Brinna…Alta, if these surges continue, we'll need to warn others about what's coming. Do you ever travel into Vornik proper?"

Brinna snorted. "Not if I can help it."

"But if you had to? To tell the stories?"

She fiddled with the broom handle. "If you think it will help them listen, I'll do it. I'll tell whatever stories I must." The Alta of the Cedar Fane then turned to her spirit. "All right, you lump. What am I calling you?"

"Do I need a name?"

"I can think up more insults if you like."

"Cedar, then."

Aspen stepped up. "It's nice to meet you, Cedar," they said. "Will you…speak to the other spirits for me? About the wave?"

Cedar looked down their long nose at the younger spirit. "If I must, wanderer."

Aspen grinned and wrapped their arms around the elk's neck. "Thank you."

Before the spirit could react, Aspen bounded off to walk beside Emry, taking the arm that Cal had not claimed. "See, they're not so bad."

Emry squeezed their hand. "You're a good friend, Aspen. Thank you."

TWENTY-FIVE

Cal held Emry's arm all along the walk from the fane. He said nothing, expecting her to move away when they entered the carriage —but she sat right next to him, holding fast to the hand he had almost lost. Unsure of how to react, he settled for looking out the window and holding his arm very still—as if a single movement would make her realize who she was touching and let go.

But she only released him when they reached her rooms, where she dropped her satchel and immediately turned back around for tea. "Green? Breakfast? Mint?" she called from halfway out the door.

"Um—"

"Chamomile, that would be perfect. Be right back!"

As her hurried footsteps faded down the hall, Emry slouched on the sofa and stared at his hand, the one that had been glowing not two hours ago. Though pale and shaky, his fingers were still there— well and whole and able to hold a lute. Visions of the alternative crept into his mind, of what could have happened if Aspen and Brinna hadn't intervened. Hadn't begged a strange spirit to help save his hand and, with it, his future.

Emry looked up. His little savior was sitting on the coffee table, holding up their own hands and concentrating very hard on the space between their fingers. Forget repaying Cal—he had no idea how to *begin* repaying Aspen.

He lowered his hand and watched the spirit's efforts for a while before breaking the silence. "What are you doing?"

"I'm trying to create a shield like the spirit at the stream." Aspen's focus didn't waver. "I've got to learn how to protect things, too. Do my part."

"Right." Emry hesitated—a thought had come to him, different from the fear-mongering visions, but nearly as gloomy. "We'll need to travel to Tazlo soon, then. To get you back to your grove."

"Oh." A shadow passed over Aspen's face, and they looked up at Emry. "I suppose so."

Emry frowned. "Isn't that what you were going to protect?"

Aspen paused, then returned to their efforts. "Yes, of course."

Cal shoved the door open with her shoulder, bearing a tray loaded with tea and cookies. "They didn't have chamomile, but they did have ginger..." She looked at Aspen. "What are you doing?"

"Shields," they both said.

Aspen relinquished some of the coffee table space so Cal could set down the tray—but before Emry could inspect the cookies, she sat down on the sofa next to him. "May I see your hand?"

"It feels fine, I promise." He was about to deflect with a joke about medical degrees when she carefully rolled up his sleeve and ran a finger along his palm.

After that, his brain promptly shut down.

"...Em?"

Gods, there was the nickname again. "I'm sorry?" He looked up from his hand, where her grip slid smoothly up to his fingertips.

"I asked if you've lost any feeling in your fingers."

This would be easier if he had.

"No, no, I can feel everything," he said, trying to sound as casual as possible. Aspen stared at them from their seat on the coffee table, a smirk on their face. Fortunately, Cal didn't seem to notice as she turned Emry's hand over.

"And you'll be able to play the lute just fine?" she asked, gently curling his fingers to wrap around hers. "This was my fault. I wouldn't be able to forgive myself if—"

He squeezed her hand. "It wasn't your fault, and yes, I'll be able to play. Really." He forced himself to let go of her, if only to stop his cheeks burning, and turned to the tray. "Tea?"

CAL SPARED A MOMENT FOR A DRINK, but she was up and pacing before Emry could finish his cup.

"We'll need to get the information about the plants to the medics somehow," she thought aloud. "If I can suggest Cedar's method to that one medical student who owed me a favor last month..."

"Using all your resources, I see."

"I'm trying to save lives, Emry."

He hid a grin behind his teacup as she continued her circular route around the parlor. "Then there's the matter of the last surge. It wasn't just Jay's Bridge that was hit, but Copper Mill as well—"

"Wait, when?"

"Heard it in the hall a minute ago."

Emry's stomach dropped. "But that's even farther north than Jay's Bridge."

Aspen looked up. "Really?"

"Unfortunately, yes." Cal twisted her pencil about in her hands. "If we're to warn people that a wave might be coming, to get them somewhere safe, we'll need something like the Council involved. Fanes and spirit shields won't hold everyone—but if the Council started building south-facing walls now..."

"What sort of Council connections do you have?" Emry asked. Cal flopped into her desk chair and tapped the end of her pencil on the desk.

"For something this large? None." She bit her lip. "But...the Academy has some."

She said it as if she had touched something sticky, but Aspen failed to heed the unspoken warning. "Do they?" they asked. Cal waved it off.

"Oh, it's the old roundabout. Young academics dine with Council members, become Council aides, get elected, turn back to the Academy for their own aides. It's idiotic—"

"And inane and useless?" Emry finished for her. Cal set down her pencil with more force than was necessary.

"My advisor is friends with some of those people," she continued, a hard line around her words. "If I can convince her to give me an audience with them, they can handle the rest of the messy Council business."

Aspen sat up. "Can I help convince her?"

"Sure, you could tell me exactly when the wave will hit and what Hara's Shield is."

"But I've no idea."

Cal rubbed her forehead. "Good, my advisor's going to love that answer."

Her mutterings about the wave soon dissolved into silent thoughts as she scrawled on any piece of paper she could find. In the absence of any fancy connections or influential friends, Emry picked up his lute and sat back on the sofa. "Want me to play something?"

Cal paused. "That would be nice."

He began to strum, and though she didn't look up from her writing, her shoulders relaxed immediately, just as they had when he'd accompanied her studies back in Tazlo. Like back then, he picked a simple, calming piece—easy for her to listen to, and easy for him to play. And like back then, he nearly lulled himself to sleep with his own melody.

So when Aspen shrieked, both Cal and Emry nearly fell off their seats.

"What is it?" Cal spun around. Aspen now stood on the coffee table, a translucent sphere of energy floating between their hands like a delicate soap bubble. Warm light bounced up into their wide gaze.

"I did it!" they crowed. "Look, I made a shield!"

Emry set aside his lute, heart still hammering from the yell. "Well, I'm glad two out of the three of us can be useful."

"Incredible." Cal leapt off her seat to inspect the shield. "May I ask some questions?"

"Cal, let them breathe. They've only just done it for the first time."

Before Aspen could respond, a knock sounded at the door. Their shield bubble popped into mist that curled around their hands. "Oh no—was I too loud?"

"Nonsense. If anyone asks, I'll say you made an important metaphysical discovery. My neighbor's a philosophy student, they'll love that." Cal grabbed the door handle. "Though I'd appreciate it if you got down off my coffee table."

But when she opened the door, it was no philosophy student—it was a messenger. "Urgent letter for you, miss." He held out a letter. Emry brightened.

"Did Marko write back already?" he asked—but as that messenger turned to go, two more ran up to the door. They all looked at each other in confusion.

"Ms. Breslin?" The newest one held out another envelope. "Letter through rush-post."

The middle one held up theirs as well. "Hold on, I've also got one for her!"

"I'll take all of them, thank you," Cal said to calm the messengers. After shelling out generous tips for all three of them, she closed the door and stared at the letters in her hand.

"Is something wrong?" Emry tried peeking over her shoulder at the envelopes. Various postage stamps, as many as would fit, littered each one to ensure the fastest possible arrival. He feared the news they held inside for her. "Cal?"

When she turned around, her hands shook.

"I don't know how this happened," she stammered. "Em, I really don't know how she found me."

"How who found you?" Emry rifled through his memory in a panic. Cal didn't have enemies that he knew of. Well, given the subtle manipulations he had recently seen, perhaps she had made a few, but surely no one who'd be hunting her like this—

Cal handed him the envelopes. "They're for you."

TWENTY-SIX

EMRY'S HEART dropped down to his feet. He took the letters, glanced at the return address, and wanted to vomit.

"I...think you should sit." Aspen gently took his arm and led him to the sofa. Cal sat on the desk chair, hugging her own arms.

"How did she do it?" she asked.

"The logbook," he rasped. He hadn't even turned over the first envelope yet. "You signed the logbook back at the Halagrad nexus. You were wearing your Academy uniform. You said you were going to Vornik. That's all she needed."

Every envelope was addressed to Calliope Breslin, from one Georgiana Karic. He took a ragged breath and opened the first one with trembling hands. A piece of paper titled *For Emry* had been wrapped around the actual missive, which was splattered in ink due to a hurried, sloppy hand:

Emry—

What's happening? Hans says that you used the river routes to travel from Halagrad to Vornik. What are you doing? Where have you been all this time? Are you all right? Weir's stupid face, Emry, until yesterday I didn't even know if you were still alive.

I should have known that you'd be near Tazlo. I was going to go look for you last year, but Mum stopped me. Said if you wanted to communicate, you would. Right. See how well that worked out.

I don't even know what to write in this. Mum and Dad are fine. Marley's fine. Nana's fine. Still have no idea how you are, you idiot.

I hope you're in one piece. And I want to know who this Calliope Breslin person is. Please, please write back. Ignore that I called you an idiot.

—Georgie

Wiping his cheeks, he opened the second one.

Emry—

I wasn't sure which messenger would be faster, so I used all of them. If you don't get the other letters—what's happening? Why are you in Vornik? Where were you? Who's Calliope? Please write me back.

—Georgie

Then the third letter.

E—

My hand's tired, I really hope you got the other letters. Write me.

—G.

"What do they say?" Cal asked as he folded up the third letter.
"Here." He held them out.
"I don't mean to—"

"I don't mind."

After a moment of hesitation, she took the letters and read them. Emry placed his head in his hands, not wanting to see her expression. Once she read them, he felt her weight quietly sink into the cushion next to him.

"I know it's not my place," Cal said gently, "but I think you should write to her."

"No, not now." As she reached for his arm, he stood up and began to pace. "I'm so close. If I can nail the Guild performance in two days, and if I hear back from them, *then* maybe I can—"

Her voice grew harder. "Emry, it's been three years. I've seen you talk yourself out of writing to them dozens of times, don't think I don't remember. How many more times must you do this to yourself?"

He took a few breaths, trying to formulate a response through his growing headache—but nothing came.

"They desperately want to hear from you, Em," she continued, delicately turning the envelope around in her hand to look at the postage. "Even after all this time. They're not going to care that you're not in the Guild yet—"

"You don't know that."

"And even if they did, don't they deserve to know about the wave?"

He paced faster. "We're not even sure that's going to happen—"

"Why won't you even consider writing them?" Cal stood, her face both furious and pleading. "Why must you make every possible excuse?"

Emry's breath hitched. "I don't know, Cal, would *you* want to write to your family admitting that you're still a disappointment to them after three years of trapping yourself in a strange city, letting down the only woman you fell in love with, and failing to show any proof that it was all worth it? Because I sure as hell don't know how to get all that down in a letter!"

The silence that followed was more than he could bear.

"I'm sorry." He yanked on the door and strode out, tears stinging his eyes.

"Emry—" Aspen started, but out of the corner of his gaze, he saw Cal reach out and hold them back.

"Let him go."

TWENTY-SEVEN

Once Emry was off the Academy grounds, he didn't stop walking—he just picked a direction and went. The noise of the city was enough to drown out his thoughts until his feet carried him into the quieter neighborhoods, where the immaculate gardens and soft birdsong no longer allowed him to ignore himself. When he reached the end of the street, he took a breath, turned around, and committed to making several laps to sort things out.

He could write to his family after the performance, if it went well. If he said he was only one step away from getting that gold pin, that members of the Guild already knew his name, had heard him perform...it might be enough.

Should he mention the wave? He had to, in order to keep them safe—but would it make him sound like he had lost his mind in his three-year absence? He sighed. Probably.

Georgie had wanted to know about Cal, too, but his mother would murder him if she found out he had ruined such a relationship. He pinched the bridge of his nose. Best to hold off on that for now. Keep the disappointment level low to start.

All his planning had gotten him a little turned around, and he found himself wandering back near the Vidanya Council building. Up ahead, an energetic crowd had formed not around the Council steps, but around the Sumac assembly hall across from it. At the door, the master of ceremonies struggled to enforce any sort of decorum as onlookers loitered about the marble steps in excitement.

Emry was set to walk by them when a familiar voice called out from the side of the building. "Hey, it's the Sada kid."

Emry stopped and squinted into the shadow of the wide alleyway. "Damir?"

Damir leaned against a carriage parked sideways, smoking his pipe and wholly ignoring the gathering on the stairs. "You ready for your exam?" he asked as Emry approached.

"Yeah. You avoiding the surges?"

"So far." Damir shrugged. "I'm sure they'll pass soon."

Emry gave a noncommittal hum and gestured to the carriage. "You escaping whatever this crowd is for?"

"If only. This is just to hide Ella's path." With his pipe, Damir pointed to the tavern on his right, then the side door to the assembly rooms on his left. "She's grabbing a drink with the troupe before playing Sumac. She'll sneak in the minute before she has to go on stage."

Emry glanced back at the stairs, where Ella's fans were keeping their eyes peeled on the main thoroughfare, straining their necks for a coach that wouldn't come. "Well, I won't keep you," he said. "Have a good night."

"See you later."

As Emry turned to leave, the tavern door opened. "Emry Karic."

This was a less familiar and far more terrifying voice.

"Ms. Sorman!" He spun on his heel again. "Good evening." He nodded to the troupe behind her as well, the same dour faces that had welcomed him so warmly at the Lamb's Ear. They gave cursory nods in response, and ducked into the assembly door when Damir opened it for them.

Ella, however, remained in the street for a moment, gaze fixed on Emry. "Walk with me," she said, and turned to follow her troupe.

"Yes, ma'am." He sped up to trail behind her, throwing a nervous smile to a frowning Damir just before the man closed the door.

"Have you played any venues in Vornik during your stay?" Ella didn't look back at him as she navigated the narrow servants' passages. From what Emry could tell, these cramped hallways encompassed the larger ballrooms of the assembly hall.

"No, not yet."

"Hm." A hint of judgment tinged her voice. "It would have helped you to have other Guild members hear you play before your examination."

Emry gulped. "Understood, Ms. Sorman."

"Ella."

"Of course, Ms—Ella."

Ella shook her head as the thick stone walls narrowed even further. "Hate performing at Sumac. Such ungainly passages..."

Emry's shoulder brushed against the rough brick. "Would be pretty safe in a surge," he mumbled.

"Pardon?"

"Nothing."

Eventually, the too-warm, claustrophobic hallways dumped them out into an empty card room, closed off for the evening's performance save for servers preparing drinks. Ella wrinkled her nose—the smell of pipe smoke clung to the heavy, overly embellished curtains and the imported Selj rug. As she waved off the scent and swept into the room, the bright lines of her dress and gold bands tucked around her braids made the opulent card room look small and stale. "Like I said. I much prefer the Trellis."

Her troupe muttered an agreement and grabbed a few glasses when the servants weren't looking.

"Is the Council having you perform tonight?" Emry ventured to ask. This only seemed to deepen Ella's displeasure.

"Against my wishes, yes," she said. "Entirely useless, trying to distract people this way. As if my audience isn't going to gather at the Council steps tomorrow morning, asking why more have died in the surges." She accepted a stolen drink from her bagpiper. "Now, if the Council would actually put us to good use, like they used to..."

The drummer laughed and clinked his glass against hers. "That was only in your time, Ella."

"You remind me of that again and you're out." But Ella's eyes danced as she threatened him.

"What did the Council used to do?" Emry dared ask, hoping beyond hope that she'd tell a story. Perhaps something about secret messages, backroom negotiations, maybe even spying—

Ella just shook her head and downed her drink. "You wouldn't believe me if I told you."

The master of ceremonies, still frazzled from the chaos at his front steps, stepped into the card room and straightened his coat. "Ms. Sorman?"

She nodded and turned to Emry as her troupe filtered into the hall beyond. "Now I have a question for you. About your performance in Tazlo."

Emry froze. "Yes?"

She looked him up and down. "Your lute was not of any fine make, I could see that, but I've rarely heard that sort of sound outside of concert halls, and assuredly never in a place such as the Lamb's Ear." Her eyes pierced him. "How did you do it?"

Emry swallowed and in a wild, stupid moment, met her gaze. "You wouldn't believe me if I told you."

He didn't breathe as she paused, her face unmoving. Then she grinned and gave a bellowing laugh. "Until later, Mr. Karic."

She turned and entered the bright hall, the excited buzz of the assembly-goers enveloping her just before the door closed. Emry breathed a sigh of relief, then crept up to the door and listened through the cracks as Ella and her troupe began to perform. With her voice, he had no need to strain his ears—it shot through the door as if it were open, flooding the card room with her clear, rich sound. She didn't need a troupe behind her, or even her lute, to enchant her audience. He'd gladly listen to her sing out every mistake he'd ever made, and would still give her a standing ovation at the end.

But the servers were slowly filing back into the card room, and as their presence broke the spell of her voice, he turned around and ducked back into the side hall.

TWENTY-EIGHT

Emry's path back to the Academy felt much brighter than his path out, despite the sun having set on him during the journey. His mind was made up—he'd go back to Cal and tell her he'd write the letter as soon as his performance was over. Then maybe he'd stow himself away in a garden tomorrow to practice a little more...

He was halfway past the nexus sinkhole when a single white particle floated past his face. He stopped mid-step. "No," he breathed. "No—"

Then the earth jerked out from under his feet with a crashing sound, throwing him to the cobblestones. Panicked shrieks immediately filled the shaking plaza. As he pushed himself up, passengers scrambled out of the sinkhole stairs, a whirlwind of white spiraling up behind them.

"Oh, hell." He stumbled into a sprint back toward the assembly hall, only to find more energy rumbling along the street from the south. Those still caught in the road there got to their feet, only to tumble back down again in the wave of white. Some of them glowed instantly. "Hara take me—"

He rushed into the first stone building he saw—a cramped

little inn that had already filled with twice as many people as it could hold. Seconds after he slid inside, the innkeeper locked the door shut. Bodies slammed and pounded against the door to no avail.

"Go next door!" the innkeeper shouted and waved at the window. As they ran off, a sickening crack from outside ricocheted off the buildings—and Emry, already pressed against the window, couldn't take his eyes away from what was causing it.

The middle of the street was beginning to swell, breaking paving stones and spewing jets of spirit energy into the air. As that hill shrank, another one next to it grew, until the road boiled and snapped like an angry sea below glowing winds.

"No." Emry broke into a feverish sweat. His hands suddenly felt very distant from the rest of him. "Let me out, I have to get back to Cal—"

He reached for the door handle, and the innkeeper shoved him back. "No one goes out until this is over, kid!"

But behind the man, the door—the wooden door—was beginning to pulse with pinpricks of white light. All around the innkeeper, people screamed and pushed wildly against the rest of the crowd in order to get away from it. Emry held his ground and forced himself back to reality. "Cellar." He grabbed the innkeeper's arm. "A cellar, do you have one?"

"Yes, but—"

"Get everyone down there. Now."

As the energy forced itself through the front door, the innkeeper lumbered through the crowd and threw open a back entryway. "Everyone in! But don't you dare take anything—"

The mob spilled into the cellar without question, quickly heating up the cool room. Emry crammed himself into the last spot on the stairs next to the innkeeper. "This door's made of wood, too. Do you have anything metal?"

"I've got an old sign down here—"

"Barricade the door with it."

After struggling and wading through people, they did so. Emry leaned up against the sign for good measure.

"Now what?" The innkeeper looked to him, and his grip on the sign tensed.

"We wait it out."

The panic came in waves. Every time something crashed outside, or the cellar wall swelled, shouts and tears filled the dark room. Emry folded into a seated position against the cool metal of the sign, wracking his brain to remember the exact layout of Esther Hall. The building was made of brick, but the doors were made of wood. What if Cal wasn't with Aspen for some reason? Aspen not with Cal? What if Aspen couldn't create a shield again?

More faces flashed through his head, faces of people who wouldn't be anywhere near a spirit to help them. If this was it, if this was the white wave itself, where was his family right now? Where were Georgie, Marley, Mum, Dad, Marko, Stef? His brain pictured them caught in the energy, feeling the pain that had once coursed through his hand, and he tried to look away or shut down his mind, but he couldn't. They were falling in front of him, screaming in pain—

Then the rumbling stopped. The walls smoothed out. The roads, for a brief moment, went quiet.

When the innkeeper looked to him again, Emry nodded, moved the sign, and peered out. The front door had stopped glowing, and through the windows, the last of the energy was dissolving away into the air.

"It's over," he called back into the cellar and rushed to the front door. As soon as his trembling fingers opened the lock, he burst out onto the street, gasping in the freezing cold air.

Vornik's panic had only just begun. Ahead of Emry, a hackney had overturned, its driver and passengers limping next to it. A building farther down the street had caught fire, pouring both smoke and its refugees out onto the torn road. Others left stranded in the open during the surge now writhed on the broken cobblestones, their bodies glowing white. Some of them stopped moving while Emry watched.

"Help!"

The call came from a man clutching a sack near the carriage, who found himself trapped between two remnants. Though still amorphous in shape, they flowed more quickly than the weak ones outside Halagrad, slithering like gauzy snakes along debris and over bodies. One veered right and struck out at an unsuspecting rat trying to sneak into an alleyway. The animal squealed, glowed white, then went limp.

The other remnant reeled back and launched itself toward the trapped man.

"Hey!" Emry yelled, grabbed the nearest thing—an overturned stool outside the inn—and launched it at the remnant. The stool flew through the attacking mist, tearing its delicate form to shreds.

"Thank you, darling!" The man nodded and tore off down the street, still carrying the lumpy sack. As he ran, something small and sparkling fell out of the bag and clinked on the stones.

"Wait, you dropped something!" Emry reached down for it—but the man had somehow scrabbled up to a roof, already sprinting away across the shingles.

At first, Emry grimaced, thinking he had helped a thief get away with some valuables—but when he turned the little trinket over in his hands, he saw it was just a simple glass bottle, thick and stoppered with a metal cap. The sparkles came from a swirl of spirit energy trapped inside it, the particles bouncing around in the glass until they were blurs.

"What the..." He flipped over a tag at the neck, attached with twine.

Test #28, Bottle 10

> *If Found, Please Return to Mr. Devrin Gray*
> *Do Not Open!*

More shouting from the fire down the street dragged him back to the present, and he pocketed the bottle before setting off toward the Academy. Mr. Devrin Gray would have to wait a moment to get his bottle back.

An anxious pounding in his head began as soon as the campus came into sight, and grew worse once he ran through the gates. The entrance, once lush and haughty, was now framed by black trees bent all the way to the ground, their dead branches brushing up against jagged shards of earth. The quad beyond it seethed in a palette of dark blue as students rushed to find each other, sobbed into each other's arms, or called out the names of their friends. Scraps of their conversations whipped past Emry's ears, distracting him from his search.

"My brother, have you seen my brother?"

"They're opening up the south hall as a medical wing, you can take her there!"

"Just got word, my cousin was ten blocks north of here, they didn't see it at all—"

Emry let out a ragged breath—so the surge hadn't struck all of Vidanya after all. His family was safe.

But he couldn't yet say the same for his friends here.

"Cal?" he called. "Aspen?"

Someone turned at the first name, a whirl of pigtails and fear. He stumbled up to her without thinking.

"Marie!" he said. "You all right? Have you seen Cal?"

"I think so." Marie was already clutching two of her other friends. "I saw her running out of the hall with the other one—the one with the lute."

"When?"

"After the quake stopped—"

"Thank Hara." He rushed away, but lost momentum in the crowd. In the sea of faces, there was no telling anyone apart, no discerning where they could have gone. He searched for a high point

—the cracked ivory steps of the music building—and joined several others who had the same idea.

"Cal!" he forced out a hoarse shout. "Aspen!"

But this was no stage, and his voice melted in with the desperate cries of the other students. Some of them succeeded in their search, stumbling down into the arms of their missing loved one as they washed up like castaways at the base of the steps. Others gasped and rushed off as friends climbed the stairs and delivered news—though good or bad, Emry couldn't hear. He wasn't even hearing his own voice anymore. "Aspen! Cal!"

"Em!" Someone drove a determined line through the crowd, shoving their way toward the base of the steps. "Stay there!"

His legs nearly gave out when they emerged from the fray, no injuries visible. Aspen reached him first in a flurry of outstretched arms.

"Aspen, are you okay?" Emry asked, hugging them to his chest. The spirit's babbling answer was muffled against his waistcoat.

"I used a shield to keep Cal safe, but we didn't know where you were or how to find you and we—we got really scared—"

"I'm okay, it's fine."

"No, it's not fine!" Aspen pulled away and looked up at him, tears welling in their eyes. "I wasn't there to protect you!"

Emry's heart caught in his throat. "Protect me?"

"Yes, you and Cal! You're my"—they wiped their cheeks and hiccupped—"you're my grove right now, and I've got to make sure you don't get eaten by a remnant, or—or a bear..."

"I'm sorry, Aspen." Emry held their shoulders tightly. They felt so small, so terrifyingly small, in their little human form. "I promise I won't run away again."

"Good." Aspen gave him a teary smile. Emry took a breath and let go of them to face Cal.

"I think I owe you an apology as well—"

She closed the gap and wrapped her arms around him. "I'm just glad you're not hurt," she said. He could feel her arms shaking, and he tightened his embrace. "Where did you go?"

"I hardly know—some inn close to the nexus. Got in before the..." He looked down at her. "The roads. Did you see them?"

She nodded against his shoulder, then stepped away and folded her arms against her chest. "You should see the lawn around the hall, everything is completely ripped up. So many people didn't get inside in time, I could see it through the windows. And the medical building—I told them about the plants, but it's already over-whelmed..." She trailed off. Emry took her arm.

"Are your rooms still intact?"

"They're fine, thanks to Aspen."

"Let's go, then. It's no use staying out here."

He quickly found that the state of her quarters wouldn't afford them any peace, either. The fallen desk chair, the coffee table turned on its side, and the spilled tea soaking into the rug all made him feel worse that he hadn't been there when it happened.

Cal reached to pick up the table, but he gently stopped her. "I think you should get some sleep," he said. "I can clean up."

To his surprise, she didn't argue with him and went up the stairs without a word. A hand pushed on his back, and he glanced over his shoulder to find Aspen nudging him toward the steps. He nodded and followed Cal up.

As he suspected, she was just sitting on the bed, staring into the distance.

"Is there anything I can do?" he asked. She shook her head and absently reached for the blanket beside her. He walked over, helped pull it over her shoulders, and sat on the edge of the bed with her. He would have let the silence fill the space, if it weren't for the students still shouting outside.

"You know, not ten minutes before it hit, I was talking with Ella Sorman." He tried to keep his voice low while speaking over the tumult. That simple conversation in the card room felt like it had been a week ago.

Cal toyed with the edge of the blanket. "Really?"

"She was playing at Sumac Hall. Happened to see her on her way in."

"Hm."

Another marred silence—then Cal shed the blanket and stood.

"I have to talk to my advisor immediately," she said. "I may not have all the answers she'll want, but I've got to go to her with something."

Then Emry remembered the weight in his pocket, and he pulled out the spirit bottle. The energy inside had lost none of its fervor, still ramming itself into the glass walls. "What if there's someone else out there connecting the dots?" He handed the bottle to her. "Someone else seeing where we're headed?"

She took the bottle and read the tag. "Test twenty-eight... Where did you find this?"

"A man dropped it outside the inn, after I got a remnant off his back. He was running along rooftops when I last saw him. You think he can help us?"

Cal chewed her nail as she regarded the bottle. "Another person researching surges..." She flipped the tag over. "The return address says he's just outside of Vornik, and if he's running experiments, he may have some connection to the Academy." The idea made her stand up straight. "I'll ask my advisor about him, then we can visit this address to see what he knows—"

She started for the door, but he took the bottle from her hand first. "Ah—not before you get some sleep." He slipped it back into his pocket. "Please?"

Her glare didn't hold nearly half the staying power it usually did. "Fine. We'll search in the morning."

TWENTY-NINE

THE ACADEMY CANCELED all lectures the next day, and Emry and Aspen had to follow Cal closely to not lose her in the shuffle of a disordered campus. Some students were huddled together, like they had been last night. Others walked around and surveyed the damage in a daze, while yet others packed suitcases to leave. Even some of the local parents had descended to gather up their children and whisk them away. Emry couldn't help but think of what his younger sister Marley would have done in this situation, if she were still at the Academy. If she would have been huddling with her friends, or if his parents would have already packed her things and taken her home.

"Cal"—Aspen tugged at her sleeve as they hurried into a cracked building—"do you need me to talk to the advisor, too?"

"No," she said too quickly, then tried to soften. "I'll talk to them. Please, wait here."

She left them on a bench in the hall, but the tense atmosphere remained, as every student around them came to the same horrifying realization that none of this was over.

"But the papers said these were supposed to be done with days ago," one woman whispered fiercely to her friend as they passed by the bench. "Everyone said so—"

"Where do we go, then?" her friend asked. "You saw what happened to Shay when he didn't make it through the door in time."

As they rounded the corner, two robed professors crossed in front of them. "Six students in her lecture—"

"Six?"

"Yes, all in the medical wing right now. Three of them aren't"— the professor's voice broke—"they're not expected to..."

Emry slouched down on the bench as grief and fear settled into the hallway like a smog.

"Emry?"

"Yes, Aspen?"

The spirit fidgeted. "Do you...think you're still going to play tomorrow?"

It took him a moment to even recall what Aspen was talking about.

"For the Guild?" He passed a hand over his face. Just the thought of it weighed him down even further. "Aspen, I've no idea."

His eyes grew heavier the longer he waited, and he was close to napping on the bench when Cal reemerged, her face grim. "Well, I wasn't wrong about Mr. Gray's Academy connection," she said. "But I wasn't right, either."

Emry pushed himself to stand. "Could we get some coffee before you explain to me what that means?"

WHILE THE COFFEE was too bitter to be of assistance, the cold air buffeting the off-campus drink stall helped wake up both Emry and Cal.

"Our Mr. Devrin Gray is an ex-Academy student," Cal explained as they walked toward the carriage stop. "Enrolled under a different name, so it took a moment to find the files. He never graduated, though he received top marks in all his classes before he left."

"Why did he leave?" Aspen asked. They held Cal's second cup of coffee, swirling it around like she did with her own.

"They rejected the premise of his thesis. Rather than change it, he left." She gave a humorless laugh and sipped from her cup. "Do you want to know what it was on?"

"What?"

"Surges."

Though their walk bore them away from the chaos of the campus, their destination was no better. It seemed half the city was at the carriage stop, all waiting for coaches that wouldn't show.

"The roads to the east and south exits are too damaged, you can't go that way!" one manager shouted at the crowd. "West is your only way forward at this point!"

All around them, customers clutching suitcases and hat boxes grew angrier and louder. Cal pulled Emry and Aspen aside. "How do we feel about walking to Mr. Gray's?"

She took the second coffee from Aspen. Emry handed the spirit his bitter cup in replacement. "I thought you said it was outside of Vornik?"

"Not that far outside."

"It's still a day's walk. We'd hardly get a chance to explain before we'd have to turn around again." He frowned. "You know...I think there's an independent river route that would get us there faster, if you're willing to walk to that."

"Independent?"

"Disconnected from the nexus. Hardly more than a stream, really, and no more than a few miles long. No runners, you just drop a coin in the box and row your own way."

Cal shivered. "Who would want to row in those dark caves all by themselves?"

"Folks in the small towns, mostly. They can get about their

villages faster, and we don't have to spare runners to babysit them." Emry grinned. "Incidentally, they're also very good for racing."

"Emry."

"I promise, if I row, I'll go very slowly." He jerked his head toward Aspen. "Can't have my lute falling out."

"*Emry—*"

"Can we go in a boat again?" Aspen tugged on Cal's sleeve. "Please?"

Cal sighed, then downed her second cup of coffee. "All right."

Aspen's excitement about the boat ride only grew as they headed to the independent route entrance, stepping over broken curbs and fallen signposts as they went.

"Have you rowed for very long?" Aspen nudged Emry's arm when the cave entrance, hardly more than a gap in a hill, came into view.

"Practically my whole life," Emry said. Now that he was about to row again, he felt an odd bounce in his step.

"Have you ever fallen out?"

"Of course. Mostly on purpose, to know what to do when it's not on purpose."

"And who taught you to fall?"

His pace slowed again as he remembered the letters sitting on Cal's desk. "Um..." He rubbed the back of his neck. "My father and my older sister."

Aspen's eyes grew wide. "You have *sisters—*"

Emry quickly lit the torch provided for them inside the cave entrance. "Watch your step, both of you. It'll be slippery down here."

As was usually the case with the independent routes, there was more to this little village cave than first met the eye. Once they reached the bottom of the first slope, the natural passageway expanded into a chasm, leaving only a bridge between them and rushing waters far below.

"Is that the stream we'll be using?" Aspen leaned over the railing. Cal froze.

"No, no." Emry gently guided Aspen away from the railing and glanced down at the water. "Rough water like that is far too dangerous to use for passengers, or even the emergency routes." Something about the fresh chill of the cavern loosened his tongue. "But you know—smugglers do use branches like this for getaways. It works, too, as long as they don't hit a flood or a rockslide. Or get caught, of course." He grinned. "I could tell you a story about Ben Ten-Fingers and how he almost got out of Copper Mill alive with this huge diamond necklace—"

"Yes, please!"

"No, thank you," Cal said crisply behind them. Emry laughed.

"I'll tell you later, Aspen."

They crossed the chasm and descended another slope until they reached a simple rowboat drawn up on a bank. Emry dropped the requisite coin in the lockbox, lit the provided lantern, and set to work inspecting the vessel. Finally, something both familiar and decently useful.

"Aspen, you'll have to hold the lute for me," he said as he finished his survey—overall, the boat was in good shape. "Cal, you can take my cloak. It'll be cold in the tunnel."

Cal approached the boat slowly. "And you're sure this will be safe?"

"Ye of little faith!" Emry hummed as he affixed the lantern to the front of the boat and helped her in, right foot first. "I'll have you know that my cave-running license is still good for another two years."

"Hm" was all she said. Aspen snuggled into the boat next to her, now wearing their own projected version of a traveling cloak. Unsurprisingly, it was made mostly of leaves.

"Cal, can you teach me how to read along the way?" Aspen asked as Emry rolled up his sleeves. Cal didn't answer right away, and he looked up to find her staring at his forearms. He worked very hard to stifle a surprised laugh.

"What did you say?" She shook her head and turned to Aspen.

"Sorry, I think it'll be too dark for reading. Perhaps when we get back to campus."

But it clearly wasn't too dark to watch Emry as he rowed. Her eyes would drift to his arms, then dart back out to the black waters every time he returned her gaze. The pattern got so predictable that even Aspen caught on. "I don't get it," they said. "Is something wrong?"

"No," the humans answered quickly—Cal biting her lip, Emry hiding a foolish grin.

Halfway through the tunnel, his mind wandered away from the regular pattern of rowing and stumbled upon an idea. If she could look effortlessly beautiful in the sunlight and massage his hand without a second thought, surely he could have his own tiny bit of fun, couldn't he?

"This boat doesn't have a dry bag, does it?" he asked, already knowing it didn't. His passengers looked about dutifully and shook their heads. "That's too bad, I thought it might have some gloves in it. Ah, well."

Taking his time, he slowly slid off his cravat and held out the cloth to Aspen. "Tear that in two for me, would you?"

Aspen took a finger, turned it into a claw, and ripped it clean down the middle.

"Rather unsettling, but that works. Thank you." He wrapped the two strips of cloth around his palms and resumed rowing, but not before making absolutely sure his shirt was open at the collar. On the other side of the boat, Cal cleared her throat.

"What's that up ahead?" she asked, her voice sounding rough. Emry twisted to look ahead, and beamed when he saw the green light. He couldn't have planned this better if he'd tried.

"Oh, I know what that is."

"What is it?"

He just shook his head and kept rowing. "I'm not going to ruin the surprise."

"You know I hate surprises!"

Emry started laughing. Cal grabbed his knee—an excellent, if unintended, riposte on her part. "Emry Karic, you tell me what it is right this instant—"

"But Cal, you're going to love it!"

"Really?"

"Truly, I promise. Here"—he lifted the oar out of the water—"you're going to want me to slow down."

As the boat drifted around a bend in the tunnel, Cal looked up and gasped. "Weir's eyes..."

"Literally." Emry leaned back. Up above them, the normal darkness of the cave ceiling shimmered with thousands of tiny green lights, as if someone had trapped the entire night sky in the tunnel. He dug the oar into the silt below them to slow down the boat, letting Cal admire the brilliant twinkling.

"They're the not-flowers we saw in the Halagrad nexus." Aspen craned their neck to take it all in. "What did you call them?"

"Glow-worms," Emry said. "We're very lucky to see them like this, at their full strength. A few days from now, and they might be too dim to see at all." He watched their glow illuminate Cal's face. "You want to see what they can do?"

"Of course," she breathed.

"Aspen, could you take out the lute for me?"

Aspen handed him the lute, then looked back and forth between them. "You know, um—being in the lute when you play is nice, so I think I'll go in there for a while, if that's all right."

The spirit promptly disappeared, leaving just the two of them in the boat.

Emry silently thanked Aspen and plucked a single chord. Above, the glow of the little larvae rippled out in a ring pattern, and Cal gave a delighted laugh.

"Want me to play a song for them?" He kept his voice low. She smiled.

"Yes, please."

Then, in a move that surprised himself, he took her satchel and placed it carefully behind her head.

"Lean back," he said softly. She nodded and did so, her eyes locked on his as she moved. Careful not to shift the boat, he returned to his seat and began to play her old favorite.

When they were dating, Cal had insisted that "Tree and the Stream" required no lyrics. For her, it already painted the picture it needed to—one of the old willow by her family's house, its long branches trailing in the water next to it. Whenever Emry played the piece for her, he imagined he was taking her back there in some way. That when she smiled at the melody, she was thinking about the tree's gentle shade, or the stream's quiet company.

He desperately wanted to know what she was thinking now as she smiled up at the glow-worms, dancing and swaying along with the music. Their glow rippled in mesmerizing patterns as Emry played, each note drawing a different shape in the light. Diamonds spread outward at the chorus, while the verses undulated in airy circles. And when the chords clustered together, a kaleidoscope of glowing lines above cast their swirling light on the waves below, until the visual duet made it feel like they were floating within the night sky itself.

Then as Cal pulled the second cloak—his cloak—up to her chin and gave a small, contented sigh, he realized this little plan of his had utterly backfired. This single performance couldn't possibly sway her opinion of him—but when it came to the state of his own feelings, he was going to end the boat ride in a much deeper hole than where he had started.

THIRTY

Aspen reappeared in human form as Emry emerged from the tunnel, the warmth of the midday light feeling less reassuring than it should have.

"So?" they whispered and glanced ahead at Cal, who was leading them down a wide dirt road. "Did the music work?"

Emry shook his head. "I'd forget about it, Aspen," he whispered back. "Really, it was a stupid mistake."

"Did she not like it?" Aspen set their hands on their hips. "Well—okay, there's other things you could try. There are these birds that, when they find their mate, they do these dances—"

"Aspen."

"Or you could build something for her, maybe with some twigs and flower petals?"

Emry stopped walking. "Aspen. Drop it."

Aspen searched his face for a moment, then trudged ahead to join Cal. "Humans are so frustrating."

Cal soon veered off the main thoroughfare down a more overgrown road, the trees and fences hemmed in with wild undergrowth and ivy. When the tree line opened up to reveal their destination, she stopped, checked the address on the bottle, and sighed. "Well, this is it."

Once upon a time, it may have been a nice house. A merchant's place, perhaps, for the grounds boasted no field or orchard that Emry could see. But whatever merchant had once filled the mansion with family, friends, and servants had long since abandoned it. The entire structure leaned, the roof bowed, the windows sagged. In short, it looked tired of existing.

But Mr. Devrin Gray seemed to have no interest in renovating the place to its former glory—in fact, he seemed to have made it worse, at least on the outside. Glass bottles tied to metal stakes dotted the yard and hung off the eaves, their unstoppered openings all facing south. He had also covered the south-facing side of the house in an ugly array of metal—signs, rods, wheels, anything and everything until the siding completely disappeared under a mess of black and rust.

"All right." Cal turned back to them, weighing Mr. Gray's lost bottle in her palm. "Let me go first. I'll explain that I'm studying surges and would like to ask him a few questions. Aspen, you can say you're my associate. We'll see if he knows anything about the wave, when it may hit—"

Aspen groaned. "Associate?" they said. "I don't want to keep lying! That's not going to get us anywhere!"

"Aspen, we don't know anything about this man—"

"He's studying surges. What more do you need to know?" Aspen threw up their arms. "I swear, both of you today..."

Cal looked to Emry. "What did *you* do?"

Before Emry could answer, the door to the house flew open, revealing a man with bronze skin, black hair, and a grumpy countenance.

"Listen," he barreled out, waving a slip of paper above his head, "I'll have you know I've got three more days to pay this off before you come knocking down my door!"

Cal quickly regained her wits. "Sir, you misunderstand—we're not debt collectors."

"Then get off my property. You're endangering my experiments!" He made a sweeping gesture toward his lawn structures.

"I'll handle this." Aspen grabbed the bottle from Cal's hand and strode right up to the man. "Are you the Mr. Devrin Gray from this bottle?"

The man frowned. "Yes."

Aspen handed him the bottle. "Hello. My name is Aspen. I'm a spirit. Do you need proof?" They stomped the ground, and dandelions burst into life all around their feet. "There. May I come in? My associates and I have questions about your surge research."

Devrin Gray stared at the flowers. Tilted his head. Opened his mouth, closed his mouth. Then stepped aside and gestured to the door. "Do spirits enjoy tea?"

If Emry was at all off-put by the exterior, he shouldn't have been surprised by the interior. It was as if Mr. Gray had ransacked the town at the other end of the road and thrown every one of its possessions into the house at random. In the foyer alone, Emry narrowly avoided tripping over a trunk full of bottles, only to smack his head on a tea kettle hanging from the chandelier. Ahead of him, the host took no notice, instead muttering to himself as he led them inside.

"If spirits are...then how would they interact with the surges, if trees absorb the...unless? No, that can't be right." He stopped, then seemed to remember that he had guests behind him. "Sit, sit, I'll be right back."

He waved them vaguely into a parlor, then grabbed the hanging kettle and disappeared. Still rubbing the impact spot on his head, Emry took one look around and opted to stand. Every chair in the parlor had books or clothing piled on top of it.

"Cal, how fast can we get out of here?" he mumbled. Cal was too busy staring in confusion at the single shoe balanced on the grandfather clock to respond.

Aspen, however, was thrilled.

"Look at all this!" They rifled through everything they could get their hands on. "What is that? What does this do? Cal, have you read any of these books?"

Devrin swung back into the room bearing a loaded tea tray. "One moment." He shoved a pile of candles off the coffee table with his foot to make room for the tray, then poured them all tea. Cup in hand, he sat right on top of a pile of clothing on the sofa and crossed one leg over the other. "Now. Before I start interrogating you—who are these associates of yours, Aspen?"

The man of the hour, who appeared to be just a few years older than them, fit in well with his style of decor. His outfit looked like he had picked the finest pieces of his wardrobe at random and then never took them off. Scuffed riding boots, coffee-stained brocade vest, dirty gloves with—was that gold detail?

Emry took a risk in trying the tea. The risk paid off—it was delicious. "Emry Karic," he started the introductions. "Aspen's roommate."

"I'm living inside his lute." Aspen pointed proudly at the lute case.

Devrin slurped his tea. "I'll have questions for you later. You?" He looked to Cal.

"Calliope Breslin, Academy student."

Devrin grimaced. "I have no questions for you. Now"—he set down his cup and leaned toward Aspen—"how did you find me?"

"I didn't. Emry did." Aspen looked to Emry, who shuffled in place.

"I was the one who threw the stool at the remnant last night."

Devrin's face broke into a grin. "Oh, that was you!" He looked Emry up and down. "Now I have more questions for you."

Emry choked on his tea. Cal stiffened. "Mr. Gray, we have some—"

"Do call me Dev."

"Dev, we'd like to inquire about your research on surges," she said. "We have reason to believe that a much larger one is coming."

"And let me guess." Dev gestured with his cup. "You need to make a presentation to the Academy so they can get the Council to do something about it?"

Cal hesitated. "As a matter of fact, yes, I—"

"Good luck with that." Dev stood up. "You're better off making your case to the cow down the street."

He grabbed the tray and walked away. Cal was on her feet before Emry could open his mouth to scoff.

"Wait!" She followed him out. "You already know about the larger surge, then? The wave?"

"I suspected something," he called back. Emry and Aspen looked at each other, then rushed to catch up, until they were all following Dev like ducklings through the cluttered hall. "I must say, it's both gratifying and concerning to hear a confirmation, though you'll need to divulge your methods."

"Then you understand the need to get the Council to do something about it," Cal said.

"Oh, I'm not arguing with that part, darling." He led them into the kitchen, where he set to work refilling the teapot. "I just don't think the Academy's going to help you."

Cal folded her arms. "Just because they rejected your thesis doesn't mean they won't listen to me."

"Cal!" Emry gaped at her. Dev smirked.

"They told you about that, did they?"

Aspen stepped in before Cal could continue. "How did you suspect that a wave was coming?"

Dev leaned back against the counter and sipped his tea. "I'll show you mine if you show me yours."

Cal rolled her eyes, then dug into her satchel and pulled out her notebooks. "As a scientist, you might think the origin of this information is a little unusual—"

"I like unusual." He gestured with his teacup. "Go on."

He came around and peered over her shoulder as she spread out her notes on the kitchen table, with her filled map at the center. As she explained the evidence in Brinna's stories and the scope of what they feared was coming, his smirk slipped away.

"I admit, I..." He flipped through a few of the pages. "I didn't anticipate an event of quite this magnitude. I suspected it could go as far as Copper Mill—"

"Which it already has."

"And it made me hope that we could possibly be done for this cycle," Dev finished. "But the build-up under the earth that I saw in Vornik, and the samples I managed to gather from last night..." He drummed his fingers on the table, then strode off toward the staircase, leaving the others to trail behind him again. "I may not know what exactly *causes* the surges yet, but the evidence I've been collecting is clear about their aftermath. I've been gathering them for over ten years now, mostly from this area."

He climbed the stairs, easily dodging the detritus thrown about the steps. "There are a precious few others who have sent me samples from west Vornik and Selj. Not that I'll get more any time soon, given the state of the rotting roads..."

He threw open the door to a long room flanked with floor-to-ceiling shelves. Unlike the rest of the house, this room was immaculate. Glass bottles of varying sizes formed perfect lines at each tier, all precisely labeled and glowing at various intensities. As they stepped inside, Dev scribbled something on a card and placed Emry's bottle on a shelf at the far end.

"No, no, that won't do." Dev waved them over as they started to wander. "Come here, you must start at the beginning."

THIRTY-ONE

THEY GATHERED around Dev to look at a bottle that held nothing but a hacked-off chunk of tree.

"Ten years ago, taken from Oakvane, a few miles north of here." He tapped the glass. "One of my best samples."

They stared at it for a moment—then Aspen smiled and tapped it, too. "Ah," they said. "It's quite nice."

"Oh, definitely." Emry nodded. "Why…is it nice?"

"The tree's absorbed the energy from the surge." Aspen looked to Dev. "How long did it take?"

"Five years. Look." Dev dragged them over to another set of bottles, all dated from the surges five years ago. They, too, looked empty save for bits of wood. Aspen leaned close to them.

"It's completely absorbed, I can feel it. It feels…" They trailed off. "I don't know how to describe it."

"May I take notes?" Cal was scrambling to find an open margin in her notebook. Before she could make a mark, Dev yanked the pencil out of her hand.

"Do you promise not to steal my research and revolutionize Thalis with the potential wonders of this unique source of energy?"

Cal tried to swipe at her pencil, but he held it above her head. "I'm more concerned with Thalis surviving the week," she countered. "What do you take me for, a thief?"

"No, I take you for an Academy student. Spirit, do you vouch for this woman?"

Aspen frowned. "Sorry, what's vouch? Whatever it is, it sounds awful. Please give her back the pencil."

Dev handed the pencil back to her and continued his tour. "Right, so you've seen my older samples. These"—he stopped at a shelf—"are from a week ago."

The energy here still drifted within the glass, sparkling faintly. The wood inside sat undisturbed.

"And these are normal from your observations?" Cal asked as she wrote.

"Perfectly. Just what I'd expect from a surge, given my limited observations. But these..."

He didn't have to say much else as he led them deeper into the room on the other side. With each passing day of research, the energy within his samples grew denser, more volatile. More of the wood blackened and twisted within the glass. By the time they reached the end, where yesterday's samples had been lined up, every chunk of tree was dead, and the particles slammed the glass in their attempts to get out. Emry looked at these samples and swallowed. Beside him, Aspen's form went translucent.

"These cards..." Cal walked back and forth between the various samples, checking the labels against her notes. "You wrote down which cities were hit during each surge?"

"All the names I could get from the papers, yes."

Emry squinted at the cards—though he couldn't make out the specific names farther down the shelves, the lists clearly grew longer with each day's sample.

"You missed one here." Cal pointed at a bottle. "Bennli was hit here, too." She flipped to a page in her notebook and showed Dev. "But it doesn't break the pattern you've clearly tracked."

"Doesn't break yours, either." Dev nodded to the map in her notebook. "I wonder…" He walked over to the window, his voice soft. "What do you think it'll be like? The wave, as you called it?"

Cal closed her notebook. "Deadly, I expect."

"I think it'll be fascinating."

Cal glanced uncertainly at Emry, whose thoughts were immediately clouded with dead trees and shimmering bodies on the street. But before either of them could argue, Dev shook his head and turned around. "But deadly, yes, you're right. I'm afraid our combined research does not lie about the lives on the line." He pulled out a chair from a desk by the window and sat, the chair back facing them. "So, Academy, what do you need?"

"Pardon?"

"For your presentation. Surely, you're lacking in information, or else you wouldn't have come to me. What do you need?"

Cal stood up straighter. "There's no way the Academy or the Council will take any action without knowing a timeline. I need to be able to estimate for them when the wave is going to hit."

"And Hara's Shield," Emry offered. "We'll need to have some idea of what that is. Otherwise, where is the Council going to send everyone in the north?"

As soon as the words left his mouth, his stomach twisted into a knot. Senne, of course, was in the north. His family was in the north.

"Well, I don't know anything about, what did you call it? Hara's Shield? But"—Dev gathered papers at the desk—"I could devise some sort of calculation to estimate when the wave will strike. I was in the middle of calculating the distances between the affected cities when you dropped in…"

As their conversation dissolved into things Emry couldn't quite track, he sidled over to Aspen, who had gone over to stare at the earliest samples on the wall.

"I'd say a copper for your thoughts," Emry half whispered, "but I'm afraid there isn't a fane around here to drop a coin in, so…" When Aspen didn't respond, he nudged the spirit's shoulder. "Hello?"

"Oh. Hello." Aspen roused as if from sleep. "I was just...thinking."

"About?"

"About my memories," they said. "I don't remember a whole lot before Addie. Everything was the same, so I guess I didn't need to remember much. But I do recall...something like this." They pointed at the piece of wood in the bottle. "Growing. Like something was building me in little pieces."

"Maybe..." Emry paused. "Maybe you're like a stalactite."

"A what?"

"You saw them. The big stone teeth in the caves."

"Oh! Yes." Aspen brightened. "How do those grow?"

"Just like you, little by little. Water drips down slowly, and the mineral deposits form the stone. Could take thousands of years."

"I'm not *that* old." Aspen elbowed him, then fell back into thought. "Suppose that's why the remnants don't work?"

"Hm?"

"Well, they didn't form right. Spirits can't take shape in a day. They have to grow, like anything else. So, when remnants try to bond, they sort of...kill things."

"Or almost take people's hands off."

"Or that."

"What do you mean, take off people's hands?" Dev looked up from a paper. "I haven't observed anything like that."

"Emry's hand got caught in a surge several days ago," Cal started, and quickly explained Cedar's healing method. Dev's eyes went wide.

"Incredible. You know, I was considering testing energy resilience across tree species—perhaps within spirit groves first— but to think that it could be variable within humans as well? This opens up a whole new line of—"

Cal raised her eyebrows. Dev refrained from reaching for a pencil and held up his hand instead. "Yes, yes. Calculating when the wave will strike..."

Their conversation elevated back into mathematics and left

Emry behind again. He found his attention drawn to the most volatile bottles on Dev's shelves, where the angry energy still flurried. After all he had seen, he could easily imagine it covering roads, forests, mountains. Then he imagined it covering his house in Senne, choking the garden, pushing through the doors. His palms went cold.

"You know, I'm not going to be of much use here," he said to Aspen, nodding over to Cal and Dev. "I'm going to try to think more about Hara's Shield, or…something."

He left the room and wandered about the second floor, knowing full well that if Cal couldn't solve the problem of Hara's Shield, he certainly couldn't. He tried not to think about his family and instead focused on everything else he saw and heard. Fortunately for him, the conversation coming from Dev's laboratory was just as varied as the objects he was trying not to trip over.

"So, tell me," Dev interrogated Aspen, who sat on the desk and swung their legs, "precisely what do you think about when you grow plants?"

"I don't know. What do you think about when you breathe?"

"Amazing."

When Emry next passed by, Dev and Cal were chattering and passing papers back and forth.

"What do you think?"

"Not bad, Academy. Perhaps that place has hired better professors since I left." Dev frowned. "You know, you do look familiar. Did we ever take a class together?"

Cal hid a grimace. "I would have remembered if we did."

The third time Emry reached the doorway, a warm light rippled through the room.

"This is the shield I can make…"

"Incredible!" Dev was a blur as he moved around Aspen and the glowing shield. "How long can you hold it? What can pass through it? How big can it get?"

"You should have seen the one from the spirit at the stream." Cal was eagerly measuring the sphere between Aspen's hands. "It had to be at least ten yards across. Quick, get a timer going."

It was on his last lap around the house when Emry found something remotely comforting—a lute, scratched and half-buried under several coats and an empty flowerpot. He picked it up and strummed it. Not a great instrument, by any means, but it could carry a melody after a bit of tuning. He went back to the doorway and held up the lute. "Dev, do you play?"

"Oh, that!" Dev looked up from a page full of numbers. "Was wondering where that was. Meant to learn, but never quite got around to it." He brightened and leaned against the desk. "Are you going to play for us? Would be awfully handsome of you."

Cal glared at Dev—but as much as Emry wanted to stay and overanalyze the look on her face, he shook his head and pointed down the stairs.

"I should really go practice, in case I've still got that, you know, thing." As if thinking about that would help untie his stomach. "I'll just...be down there with your lute, if you don't mind."

"Emry's going to be a part of the Guild one day," Aspen bragged as he descended the steps. "He's amazing."

He spent a few minutes trying to find a place to sit somewhere on the first floor, then gave up and walked out the door into the cool afternoon. Before he really thought about what he was doing, he was standing at the mouth of the river route tunnel, then hopping into the boat, then rowing himself out into the calm waters.

Once away from the banks, he brought in the oars and filled the air with a few aimless riffs on the lute. He knew he should be practicing something more legitimate, but none of the formal pieces he had decided on for Ella and her peers felt quite right in a space like this. In the rare instances where he had run routes with both of his sisters, they had requested he sing silly songs to bounce off the tunnel walls, or create tunes for rhymes they made up on the spot. Their laughter and dancing used to rock the boat back and forth, until Emry had to stop singing to hold on.

"Hey, Aspen," he said, "you want to hear that story—?"

He looked down at the lute and remembered that this was Dev's instrument, not his, and Aspen wasn't here. He slouched as an unexpected wave of sadness struck him. If this was what his lute would be like after Aspen returned to their grove, he didn't want it.

The meandering river guided him farther out, and when he reached the glow-worms, he took an oar and dug it into the silt. As the boat slowed to a stop, the worms twinkled at him as a silent, patient audience, and he lay down in the boat to play one song for them.

When the gods begin to fight,
    Through ground, rivers, trees, and light
    Dance your way to Hara's shield
    Follow her voice, she will not yield

Unlike the last piece, the glow-worms reacted to the music in a much more stable pattern. Little triangles shivered up at the top of the display, then formed wiggly lines that branched out like veins—two north, three south, a lopsided diamond shape in the center. Emry gave an amused hum. It almost looked like the Sumac river route he'd had to memorize as a boy.

He paused, repeated the last verse, then sat up straight.

It *was* the Sumac route he'd had to memorize as a boy.

"Shiro's hairy foot..."

He started the song over, repeating bars and taking careful note of the other patterns that flashed around the lines. The triangles he understood—those were the northern mountains, surely—but the five little circles that expanded out inside them, he didn't understand. What in Hara's name was *inside* the mountains that would be of any signif—

"Caves." He grabbed the oar. "Cold and dark. It's not a stupid structure, it's a cave system—"

He rowed as fast as he could and sprinted back to the house. "Cal!" He burst through the front door of the mansion. "Aspen!"

Muffled voices floated from somewhere far down the hall on the first floor. Afraid the circles on the map would slip out of his mind, he dashed upstairs, scrawled them out on a scrap of paper from the lab, and ran back down toward the voices.

As he rushed over, he realized the conversation was coming not from the first floor, but from the lawn out behind it. Metal sheets had been dragged from the side of the house to the yard and stuck into the soil, creating a makeshift wall in the dead grass. Emry could barely see Dev and Cal's heads sticking out on the other side of it, but Aspen was in full view on the near side. They stood opposite a series of bottles—big ones, larger than growlers in size—clamped sideways onto a table. The spirit energy inside them buzzed in the glass like wasps.

"Okay, go!" Aspen shouted, and the scientists ducked down. A cord hiding in the grass went taut, yanking out the stopper on one of the bottles. The energy burst out and barreled toward Aspen.

"Aspen!" Emry started, but the spirit threw up a shield just as the blast reached them. With the particles still pelting the barrier, Aspen slowly walked backward until the tiny surge lost steam and dissipated. Something clicked, and a hand popped out a ruler from behind the wall.

"Got the time?"

"Yes. What was the distance?"

"Three yards."

Cal popped her head up over the wall. "How are you feeling, Aspen? Ready for a bigger one?"

"Yes!" They gave her a thumbs-up. Emry tensed and opened the door to the yard. Cal disappeared again, and Dev began to count down.

"One, two—"

"Hold on, hold on, what do you mean a bigger one?" Emry called.

Cal popped up again. "Emry, get back inside!"

"*Three!*"

Many cords in the grass whipped up this time, releasing the energy from the remaining bottles. Aspen whipped up the shield a millisecond before they struck, and their heels immediately dug into the grass as the force shoved them back.

Emry waited for the energy to dissipate, but it kept going, pushing Aspen much farther than before. The shield flickered once.

"Aspen!" he shouted. The spirit didn't seem to hear. They bent forward, eyes screwed shut with the effort of keeping up the barrier —but the shield flickered again.

"Hara take me." Emry sprinted across the grass and tackled the spirit just as the shield disappeared. They tumbled across the lawn until Emry's body struck the flimsy metal walls.

"What the—" Dev's head poked up over the wall. "What in Shiro's name are you doing? Oh, Cal, the energy's gone."

"Time!" Cal called, then appeared around the metal sheet. "Em, are you all right?"

Emry rubbed the back of his head and winced, the ringing sound of the metal still reverberating in his ears. "I'm fine. Aspen?"

The spirit scrambled to their feet, dusted themself off, then reached out a hand toward Emry. "You didn't have to do that. I had it, you know."

"You did not have it." Emry accepted the hand up, then glared around at all of them. "What were you thinking, making Aspen do something like that? You could have hurt them—"

"It was their idea!" Dev gestured. Emry looked to Aspen, who raised their hands.

"What? I needed practice with the shields, and they needed the data!"

"I wouldn't let anything happen to Aspen, you know that." Cal reached up to sift her fingers through Emry's hair. "Are you sure you're unhurt?"

He hoped she couldn't feel the heat coming off his cheeks. "Yes, I'm sure."

"Last time you told me you were fine, you almost lost the use of your hand."

"Well, I'm not getting my binder in a twist. I'm sure his pretty head is fully intact." Dev vaulted over the wall and handed Cal a piece of paper. "Double-check these calculations, if you please."

Emry then recalled why he had run out to find them in the first place. He retrieved the map he had dropped at the back door and held it out toward them. "Wait, wait! I think I found out what Hara's Shield is."

"Really?" Aspen stared at the paper. "Hara's Shield is...some lines?"

"No, no, that's the Sumac river route. Listen, I went back to the glow-worms, played the song, and they lit up, like earlier today—but *this* was their pattern."

Cal looked up from Dev's string of numbers. "The glow-worms showed you a map of the Sumac route?"

"Not just the route. It also showed these in the mountains." He held up the paper and pointed at the little circles.

"In the mountains," she repeated—then it clicked for her. "Caves. That's the Alacova cave system near Dawnstone."

Aspen rushed behind the wall and reemerged with Emry's lute.

"When can we get people up to the caves?" they rambled. "I do hope they're not as cold and dark as Brinna's stories. How many humans live up north? A hundred, you think?"

"A few more than that," Emry said, his words firing just as fast. "The Council will need to find a way to close off the cave openings first. And make sure the system isn't connected to the river tunnels, or else the energy could get in that way. But if we tell them to evacuate now..." He turned to Dev and Cal. "How much time do you think we have?"

Cal reached the end of the calculations and looked up at Dev in fear. "Are you sure these are correct?"

"I'm always correct."

Cal swallowed and looked at Emry. "We've only got four days."

CHAPTER

THIRTY-TWO

"No, don't phrase it like that, they're not going to pay attention if you do."

Cal and Dev paced in circles around the parlor, like vultures floating impatiently over a carcass.

"Fine, then how should I start it?" Cal crossed her arms.

"Throw some big words at them, it'll make them feel smart and important at the beginning. *Then* hit them with the information." Dev paused to refill his tea. "Trust me, I presented to the Academy many times before leaving that hellhole. At the very least, I can tell you what not to do."

As Cal ran through her presentation for the fifth time and Aspen rested in the lute, Emry found himself in a mental rut. He had planned out how to get Aspen back to Tazlo, with time to make sure Marko and Stef found a safe place...but everything beyond that was blank.

"Cal, where are you going to go?" he asked as she broke for tea. "After you make your presentation, I mean."

"To Tazlo, to make sure Aspen gets to their grove all right."

"After that?"

237

Cal took a sip. "Dawnstone, to meet my parents at the cave system. I'll send them a letter tonight."

"Right, right." Bile rose in his throat. He had some letters to write, too.

"And what about after that?" Dev swirled a spoon around his own teacup. "Surely you'll be graduating from the Academy soon?"

"Oh." Cal hesitated. "Not just yet. I've still got a few courses I'd like to take..."

Emry's twinge of annoyance was brief this time—a dull spark, easy to shrug off. "What sort of classes are you looking to—?"

Then Dev cut him off, dropping his spoon on the saucer with a clink. His eyes were locked on Cal. "Wait, I know where I've seen you."

Cal narrowed her gaze over her own cup. "On campus?"

"No. Hasek's election three years ago. You were a volunteer, weren't you?"

It was Cal's turn to choke on her tea as Dev continued blabbering.

"Yes, I thought I recognized your voice! Flyers at the square and all that, right? I recall someone beating the opposition's aide so soundly in a debate, I thought they were going to cry. The victor was you, wasn't it?"

Cal looked as if she wanted to sink into the discarded jackets covering the couch.

"I don't know what you're talking about," she said, a warning edge on her words.

"No, no, it was definitely you!" Dev had resumed his circular pacing, while she remained in place. "Your stance was on maximum working days, wasn't it? Too bad Hasek didn't actually believe all that campaign talk..." He drained his tea. "What on earth are you still doing at the Academy, then?"

Emry's annoyance flared, but not toward Cal.

"Studying what she wants to," he cut in, his words as sharp as hers. "Now, I believe Cal wanted to go through the presentation one more time?"

If Dev felt a hint of the chill coming off either of them, he made no sign of it as he waved them on. "Sure, sure, run me through the presentation again..."

Another hour wore on before Dev deemed the work fit for an audience and opened the front door. "Good work. Go, and if you happen to catch any samples during the wave, do send them to me."

"Are you really going to stay here for it?" Aspen asked from the lute as Emry followed Cal out the door.

"Of course, I am! I'm already set up, aren't I?" Dev waved out at the bottles posted across the lawn. "You come back around for tea, all right, Aspen?"

"Definitely! Thank you, goodbye!"

Dev closed the door.

"I like him," Aspen said.

"He's an absolute madman," Cal said, and turned back down the path, muttering something about impertinent questions under her breath. Her low complaints soon faded into a grumpy silence that not even Aspen could break, despite their best attempts to chat in the tunnel and on the walk back to the Academy.

"Emry, can you tell me about the Ben Fingers and the copper necklace now, please?" Aspen asked as they walked through the campus gates. Emry laughed, which didn't seem to help Cal's mood.

"Ben Ten-Fingers and his failed adventure out of Copper Mill?"

"Yes!"

"All right." Emry cleared his throat. "Well, first you need to know that Ben Ten-Fingers was a prince among thieves in Copper Mill, which used to have more thieves than leaves—"

Aspen gasped. "No."

"Yes."

"But that's so many!"

"Exactly. Well, the place has gotten a little better since then."

Emry waved a hand. "Anyway, when some dumb Councilman wanders into town with a diamond necklace—"

"Can we not talk about dumb Councilmen right now?" Cal burst. "Any more mention of them and I'm going to turn all of you into dumb Councilmen!"

Emry and Aspen stopped as she stormed into the administrative building for the second time that day. Aspen tilted their head.

"Can she really turn us into Councilmen?" they asked. Emry set a hand on their shoulder, guilt rising in his throat.

"Give me a moment, I'll be right back out. Cal, wait!"

He caught up with her in the hall, where she turned on her heel.

"*What?*" The word bounced sharply across the marble floor.

"I just wanted to say," Emry started, then let out a breath. "I wanted to say I'm sorry. Dev shouldn't have pestered you about being at the Academy, and I shouldn't have, either. You can do whatever you like, whether that's Council work or reading every book in the library. And I know you already know that, but..." He rubbed the back of his neck, then dropped his hand. "I was wrong, and I'm sorry."

Cal maintained her stiff posture, but glanced down at the floor. "Apology accepted." Her response fell more softly this time. "I appreciate it."

When Emry exited the marble hall and stepped back into the light, the campus was much quieter than when they had left it that morning. Everyone had either left or retreated inside, finding no pleasure in being outside amongst the dead trees and shards of broken earth.

The longer they waited in the eerie silence, the more Aspen fidgeted, until Emry nudged them and nodded to a bench. "Come on, she might be talking to her advisor for a while. I'll tell you the rest of the story while we wait."

"Yes, please." Aspen eagerly followed him, stepping carefully over the half-crumbled sidewalk. "How did Ben steal the necklace from the Councilman?"

"Well, there were actually three separate thieves all planning to steal the necklace on the same night…"

When Ben Ten-Fingers finally met his watery demise in the smugglers' cave routes, Cal still hadn't emerged from the building—so Emry grasped for any other story he could recall from his father. The words stung as he told them the way his father had—but the tales kept Aspen's attention away from the quiet destruction around them, and he kept going until Cal finally reappeared on the quad.

"Cal!" He stood and waved her over. "How did it go?"

She picked up her skirt to step over a few cracks in the path. Emry took the opportunity to search her face—it was still serious, but no longer grumpy.

"My advisor was…skeptical, but I convinced her," she said. "She's going to call in favors to get me an audience tomorrow morning. If she can manage it, every Council connection she has will be there."

"And they'll take it from there?"

"With any luck, yes." She twisted her necklace. "They're not going to take this sort of thing lightly. I'm not sure I'll even have an advisor anymore if this doesn't go according to plan."

"It'll be fine," Emry said. "You practiced with Dev. You have the evidence you need—"

"And you're Cal." Aspen grinned up at her. "You'll do great."

"Thanks, Aspen." She squeezed their arm. "I think I'll feel better after I run through it a few more times…walk with me as I check the mail?"

"You think mail is getting through, with the state of the roads out there?"

Cal shook her head. "It's just a habit. It'll make me feel better, if nothing else."

As they entered Esther Hall—more populated, but still quiet— and let her veer away for the mail, Emry juggled ideas on what could help her while she practiced. She needed a fresh notebook, to be sure, but he didn't have the money for that. He did have enough coins for some coffee, though, or some cinnamon skewers from that stall a block away. If they were even open, post-surge...

A shriek crashed through his thoughts, and Cal came rushing back around the corner.

"Em, open it!" She shoved a crisp envelope into his hand. He ripped open the card and scanned it. At first, he relaxed—it wasn't Georgie's handwriting this time—but then the contents made him freeze up again.

"They're keeping on the Guild test for tomorrow—but changed the location?" He looked up at Cal, who had been standing on her tiptoes to read over his shoulder.

"Sumac Hall's windows got blown out last night. Check the address." Cal grabbed his shoulder. "That's Ella Sorman's place."

Exhilaration and fear swept through him. "But—but I haven't practiced enough—"

Cal pressed a key into his hand and pointed him up the stairs. "Go on up. I've got to get something."

"Get what?"

"You'll see, just go!"

When they reached Cal's quarters, Aspen resumed their seat on the coffee table and Emry opened the windows. Though they had cleaned her place last night, the parlor still smelled strongly of the spilled tea from yesterday's surge.

"Have you decided on what you're going to perform?" Aspen asked. Emry shook his head.

"Haven't quite narrowed it down yet," he said. "If I play the options for you, would you tell me which one you like best?"

"Of course." Aspen propped their head on their hands to listen. It took a moment for Emry to calm his hands and focus, but he slipped into the rhythm soon enough, and played through each of his favorites. But the spirit wasn't much help, for they had the same reaction after each piece.

"That one was so nice." Aspen smiled. "Could you please play another?"

Emry laughed and shook out his fingers. "That's all I've got, Aspen."

"Really? What about some of the songs you played in Tazlo?"

"I'm not going to play those for the Guild."

"But for me? Please?" A hint of desperation weighed on their voice. Emry wondered at the reason, then slouched when he realized it. He set the lute aside and leaned forward.

"Aspen, this won't be the last time you'll hear me. I promise I'll visit your grove and play for you when we're back in Tazlo."

Aspen nodded, their eyes shining. "Promise?"

"Absolutely."

"Took long enough, but this should work..." Cal cut in as she opened the door behind them, clutching a bundle of fabric against her chest. Before Emry could react, she dropped the bundle into his arms. "Here, try these on while I find some polish for your shoes."

He carefully separated the bundle into its different pieces: a waistcoat, a jacket, a completely spotless cravat... "Cal—"

"I told you I wouldn't let you perform in those rags, didn't I? I managed to borrow it all from someone Marie pointed me to. I think he's your build..."

Emry ran a finger over the elaborate pattern on the waistcoat. "You're far too generous."

"No, Gareth from Marie's provincial law class is far too generous. Try it on and come down when you're done." She pushed him toward the stairs.

Emry felt silly as he closed the door to her room and changed into the borrowed clothes. Though Gareth was clearly a bit of a paisley-adoring dandy, he was at least a responsible one. He couldn't remember the last time he had worn anything this nice, or this clean.

"Cal, could you help me with the cravat?" He fussed with the cloth as he walked back down the stairs. "I have no idea what the

Vornik style is these days. Stef made fun of me last time I tried the Tazlo knot…"

"One moment." Cal was hunched over her desk, dashing out a letter. Once she was satisfied, she set down the quill, stretched out her fingers, and turned around to survey his look. She froze as soon as she saw him.

"That bad? Really?" Emry started back up the stairs. "I'll go change—"

"No, no. You look…" She came over and took his arm to turn him back around, then smiled up at him. "Perfect. You look perfect, Em."

"Oh." All the silly, fleeting confidence he had felt back in the river tunnel was gone. After a moment of staring at her smile, some vague part of his brain informed him that he should probably say something. "Thank you."

Nailed it.

"You said you needed help with the cravat?" Cal asked.

"Yes, tying the knot—I mean, um, tying the, you know."

Over on the sofa, Aspen slapped a hand to their face.

As Cal stepped closer and pulled slowly at the cloth draped over his neck, Emry immediately regretted asking for assistance. Was this payback for what he'd done in the tunnel? Or was she truly not aware of the effect she had standing this close to him, so close that he could feel her breath on his neck? No, she had to be aware. She had done this to him intentionally all the time back in Tazlo. She'd pretend to fix his collar, he'd grab her waist, pull her close, lean down…

She stepped away before his memory could torture him further.

"Is that all right?" she asked. He leapt on the opportunity to break away from her and search for a mirror.

"Which knot did you do?"

"The Vornik one."

He found a mirror by the front door and held back a sigh. Of course, Vornik used overly elaborate, puffy knots. "It's a bit foppish."

"I can try another one—"

"No! No, no. All good, thank you." She walked toward him, and he scrambled for a distraction. "So—you've got your presentation tomorrow before my exam, right?"

"Oh—um, yes." She stopped. "I should be back in time to accompany you to your exam, but we'll need to head to Tazlo after that."

Aspen's head whipped up. "Tazlo? So soon?" they said. Cal nodded.

"I'm sorry, Aspen, but if you want to get back to your grove in time, we'll have to leave right away. And I'll need to head to Dawnstone right after that—"

"No."

They both looked at Aspen, who was now standing in the middle of the room, their lower lip trembling.

"What do you mean?" Cal asked.

"I'm not going back to my grove." Their voice broke. Cal softened immediately.

"But if you want to protect it, you have to—"

"No!" Aspen's face crumpled. "I can't go back and just sit there, not knowing if you're alive or not, I can't!"

The spirit dissolved into tears, and they both rushed to hug them.

"No, of course not, we'd never make you go—"

"We're happy to have you stay with us, truly."

Emry pulled the spirit close, then glanced up at Cal. Her eyes were already searching his face, and Emry knew what she was going to ask next. "I'll be going to Dawnstone, but...Emry, where are you going to go?"

There was only one answer left.

"I'll meet my family in Dawnstone, too," he said. Aspen, who had latched on to his waist, looked up at him.

"Really?"

"Are you sure?" Cal touched his shoulder. He nodded, trying to convince himself as he spoke.

"They'll be safest in the caves, and I'll have that Guild exam under my belt when I see them. It'll be okay. It'll..." He let out a breath. "It'll be enough."

THIRTY-THREE

THE NEXT MORNING, Cal made her usual trip to the dining hall to forage for their favorites—coffee, tea, fruit dumplings, plus an extra for Aspen to hold while the humans ate. Aspen took theirs as soon as she set down the tray, but Cal and Emry just stared at the food.

"Are you both feeling all right?" Aspen said as they inspected the pastry. "You know, when bobcats get sick, they don't eat very much. Then they hide from predators until they get better or die—"

"Fine, fine." Cal took her dumpling and bit into it. Emry shook his head and wandered over to the desk, where he had gathered a bundle of paper and envelopes from Cal's stockpile the night before.

"Have you finished writing your letters yet?" Cal asked from the sofa. "We'll need to send them today if we want them to get anywhere. Once the Council starts telling people what to do, the post will be overwhelmed."

Cal's stack of letters sat patiently at one end of the desk, waiting to be sent to her circle—parents, grandparents, cousins, friends. Emry sat and rolled a quill between his fingers. "I'll get them done before we leave."

The words came to him slowly, but after an hour or so, he was able to add his stack to the pile—Marko, Stef, Bron...

He flexed his fingers and stared at the one piece of paper he had left. The only thing he had written on it was the letter *G*.

"Em." Cal brushed her hand against his shoulder. "If you dress now, I can help you with your cravat before I go."

He nodded, pushed the paper away, and left the desk.

"You sure you want to walk with me to Ms. Sorman's?" he called down as he dressed. "If you've got to pack—"

"Walk? You think you're *walking* to her place?" Cal's voice floated up the stairs. "No, I'm ordering you a carriage. Walking up to her doorstep, how ridiculous..."

Emry bit back a smile as he fiddled with his coat. "Fine, then let me pay for it."

"Absolutely not."

"Okay, now who's being ridiculous?"

"Still you." Her voice was much closer now. Emry jumped and turned to find her leaning against the doorway. "Come on, let's have a look at you."

She walked up to him, straightened his coat, then began to work on the cloth at his neck, just as she had the day before. For once, he was thankful his nerves were smothering all of his other emotions.

"There." She stepped away and turned him toward the mirror in the corner. "How do you like it?"

Unlike the puffy confection from earlier, this style was simple, straightforward, and familiar. A bittersweet feeling grasped his throat. "You did the Senne knot."

"Is that all right?"

He swallowed and nodded.

"Hey, Cal?" Aspen called from the stairs. "You told me to tell you when the clock looked a certain way, and it looks a certain way now—"

"Thank you, Aspen." Cal brushed some nonexistent lint off Emry's shoulder. "Well, I have to go..."

Going out on a limb, Emry took her hand and kissed it gently.

"Best of luck, Cal. I'm so proud of you."

She squeezed his hand before he let go, unable to quite lift her gaze to his as she smiled. "It's an important day for both of us. I'll see you soon."

After she left, Emry stared at his blank letter for a while. Paced around. Sipped some cold tea. Then finally settled on pulling out his lute and riffing on a few pieces. There wasn't much point in practicing now, but there was some comfort to be found in weaving his favorite chords together. Aspen sat cross-legged on the table, holding a cold cup of coffee with both hands. Though they said nothing, Emry could tell they were holding in a question. They were watching him too intently, their lips pressed into a line. "Yes, Aspen?"

Aspen set down the cup. "Now that I'm not going back to my grove, could you teach me how to play the lute?"

"No."

"No?"

Emry grinned. "Because you'll learn far too quickly and put me out of a job."

"I won't! I won't, I swear—"

"I'm kidding." He nudged the spirit's knee. "Of course, I'll teach you how to play. You do live inside this thing, after all. Here, want to start now?"

He walked Aspen through all the parts of the lute, how it created sound, how it tuned. Once they seemed to have a grasp on that, he handed over the lute itself.

"Okay. Put one hand here, and the other hand here..."

Aspen shifted their hands, holding the instrument gingerly. "Did you ever teach Cal how to play this?"

"Oh, I tried once." He recalled her nearly throwing the thing in frustration, and held back a laugh. "She, ah, prefers listening, rather than playing herself. But you should ask her to sing for you sometime. She has a lovely voice."

"Will you ever sing with her?" Aspen's gaze was pleading. Emry's smile faded.

"Maybe one day." He focused on Aspen's hands. "Now don't put the weight on your left hand. You'll need it to move freely to play. And keep the lute tilted up a bit, like this."

"Why?"

"Helps with the projection. Here, let me adjust the strap for you—"

The door blasted open with a string of curses, and he nearly slapped the lute up into his own face.

"Cal?" Emry scrambled to his feet, Aspen following suit. "What happened?"

"Dev was right." She threw her satchel onto the ground and paced back and forth, her breathing still shallow even as her voice grew. "That infuriating man was *right*."

Emry's stomach dropped. "They didn't listen?"

"Of course, they didn't listen!" Cal ran her hands through her hair. "Apparently it didn't matter that hundreds of people died in the surge two days ago. They didn't trust the data, completely disregarded the pattern in the narratives, kept spewing nonsense about peer reviews and vetting, which would take months, when we only have days before the rotting world ends—"

"Are you sure you don't have any others you can go to?" Emry grasped at straws. "Anyone else connected to the Council itself?"

"I thought about that, I went through everyone, I just..." She let out a grounding breath, kicked her satchel for good measure, and downed the cold coffee on the table. "I'll think of something on the carriage ride over to Ms. Sorman's. I've got to."

An idea crashed down on him as soon as he heard the name. A terrible one, one that made his insides churn and his throat tighten. But now that it was in his head, he couldn't let go of it.

Cal reached for the door. "We should leave now, if you're ready."

He hadn't been less ready for anything in his life—but he put on a brave face as he picked up both the lute and her beat-up satchel. "Let's get this over with."

THIRTY-FOUR

As Cal huddled inside a cloudy brainstorm on the carriage ride over, Emry's own thoughts settled into his stomach in a nauseous sort of pain. Three times he considered making the carriage stop so he could vomit out the few sips of breakfast tea he had managed to get down that morning.

"Emry?" Cal finally looked at him. "How are you feeling?"

"Fine."

When he didn't meet her gaze, she touched his knee. "You're going to be excellent, I know you are."

"They already know you're great," Aspen said. "What's there to be nervous about?"

He closed his eyes and nodded.

As they approached Ella Sorman's place, Emry saw that Cal had been right that morning—he would indeed have looked ridiculous simply walking into her courtyard. He couldn't imagine striding through the complex iron gate, nor past the elegant fountains and greenery that lined the sun-warmed stone plaza. And there was no way he could have just strolled up and knocked on the intricately carved door at its far end.

As the carriage door opened, Aspen disappeared into the lute, and Cal leaned forward to catch his hand. "Best of luck, Em," she said, eyes crinkling as she smiled.

Emry took an uneven breath and handed back her satchel. "No need to say goodbye. You're coming with me."

"What?" She frowned at it. "I don't understand."

Before she could protest, Emry grabbed the lute case and led her out of the carriage.

"Emry"—Cal's voice pitched high—"I am not at all dressed to meet someone like—"

"Mr. Karic?" a man called out. At the top of the marble staircase, a butler filled the doorway with his humorless gaze.

"Yes." Emry kept a shaky hold of Cal's hand and continued forward.

They entered the soaring foyer, the butler giving them just enough time to be dazzled by the chandelier and plush rug before ushering them into a summery drawing room. In any other scenario, this room would have been comfortable and welcoming—bright sunbeams, pillowy furniture, plants and flowers giving vibrance to every ivory-wallpapered corner. But once Emry saw the line of chairs in the middle of the room and the single person sitting there, his chest constricted.

Ella Sorman's deep voice flooded the room. "Good. I see you're still in one piece after recent events."

Ella herself looked no worse for wear, with her vivid colors and regal pose—save for her left arm, which she held rather stiffly.

"Ella." He gave a short bow. "I trust you made it out safely as well. The surge must have hit while you were still in the hall, and I heard the place sustained damage—"

"You were right," she said. "The servants' halls in Sumac turned out to be quite safe during a surge. My troupe and I are still in perfect condition, thanks to you." She stood, the silk of her kaftan whispering against the chair. "I decided I owed it to you to keep our appointment."

Emry inclined his head again—it was the most movement he could manage, given the wave of anxiety that was paralyzing him. "Thank you, that's incredibly generous of you."

"Karic." Damir's voice preceded him as he wandered in from the hall. "Still alive, yeah?" He frowned at Cal, who was standing like a surprised deer in Emry's shadow.

"Afraid so." Emry looked to the empty chairs, which he supposed he should feel grateful for. The smaller the audience, the easier this would be. He could hardly hear his own words through the pounding of his heart in his ears. "Will there be other Guild members attending?"

Damir lingered in the doorway to glance out the window. "Supposed to be. Late due to the state of the roads, I imagine."

"I don't believe they'll be necessary. I won't be performing today."

As soon as he said it, the nerves flooded out of him. That was it, it was done—there was no taking it back.

Every head in the room whipped toward him.

"Ella," he rushed, "you mentioned the other day that you wanted to do something about the surges, actually *do* something." He stepped back to bring Cal to the front. "My associate Ms. Breslin has been researching these surges and has an evacuation plan she'd like to propose to the Council. Ella, there's a bigger surge on the way, a much bigger one, and this is the only way we can save everyone."

A long, stunned silence. Damir was the first one to speak.

"Karic, have you lost your mind?" he said, then threw up his hands and turned away. "All right, I'm calling off the other Guild members. Ella, remind me not to recruit anyone from Tazlo again."

As he sauntered out the door, Ella's steely gaze landed on Cal. "Ms. Breslin, are you a professor?"

"A student, ma'am, fifth year." Calliope curtsied. Ella's lips pursed.

"And how long have you studied these surges?"

Cal swallowed. "A—little while, ma'am, but—"

Ella sighed and stood. "I believe that's enough. Mr. Karic, I'm afraid I'm going to have to ask you to—"

"Ms. Sorman, your hand."

This was a new voice. Ella glanced around to see who it was, while Emry and Cal froze in fear.

"Your hand, may I take a look at it?" Aspen appeared as a human next to Emry, dressed in an identical coat and vest. Ella blinked.

"Were they standing behind you?" she asked, while Aspen strode confidently over to a fan palm in the corner and plucked off a leaf. Now that Ella was standing, Emry could see that a part of her wrist glowed dimly.

"You got your hand stuck in the surge, didn't you?" Aspen continued, holding up the leaf. "I can fix it. Please sit, it'll only take a moment."

When Ella looked to Emry and Cal for an answer, Cal nodded in encouragement.

"This is Aspen, our...other associate in our research," she said. "They're not wrong, ma'am. They know how to heal your wrist. Please give them a chance—the harm the spirit energy can do to your wrist is severe if you let it continue to bond."

"Spirit energy?"

"Yes, ma'am."

Ella took a long moment to consider the trio that now surrounded her—then sat and gave a stiff nod in Aspen's direction. "My physician has not yet found a treatment for this...spirit energy." There was a hairline crack in her strong voice. "And I saw the bodies consumed by it the other night. If your associate has a solution..."

"Quite an easy one," Aspen said brightly and sat down next to her. "If you could hold out your wrist, please?"

She did so. Her ring bearing the Council insignia flashed in the sunlight, just as bright as the spirit energy digging under her skin. Aspen wrapped the leaf loosely around her wrist. "Close your eyes. You can feel the energy, right?" She nodded. "Because your body hasn't yet rejected it, you're going to need to give it a push. It'll sting a bit, but it'll save your arm."

Her brows lifted. "Save my arm?"

"Yes, ma'am. Now, close your eyes and breathe. One, two—"

Ella exhaled, then flinched, as if a bee had stung her. The leaf flashed and smoked, and the glow at her wrist faded.

"How does it feel?" Aspen pulled away the leaf. She twisted her hand a few times, the bangles on her wrist clinking together.

"Quite sound." Ella frowned. "How did you learn this?"

"My friend Cedar healed Emry when he got caught in a surge." Aspen set aside the leaf. "Apologies for disrupting your plant. Here, let me grow it back."

They walked over, patted the plant, and a new frond curled into place. Everyone was silent for a moment.

"Ella"—Emry cleared his throat—"the other day, you asked me how I achieved the sound that I made back at Lamb's Ear."

Ella tore her eyes away from the plant. "I did, yes."

"If I told you that Aspen was a forest spirit living inside my lute, would you believe me?"

Ella paused, then strode over to the door. Emry squeezed his eyes shut. He knew he shouldn't have said it, he knew it, he'd ruined Cal's only shot—

"Everything all right, ma'am?" the butler asked from the hall.

"Quite. We will be a moment. Some tea, please."

She closed the door and gestured to the chairs. "Ms. Breslin. Your research, if you would be so kind."

Emry quietly set his chair farther back from Cal as she stepped through their findings, chiming in only when she needed assistance recalling a lyric or a story. He couldn't help but glance at Ella every time they ventured into new, more absurd territory—ancient stories, glow-worm maps, destructive waves from thousands of years ago—but every time he thought she might kick them out, she instead leaned in closer.

"How many people will the Alacova system hold?" she asked as she pored over Cal's map.

"Enough for three full cities to evacuate, if they spread out across all the accessible entrances."

"Not nearly enough for all the cities within range of the wave."

Cal flipped a page in her notebook and pointed with her pencil. Her words ran fast, but clear. "If the surges continue at this pace, most cities won't have time to evacuate that far anyway. Every town below here"—she gestured to a dotted line across the map—"will need to fortify rather than evacuate. Even those above that line will still need to fortify for those unable to leave."

Ella drew a finger over the notes and tapped them thoughtfully. "You mentioned the pace of the surges. How long do we have until the wave comes?"

Cal pulled back her pencil. "Three days, ma'am, after today."

Ella nodded, sat back in her chair, and looked out the window with a furrowed brow, while Cal remained rigid in her seat. Aspen tapped their fingers on their knees. Emry didn't dare breathe.

When Ella stood up, they all jumped.

"As many questions as I'd like to ask your spirit associate here"—she nodded to Aspen—"I'm afraid we have no time to lose regarding this wave. Come with me to the Council, Ms. Breslin, and I'll make sure they put your plan into motion."

Cal scrambled to her feet. "Come with you? Right now?"

But Ella was already opening the door. "Ready the carriage at once," she ordered someone in the hall. Cal stepped forward, eyes gleaming with excitement.

"Ms. Sorman—"

"Ella."

"Ella, I have other associates who should present this with me.

Mr. Devrin Gray and the Alta from the Cedar Fane. They're both close to Vornik. If I could contact them—"

"Give me their addresses and I'll send for them myself."

"And you're sure the Council will let us speak at such late notice?"

Ella waved a hand. "Oh, this won't be the first time I've barged in on them with demands, and it won't be the last. Now, if you'll excuse me." She started to sweep out of the room, then laid a hand on Emry's shoulder. "Thank you, Mr. Karic. It seems I have only increased my debt to you."

Emry forced a smile, then turned back toward Cal and Aspen. Now that it was over, truly over, a harsh tightness grew in his throat, and he desperately tried to swallow it down. Ella had listened, hadn't she? Cal's plan was heard, would be acted on. That mattered far more than some stupid Guild pin.

"Cal, can I come with you?" Aspen was begging her. "I've never seen a council before."

"I don't know—"

Emry shoved the lute toward Cal, clenching his jaw to fight back tears. "Take them. Aspen, you can watch, but you have to stay in the lute. I'll head back to the Academy, pick up your luggage, and meet you outside the Council building as soon as you're done."

"Emry..." She set down the case and pulled him into a hug. "Em, I don't know what to say."

He had to hold his breath to keep himself together. "Please don't worry about me." His voice came out as barely more than a whisper. "You've got a Council to focus on."

"Ms. Breslin?" The butler reappeared at the door without so much as a footfall. Emry pulled away and nodded to Cal and Aspen.

"See you soon," he said, and brushed by the butler to escape. He was climbing into the rented hackney when Ella's magnificent coach, four horses strong, came into sight. As his carriage rolled away, he could vaguely hear Aspen chattering from the gleaming front steps.

"Can I ask Ms. Sorman some questions on the way?"

"Not too many, please. I don't want to annoy her."

"...Hey, Cal?"

"Yes, Aspen?"

"He's not going to be joining the Guild, is he?"

Emry dropped his head into his hands and sobbed.

THIRTY-FIVE

ONCE EMRY WAS in Cal's room, he mustered the strength to change out of his borrowed clothes, lay them out carefully across the bed, and scrawl out a few lines on his abandoned letter.

Georgie, Marley, Mum, Dad—
   Meet me in Dawnstone immediately.

After finishing the missive and staring at the paper, he went over to the sofa and collapsed into sleep.

When he woke, he resembled mud in both his thoughts and movements. His eyes were dry, his throat raw, his limbs heavy. The remains of the coffee on the table were beyond inedible, but he took a few sips anyway. It didn't help.

The only thing that did startle him awake was the darkness cloaking the window.

"Oh, gods." He sprang to his feet, scrambling for a clock. "How long was I out—"

Cal's luggage was already packed and waiting by the door,

leaving just his satchel to shove things into. A rare moment of fore-thought led him to open Cal's case, grab her cloak, and sling it over his shoulder as he rushed out the door.

He reached the square after a hurried stop at the post office, and as usual, a crowd surrounded the Council building—but today, they were surprisingly quiet. There was no one on the steps to yell at, so instead they waited, watching the front doors for any kind of move-ment. He pinpointed a group he thought might divulge the most information—a fiercely whispering group of ladies at the foot of the steps, their eyes constantly darting to the door.

"Pardon, what's going on?" he asked them quietly.

"Ella Sorman's in there." The leader of the group jerked her head toward the building, her eyes wide. "Something to do with the surges."

"Ah." He let out a small sigh of relief. Cal and Aspen weren't out yet after all. "Thank you."

There was nothing left to do but wait along with the crowd, so he set down Cal's luggage and sat on it until the murmuring of the square spiraled up into shouting.

"Ms. Sorman!" Several journalists at the door leapt to their feet. "Ms. Sorman, what exactly did you discuss with the Council?"

A wise woman, she descended down the steps in perfect poise, saying absolutely nothing. All she did was give one gracious nod to the crowd before disappearing into her coach farther down the street.

Mr. Devrin Gray, on the other hand, could be heard loud and clear through the open doors despite being inside the building. He had changed from his brocaded number into gold-buckled boots and a brilliant blue vest—though Emry thought he saw a tea stain on it.

"You must make sure they're south-facing fortifications, you understand?" he rambled at an overwhelmed Councilman. "And while you're building them, is there any chance I could install some experimental equipment? It will all be up to code, of course, once I establish the code for this sort of research, as I *am* the premier researcher in this emerging field of science—"

Cal and Aspen were both absent from the doorway, and if Emry hadn't moved to find a better view, he might not have caught them. As reporters mobbed the front steps, his friends were sneaking out the side of the building, Brinna hobbling at Aspen's elbow.

"By Hara, must they make so much rotting noise..." Brinna grumbled as they walked down the alleyway. She had swapped her broom for a proper cane, but hadn't changed out of her scowl. "What's the fastest way out of this city?"

"Ms. Sorman has already paid for a carriage," Cal reassured her over the din. On the steps, a harried Councilwoman addressed the journalists.

"The Council has been monitoring the surges over the past week, and has reason to believe that a much larger surge will be coming our way within four days. We will begin protective measures immediately for the city of Vornik and all cities south of Thisby. For all cities north of Thisby—"

Both the journalists and the crowd dissolved into questions after that, and Emry couldn't hear the rest of the speech. He jogged to meet the others in the middle of the alley. "Brinna, it's nice to see you again so soon."

"Yes, yes. Glad to see you're all still alive," Brinna muttered. "Which way is the damn carriage?"

Cal pointed. "Just down that way—"

"Thank you. Now, continue to stay alive, and come make an offering at the fane sometime. Cedar won't act like it, but they'll appreciate it." She immediately shuffled off toward her escape from the noise.

"Say hi to Cedar for me!" Aspen called.

"I'll fit it in amongst the many other things I have to say to that spirit," Brinna called back, then waved and disappeared around the corner. Emry waved back, then tried to gather as much enthusiasm as he could for Cal. When he turned and saw the look on her face, it wasn't difficult. The glow of her success spilled out of her expression like sunlight.

"Congratulations, Cal." He hugged her with his free arm, grinning into her hair. "How did it feel, going to all the hot-air Council members and shoving it in their faces?"

"It was amazing!" Aspen bounced around them. "You should have seen her, there were so many people, and Ella yelled at them for a bit, but then Cal went up there and—"

Cal laughed; the sound vibrated against his chest.

"All right, Aspen, he doesn't need all the details." She pulled away, but couldn't contain her smile as she took her suitcase from Emry's hand. "It was...satisfying. Even if they're trying to pass it off like they've known about the wave this whole time."

"Of course, they are."

She still glowed, and Emry didn't realize he was staring until Cal gestured with her suitcase. "Shall we...head to the carriages?"

Emry shook his head and handed over her cloak. "I've got a faster way to Dawnstone—but you'll have to handle a bit of rough water."

Cal frowned as she and Aspen followed him out toward the nexus. "Rough water? I thought all the river routes out of Vornik were fairly smooth."

"All the ones you've taken are."

With Emry leading the way, the three of them pushed through the crowd and slipped down into the sinkhole—but instead of waiting in the growing line at the passenger docks, he stopped farther up the tunnel and handed Cal the lute. "Stay here for a moment."

"Hold on—Em, are you sure you're all right with this?" Cal searched his face. Emry looked around at the docks and drank in the one silver lining to his failure—he had no reason to hide from the caves anymore. He could look at the tunnels without wincing, at the boats without pain.

Well...less pain.

"I'm okay with this." He kept his voice firm. "Really, I am. Now stay, I'll be back in a moment."

He turned and walked into the boathouse.

Every boathouse across Vidanya was more or less structured the same way. Lamps all around the room threw soft shadows across the manager's desk at the front, the card table to the side, and the neat stacks of spare equipment in the back. The Vornik crew had chosen to dress up their little space with a wooden pallet on the wall, painted white and decorated with scraps of paper nailed to the planks. As he got closer, he could see there was an artist among the crew—someone had done little sketches, hardly more than gesture drawings, of passengers, the manager, and their fellow runners.

His mouth twisted into a bittersweet smile when he saw a familiar face sketched out in the corner—his father, standing at the edge of the docks, clearly laughing at something the manager had said.

"Excuse me, sir?" the manager said as he ducked into the house. "You're going to have to wait in line like everyone else—"

"Oh, I'm not a customer." Emry reached into his pocket and dug out his license, a lacquered wooden card with his name and credentials burned into it. "I'm looking for a job. You need anyone to run the gray medical route?"

"Oh, um..." The manager looked flustered as soon as he saw the name on the card. "Yes, Mr. Karic, we've got a shipment of emergency supplies going up to Thisby, but I've got Amelie down to take it in ten minutes."

Over in the huddle of runners playing cards and waiting for their next call, Amelie's head popped up. Emry recognized her as the woman who had rowed them out of Halagrad.

"I thought he looked familiar." She sighed and slipped a card to another player. "I'm not about to argue with a Karic. I learned my lesson from that sister of his. Let him take it."

The manager scratched out Amelie's name in his book and

reached for a coin purse, but Emry held up a hand. "I'll do it for free. Has the boat been inspected yet?"

"Not yet. Can you do it?"

"Of course."

"Right, then." The manager nodded to the door. "Cork vests are to the left of the dock. Safe running."

Emry left the boathouse and led Cal and Aspen down a side tunnel, away from the main docks and toward the sound of rushing water. "I've gotten approval to run some supplies up to Thisby," he explained as he jogged down a set of stairs hewn out of stone. "From Thisby, we can take the purple medical route to Copper Mill, then passenger green to Dawnstone. The first two are long routes, but between the rapids and lack of other stops, they're our fastest option."

"How safe are they?" Cal's trepidation bounced off the stone walls as they reached the dock, a tiny spit of wood tethering a single boat. Though the rapids couldn't be seen from their viewpoint, the looming sound of them filled the narrow cavern.

"As safe as I can possibly make them." Emry grabbed two cork vests off a rack and handed one to her. "Just remember to hold on to the lines with both hands and lean in when I say so."

He dove into checking the boat and securing the luggage, conflicted about how easily it all came back to him, how his fingers hadn't forgotten the knots or the routine. He told himself it was a good thing—this trip mattered more than any other route he had ever run. He had already failed his family once today, and that was more than enough.

Behind him, Cal edged her way toward the dock, eyeing the water with skepticism. "What if I fall out?"

"If you fall out..." He straightened, double-checked the ties on her vest, then pointed to the safety lines running around the boat. "Grab those ropes and face the boat if you can, so I can pull you in. Otherwise, keep your nose and toes above the water and point your feet downstream."

"What if *I* fall out?" Aspen was already perched in the boat, trailing a finger in the water.

"Turn into a fish or something." Emry turned back to Cal and set a hand on her shoulder. "Listen, we don't have to do this if you don't want to. We can still get on the passenger route in an hour or so—"

Cal shook her head. "No, I trust you. Let's go."

THIRTY-SIX

Aspen shrank down to their terrier form so the humans could cram themselves in between the medical supplies, luggage, and lanterns hanging at both ends of the boat.

"You'll want to hold on right away," Emry advised as he paddled them out. "If I'm remembering right, the first part of this route is the roughest." Cal immediately grabbed the safety lines in a vise grip.

As the river current picked up, the boat lurched forward, and the lanterns at both ends swung wildly. Emry caught the briefest of peeks at the low, spiked ceiling and tight walls before darkness and the spray of the rapids encompassed them.

"How much of the route is like this?" Cal shouted over the roar of the water as the boat rocked.

"Just the first third!" Emry wiped spray from his eyes. The lanterns gave a spotty view at best, so instead he latched on to the echo of the water, attuning to the distance it implied. "Lean in!"

"What?"

As he suspected, the lantern light caught the edge of a rock ahead of them. "Lean *in*!"

He reached for her shoulder and pushed forward, then grabbed the handle of the paddle and shoved it down to the floor of the boat. The impact of wood against rock vibrated up through his boots, and his knuckles scraped against the floor—but a breath later, they were up and over the block, with all three passengers still on board.

"Everyone good?" Emry straightened.

"I hate this!"

"You're going to love this drop, then!"

Cal shrieked as the boat plunged downward. Emry shook off the spray and reassessed the tunnel—the walls had expanded outward and dropped into the darkness, leaving him nothing but the silhouettes of pillars and stalactites to veer around. He mentally hurried through what this next part of the route had felt like on past runs. "Aspen, how well can you see in this?"

Aspen hopped onto his shoulder in owl form. "Better than you."

"Okay, show-off, can the broadside of this boat fit between the walls?"

"Yes."

"Before the rocks up ahead?"

Aspen ruffled their feathers. "Yes, but how did you—"

"Hold on!"

As the tip of the next rock rushed into view, Emry twisted the boat with all of his strength—instead of a sharp head-on impact, the boat spun off the rock, guiding them more gently into a smoother stretch of water.

"All still here?" He looked back to catch Cal's death glare. "What? I thought I did a pretty good job with that last one."

"Well, I had fun." Aspen hopped onto Cal's knee and shook water off their feathers. "Can we do that again, please?"

To Cal's dismay and Aspen's delight, they alternated between pools and rapids for another hour before finally shifting into a smooth stretch of water.

"No more rapids for today, I promise," Emry panted, his wet curls sticking to his face. "You can take a nap and we'll be there before you know it. Hand me that dry bag?"

"I don't think I can take a nap after all that," Cal grumbled, squeezing out her hair with a handkerchief. Once the cloth was thoroughly sopping and useless, she sighed and passed him the small bag he had stuffed in with the emergency supplies. He gave what he hoped was an apologetic smile and rummaged around for a pair of fingerless gloves.

"Did you do this sort of route often?" Aspen asked, wide owl eyes absorbing every inch of the cavern in excitement. They had outright cheered during the last drop.

"At least twice a month, when I was in Senne." Emry rinsed his hand in the water, then winced as he yanked the gloves over his marred knuckles. "My sisters used to be the emergency runners, but someone had to fill in when Georgie got too busy and Marley went off to the Academy."

"And they were the ones to teach you all this?" Aspen brushed the paddle with their wing. "I wish I had a family to teach me things. What else did they teach you?"

Too many painful responses came to mind. Emry hesitated as he flexed his cold fingers.

"My mother taught me how to ride a horse," Cal interjected, glancing at him. "And how to dance the cotillion, how to draw up a financial chart..."

Emry regained his grip on the paddle, relieved to let her take over the conversation. "Has your mother sold the business yet?" he asked.

"'Course not, she doesn't really want to. Though my father would love to see her step away from her desk at some point."

"I thought your father couldn't be dragged away from his library?"

Cal gave a small laugh and propped her chin on her palm as Emry paddled them forward. "He did build another wing of it this past summer."

"Ah, but does it have a reading nook for you?"

She rolled her eyes. "He claims it does, but I haven't seen it yet. If he made one, it's probably covered in books by now." Her attention drifted to the river. "You know, they really wanted me to study closer to home after I left Tazlo. They were thrilled when I moved to Vornik..." She trailed off, watching the water ripple gently along the side of the boat. When Emry caught her gaze, she straightened and changed the subject with a false smile. "I'll have to teach Aspen the cotillion as well. I can't possibly introduce a spirit to society without them knowing how to dance."

Before Emry could guess at the thoughts she was locking behind the smile, Aspen puffed out their feathers and hopped forward. "Oh, yes, please. Emry did say you were the best dancer."

Emry's cheeks warmed despite the river chill. "I did tell Aspen you'd teach them," he mumbled. "Poor spirit was trying to get lessons from me."

Cal smiled. "And how many times did you step on their foot?"

"Only twenty."

"A record for you, then. I congratulate you."

Emry laid an insincere hand on his heart. "Thank you, Ms. Breslin, you're too kind."

She shook her head and turned her smile to the water—then just as before, the smile faded, her thoughts swirling along with the river. Emry frowned—nerves about the wave, perhaps, or worries about her parents' journey. He let the boat fall quiet and paddled them on. Whatever the thoughts were, he could trust them to surface eventually.

THE BLEARY-EYED MANAGER in Thisby accepted the supplies with a grunt and a dismissive hand wave toward the exit. Built into a shockingly deep sinkhole outside of town, the zigzagging stairs of the Thisby nexus bore them up past an array of carvings in the endless stone wall. The artist had followed the natural striations of the stone and tiny waterfall trickles to illustrate trees, clouds, stars, and lightning bolts.

"Brinna told us about this one," Aspen said, pointing to a snarling wolf chasing a hare right above their head. "How Hara had turned into a rabbit for the day, and Shiro sent a wolf to eat her up. But Weir didn't want him to, so he threw all his stars down at the trees to blind the wolf. And the trees, they…"

Aspen fell silent, their fingers lingering along the carving of twisted, dead trees. Cal took their arm and led them up the stairs. "But Hara escaped, didn't she?"

"She did."

"See?" She smiled at them. "It all turns out fine in the end."

To Emry's relief, Thisby did not yet share Aspen's anxiety, nor Vornik's chaos—the town was blissfully, ignorantly asleep when they arrived. From the top of the nexus stairs, he could see the full stretch of the quiet little town curled atop a hill, its twinkling lights blanketed in a light settling of mist. The fog thickened as they walked in, gray breath against gray cobblestones and gray buildings. The only spots of color were the warm orange brushstrokes of the street lamps, flickering silently in the muted night. Not even the lamplighter made a sound as they shuffled along to check the little flames.

"You're in late," the lamplighter said when they caught sight of the trio, their voice as soft as the mist. "If you're looking for a place to stay, there's an inn up the street, the—"

"The Great Elm?" Emry finished for them, then winced. His voice was far too loud for the silent street.

"That's the one." They tilted their cap. "Sounds like you know where you're going. Have a good night."

As the lamplighter strolled off into the gray, Aspen looked up at Emry.

"Thisby was the first place I went after leaving Senne," Emry explained more quietly. "Stayed at the Elm until I couldn't afford it, then played there a few times. I'm sure they won't remember me."

Unfortunately, the owner's face lit up as soon as he stepped into the drowsy warmth of the inn.

"Mr. Karic!" The woman, rosy and round, spread her arms wide, though she contained her voice for those sleeping above. "Hara bless me, a face I never thought I'd see again."

"Mrs. Portsmouth." He choked out a smile. "How are you?"

"Just fine, dearest, just fine," she said, already writing his name into her ledger. "So wonderful to see you well. Goodness, you left in such a hurry all those years ago, we weren't sure if you were all right! And oh, did we miss the music." She placed a hand at her chest and looked up at the sky. "By Weir, we haven't had such a singer in these, what, two years?"

"Over three," he said softly, as an odd pain curled around his heart and slipped down through his arms. When he had last performed here, he had only been away from home for a few months. He'd had money, a well-functioning lute, and the foolish self-assurance that he'd be back home within the year. Now, he had...what did he have?

Cal stepped forward. "If we could get two rooms, please."

"How many nights?"

"Just tonight. I'm afraid we're only passing through."

Mrs. Portsmouth's smile faded. "Oh, I'm sorry to hear that. I was dearly hoping we could hear you play again."

She handed over the two keys and seemed about to ask more questions until Cal took Emry's shoulder and guided him up the stairs. "The Council messengers could be here by dawn, if they send their fastest riders," she murmured as she opened the first door and handed him the key to the next one. Emry nodded, still mired in the dull pain.

"We'll set out at dawn, then. I don't want to be here..." He meant to say "for the chaos," but didn't see the need to finish the sentence.

"Are we going to go through the rapids again tomorrow?" Aspen whispered. Emry mustered half a smile for them.

"A few, yes."

The spirit grinned. "Excellent! I'll see you at dawn," they said, and slipped into Cal's room. Cal paused halfway in.

"Em, could we...talk in the morning?"

Her thoughts had surfaced faster than he'd anticipated. The idea of any kind of discussion exhausted him, but he managed a nod. "Sure," he mumbled and shuffled off to his door. "Goodnight, Cal."

CHAPTER

THIRTY-SEVEN

As Cal had predicted, Thisby's quiet ignorance shattered as dawn burst in with ill news from Vornik's riders. From under the pillows, Emry could hear the panic of people shouting and horses galloping out of town. He could only imagine the stream of people who would be lining up at the boathouse, backing up the stairs, trailing out of the nexus...

He rubbed his eyes, tried to push himself up, then collapsed back onto the pillow with a harsh wince.

"Shiro's hairy *foot*." That was one thing he hadn't accounted for on this cursed trip. After years away from cave running, his entire body ached, as if he had repeatedly rammed himself into a wall the night before.

Slowly, he tried to get out of bed, only to fall to his knees on the floor. It took an immense amount of willpower and cursing to get himself into a bath, which at least gave him the ability to limp about the room before Cal knocked on the door. "Emry?"

"Hara take me." He wasn't ready for this, especially not now. He tried to pick up his satchel, but his arm refused.

"Em, are you all right?"

277

"...No."

Cal and Aspen opened the door to find him leaning against a wall, still in just a shirt and breeches, trying and failing to fully extend his arm. He sighed and rested his head against the wall. "Everything hurts."

"I was afraid it might." She set the lute down and took his arm. "Do you think Mrs. Portsmouth might have some willow bark tea?"

Emry gave a single, pained laugh. "Trust me, her tea would only make this worse."

"What about moonflowers?" Aspen bounced on their heels. "All you have to do is chew the petals. Here, I'll grow you some!" They rushed off before Emry could decline the offer.

"Be careful with all the people out there!" Cal called after them, then closed the door. "Let's just hope they don't try to grow it in the middle of the street or something..."

As she led Emry back toward the bed, he glanced out the window to find green-jacketed Council representatives waving frightened people this way and that. "Cal, we don't have time for this—what if they overwhelm the docks?"

"I'm not letting you row in this state. You'll send us all into the water," Cal said firmly and sat down on the edge of the bed. "Now, lie down and take a deep breath."

As he did so, he noticed that she had pulled her hair back in two sleek twists—a cautionary measure against the rapids to come. He gave a small smile at a tiny blue flower peeking out of one of the braids.

Then she took his arm and dug hard into the muscle.

"Ow ow ow—" He tried yanking his arm away, but she grabbed it back.

"It's going to help!"

"Not if it kills me first!"

"Such a baby..." But Cal was laughing as she resumed massaging his arm, her touch a little lighter than before. Emry laid his other arm over his face to muffle his sounds of pain. "It's been years since you did a route like that, right?"

"Mm-hmm."

"Must really hurt, then."

"*Mm-hmm.*"

"If you need to rest a day…"

He let his arm slide off his face. "No, I'm getting you to Dawnstone when I said I would."

The shadows across her face deepened as she moved to his other arm. He waited for her to say something, but her fingers shifted up his forearm in silence. He jumped to fill the quiet, if only to distract himself. "You wanted to talk about something this morning."

"We don't have to do it now—"

"Well, I can't go anywhere. Might as well."

She paused with her hand on his wrist. "I wanted to apologize."

"For what?"

She looked down at his arm and resumed her massaging, but her motions were gentle this time. If he were a hopeful man, he would have called them loving.

"A year ago in Tazlo, when you told me why you couldn't come with me to Vornik, and I made you choose…" She paused to let out a broken breath. "I shouldn't have given you an ultimatum like that. You had already suffered for so long under one. You explained everything to me, you reassured me that you loved me, and then I turned around and…" She turned to the window, her voice cracking. "I regretted it the moment I arrived in Vornik without you, and I never said a word."

He scrambled to deflect, even as his heart stumbled. "Cal, please. You weren't wrong for leaving behind a cowardly musician. I'm sure all your friends were urging you to dump me and find someone better the whole time. I should've been a passing fling at best—"

"Is that really how you think of yourself?" She turned back to him, her eyes welling. She seemed unaware that she was clutching his hand to her chest. "After everything you've done? After everything you just gave up?"

Hot tears pricked at the corners of his eyes. "I've hardly done anything—"

"You saved your family." She gestured out to the window. "You saved *them*. Without a second thought, and you—you have the audacity to call yourself a coward, a passing fling? Gods, Emry—"

She leaned down, wiped away a tear on his cheek, and kissed the spot where it had been. The fleeting sensation rippled like a wave down to his toes, and if anyone had told him he was floating, he would have believed them.

Her face hovered inches away from his, searching his expression. He gave her a breathless smile, pulled her back down to him with his free hand—for the other one was still tangled in her grasp—and pressed his lips against hers.

She immediately relaxed on top of him, letting go of his hand to run her fingers through his hair. In turn, he wrapped his arms around her waist and shoulders, ignorant of the pain every movement caused him. As she deepened the kiss, the noise out in the street no longer meant anything, nor the clicking of the door handle as it turned—wait—

"Okay, I think I grew too many flowers, but that means we'll have some extra in case—" Aspen looked up from the bouquet spilling from their grasp and immediately threw the flowers into the air. "Oh gods, I'm sorry!" They stumbled back out of the room and slammed the door closed with a wail. "I've ruined it, they're never going to forgive me, ever—"

"Aspen!" Cal called out to the door, but only the sound of retreating footsteps answered her. Emry burst into laughter. Cal pushed herself off of him, trying and failing to maintain a frown. "It's not funny, they're going to run off with your lute!"

"And you think I can run after them in this state?" Emry flinched as the laughter strained his aching ribs. "Go get them and tell them it's okay—"

"Fine. You eat one of these things while I'm gone." She picked up a moonflower and tossed it at him, grinning. "You fool."

As she ran off calling the spirit's name, he plucked a few of the gray petals from the bloom, chewed on them, and gave an involuntary shudder. The bitter notes of mint and anise attacked both his mouth and sinuses, but Aspen hadn't been wrong—a few minutes later, the tension in his limbs subsided, allowing him to finish dressing and walk down the stairs with minimal pain.

"Mr. Karic, have you heard?" Mrs. Portsmouth called to him right away, trying to juggle the keys from all her guests rushing to leave. "Another surge, this far north? And something about a defensive wall? Surely it can't be as bad as all that—"

"I'm afraid it is, Mrs. Portsmouth." He looked around. "Do you have a cellar?"

"Of course."

"Go down there for any surges you feel, and make sure you've got something metal to block the door. You'll be safe down there, I promise. Now, if you'll excuse me"—he slid the key back to her over the counter—"it was lovely seeing you, but I have to find my..."

He wasn't sure what to call her anymore, so he just nodded and stepped out into the chaos of the streets.

"Emry!" Cal waved at him from farther down the street, her hand on Aspen's shoulder. Emry ducked and weaved his way over to them, trying to block out the fear in everyone's voices and faces.

"Those flowers you brought worked great, Aspen," he said as soon as he reached them, and held up his satchel. "I've got the rest in here. I expect tomorrow's only going to be worse—"

"You're sure I didn't ruin everything?" they cut in, wringing their hands. Emry laughed and shook his head. Next to the spirit, Cal bit back a smile.

"No. I promise, everything's fine. Come on, you wanted to go through more rapids today, didn't you?"

Aspen gave a great sigh and adjusted the lute on their back. "Yes, I very much do, please."

Thisby's morning manager was far too swamped to even take a look at her logbook when Emry ducked in to inquire after the purple route.

"Half my runners just up and left at the news, so go ahead. Medicine's already on the boat." She waved him off. "Safe running or whatever."

Having already sent Cal and Aspen down the emergency tunnel, he could hear their voices echoing up at him as he descended past the curtains of stalactites to the narrow dock.

"And no one's going to turn into anything?"

Cal laughed. "No, Aspen."

"Turn into what?" Emry slipped on his cork vest and resecured the medicine to the boat. Aspen sat on Cal's shoulder as a mouse, flicking their little whiskers as Emry worked.

"A prince, or a princess, or a toad, or a fish," they rattled off. "Addie's stories had so many things happen when people kiss, I wasn't sure what to expect."

"Ah." Emry stepped into the boat, checked Cal's vest, then kissed her cheek. "See? No magical transformation. She's perfect already."

Cal smiled and hid her face. "Hara take me, what have I done?"

Emry winked at Aspen and grabbed the paddle. "Might I remind you that she chose this not once, but twice."

As he guided them out, the noisy tumult of the main Thisby docks spilled into their little oasis, bringing them back to reality. Cal looked back and pulled her cloak tighter around her.

"Do you think Copper Mill will be like this?" Emry asked, paddling them out faster.

"If we had left right at dawn, perhaps we could have beat the messenger, but..." Cal shook her head. "I'm not sure. We should prepare ourselves."

They fell into silence for a while as Emry navigated the rapids, leaving space for the rushing water and his intermittent commands. The pools here were all too brief, giving him no moment to breathe before throwing him into more rough water. Halfway through the route, he winced and gestured toward his satchel. "One of those flowers, if you could."

"Do you need to stop and rest?" Cal asked as she plucked a few petals and handed them to him.

"No banks to stop at along this route, unfortunately." Emry paused to keep himself from gagging on the petals. "But this pool will last for a while, and we're coming up on the best part of it." He nodded to the soft light beckoning them from around the corner.

"More glow-worms?" Aspen leaned forward.

"Not quite."

The waters bore them into the light of a giant sinkhole, much wider and more layered than any of the nexus openings or the shafts near Halagrad. This one crisscrossed the downpour of morning light with natural bridges, all dripping with moss, foliage, and sunbeams.

But it wasn't the sinkhole itself that Emry was looking forward to. It was the light, bouncing off the surface of the river and all down the tunnel until it reached a bend in the cave. Not only did this illumination give his eyes a respite from squinting, but it also unveiled a display of natural artwork that otherwise would have remained cloaked in darkness.

Brushstrokes of stripes, blue and brown and green and silver, painted themselves over the ceiling and down into the waters. As the stripes flowed over the undulations of the rock, they warped into whorls and circles that, when combined with the constantly shifting reflection of the water, were almost dizzying to look at.

"Is it like this all through the caves here?" Cal asked, twisting to take it all in. Emry paddled back to slow them down.

"Difficult to tell, but I think so."

"I wonder what it would be like to be a cave spirit," Aspen mused aloud as they watched the reflections play on the ceiling above them.

"Seeing how much you enjoy the rapids, I imagine you'd like it," Emry said. "Though river weed doesn't afford quite the same view as a tree."

"I guess so." The spirit dipped their hand into the water, their fingertips brushing up against the tops of the river weed that waved beneath the surface. "Your family really sees stuff like this all the time?"

"They do."

"What are they like?"

Emry wanted to say that Aspen already knew what they looked like. That when Aspen copied Emry's appearance, they had copied Georgie's curls, too. And Marley's dimples, and his father's freckles, and his mother's eyes—

Cal jumped in once more. "Aspen, he may not want to talk about them."

"But we're meeting them tomorrow." Aspen lifted their hand from the water. "Aren't we?"

Emry loosened his grip on the paddle. Aspen was right. Avoiding them now wouldn't ease the pain of seeing them tomorrow.

"I suppose I can tell you a bit about them," he said quietly. "You already know that Georgie's a part of the boat business, and Marley is—was—a student, like Cal."

Cal gave him a soft, encouraging smile. "What did she study, again?"

"Marine science. Well, that's the study she started with. No idea if she ever switched."

"And she's graduated?"

"She would have last year, I think..." He trailed off. He usually tried not to think about the missed milestones. Georgie's birthday had been last month, Marley's was coming up in two. Were they dating anyone? Shiro drag him to dust, was there a chance they had gotten *married* without him?

"And Marley's your younger sister?" Cal continued. A pang wormed its way through his ribs, but he pushed past it.

"Yes. And Georgie's older." Gradually, their boat left the sunlight of the sinkhole, dropping them back into darkness. "You'd like them, Cal. A lot. They're smart, driven, better than me at everything—"

"That can't be true. Do they play any instruments?"

"No, but I swear that if Marley had ever let Dad teach her the lute, she would have gotten into the Guild by now. She's just so..." He sighed. "Marley's not going to make sense to you until I tell you about how she beat my Nana at Spirit's Cross when she was six."

Aspen looked aghast. "She beat a spirit?"

"No, no, it's a game. I'll have to explain that, too..."

But it wasn't enough to tell Marley's story. Marley's casual cunning quickly led into Georgie's competitive streak, which then flowed into her almost burning the house down in an attempt to make pies that were better than Nana's, which *then* veered off into how Nana refused to teach her grandchildren her secret pie crust recipe until all of them could beat her at Spirit's Cross, like Marley...

The Copper Mill emergency dock, nestled between natural pillars, appeared just as Emry thought of ten more stories he had spent three years willing out of existence.

"Mum's birthday five years ago." He jumped out onto the dock to secure the boat. "Separately, everyone thought it was a good idea to secretly bake her a cake in the middle of the night. I got to the kitchen first, and Georgie's a liar if she tells you anything different. Georgie got there second and threw flour at me for being first. Marley got there next and thought I had stolen her idea somehow, so she took the eggs away. Dad came in and took them back, but then tried to start a bidding war for the milk—"

"Did your mother get a cake in the end?"

"Absolutely not. She got a kitchen disaster and four nincompoops covered in cake batter for her birthday."

Their laughter was quickly drowned out by shouting beyond the docks.

"I'll go look ahead." Aspen grabbed the lute and sprinted up the wooden stairs that led to the tunnel beyond, leaving Emry and Cal to unload the medicine.

"Thank you for telling us about them." She squeezed his shoulder. "I'm sure it wasn't easy for you."

He caught her fingers and gave them a brief kiss. "It was all right. It...it helped. Really."

Together, they carried the supplies up into the main passageway, where they needed no scout to tell them what was going on.

"Please, come back later!" A manager down by the passenger docks waved wildly to the crowd, which stretched from the boathouse all the way past where Emry could see down the tunnel. "We won't have any more boats until more passengers come up from the south!"

"I don't think we quite beat the news," Emry muttered after they dropped the supplies off, the echo chamber of the cavern over-whelming with the reverberations of shouting and panic.

"You said the Copper Mill docks don't have an emergency route going north?" Cal kept a tight grip on his arm as she looked around for Aspen.

"Not to Dawnstone, no. We'll have to stay somewhere for a few hours until the passenger boats open back up."

But once they got halfway up the tunnel, Aspen came rushing down toward them. It was fortunate they were moving too fast for the passersby to notice their flickering.

"We can't stay here," they panted once they reached Emry. "We have to get a boat, now."

"There aren't any right now. We have to find somewhere to—"

Aspen shook their head vehemently. "No. Not here. We can't stay here."

THIRTY-EIGHT

CAL SHIVERED AT HIS ARM, and Emry had to push back against the passengers choking the tunnel. "Let's get into the sun and figure this out." He covered her hand with his and led the way out.

When they emerged from the nexus, they saw why Aspen was in such a hurry to evacuate. Every building—house, store, inn—was made of wood. In normal circumstances, the town would have had a rustic, fairy-cottage feel to it, with the rich browns of the buildings melting into the pines and dappled afternoon light.

Today, the entire place looked like a death trap.

"Okay, I see what you mean." Emry looked around. "Maybe there are some carriages left or something—"

"No carriages," said one woman holding a hatbox and a three-year-old in the boat line. "They all left this morning, and not a one's come back."

"I've got my boy waiting at the stop, just in case." A burly man behind her jerked his thumb over his shoulder. "Others have started walking to Fanestown some miles out, but I hear bandits are waiting out there, taking advantage of the evacuees headed that way."

Despite their gloomy words, Emry found their northern accents oddly comforting. "Thank you, we'll, um..." He turned back to Cal and Aspen. "I'm not sure what to do."

"I'm not feeling prepared to fight bandits"—Cal glanced nervously at the road out of town—"and I don't believe any carriages are coming back. The boats are still our best bet out of here."

Emry looked to Aspen, who shifted the lute strap crossing their chest.

"If we need to stay here, I think I could protect us if a surge comes," they said. "But we'll take the boats as soon as we can get them, right?"

"Definitely." Emry held out his hand. "You save your energy inside the lute. I'll carry it for a while."

But after an hour of walking, every inn in town had turned them away, either overtaken by customers or boarding up to evacuate. Emry lagged behind the others, his waterskin empty and his satchel devoid of food. The acorns scattered along the road suddenly looked tempting, and he regretted not eating anything the day before.

"What if we just sit under a tree or something?" He gestured vaguely to the forest. "Grow some berries, take a nice...seven-hour nap..."

Thunder grumbled above. Emry passed a hand over his face.

"You looking for a place to stay while the boats come in?" someone called to them—a hunched old man, sitting on a stool in front of a weathered barn. "Got a couple families staying here. Ten gold for the night."

Cal balked. "Ten gold, are you serious?"

"S'either that or the streets, miss."

Emry took her arm. "Come on, Cal, let's—"

A hansom cab burst around the corner and careened toward them. Emry had to shove Cal off the road to avoid the wild-driven horses, their vehicle overflowing with stolen goods and men bearing muskets.

Cal handed the man the coins. "We'll take it."

They grabbed a spot in the corner of a hayloft overlooking the rest of the barn. Like the man had said, several small families were already huddled in stalls between the sheep and the donkeys, keeping watchful eyes on the entrance and trying to hush their babies.

"Knew I shouldn't have put Copper Mill on the route," Emry muttered.

"Why not?" Aspen asked as they ventured out of the lute to explore the loft. Emry gathered some hay together and collapsed down onto it. The thin layer of straw let him fall directly onto the bumpy wooden slats underneath.

"You remember how Copper Mill used to have more thieves than leaves?"

"But you said it got better since then."

"I said it got *a little* better since then."

"But those are just stories, right?" Cal sat down next to him. Outside, a gunshot pierced the air and sent several of the toddlers below into a tizzy. Cal grabbed Emry's hand.

"Not the way my father tells them," Emry said.

Aspen immediately shifted into their wolf form and planted themself squarely between the ladder and their companions. "You rest. I'll keep watch."

Aspen didn't have to tell Emry twice, and he quickly slipped into a hazy sleep. Every now and then, as a baby shrieked or a donkey brayed, he would wake and find Aspen missing.

"Checking the boats," Cal would explain, or, "Attempting to find a berry bush to bring into the barn." One time, she actually did have some berries for him, though Aspen had gone back to check on the boats again. It wasn't until Emry had woken up for good that he found both of his companions in the loft, whispering to each other.

"The line still goes to the entrance," Aspen mumbled, "and there's no one left in this barn. We're not staying here for the night, are we?"

Cal glanced out the window at the sunset. "No, it's not safe here."

"Should we start walking to the next town, then?"

"I don't know if he can walk that far."

"I can walk—" Emry sat up, then cursed and dragged himself over to the wall to lean against it. His shoulders had knotted up as he slept. "I think I can still walk..."

"We're not walking." Cal grabbed their waterskins and headed down the ladder. "I'm going down for water. Aspen said there's a well out back."

As soon as she left, Emry reached out for Aspen. "A little help up?"

Aspen pulled him to his feet so he could limp his way over to the satchel and grab a moonflower. He stared at the half-crushed bloom. "What would happen if I ate this whole thing?"

"Please don't."

"Fine." He chewed a few petals as fast as he could. "If I eat enough of these, I bet we could get to the next town just after night-fall. Find some sort of stone place to hide in, walk back to the nexus in the morning..."

Below them, Cal swore and rushed inside. "Hide!" she whispered as she clambered back up the ladder. Emry looked around.

"Where do you expect me to—"

"How many horses in there?" a gruff voice called out beyond the entrance to the barn, while a few men peered inside.

"None, but there is a donkey."

"Fine. Take it and check for anything folks left behind."

Three men jogged into the stables, muskets slung on their backs. Aspen shifted into their wolf form and growled, but Emry pulled them back.

"Aspen, get into the lute. Cal, did you see the owner out there?" he whispered, leaning forward to keep an eye on the men while maintaining one arm around Cal. She shook her head.

"No. Bet you he ran off as soon as the other families left."

The donkey trotted out, but the same gruff voice from before made one of the men linger. "Check the loft, too."

The last man turned toward the ladder. They both sprang to their feet, searching around them and whispering frantically.

"Do you have a weapon?"

"Cal, do I look like someone who owns a weapon?"

They froze when the thief reached the top and raised his musket at them.

"We don't have anything." Emry quickly stepped in front of Cal, his hands held up. The man nodded to their luggage.

"Don't want any trouble. Kick those over."

Emry toed his satchel over first. The man grabbed it. "Suitcase, too. And the lute."

The hay behind them rustled, and a low, rumbling growl filled the air. The thief pointed his gun at the hay.

"Call off your dog."

"Aspen," Cal warned. The hand she had laid on Emry's back shook, and he wondered if she could feel his panicked heartbeat through his clothing.

The rumbling only grew louder.

"I said, call it off," the thief started—then his eyes grew wide and traveled upward. A shadow fell over Emry as a mass of fur brushed by his shoulder.

Aspen's wolf form, now a full head taller than Emry, padded past them and bared every one of their glimmering teeth at the man.

"What the—?" He lifted his musket and aimed. Before he could pull the trigger, Aspen flashed in front of them, ripped the gun out of his hands with their teeth, and tossed it like a toy over the side of the loft.

"Fetch," they growled.

The thief half fell down the ladder, grabbed his musket, and streaked out of the stables. "Nothing up there, let's head out!"

Emry remained rooted in front of Cal until the sound of hooves and voices faded away. "Time to go?"

Cal grabbed her luggage. "Time to go."

THEY SPRINTED over to the nexus in the moonlight, only to find the crowd gone and a woman closing the gates.

"You can't be closed yet—you've got another hour left!" Emry started—but this woman wasn't the boathouse manager from earlier.

"That's right, the routes will remain open through the night"—she secured the gate and winked at them—"if you have twenty gold to spare."

"*Twenty*—?" Emry spluttered and looked over to Cal, who grimaced and shook her head. He then saw the armed people wandering about in the tunnel ahead, and set his jaw. "Never mind, let's go."

"Do you need me to be a wolf again?" Aspen asked from inside the lute.

"No, thank you. We'll find another way," Emry muttered as he strode toward nowhere at all. "I cannot—I *cannot* believe I'm saying this—but my father will hear about this. Taking an entire nexus hostage..."

Aspen popped up next to Emry and pointed. "Do you think they know another way?"

Emry and Cal followed their finger to catch several people sneaking under the bridge to the nexus, disappearing into the brush that overflowed below. The woman on the bridge took no notice of them as she retreated back into the tunnel.

"Good question." Emry started after them. Cal grabbed his arm.

"Wait. Aspen, is there any way you can follow them silently?"

Aspen shifted into an owl form and flapped off, wings perfectly quiet as they dove under the bridge. After a few minutes, they sailed back over and hit the ground as a human. "Question—is it bad to steal from people who are already stealing?"

THIRTY-NINE

As clouds erased the available moonlight, Aspen led them down into the brush to show them where the others had gone—a narrow horizontal slit of a cave entrance, just big enough for a human or two to slip through if they crouched. As it was mostly hidden by overgrowth, Emry had to focus hard to see the flaring lights within, or hear the muttering of voices over a low rush of water.

"It's got to be a smuggler's route," he whispered as they took shelter behind a bush. "And you said they have a boat in there?" Aspen nodded. "Did you see a dock?" Another nod. He breathed a sigh of relief.

"What does that mean?" Cal asked, her gaze tracking every flash of the torchlight within the cave. The voices inside briefly rose in pitch, and Emry held his response until the murmurs faded again.

"Most smuggler's routes don't have actual docks," he said. "Even if they managed to sneak all the materials in and build the thing, it'd be too much of a giveaway. If this one does have a dock, it means we're looking at the closed emergency route this place used to have."

"And it goes north?"

"Directly to Dawnstone, drops out into the main route from

Strava to the west. Must have made it a fairly profitable route when it was open."

They all ducked as a newcomer slid down into the brush, an overstuffed bag swinging from their shoulder. Its contents clinked together loudly, and they hurried to still it, whipping their head around to ensure no one had heard them. For a moment, they looked straight at the bush the trio was crouched behind. Emry's grip on Cal and Aspen's shoulders tightened.

Then the thief crouched low, adjusted their bag, and slid through the cave entrance. The voices within the cave rose again to welcome them, followed by the muffled clank of loot being tossed onto a pile.

Cal kept her voice as low as possible. "Why'd they close off this route to begin with?"

"Can't remember. But if smugglers are using it now, it's got to be mostly runnable." Emry leaned forward, eyes straining to see any details within the cave. "We just have to get them out somehow..."

"Oh, that's easy." Aspen shrugged, shifted into owl form, and dove toward the hole.

"Stop!" Cal whispered harshly and reached for them, but it was far too late—Aspen had already swooped in. Seconds later, wolfish growls echoed loudly about the cave.

"What in Shiro's—"

"Shoot it!"

Gunshots rattled the air.

"*Aspen!*" Emry launched out from behind the bush. He made it two steps before crashing into another panicked person—the newcomer, now scrambling back out of the cave with a torch. As they flew backward, the torch fell into the dead foliage behind them and immediately bloomed into a blaze.

"Rotting hell!" The thief scrabbled up the hill, away from the flames. Emry grabbed the torch, staggered back from the smoke, and swung the light toward the cave.

The thieves had lined canvas sacks and wooden crates next to the warped dock, the loot tossing shadows across the lumpy walls. A streak of a wolf sprinted past the loot, barking their head off—then a spray of bullets followed their heels, piercing the water at the edge of the dock.

Emry panicked and looked at the torch.

"Aspen! Turn into a fish or something!" he yelled, and threw the torch through the hole. It landed right onto the pile of canvas and wood, which flared up in an instant.

"What are you doing?" Cal rushed up and dragged him away from the growing brush fire by the entrance.

"Smoking them out!"

"Aspen's in there—"

"I know they're in there, they're still running around as a damn wolf!"

They dove back behind a shrub as thieves poured out of the hole, coughing and spluttering. Some of them had dropped their torches in the escape, sending more flames licking up the cave walls both inside and out.

"Get in there!" Cal handed him the lute case and pushed Emry inside. He slid down to the uneven floor and immediately shielded his face from the smoke trying to escape outward.

"Aspen?" he shouted.

"Over here!" The voice came from a fish frantically circling the boat. "We got them out—"

"I know, stay there!" Emry threw the lute onto the boat and squinted through the smoke for any sign of a cork vest. Cal slid in behind him, already shielding her face with her jacket.

"What do you need?"

"Unmoor the boat and light the lantern if it's got one!" He gestured to the dock and weaved through the flames to find what he sought—two crumbling cork vests, seconds away from catching fire.

"Em, never mind those—"

"No, keep unmooring, I'll be right there!" he shouted, then coughed and covered his mouth in the haze. With his free hand, he grabbed the first vest and slung it over his shoulder. His fingers were inches away from the second when the fabric of the vest burst into flame. He yanked his hand back with a shout.

"Em!"

"I'm fine!" As the smoke thickened and his eyes burned, he stumbled back to the boat and felt around for the ropes while Cal climbed in.

"Aspen, get in the boat!" she choked out the words against the smoke. The lute rocked as Aspen retreated into it. "Emry, you too—"

"Got it!" He tossed the last rope into the boat, grabbed the paddle, and leapt in, the force of his jump pushing them away from the docks. Though he paddled them away as fast as he could, their coughs continued to rattle through the cave, even after the glow of the dock fire had disappeared around a bend. Slowly, the clear, cold air of the river replaced the acrid smoke in their lungs.

"Aspen, are you all right?" Emry called, rinsing his stinging eyes with river water. "The bullets didn't hit you, did they?"

"Oh, they did."

Cal gasped, and Emry whipped around. "What? Are you bleeding?"

Aspen appeared as a terrier sitting between him and Cal. "Of course not. Spirits don't bleed."

Indeed, the spirit looked fine, if a little transparent. The momentary panic sent Cal into another coughing fit.

"Weir's eyes, you can't just say things like that..." she managed to get out between coughs. Emry waited for the fit to subside before helping her into the cork vest he had saved.

"Hold still, hold still..." he muttered as he worked at the ties, his throat feeling ragged. When she offered him her waterskin, he downed half of it.

"What's this route like?" Cal had to pull the vest away from her neck to keep taking in deep breaths while he drank.

"I don't know, it closed before I started doing runs." Emry handed back the water and turned to the light from the single lantern at the front of the boat, keeping an ear out for rapids. "All I can say is that it'll be a few hours until we get to Dawnstone."

"And then no more boats?" Aspen's tail stopped wagging.

"No more boats. Though I bet you Georgie and Marley would love to take you on a ride someday."

They remained like that for a long time, navigating between stalagmites and gulping in as much of the clean air as they could. Emry was groggily estimating how much of the route they had gotten through—half? No, three-quarters, at least—when the boat shuddered up against a stone pillar. Cal, who had dozed off in an uncomfortable pose against the side of the boat, jumped and fumbled for the safety lines.

"Sorry!" Emry called back to her. "I thought I had avoided it..." He paddled harder away from the stone, only to find new, choppy waves pushing him up against it. Up ahead, the tunnel started to glow. "Um—Aspen?"

Aspen set their paws on the side of the boat. "Cal, sit next to Emry and take the lute."

Cal slung the lute onto her back and wrapped her arms around Emry's waist. Her cold hands at the edge of his shirt took him by surprise. "What—"

"You don't have a vest on! What if you fall out?"

"I'm not going to fall out!"

"Emry, hold on to the stone!" Aspen called. Emry grabbed the pillar and yanked the boat up against it as a shimmering barrier swept over their half of the vessel.

Seconds later, thousands of glowing streams of energy pelted the barrier like rain, and the pillar shook under his grip.

"This can't be it, this can't be it, it's too early," Cal mumbled and drew closer to Emry as the waves climbed higher, splashing over the sides of the boat with cold fingers. He tightened his grasp on the pillar and squeezed his eyes shut against the blinding light, silently mimicking Cal's mantra.

But the surge was gone as quickly as it had come, leaving nothing but fizzling trails of spirit energy roaming around the stalactites above.

"You were right, Cal." Emry squeezed her hand, which had latched onto his chest. "It was just a small one."

But as the last bits of energy faded and plunged them into complete darkness, he slumped. The surge had blown out his only lantern light. "Cal, is there a dry bag in this boat?"

She let go of him and took off the lute to search behind her. "I don't see one, no."

"Great."

"Here." Aspen, now in human form, climbed to the front of the boat and held out their hands, where a tiny sphere cast an eerie light across the calming waters. "Will that work?"

"How long can you hold it?"

"As long as I need to."

Emry resumed paddling, his eyes adjusting to the new light. "What would we do without you, Aspen?"

"Die?"

"Well, yes, but—"

"Is that another one?" Cal froze. Emry's head snapped up, but the white glow she was seeing up ahead moved differently—as if something was slowly shimmering over the walls ahead, rather than barreling toward them.

"I don't think so..." Emry slowly forged ahead until the boat turned around the bend, and the sight confirmed his fear.

Three remnants morphed and bubbled in uneven patterns around the stalactites ahead. As they disturbed the ceiling, flurries of bats hurried away from them in a whirlwind, rushing to form a flying river of their own just above the boat. One of the remnants lashed out at the river, catching one of the unlucky bats at its edges. All the veins in its wings flashed white, and it flew as hard as it could until it dove and perished amongst the stalagmites below.

Those in the boat all ducked down to let the remaining cloud of claws and wings pass—but when that was gone, the other two remnants remained. Still silent, still floating.

"I can take them," Aspen muttered, crouched low with the light sphere between their fingers.

"No, you stay there with the light. I think we can get past them." Emry paddled forward as he picked up on the sound of rushing water downstream. "We can lose them in the rapids if we keep going—"

The remnants dove for them, and Cal screamed. Emry yanked up the paddle and lashed out at the one aiming for her head. As he struck, its silvery threads splintered and dissolved around the blade.

But the other one veered at the last second and slammed into his arm. He yelped, fell back against Cal, and dropped the paddle into the water.

"Shiro's hairy—get *off!*" he shouted at the light now burrowing into him, while his arm flashed in bursts of pain and numbness. Cal grabbed the paddle before it floated out of reach and slapped at the remains of the remnant. Though it fizzled away easily enough, Emry's arm continued to glow.

"Emry?" Aspen twisted to look at him, their fingers loosening around the light.

"Aspen, keep the light up!" Cal leaned over the side of the boat. "Hold on, hold on..." She reached down into the water and yanked up some river weed from underneath the surface. As she wrapped it around his arm, Emry felt around the boat with his good, if shaking, hand.

"Cal, give me the paddle."

"I'm almost done—"

"Too late for that!" He pointed ahead. White water flashed and sprayed in the light of Aspen's shield. Cal handed him the paddle and grabbed the safety lines.

"Can you still row?"

"We're going to find out!"

The boat gave a sudden lurch as the rapids launched them

forward, and only his hearing and the shield's shuddering light gave him time to react to what lay ahead. He cartwheeled the boat off a rock, only to be sucked into a stomach-heaving drop a moment later. As he wiped the spray from his face, he cursed and swerved again—a churning undercut swept by them, far too close for comfort. And with each stunt, his right arm stiffened more and more.

"All still here?" he panted when the last drop mercifully let them out into a pool.

"Here."

"Me!"

He took a few deep breaths, tightened the river weed around his arm, and forced out the burrowing spirit energy in one swift push. As the energy flashed out, he swore at the blast of pain that shot up to his shoulder, and tossed the plant aside.

"Is it out?" Cal set a supporting hand against his back as he slouched.

"Yeah." The arm still hung heavy at his side. "I'm gonna need a second. We should be dropping out near the Dawnstone docks any minute, I think."

Aspen pointed ahead. "Then what's that?"

A roar of water drowned out his next curse.

FORTY

SCARCELY TEN HEARTBEATS ahead of the boat, a massive rockslide obstructed half the tunnel. The sloping pile of striated rocks, soil, and vines tumbled from the broken ceiling and broached the river, shoving angry water up and over what had already been a dangerous drop in the route.

"This is why they closed it." Emry scrambled for the paddle, fear tightening every muscle in his body. Any runner knew this was death he was looking at. "This is why—Hara take me—Cal, tie the lute to something. Aspen, get inside."

"But you need the light!"

"I'll use what's coming in from the ceiling."

"You can get us through this, right?" Cal frantically wrapped rope around the lute. Emry's grip on the paddle shook hard, and he couldn't look back at her.

"The most I can do is get us past the undercuts. You ready?"

"No!"

"Kneel down, grab the ropes, and don't you dare let go!"

"Em—"

Her call dissolved into a scream as the boat fell out from underneath them.

The brief sense of weightlessness only made the bottom of the drop hit harder. A wall of wood and freezing water slammed into him, ripping apart his white-knuckled grip on the ropes and knocking him into the spray. There was no time to reach for the edge of the boat, or yell, or even draw breath before ice water flooded his nose and mouth, and wrapped around his limbs. The drop had claimed him.

The force of the waterfall shoved him down into the roiling current at the base of the rockslide. At first, his instincts made him fight to the surface, struggling against the downward push—but the deep chill only paralyzed him further. He wracked his brain to recall anything beyond panic, beyond the last of the air in his lungs. *Relax* was the only word that came to him—in his father's voice, his sister's voice.

With his last handful of wits, he let go. He sank deeper into the cold, until the lower current grabbed his body and dragged him out into open water beyond.

He broke through the surface just as the last of his breath slipped away.

"Cal!" he gasped and coughed, straining to see the silhouette of a boat, a person, anything in the darkness. "You there?"

The water was calmer here, but just as freezing. Something bumped his head. He jolted and turned, only to find the paddle bobbing next to him. He slung his bad arm over it and kicked forward.

"Cal? Aspen?" Water blocked his ears, and the last light of the sinkhole slipped away, leaving him in total darkness. His breath came in shorter and shorter, his limbs losing the strength to move. Relaxing wouldn't get him any farther.

"Help!" he shouted before his mouth dipped under the surface. He struggled to get more of his body onto the paddle, only to slide off of it again. His next gasp swallowed water, and he had to choke out the word. "*Help—*"

As he sank, heavy rope landed hard on his shoulder.

"Grab it!" Aspen shouted.

He clutched the rope with his good arm and let it pull him back up to the surface as Aspen reeled him in. Seconds later, a pair of hands dragged him over the side of the boat, dropping him next to another sopping wet figure.

"Next time, I'm going to tie *you* to the boat," the flickering spirit huffed and retreated back into the lute next to Cal, who was curled up on her side, coughing and shivering violently. Up ahead, light began to filter back into the cave.

"Did you fall out?" Emry reached for her, shaking with relief. She was here, she was breathing. Cal nodded through her next cough and opened her hands.

"Didn't let go of the rope..." He could dimly see the red marks streaking her palms. "Aspen got me back in. I couldn't see you, but I could hear you shouting—"

She bent over in a coughing fit, and Emry slowly pushed himself up to his knees. They weren't safe quite yet.

"We should be on the main route from Strava now. If we don't get up to the surface and dry off soon, we'll freeze to—"

The boat shuddered and threw him back down to the floor as wood collided with wood. Somewhere to his left, a few strangers shrieked.

"What in Hara's name—?"

A cave runner popped his head over the side of the boat. "Where did you come from?"

Emry let out a breathless laugh. "Copper Mill." With effort, he pulled himself up to his knees again, to discover that they had collided with a very confused passenger boat from the south. "Nexus was taken hostage, smuggler's route was the only way out—"

"Taken *hostage*?"

"Hitch us together and get us to the docks. You have any dry cloaks?"

The runner immediately tossed him the dry bag. Emry caught it with trembling fingers.

"You both fall out?" The man made quick work of the ropes.

"Rockslide drop, completely un-runnable."

The runner's jaw dropped. "Weir's eyes, you're not even wearing a vest—how are you alive?"

"Get us to the docks or we won't be for much longer."

Emry untied Cal's cork vest and threw any dry cloth he could find over Cal and himself. She immediately curled in and leaned hard against him. Not wanting his wet sleeves to soak her new cloak, he kissed her forehead and folded his arms against his chest. "We'll get inside very soon."

The docks were only a minute out, and as soon as the lanterns came into sight, the runner cupped his hands around his mouth. "Rogue vessel and two swimmers from Copper Mill!"

The boathouse manager rushed out to the edge of the dock, blankets in hand. "Names?"

The runner looked at Emry.

"Emry Karic."

The man's eyes widened as he grinned. "It's Karic's boy! He made it!"

The manager turned to someone farther up the path. "Go tell Eddie and Georgie he's here! Anyone with him?"

"Breslin, Calliope Breslin—"

"Calliope Breslin!"

The manager turned again. "Tell 'em she's here too!"

Emry winced at all the shouting and looked down at Cal. "Can you walk? Does anything hurt?"

She shook her head through the shaking. "Just c-cold—"

"I know, we're going to get you in front of a fire." He untied the lute and helped her up as the boat bumped against the dock.

"Mr. Karic, do you need help?" The manager threw a blanket over him as soon as he stumbled out.

"Where's the nearest inn?"

"Just across from the entrance."

"We're close, Cal, we're real close." He slung her arm over his shoulder and limped along the path. "Aspen, you hero, you still there?"

The lute vibrated weakly. "I'm tired."

"I believe it. Cal, say something, you with me?"

"Mm-hmm." She nodded, her lips tinged with blue. Emry's insides splintered.

"I'm sorry. This is all my fault." He kissed her hand at his shoulder and brought her out into the moonlight. "We're almost there, I promise."

Even with the moonlight, Dawnstone was dark—Emry hardly took in more than the crowds around him and the cobblestones threatening to trip him. He pushed past the huddles of confused, aimless refugees wandering the streets, keeping his focus on the doors of the inn ahead. But his knees gave out as he turned the handle, and together they fell into the warmth of the inn, icy puddles forming on the wood below them. He looked up, his arms shivering. "Blankets, please, someone..."

"Got it!" The innkeeper in the back sprang into action, as did two other groups of onlookers on opposite sides of the inn. To his left, a couple sitting near the fireplace gasped and leapt out of their chairs, their eyes locked on Cal. The woman had spilled coffee on the man's book as she stood, but he took no notice.

To his right, a gaggle of people thundered down a narrow stairway, a wall of curls and freckles shoving anyone and anything out of their way in a beeline for Emry.

FORTY-ONE

"Calliope?"

"Emry!"

Their families tore them in different directions. As Cal slipped out of his grip off to the left, his parents were suddenly on their knees in front of him, pulling him into their arms. He only caught a blurry glimpse of their faces, ones he hadn't seen in years, before they buried him in a tangle of hugs and tears.

"Oh, my son—"

"My baby boy—"

"Mum, Dad, he's gonna freeze to death." Georgie elbowed her way in, all fierce curls and wide cheeks, and threw a blanket over his shoulders. As she dried his hair with the corner of a blanket, Marley slid across the floorboards and latched onto his arm, tears already streaming down her freckles.

"Emry, I didn't think I was ever going to see you again," she sobbed into his sleeve. He leaned in against all of them, his tears hot against the river water soaking his face.

"I'm sorry, I'm so, so sorry—"

They huddled together in a single mess, blockading him from anything other than their embrace. He had missed it, he had missed all of it—the fuzzy curls brushing his face, the embroidered coats under his fingers, the tangle of their voices. He could have knelt there forever in a pool of bitter, guilt-ridden joy, if Georgie hadn't had the wherewithal to lift him to his feet.

"Let's get you changed. You smell like a cave," she grumbled and led Emry towards the steps. His father quickly grabbed his other arm for support, and he was thrown into a new sort of chaos—his family's questions.

"The runner told us you arrived by the old Copper Mill route, but that can't be possible, can it?"

"Are you hurt?" Marley squeezed past them up the stairs to get the door, while his mother pulled a dragging blanket up over his shoulders.

"Emry, who was that woman you were traveling with?"

"Did someone grab Asp—the lute?" Emry tried to turn his head against the growing pile of blankets on his back.

"I've got it!"

"Thanks, Mar."

They collectively burst into the room, everyone chattering, arranging chairs, and asking questions on top of each other. After making him change into dry clothes, Georgie shoved him into a chair near the fireplace and stoked the sleepy embers by his feet. For the first time in all this, he had a moment to actually observe his older sister. She was scowling, and the remains of the fire illuminated the circles under her hazel eyes—but her gaze softened when she looked up at him. "You going to survive?"

"If I don't melt under all these blankets, yes."

She grunted and tossed a log onto the fire. Emry gently nudged her with his foot. "Georgie...thanks for not giving up on me."

She stood and folded her arms. "Don't get me wrong, I still want to strangle you with a lute string."

"That's fair."

"But..." She sighed. "I knew you'd make it back. Maybe not after three years. But I knew we'd see you again."

Then Emry's mother, Tessa, swooped in to inspect his head, her signature worry line sharp between her eyebrows. Just the sight of it made him tear up again. "How are you feeling?" she asked. "Any pain? Dizziness?" She turned his head, then felt his arms through the blanket.

"Really, Mum, I'm all right."

"He must be in shock," Edward Karic muttered behind his wife, pacing and pulling at his beard. "I've seen that route myself, down through the sinkhole. It was barely runnable *before* the collapse—"

"What was it like?" Marley peeked around her mother, perched on a chair across from Emry. "Was it exciting?"

He couldn't help it—he grinned at her. "Well, if you count the smugglers we had to get past..."

"There were *smugglers?*" She leaned forward. "Tell me, how many were there? What were they stealing? Did you have to fight them off?"

"Kind of—"

"Really?" The color drained from Tessa's face.

"I didn't have a choice, Mum, people had taken the Mill nexus hostage!"

His father whipped around. "They had *what?*"

"Yes! Closed the gates, charged twenty gold for a ride out!"

"Rotting hell," Georgie spat and made to grab her cloak. "I'm taking the next carriage out of here down to Mill."

"No, Georgie, you can't." Emry reached out for her. "We don't have time."

The other Karics went silent, letting the sounds from outside float in through the windows—travelers filling the streets, soldiers shouting about evacuation zones. Tessa closed the curtains. "Dear, how did you know about...all that?" She turned around. "Your letter arrived before the Council runner did."

"And it contained far more information than they had." Marley's eyes narrowed at him. "Are you secretly a spy? Is that what you've been doing all this time?"

"No, Mar, I..." Emry trailed off. He had finally reached this point —all of them were looking at him for an answer, and he had nothing. The blankets weighing him down felt like stones. "I'm not anything."

Once the words started, they wouldn't stop, and he fished himself out of the blankets to explain.

"I'm not a Guild member—I tried, and I wasn't going to come back until I was, just like you said—and I didn't mean to stay away for so long, and I didn't mean to wreck everything with Cal, and I didn't mean to bring about the apocalypse—"

A new voice filtered out from the lute case. "All right. If we're talking about the wave, you can't take all the blame yourself." Aspen appeared next to Emry and set a comforting hand on his shoulder. "But I don't know about the other things." They looked up at the Karics and smiled. "Hello! I'm Aspen, I live inside Emry's lute. I've heard so much about you all, it's very nice to finally meet you."

All at once, everyone's heads turned to Emry. Georgie grabbed a poker from the fireplace.

"Emry?" she said in a warning tone. He held up his hands and gave a nervous smile.

"Georgie, it's okay. Aspen, please sit. I should start from the beginning."

He started the story with the day he took Georgie's lute and left Senne—

"Still can't believe you took my lute."

"It was basically mine, you never played it!"

"I was going to one day!"

—and summarized most of the years he had been gone. Floundering first in Thisby, then Foxhill, then Tazlo. Meeting Cal, breaking up with Cal. Playing at the Dancing Rabbit the first night of this year's Sada.

As soon as Aspen made their debut, Emry had to work harder to keep the narrative on track. "So, we go into the Academy building, and of course I run into Cal—"

"Oh, that was fun. She's so smart." Aspen bounced in the chair they had dragged over. "Did you know that she's studied astronomy *and* calculus *and* physics *and*—"

"Aspen, please let me finish before we start going through Cal's superlatives." Emry saw his mother rub the worry line on her forehead, and tried to move forward quickly. "I run into Cal, but right when she's about to kick me out of the library, Aspen comes in..."

His family leaned in when he got to the Lamb's Ear performance.

"Impressive? Is that really what she said?" Tessa beamed. "Weir's eyes, Emry."

Marley frowned. "But you said you weren't a Guild member."

"I'm getting to that."

This only confused them more when Emry recounted the card he'd received.

"They asked you to play for them?" Edward looked up as he stoked the fire. "Hell, you're a shoe-in after that!"

"Right?" Aspen gestured. "He's so good!"

That pain was coming back again, trickling through Emry's arms and settling in his hands. From across the fire, Marley was catching on. "Let him continue," she said quietly.

Emry found himself hesitating more the closer he got to the end of the story. "Then...then Cal goes off to present to the Academy, and I prepare for my Guild test..."

"So you took the test." Georgie leaned in from the edge of her seat. "And then what happened?"

"Nothing."

"Nothing?"

Emry took a breath. "The Academy had shut down Cal's proposal just the hour before—her plan was going nowhere. I knew Ella wanted to actually do something about the surges and had pull with the Council, so I…" He fumbled with the edge of a blanket, unable to meet their gaze. "I declined to perform and asked Cal to propose her evacuation plan instead. And it worked. And…now we're all here." He nodded out to the window, to the chaos outside. "Us and half the province."

They all fell quiet again until Emry couldn't stand it.

"Well, the floor is open now," he tried to joke in a breaking voice. "Time for some disownment, I think? Maybe a few eternal curses for good measure?"

They still said nothing. He gave up and stood, piling the blankets on the chair. "Come on, you must have something to say after over three years of utter disappointment." Tears burned his eyes. "Just get it all out now. You can say I told you so, I fully admit it! I didn't make it on my own, I nearly got my ex-girlfriend killed in a drop, I barely got *myself* here in one piece, I…" He dropped his arm from his gesture at the door. "Please, why won't you say anything?"

"Emry." His mother stood, her eyes shining. "We know you. Is there anything we can say that you haven't already told yourself a thousand times?"

Aspen looked at him. Emry wiped at his cheeks. "No."

"Yes, there is." His father stood as well. In the firelight, he truly did look like an older mirror image of Emry as he walked over and placed his hands on his son's shoulders. "We love you, we're proud of you, and we're so happy you're with us."

FORTY-TWO

Eventually, the Karic family attempted to catch some sleep before dawn. After much insisting, Emry took the chair near the fireplace, leaving one narrow bed to his sisters and the other to his mother. His father claimed he would take the sofa, but he was still awake when Emry finally fell asleep, and at one point in the night, Emry briefly surfaced to find that someone had moved him from the chair to the sofa.

But the anticipation of the next day was stronger than their collective exhaustion, and by dawn, they were all awake again, murmuring softly over the rationed dregs of the inn's coffee and a few day-old pastries.

"Emry said you studied marine biology," Aspen stage-whispered to Marley as she sat at the card table near the door.

"I did." Marley perked up as she drained the last of her tea. "Do you know what that is?"

"No."

"It means I studied the oceans, the fish, the seaside caves—"

"Could you teach me about fish? I didn't have any at my grove."

Aspen's fingers tapped on the table. "Wish I did, though. I like the way they swim."

As those two continued their whisperings, Emry stretched on the sofa and found another low conversation murmuring by the window.

"I went out to check," Georgie muttered into her coffee as she stood next to Tessa. "They say we're in evacuation zone ten, which is supposed to leave in four hours."

"Will that give us enough time?"

"I already tried to see if we could sneak out another way, but they have all the roads monitored. Meant to avoid a stampede, I guess." Georgie opened the gauzy curtain to eye the Council soldiers below, where they waved around pieces of paper and directed crowds this way and that. "But if I find another way out, we're taking it."

Emry looked about the room—Edward Karic was nowhere to be seen.

"Where's Dad?" he asked the room at large. Tessa immediately abandoned the window and took a cup of pungent-smelling tea from the side table.

"Drink this, you're sure to be sore."

She had added a drop of honey to the willow bark tea, but the drink was still bitter as it coated his throat. He feigned a smile and tried not to taste it as he drank the rest. "Thanks."

She shifted a sleep-addled curl from his face and kissed his forehead. It did more for his aches than the tea ever would. "Oh, I did miss you, love."

"I missed you too, Mum." He set down the cup and gave her a knowing smile. "But I'm afraid you haven't told me where Dad is."

Tessa hesitated. "He's off to find the Breslins. He wanted to apologize for the trouble you ran into at Copper Mill."

"What? Why is *he* doing it?" Emry jumped to his feet. "I should be the one apologizing, I ran the route—"

He winced as he started for the door, and his mother guided him back down.

"Wait and let the tea settle first," she said. "It's going to be a long walk to the caves, as far as we can tell. You'll have plenty of time to talk to the Breslins on the way there. But…" She checked the pocket watch Georgie had left on the side table. "I suppose I should make sure he's not talking their ears off. You know how he can get."

After draping him in an unnecessary blanket and handing him the last pastry, she swept off to find her husband, leaving him with two sisters who immediately turned their hungry shark eyes on him.

"Oh, you can talk *to* the Breslins on the walk over, but…" Marley dragged a chair over to the sofa and plopped herself down. "We can talk *about* the Breslins now."

"Spill it." Georgie leaned over the back of the sofa. Emry stuffed his breakfast into his mouth before she could grab it. "Come on, what's Cal like? I didn't get a good look at her when you two came in, and you left out all the damn details last night."

Emry reached out toward Aspen. "Aspen, help me out here—"

"Help you with what?" The spirit was shifting the lute strap over their shoulder. "I was going to go outside to check on things."

"Why?"

Aspen fidgeted. "Well, the shouty person out there hasn't been shouting recently…"

Georgie glanced out the window. "The soldiers are still in the square, but if you must…" She dug around in her pocket and tossed Aspen a few coins. "See if anyone's selling more turnovers out there, will you?"

"Georgie, I haven't taught them about money yet—"

"Whatever, just throw the coins at the person behind the stall and see what they give you."

"Check on the shouting, throw the coins, get the breakfast," Aspen rattled off, then left before Emry could correct them on any of it. He sighed and rubbed his eyes.

"You're a bad influence, Georgie."

"Oh, and you've been teaching them morals, have you?" Georgie dragged over a chair to sit next to Marley. "All right, enough dallying. Tell us about Ms. Breslin."

Emry leaned back and folded his arms. "I won't say a word until you both tell me what you've been up to the last three years."

Georgie scoffed. "Nothing, Senne is boring. Marley?"

Marley sipped her coffee. "I agree, I've done nothing but eat chocolates and stare out the window. Your turn, Emry."

"No. No no no"—he waved his hands—"Mar, you went to the Academy! You graduated! You can't tell me you don't have any stories for me, that's just—you've got to give me something!"

Georgie gestured to Marley. "Fine. Tell him about that exploration gig you landed."

"Please do." Emry leaned forward. Marley rolled her eyes in a poor attempt to conceal her excitement.

"It's not much—just a cave expedition out on the western coast of Selj. They need someone with both cave and sea experience to look for new species of bats, and they want me to start as soon as their flooding season has ended..."

It didn't take much interrogation to uncover that Marley's Academy experience had glittered with things like this—offers, accolades, influential friends. Not that Emry expected anything different, of course.

"Now, Georgie." Emry turned to his older sister. "You can't tell me you stared at ledgers for three years, because I know you didn't."

"No, *Georgiana* has been getting suitors." Marley nudged her sister, who sharply elbowed her back.

"All they want is a piece of the family business," Georgie explained it away with a wave of her hand. "I'm just having fun stringing some of them along."

Marley tapped her chin and looked about the room. "That doesn't explain the hour you spent away from the Lins' dinner party with that Ms. Castaic..."

"Mar."

"Or that man from the Izar Night ball, who seemed to like the gardens an *awful* lot—"

Marley shrieked when a throw pillow slammed into her face.

"Once I kill Emry, you're next, you little—"

"Children!" Emry laughed and raised his hands. "Children, behave!"

But his command went ignored, and he happily sat back as their kerfuffle ran its course.

"Right, anyway." Marley swept her hair back into position. "This Calliope Breslin of yours."

Emry gave a tired sigh. "Cal."

"Ooh, *Cal.*"

"Mar, I swear to Hara—"

"Sorry, sorry. Continue. What's she like?"

Emry bit his lip, unsure of where to start. "Well, she's an Academy student. She's brilliant. She's beautiful. She's—"

A knock sounded on the door.

"Em? Are you in there?" A hesitant voice called out. "I wanted to check in on you..."

Emry froze. "She's at the door."

His sisters leapt out of their seats.

"Fix your hair, it's a mess—"

"She calls you Em? That's adorable—"

"Georgie, get your hands off my head!"

By the time he managed to open the door, Emry was afraid Cal had given up and left—but she was still standing there when he opened it, a nervous smile pasted to her face. He let out a breath he hadn't realized he was holding. Other than the bandages on her hands, she looked no worse for wear after last night's events.

"I hope I didn't wake your family," Cal said as she glanced through the doorway.

"No, no, I was just talking with my sisters—"

"Who are leaving!" Georgie took Marley's arm and dragged her out of the room. "Calliope, hello, it's very nice to meet you, but it's past time we check on our parents."

"Oh, they're downstairs with mine, actually"—Cal began to back away—"but really, I didn't mean to intrude—"

"No, we want you to, please go ahead!" Georgie waved her in and disappeared down the hall. Cal turned to Emry and clasped her hands together.

"Georgie and Marley, I suppose?"

"I promise I'll properly introduce you all at some point. But, um..." He stepped aside to let her in and quietly closed the door behind her. "How are you feeling? I'm terrible, I didn't check on you last night."

He took her hands in his and gently turned them around to inspect the bandages. She shook her head and pulled her hands away. "I'm fine—and please, if a Karic apologizes to me or my family one more time today, I will scream."

"I—" He stopped himself. "All right."

"So?" She looked up at him expectantly. "How did it go? With your family?"

A stupid, uncontrollable grin spread across his face. "Turns out they still love me, if you can believe that."

Cal wrapped him in a tight hug, laughing into his waistcoat. He breathed in the sound to savor it. "Em, I'm so happy for you, I knew it—"

"I know. You certainly did tell me so." He gently squeezed her shoulders. "Thank you, Cal."

When she finally withdrew, she glanced around the room. "Where's Aspen?"

"Out checking the square. I think they're nervous about the wave."

"Right." Her light faded, and Emry regretted bringing reality back into the room. "I went out to check myself, a few hours ago. Of course, the local council evacuated zone seven before zone six, and forgot to include a whole street in zone four. I heard people yelling about it before the sun was even up. And we've only got a few more hours until we…until the…" She wandered over to the bed and sat on the edge. "We should talk, then."

Emry swallowed. "Okay. What about?" He remained by the door, his chest seizing up again. This was it. This was when she would admit it, that she didn't actually want to spend her last few hours near him—

"About how I still love you."

Oh.

"…Emry, you're supposed to say something after that."

He realized he was staring at her with another grin on his face and tried to shake himself out of it—but there was no getting rid of such a feeling, not when it had already dug in deep years ago. "Do I need to say something, or can I just come over there and kiss you?"

She smiled. "If you don't, I'll be disappointed."

She didn't have to tell him twice—he was over there in a heartbeat, cupping her face with both his hands, feeling the upward curve of her lips against his.

"I still love you, Cal," he murmured between kisses. "You know that, right?"

"I may have suspected…" She gave a small gasp when his lips trailed her jawline. As he journeyed back up, she leaned back and pulled him down on top of her.

"Cal"—he stifled a groan when her mouth strayed to the pulse at his neck—"we shouldn't get too ahead of ourselves…"

She paused. "Says the man who tried to seduce me in a rowboat using nothing but a cravat and a lute."

"It worked, didn't it?"

Her soft laugh reverberated against his skin and sent a shiver down his spine—but she reluctantly came back up and kissed his cheek. "I suppose you're right. We should go see our families before they start to look for us."

She managed to steal a few more kisses before they left the room and descended the stairs, where they found themselves at the mercy of an overcrowded inn.

On any other day, the front room would have felt cozy—chairs circled around the fireplace, a few tables scattered off to the side under yellowed paintings of the Sea Mountain range. Though there was no stage, Emry could imagine that the corner by the windows would do in a pinch. But through the mess of people all glancing out the window for their turn at evacuation, it was difficult to see even the paintings higher up on the wall, much less the families they sought. Edward Karic, standing a few inches above the rest, flagged them down to a scrappy collection of tables they had shoved together to fit them all.

"Glad you could make it down," he said, throwing Emry a pointed, but not unkind, look. "Sit, sit. This is the last of the bread they've got."

As Cal weaved her way past Emry, two others at the table stood, their eyes on him.

"Ah, this is Mr. Karic?" A man bearing thick glasses and Cal's nose held out his hand. "It's good to finally meet you. We've heard so much about you at this point."

Emry swallowed and took the hand with as much courage as he could summon. "Mr. Breslin, I was told that I'm barred from apologizing for Copper Mill, so I'm going to have to trust that my father conveyed our regrets well enough."

Mr. Breslin laughed, revealing that he also had Cal's smile. "Indeed, he did. We're just happy Cal is here with us."

Next to him, his wife extended her hand as well. It only took a brief glance to see where her daughter had inherited her eyes and perfect posture. "Mr. Karic," she said, "given what Calliope has told us about you, I daresay it's an honor."

He grinned. "Then I'd love to hear what lies she's told about me."

They all sat, passing out the stale pieces of bread and last swipes of butter from the kitchen. Despite the dread simmering around them, their chatter made the huddle of tables feel like a normal supper. He wanted to settle into it, to pretend these faces he loved hadn't gathered because they were all in imminent danger—but as he accepted half a crust from Marley, he found he couldn't relax. There was something missing.

He passed his piece of bread off to his mother and stood.

"Where are you going?" Tessa touched his arm as he untangled himself from the bench.

"Aspen should be here. I'm going to go find them."

Cal looked up. "How long have they been gone?"

"At this point, I could hardly tell you—but I'm sure they haven't gone far. I'll just be a moment—"

"No need." Georgie's eyes locked on the door, her bread halfway to her mouth. Across the room, a wispy shape of a human carrying a very real lute case was slipping and ducking their way through the horrified crowd as fast as they could.

"The caves," they panted as they skidded to a halt in front of Emry. "It's the caves."

Emry went cold—he had never seen Aspen so transparent.

"Take a breath." He reached for their shoulder, but his hand passed through it. "It's all right—"

"No, it's not all right." Aspen grabbed his arm, their eyes shining with fear. "The caves are full."

FORTY-THREE

The room erupted in panic as soon as the words left Aspen's mouth.

"Upstairs!" Edward shouted over the din and pulled Tessa along toward the staircase. Tessa latched onto Georgie, who grabbed Marley. Marley reached for Emry, but a family of four barreled in between them, knocking their hands aside.

"Aspen—" Emry turned to the spirit, but they had already ducked back into the lute. He caught the case before another wave of families rushed past the table, knocking him toward Cal. She grabbed his hand, then her mother's, and without another word, they fought their way up the stairs and into the Karics' room.

"What do we do?" Marley asked as they closed the door. "Can we hide in the nexus?"

"The river caves aren't safe—the energy's been traveling through them," Emry said. "Does this inn have a cellar?"

Mrs. Breslin shook her head. "Already reserved for those who can't make the walk."

"Hey—" Aspen's voice floated up from the lute. Emry set the lute on the table.

"Aspen, you rest, we'll figure something out."

"Are there any other caves in this area?" Tessa looked to Edward, who grimaced as he checked on the frenzy out the window.

"The only ones I know about are the ones connected to the river routes."

The lute case unlocked itself and flew open. "I think I—"

"These walls are made of stone." Georgie spoke over Aspen. "Can't we stay here and wait it out?"

"I don't trust the window frames or the doors." Cal chewed her lip. "Not in a wave as strong as what we're expecting. Unless we can barricade them with something—"

"*Listen!*"

Aspen suddenly stood on the card table, yanking a piece of paper from the lute case. They had only half thought through their translucent form—one leg was that of a wolf, the other of a deer. But the hand that waved the paper was very human. "The Council people were using this to tell everyone where to go, and they said all these places are full, but"—he handed the sheet to Cal—"their paper is wrong."

Cal took the paper and frowned. Emry caught a glimpse of a detailed print of the Sea Mountains, and the Alacova system underneath. Someone had circled the available cave entrances, then crossed them out. "Their map is wrong?" She flipped it over and scanned it a few times. "I don't understand, it looks correct to me."

She passed it off to her mother, then her father, who both seemed equally perplexed.

"Aspen, you haven't seen this map before." Emry looked up at the spirit. "What makes you think it's wrong?"

"Because it doesn't match what you drew at Dev's house," Aspen said. "You drew five circles. They only have four."

Mr. Breslin extended the map to Emry. Just as they said, someone had marked four entrances into the mountains, but the highest peak spaced between them was blank. Emry pointed to it. "You're right, Aspen. The glow-worms showed a circle there, too."

Cal grabbed the map and rushed outside. Aspen plucked the lute from the case and sprinted to follow.

"Calliope?" her mother called.

"Stay there, be right back!"

No one in the room heeded her response, and the two of them soon had a gaggle of people trailing them all the way out to the crowded square. Cal made a beeline for two Council soldiers standing uselessly on the fountain at the center, as if it were the only rock jutting out of a rushing river.

"Excuse me!" Cal shoved her way over and jumped onto the fountain's edge next to them. "Do you know what's in this area?"

"What—?" The first soldier looked down from the flask she was bringing to her lips. "How did you get my map?"

"Do you know anything about this part of the mountains?" Cal repeated. The soldier shrugged and took a swig.

"Hell no, I'm from Bennli." She nudged the soldier next to her. They looked to be a few years younger than Emry, with a five-o'clock shadow and a worried frown etched across their face.

"Yes, ma'am?" They tore their eyes off the crowd and turned the frown on them.

"You're from Dawnstone, aren't you?"

"Yes, ma'am." They glanced down at the people swarming past their feet. "I, um, haven't seen my parents go through the gate yet—"

"Tell you what, you answer this woman's question and I'll let you go find your parents. It's the least I can do before we all die." The first soldier motioned with her flask. "What was the question again?"

"We're wondering if there's any kind of landmark here." Cal demonstrated again for the second soldier. "Perhaps a collapsed cave entrance, or the remains of a village?"

"Nothing like that." They shook their head, then paused. "Though...there is an old fane around there."

"How old?"

"Uh—my mum says it's the oldest in Vidanya. Couple thousand years, maybe? It's mostly ruins now, I think."

Cal, Emry, and Aspen all looked at each other.

"Time to go!" Aspen made to jump off the fountain, but Cal caught them.

"Wait—we need to tell these people to head there as well."

Emry took in all the nervous faces around them. "Cal, what if there's nothing there?" he countered. "We'd be sending everyone out into the woods with no protection—"

A low rumbling cut him off, and the fountain sprayed mist on their legs as the water shifted. Emry took hold of Cal's arm and wildly scoped out any sort of stone wall they could hide behind—but the quake was gone in a second, leaving nothing but a more panicked crowd in the square. Many began pushing and shoving their way to the gate.

"There's no protection here, either," Cal argued. "We have to direct people to the fane now."

"But don't we have to get there first?" Aspen pointed out to the gate. "We can't direct people somewhere we haven't been."

"Don't worry about that." Below them, Georgie dug into her pockets and passed off a stack of coins to Marley. "Mar, go bribe someone for their horses. We'll get to the fane ahead of the crowd that way."

Emry grinned, while Tessa spluttered. "Georgiana!"

"Mar, I'll go with you." Edward took his younger daughter's arm. Mrs. Breslin stepped forward as well.

"I'll go as well. You'll need assistance handling that many horses."

"My dear—" Mr. Breslin tried, but the three had already slipped away into the crowd.

"Meet you at the gate!" Marley called out before she disappeared amongst the bodies pressing toward the exit.

"Mum, they'll be okay." Emry reached for Tessa, but on his other side, Georgie was making it worse.

"Give me that." She took the first soldier's flask, stole a swig, then gave it back along with the map from Cal's hands. "Start telling people to head right there. It's their last chance to make it through this alive."

"Please, can I go find my parents?" the second soldier pleaded. The first one sighed and tucked her flask back into her pocket.

"You go, I'll redirect the crowd."

The soldier dashed out into the mob.

"Is there anyone you can spare to come with us to the fane?" Cal asked the remaining soldier. "If we're able to find the last entrance, someone from the Council could help us direct others—"

The other woman scoffed. "Best of luck finding anyone not already running off."

Cal's frown sharpened. "Fine." She held out her hand, palm up. "Hand me your coat, then."

"What?"

"Your coat. I just need the color to help catch people's eyes and get them to the fane."

"So rotting needy," the soldier muttered, shrugged off her jacket, and handed it to Cal. "Have at it."

"Cal, can we go now, please?" Aspen bounced on their heels next to her. She folded the jacket over her arm and nodded.

As they jumped off the fountain and joined the fray, the soldier began wrangling the crowd with a booming voice. By the time they reached the others at the gate, the chaotic, swirling mass of people was slowly reforming into a steady stream headed into the mountains.

"Time to see if the glow-worms were right." Georgie extended a hand to Emry, pulling him up to join her on the last horse. "No pressure, though."

"Cal, are we really doing this?" Mr. Breslin asked in a low voice. Cal guided her horse out, Marley sitting behind her.

"You're going to have to trust us. Everyone ready?"

Those behind her nodded. Aspen shifted into a bird on Emry's shoulder and rustled their wings. "Let's go."

FORTY-FOUR

THE HORSES BORE them out ahead of the other escapees easily, as most of the mob was on foot, dragging wagons, or in carriages overloaded with family members and belongings. But the farther they retreated from the initial stream of people, the more they spotted the vestiges of those turned away from the other caves. Families and friends scrabbled about the forested hills in search of a stony outcropping or a sinkhole big enough to shelter themselves. Council soldiers were ripping up the flags leading to the now-full shelters, but many frantic groups blew past them anyway, as if the caves were going to magically expand by the time they reached them. And every mile or so, small quakes struck—just enough to trap them in a constant state of hypervigilance.

"The cave over there is full!" A woman gestured to them from the top of a hill, after one such quake died down. "There's no use going that way."

"How is it full?" Cal shouted up to her. "It was supposed to be able to fit half of the city!"

"Collapsed tunnel, closed off most of the cave. Turn back while you still can!"

With that, the woman disappeared over the ridge, and they pressed forward despite her advice.

"I'll go ahead again," Aspen said, and launched themself off of Emry's shoulder.

"Are you sure?" Emry called, but their bird form—a brown eagle this time—had already spiraled high into the sky. They made these trips every few minutes or so, soaring as far from the lute as they could to scan the area before diving back down. Each time, they came back a little more transparent, a sight that did nothing for Emry's nerves.

Next to him, Mrs. Breslin watched Aspen fly upward with the same fascination he had seen on her daughter's face many times. "Calliope told us about this spirit," she said, "but...well, I didn't think..." She shook her head. "I don't know what to think."

"I understand." Emry gave a small smile. "Cal almost hit them with a book the first time they transformed in front of her."

Cal scoffed. "I did not—"

"I said you *almost* did, before I jumped in. For a second, I thought you were going to hit me with the book instead."

Georgie snorted at that.

"Cal, did you ever study near Senne?" Marley asked from behind Cal on the horse.

"No, just Tazlo and Vornik. Took a practical at Bennli."

"Which one?"

"The astronomy one, after they built that telescope."

"No." Marley's eyes sparkled. "Which year?"

"Two years ago by now, I think?"

"No way!" Marley shook Cal's shoulder. "Do you know how close I was to taking that class? We could've been classmates!"

"Thank Hara," Emry said. "The professors wouldn't have known what to do with themselves."

He thoroughly enjoyed the look they both shot at him, but it was short-lived—for up above, Aspen shouted something between a bird call and a human shriek. The sound was more unsettling than the last quake.

"I found it!" they shouted as they swooped back onto Emry's shoulder. "Up ahead!"

They sped up to round the narrow, canopied road, and stopped at the foot of an overgrown deer path.

"Up here?" Cal dismounted. Her parents started to follow, but she held up her hand. "Stay with the horses and look out for others, just to be safe."

Emry handed the reins over to his father after dismounting. "I'll send Aspen to you if it's the right place. Otherwise, we'll come straight back down."

Tessa grabbed his hand. "Be careful, love."

"Of course, Mum."

Aspen was already flitting through the canopy above, turning back to the group impatiently as they trekked up the hill. Gradually, the sound of trickling water tugged at their ears.

"We almost there, Aspen?" Georgie grumbled as she hoisted herself up over a boulder.

"Almost!"

As they crested the hill, the ground smoothed out briefly, allowing just enough space for the promised ruins until the earth shot upward into a towering cliff face. In the shadow of the cliff and its dying waterfall, the fane was fittingly bleak. The only remaining structures after so many years were a crumbling stone archway and a very large, very dead pine tree. All around the archway, mossy rocks and imprints of squares in the earth acted as gravestones for other structures, ones that must have stood proudly around the tree long ago.

Emry found he couldn't look at it too long, as if it were a forced glimpse into Brinna and Cedar's eventual future.

"Does a spirit live here, Aspen?" Marley ran up to the tree. Aspen landed in one of its brittle branches.

"Not anymore," they said, their voice soft. "I can't feel anything."

"That's too bad." Marley traced the worn edges of the old cubbies carved into the archway. "I wanted to put in something nice as an offering."

Aspen flew over and dropped a seed into her hand. "Here. I will appreciate the offering on the old spirit's behalf."

"Mar, once you're done communing with nature, help us look for a cave entrance." Georgie picked her way around the ruins, searching for any kind of opening in the cliff face. "Did those old stories say anything about where to actually find the shield thing once you get there?"

"Not that I can tell. The other entrances were fairly easy to access..." Cal was right behind Georgie, extending her fingers into the waterfall to catch some of the spray. "Do you think there's anything upstream?"

"I'll check!" Aspen soared up and over the waterfall, while Cal leaned closer to the cliff face. Though the cliff's shade and crawling vines buried the details, worn decorative carvings covered the wall.

"Do you have anything like these carvings in Senne?" she murmured.

"Not really," Georgie said. "Mum and Dad used to tend to a fane before they got too busy. I don't remember anything like this being there."

"Aspen?" Emry remained closer to the archway with Marley, keeping his eyes on the top of the waterfall. "You see anything up there?"

Before anyone could answer, the ground shivered. They both grabbed the archway for support, but the quake was gone a moment later.

"Everyone good?" Georgie headed back toward them.

"Fine," Emry said, but Aspen's absence threw doubt into his response. He cupped his hands to send his voice up the waterfall. "Aspen! Come back!"

A twig snapped off to their left. They all jumped and whipped around to find a cougar limping its way down the side of the cliff.

"Asp—" Marley started forward, but Emry dragged her back.

"That's not Aspen," he breathed. Underneath the cougar's fur, white lines glowed, rippling over its muscles and leaking light out of its eyes. Wobbling and confused, the animal locked eyes with them and bared its teeth.

"Shiro's rotting beard." Georgie stepped in front of them and yanked a knife out of her boot. "Get behind me. Cal, stay near the wall. What's wrong with that thing?"

"A remnant, it's possessed." Emry tensed as her knife caught a flash of sunlight. "Georgie, don't be a hero, it'll die in a minute anyway—"

"Right, Emry, I'll just tell the giant angry cat to wait a bit!"

The cat stalked forward, then staggered back, thrashing its head as if trying to rid itself of the remnant. The light crossing its body pulsed, and in a panicked rage, it bounded straight toward them. Georgie hip-checked Marley to one side, shoved Emry to the other, and ducked as the cougar's back paws left the ground. It slammed into the arch above her—but before she could roll away, it collapsed onto her back, and her knife skidded out of her hand.

"Georgie!" Emry went for the knife. Marley yanked him back as the cougar's claws gouged the earth near it. Struggling under the creature, Georgie kicked and pushed at its ribcage. It yowled in pain, then snapped its jaws an inch away from her neck. Emry spun back to the waterfall.

"Aspen, *help*!"

"I got it!" The blur of a massive brown eagle whipped past his shoulders. As the cougar's jaws lunged again, Aspen gripped its body with their claws and hurled it toward the cliff. Yelping, the animal flew straight through the waterfall, slammed into the carving behind it, and fell still. Its glowing lines flickered, then slowly faded. White wisps escaped out of its nose and mouth and dissolved in the morning light.

"Did it get you?" Emry pulled Georgie to her feet, searching for any sign of blood.

"No, I'm fine." She reached down for her knife, slid it back into her boot, and frowned at the waterfall. The force of the cougar's impact was still reverberating through the stone. "Does that wall sound...hollow to anyone else?"

"Working on it!" Cal called—she was already knocking on the carvings, testing for more echoes.

As they all rushed to follow her, Emry joined Aspen by the body.

"Thank you, Aspen. I'm sorry you had to kill it."

"Oh, it wasn't really me," Aspen said weakly, shifting back into human form. Emry could see rays of light passing through their mournful expression. "The remnant had nearly overtaken it anyway. I'm just glad it didn't take Georgie with it."

Emry lifted a hand to touch Aspen's shoulder, but there wasn't enough shoulder to touch. "Here, let's get it away from the water-fall." He helped them drag it off to the side of the cliff. "Why don't you stay in the lute for a while? You've done a lot today."

Aspen shook their head. "I need to find the cave first."

Behind them, the others were already making headway on that front.

"The corner's over here, I can see it!" Marley pointed as Georgie cut away the vines behind the waterfall, ignoring the water pelting the cloak on her back.

"Got it." She cleared the vine near Marley's hand, then pounded the stone. The sound echoed, just as it had before. "This better be a door. Mar, go get the parents while we figure out how to open it."

"Why do I have to get the parents?"

"You run faster than Emry."

Marley rolled her eyes. "Fine." She took off, and Emry took her place.

"No handle?" He felt around the carving, which stretched up far above him.

"Not that I can tell." Georgie stepped out of range of the waterfall and ran her fingers along the seam of the carving, at the upper limit of her reach. "Just these notches up here. See, you've got matching ones on your side."

"Ropes, then." Cal folded her arms. "They used to have ropes around the door. Pull it down from the front, pull it back up from inside the cave. The ropes would block the holes from the notches, and they'd be safe inside without leaving anyone outside."

Georgie stepped back. "Smart, except for when you wait a thousand years to open the door and the ropes have all rotted away."

"What about the vines?" Cal plucked at the creeping plants. "They're about the right thickness...Aspen?"

Emry stooped to pick up the vines they had already cut down. "I think Aspen's done enough already. Why don't we—"

"No, I can do it." Aspen took the vines from him. From their hands, the plants snaked their way up the door and through the old notches.

"Aspen, once this is done, I'm building you a new fane myself," Georgie said, and grabbed hold of the bundle of vines now attached to the door. "Anyone, a little help with this?"

It took all of them, including the parents climbing the hill, to take down the massive stone door. Over a foot thick, it fell with a resounding boom onto the soil, sending dead leaves twirling into the air. As the waterfall splashed down against it, the water flowed into the stone carvings, winding down the sides and resuming its journey into the stream within a moment.

Together, they all stared into the mouth of the cave. Nothing but darkness yawned back at them.

FORTY-FIVE

MR. BRESLIN WAS first to break the silence.

"There was a family we passed." He glanced back, into the overcast light. "I think they had a lantern. I could go find them—"

"No, there's no time. Here." Aspen pushed past the group and held out their hands. Just like Emry had seen before, a tiny shield formed between their fingers—but as soon as it reached the size of a pinecone, it broke free and floated away, and another one took its place. These little orbs danced their way in opposite directions all about the chamber, illuminating what they could of the massive space.

If the cave had a ceiling, Emry couldn't see it—only the layers and layers of draped stalactites that covered the walls like scales before disappearing into the darkness above. As they sloped to the ground, the points gave way to column-like stalagmites, giants that framed a winding pathway farther into the cave. Cal squinted at one of the pillars as they crept past it, then tugged on Emry's shoulder and pointed. Though mineral formations had obscured most of the details, an old carving remained on the stalagmite—a sheaf of wheat, pointing them deeper into the depths.

Eventually, the pathway split, tempting them to stray into other chambers—but the darkness down those trails pressed a little too much, and they stuck together on the main route inward. Aspen's tiny shields led them like fireflies until they reached a wall and gathered around a tall structure.

The fane out by the tree was meant to honor a spirit, to be sure, but this one—*this* one must have been for Hara herself. Multiple archways, all three times Emry's height, converged at the end of the chamber. Though the planes facing outward had all been carved with murals, those facing inward were lined with holes.

Cal stepped forward to get a closer look, but Tessa gently touched her arm.

"It's best not to approach without an offering." Given how soft her voice was, Emry was surprised he caught any of her words at all —but the chamber bore them up easily. She walked in first as an example, stopping to pause before the archway, then moving ahead and sliding a coin into one of the cubbies. Edward followed suit, and after a moment, Emry followed his sisters in.

The offerings already within the cubbies made his coin feel unworthy. Though his ancestors might have left things like flowers and fruit in their day, the offerings that had withstood the test of time here were far more valuable. Necklaces, rings, and delicately adorned metals winked as the glowing shields floated by them. Ancient coins had been stacked carefully into several of the holes, and in others, the lustrous inside of shell fragments gleamed in the light. These, Emry guessed, had to have been prized possessions back then—the closest ocean was on the other side of the mountain range.

On any other day, Emry would have offered up a song and considered it the highest honor. He turned around, hands aching for his lute, and found Aspen hanging back at the edge of the light. The spirit was frowning up at the archways.

"Aspen?" Emry approached them quietly. "Copper for your thoughts?"

Aspen adjusted their grip on the lute strap. Apart from where the lute needed to hang across their body, they were almost fully transparent.

"I was just thinking…" they murmured, then looked at Emry with a hard gaze. "This Hara better come through today."

Then a new voice drifted in from the cave entrance. "Dad, do you see this? Come look!"

The silhouette of a child clambered over the fallen door. The sound of their voice and their little feet clomping against the stone broke everyone else out of their reverie.

"We should see how large the other chambers are," Mrs. Breslin said, keeping pace with her daughter as they strode back down the path. "How accessible they might be, how many they can fit—"

"I saw three smaller chambers, one right and two left." Cal pulled on the green Council jacket and gestured to the family gathering outside the cave. "Come in, it'll be safe here!"

It wasn't long before the one grateful family turned into three, then five, then a dozen, dissolving the silence of the cave with their voices. A few of them had the wherewithal to bring in lanterns to replace Aspen's floating lights, which doused themselves as soon as the spirit stopped to rest by the door.

"Please head all the way down and to the right! That's it, keep going!" Cal and her parents directed those at the mouth of the cave, while Georgie's booming voice kept the newcomers in line halfway down.

"No, not down there—over here! And don't step on that stalagmite, no one's got the time to clean it up—"

As another brief quake mocked them, Emry checked his family's whereabouts for the tenth time—standing near Hara's fane, ensuring there was enough space for those gathering at the back— then confirmed that Cal's parents were still close by their daughter's side. Now that Council soldiers, true ones, had begun to appear at the cave, they were parroting the directions Cal had started.

He let out a breath and swung over to Aspen, who hadn't moved from their seat at the door. More than a few refugees had noticed their ghostlike form by the waterfall, but had been too panicked to do anything more than point and whisper on their way in.

"Aspen, Marley wants you to come sit next to her in the cave," he lied. Aspen didn't take their eyes off the people streaming in.

"I need to make sure this door closes."

Emry sat next to them. "It will close," he said. "You've set up the vines, and I've recruited some people to lift it. As soon as these folks are in, we'll close the door and I'll join you by the arches."

"Em?" Cal's baggy Council jacket appeared at the edge of his vision. "We're going in."

"Good." And he meant it—just hearing her say it released a weight from his shoulders as he stood. "My family's got a spot for you in the back. And"—he gestured to Aspen—"please take this one with you."

"No!" Aspen stood in defiance. "I'm staying with Emry until the door is closed."

"And then you'll both come straight back to us?" Cal looked between Aspen and Emry, holding his arm in a tight grip.

"Of course."

"Calliope..." Mrs. Breslin glanced back into the cave. Emry kissed Cal's cheek.

"It's almost over, I promise." He squeezed her hand. "I love you."

"I love you, too."

The Breslins melted into the darkness along with the last trails of those finding refuge into the caves. Through the growing clouds, Emry could tell the sun was high in the sky, and the Council soldiers at the cave entrance were getting antsy. They soon signaled for those at the bottom of the hill to begin directing others away from the path.

"Are you sure it's time?" Emry asked the nearest soldier. Beside him, Aspen slung the lute on their back. "There's still people out there—"

A screeching crack split the air between them, and the earth jerked so violently that the waterfall itself leapt in a curve to spray anyone near it.

"Get the vines!" the call erupted from both sides of the door. Aspen reached out a hand, and the cave-side vines went taut at their command. Just as the door began to lift, Emry slipped inside to help pull. Slowly, the stone door creaked upward, plunging the chamber into deeper and deeper darkness.

"Aspen, get in here!" Emry shouted. The spirit jumped through the slim opening.

"Emry Karic!" Georgie's voice thundered from the back of the chamber. "Are you inside?"

Aspen tossed up a tiny glowing sphere in response while Emry continued to pull the door closed.

"Almost there..." The soldier off to his left motioned them back, then froze. "Wait, *wait!*"

Another crack sounded above them, and dust fell through Aspen's shoulder. Emry looked up.

"Out of the way!" He leapt to push the spirit away, and just in time—far above them, the top third of the ancient door tilted along a rugged fracture as if in slow motion, then tumbled to the cave floor with a shuddering thud. As those at the front coughed from the swirling puffs of dust, light once again flooded the cave.

Screams rippled through the chamber, the walls amplifying their fear until the sound screeched in Emry's ears.

"No." Aspen looked at the beams of light in horror. "No, it's going to come through, it's going to..."

They began to climb up the door, so frantically transparent that the lute swung through their body and banged against the stone as they went.

"Aspen!" Emry reached for their ankle, but his hand swiped right through it. "Aspen, what in Hara's name are you doing?"

"What Hara's supposed to be doing!"

"You're not strong enough—"

But the spirit had already dropped down out of sight. Emry's hands trembled, his breath caught in his lungs. He looked back into the chamber.

"Emry?" Multiple voices rattled over the din. "Where are you?"

He turned away, steadied his hands as best he could, and climbed up the door. Once his silhouette reached the light, he heard the voices again, closer this time.

"Oh, gods—Emry Karic, you get back *down* here—"

He vaulted over the side and slid down into the stream, into the muddy waters and the mountain air that smelled like a storm. Ahead of him, Aspen was looking out over the hills, standing still despite the shaking ground.

"Cedar did it," they breathed as Emry approached. "Look."

All around the mountains, luminous white shields expanded to cover the forest. Some were hardly a speck on the horizon, others ballooned to cover the tallest trees. As they watched, the soil began to swell at their feet.

Aspen set down the lute at the base of the dead tree. "If they can do it," they said, "I can, too."

They set their hands out in front of them—but the shields that tried to grow there only shattered.

"Not without any strength, you're not." Emry couldn't keep his voice steady. "Look at you, you're—you're not even—"

"Then I'll attach to something else, something stronger!" Aspen searched around wildly—but the foliage around them was starting to glow white, and the canopy above glimmered faintly against the darkening sky.

Emry took a deep breath. Stopped to recall every detail of those he loved, who were standing in the cave right now. His mother and father, keeping Marley close. Marley reaching her hand out toward Georgie. And Cal—Cal with her oversized Council jacket, who had forgiven and apologized and loved him again. No, loved him still.

Emry held out his hand. "Use me."

Aspen took a step back. "No. No, it'll kill you—"

"We're going to die anyway if you don't."

A roiling wave of white crested over the farthest mountain. Then the next closest, then the next. Emry gestured again with his hand, ignoring the tears that stung his eyes. "Please, Aspen. I trust you."

The wave crashed up over the hill across the road. Aspen grabbed his hand, and his vision went blank.

FORTY-SIX

EMRY'S KNEES hit the shuddering earth, and his hand flew up to his heart of its own volition. The world had shrunk to nothing but the pain that flooded his veins.

Let me in, you've got to let me in! Aspen's voice floated somewhere in the darkness, hard to hear over the pounding in his head.

How?

Just let go, let me take control!

Emry forced out a gasping breath and relaxed into the pain, as if another current was shoving him to the bottom of the river. Anywhere he felt the spirit energy fighting to get in, he let that muscle loose. He thought the effort would release his body to the ground, but the moment he let go of his arms, something else swooped in to hold him up.

Yes, that's it—

He let go of his legs, and they stood of their own accord.

Almost!

He focused on the ache in his head and released it. Instantly, his vision returned to him.

Nothing had changed outside—leaves still whipped past his face in the storm-laden wind; the wall of white still surged up the hill. But he wasn't the one widening his stance, or holding up his palm toward it. Even his breath felt alien as he inhaled deeply, more deeply than he thought was possible, then exhaled and flexed his fingers.

As the wave barreled past the old fane, a shield burst out from his hands, arcing backward in time to guide the flow of spirit energy up and over the waterfall behind them. The river of white flooded up over them, the impact of its energy thudding like a drum against Emry's palms.

Then Aspen lifted his chin so they could both watch the deluge above his head. Blinding particles of energy stuck to the shield, as if someone had forcibly thrown the night sky upon them. As the stars tried to push through, the constant wind whipped leaves and branches against the barrier, applying an erratic, jarring force alongside the wave's unrelenting pressure. Ahead of them, the dead tree creaked and bent backward in the gale.

But Aspen's shield held strong.

You did it, Emry said, though his mouth didn't move. *How long can you hold this?*

I have no idea.

Then hands began to pound at the shield, a new force against the barrier. Ghostly palms appeared left and right; shoes kicked at the wall. Emry wanted to jump back, but Aspen kept his legs locked.

I don't understand, why can't they come in? he asked.

I had to make the shield strong enough.

The hands pounded more frantically.

Aspen, you made it too strong, you have to let them inside—

I can't weaken it, it might let the wave in!

Then can you expand it?

I can try.

Emry's breath shuddered as Aspen pulled more energy from him to expand the dome. Glowing hands quickly turned into arms, then shoulders, then bodies of people falling into the safety of the barrier as it bowed outward to embrace them. Some of them pulsated terribly, stumbling on their damaged legs or clutching torsos that burst white. Aspen waved Emry's hand to guide them behind him. They took one look at him, with his light-riddled veins and Hara knows what else, and staggered away without hesitation.

Ahead, more hands slammed into the shield.

Can you keep it going?

We won't be able to save them all.

I know that. Just try.

Aspen moved his body forward, pulling more energy with every step. Emry's heart stuttered this time, and one of his legs gave out.

That's it, I'm not going any farther.

But—

No. I'm not.

Unable to look away, Emry watched as the last remaining hands gradually stopped pounding and disappeared into the white fog. All the while, the roaring wind and the boiling earth continued around them, and his other leg gave out a minute later, sending him to his knees. *How much longer?*

We're close—look, it's starting to lift!

Some of the energy building up on the dome was beginning to wink out—but far too slowly. Emry's arms shook. *Aspen—*

We'll make it through. Just a few more seconds.

I can't.

Yes, you can.

A jolting thud shook the ground behind them, and Aspen whipped Emry's head back toward the cave. Someone—or many someones—had knocked the broken door back down to let the newcomers inside. But several people were headed the wrong way, up over the fallen slab and out into the light. They all staggered to a stop when they saw him kneeling on the ground by the barrier.

Tell them something, Emry begged.

Tell them what?

Cal screamed.

I don't know, tell them I—

Emry, I can't, I have to focus.

Georgie tried to run toward him. It took every other member of his family to hold her back.

Please—

The wind hurled a broken tree trunk at the shield, and as Aspen ripped more energy away to strengthen the dome against it, Emry lost his vision again. He couldn't see their faces anymore, but their screams kept going.

You don't have to hold on for much longer, Aspen said. *Just—just three seconds, okay?*

Okay.

Three—

His hearing dropped out, leaving nothing but a high-pitched ringing. His left arm fell to his side.

Two—

His right arm dropped.

One!

As the ground settled, Aspen let go of his body like a puppet, and he crumpled onto the soil. His senses expanded back out into the world, but for a moment, there was hardly anything to see or hear. No birds or humans spoke. Not even a leaf rustled. All he saw was the gray sky above him.

Then the full weight of Aspen's consciousness came rushing back to him, and his body railed against it with all of his remaining strength. He wanted to run, *had* to run, but the possession locked his body to the ground with darting spasms of pain.

Can you walk? Aspen's thoughts wavered. *You need to get me closer to somewhere I can attach to—*

I can't move. Emry's lungs couldn't break out of their shallow pattern. *I can't breathe—you have to get out—*

I don't have the strength—you have to push me out!

Leaves shifted around his head as several pairs of feet surrounded him. As his mind fought against Aspen, he couldn't seem to focus on their faces—but he could feel them, their heartbeats, the way their lungs caught as they looked down at him.

"Ed, tell me he's breathing—"

"Barely—Emry, can you hear us?"

"You get out of my baby brother *right now*—"

"Georgie, don't," Cal cut in. "He needs the lute. Where's the lute?"

"Over here!" Marley called fearfully. He could hear broken strings and wood jangling as she moved. Cal choked.

"Oh no."

"Calliope, what does he need?"

"Something living, a plant, anything still alive around here—"

"Emry, stay with us." He felt his mother's wedding ring as she grabbed his glowing hand. Tears dripped down onto his arm. "Please—please, we just got you back."

"Son, you can do this."

Emry closed his eyes and gasped for breath. He tried to wrap his fingers around his parents', but he couldn't move them. Pain rolled through his body in waves in a last attempt to expel Aspen, and something closed within his throat.

"Cal, I found this—"

"Put it in the lute. Um—that piece. Yes, that's it."

Someone placed a bundle of smooth wood on his chest, and through the noise of his connection with Aspen, he could feel something else—a tiny sapling, planted inside the broken rose of the lute, its roots trying to take hold in the loose soil within its new home.

Cal touched Emry's shoulder. "Aspen, this is all we've got. You have to jump now."

Emry, you have to push. Can you do that?

Though his eyes were closed, he felt them all looking down at him.

Yes.

"Come on, Aspen."

Aspen—thank you—

I'll see you soon.

He used the last of his strength to force Aspen out, sending every-thing he could toward the sapling. The broken remnants of the lute rocked violently, and Cal snatched them up before they could topple off him.

Emry gasped in his first full, desperate breath.

"Oh, thank Hara—"

"Emry, can you hear us?"

He nodded weakly and opened his eyes. His family's faces, all half-shrouded by their curls, crowded the left side of his vision, while Cal covered the right. He smiled in relief. "Everyone...okay?"

Georgie slapped his arm. "Your eyes"—she hiccupped through tears—"your eyes were glowing, and you're asking us if *we're* okay?"

Emry gave a breathy laugh, winced, and inched his head toward Cal, who was cradling the broken lute with one hand and holding his wrist with the other. "Are they there?"

She set the pieces down next to his head. "Aspen? Are you in there?"

At first, nothing. Cal's grip on his wrist tightened.

Then the tiniest and wispiest of mice crawled up out of the rose, onto the sapling's largest leaf, and wiggled their fuzzy ears at him.

"What are you worried about?" their voice echoed weakly off the remains of the lute. "I said I'd see you soon."

FORTY-SEVEN

EVERYTHING after that point was as murky as river water. Emry vaguely recalled being lifted into the carriage at the bottom of the hill, while strange voices shouted questions at them from all directions. He remembered a bed, briefly, then the sweet, swirling air of a tunnel. The steady motion of the boat must have sent him into his deepest sleep, for he didn't wake up until he was back in another bed, this one far more familiar.

The Karics hadn't done much to his room in the past three years. The windowsill was still littered with striped rocks that Marley had gifted him when she was a toddler. A music stand collected dust in one corner, while a pair of old slippers from Nana gathered an army of dust bunnies in competition. The only jarringly new element was the woman playing Spirit's Cross with Marley by the fireplace, while Georgie leaned against the mantle in boredom.

"Please, someone, make a move. It's been an hour."

"It's been five minutes, Georgie. Don't rush Cal." Marley set her chin on her hand. "Or maybe do rush her. If she makes a mistake, I might have a chance at winning this."

Fighting through a full-body ache, Emry turned over onto his shoulder and propped his head up on his hand.

"Cal, the easiest solution is to say that your piece has grown wings, then attack the other pieces from the sky," he croaked. "Then all you have to do is survive my sister trying to hit you on the head with the board. I've done it before, it's worth a shot."

"Called it! I knew he'd wake up today." Marley leapt up and ran out the door. "Mum, Dad, he's alive!"

"Awake, he's *awake*! Rotting hell..." Georgie called out the door, then strode over to feel Emry's forehead. "All right, on a scale of one to alive, how alive are you?"

Emry collapsed back onto the pillow. Every movement hurt in some way; pain signals scattered across his body and muddled together in his head. He rubbed the spot between his eyebrows with a grimace.

"Let's say...one foot still in the grave," he muttered.

"That's fair. You hungry?"

"Starving."

"Makes sense, you've been out for a week. I'll get you something before the cavalry arrives." Georgie ruffled his hair and followed Marley out of the room. Cal glanced at the door, then took Georgie's place at his side.

"Welcome back to the world." She bent down and kissed him—a careful, restrained kiss, as if he could still fall apart at any moment. A deep warmth spread through him, and he sank further into the bed. As she pulled away, she kept her hand at his cheek. "How are you feeling?"

"Feels like a spirit possessed my body or something." He tried to push himself to sit and gave up. "Cal, not that I'm not incredibly happy to see you the moment I wake up, but"—he took her hand—"I thought you would have gone home with your parents?"

Cal smiled and squeezed his fingers. "I told them I would come home once you woke up. It did help that Aspen asked me to stay— they were terrified they had broken you entirely."

"Cal's exaggerating," a voice called from beyond the foot of the bed. "But…I was a little scared."

Emry craned his neck to see where the voice had come from, and found that they had placed his broken lute—or rather, Georgie's stolen, broken lute—on a chair by his bed. The sapling planted inside it had already grown a few inches. "Aspen, how are you doing? Looks like you've found a new little grove."

"Yes! I like your family a lot. They're very kind."

Emry grinned. "I meant the plant, Aspen."

"Oh. Yes, I like that, too."

"Good." Emry froze and turned to Cal. "Hara take me—love, I've left you alone with my family for days on end with no defense. How are you? They haven't annoyed you too much, have they? If my sisters have asked you too many questions, I can yell at them—"

Cal laughed and shook her head as she forced him back onto the pillow with a gentle push.

"I've survived just fine, I promise. They've been exceedingly kind to me, even when I rudely refused to leave your side on the trip over."

He gathered enough strength to lift her hand to his lips. "I had no doubt they'd adore you."

Soon after, the cavalry did arrive, bearing food, hugs, and more questions about his well-being. After the hundredth reassurance, Emry tried again to sit up and look out the window.

"How did Senne do in the wave? You said Nana stayed in her cottage—"

Tessa yanked the curtains closed before he could get a glimpse of the outdoors. "Nana's fine, we've checked on her. She barricaded her place and refused to leave her dogs." She felt his forehead. "Are you sure I shouldn't call for a physician?"

It didn't strike Emry as odd until he began to walk—slowly, and with complaints—and Aspen declined to accompany him, not even as a mouse on his shoulder. Any questions he had about the outside world were waved away with vague comments, and when he mentioned offhand a desire to walk around outside, his entire family leapt to direct him to the garden in the back of the house.

"It's lovely this time of year! Cal will help you along." Edward opened the back door for them while Tessa conveniently blocked the path to the front door. Emry limped out, looked at all the dead, frosted plants, and turned to his walking partner.

"Cal, what's going on?"

"So lovely!" Cal said loudly, then took his arm and led him around a few hedges until they were out of sight of the windows. "Listen, your family didn't want to bother you until you were feeling better."

"Bother me about what?" He followed her to a mossy bench near an overgrown fountain—one that he may or may not have broken as a child and blamed on Georgie. "Did Senne not make it through the wave? Are we the only ones left in Vidanya? I saw Marko and Stef's letter, they said they were fine—"

"No, no. Not quite that." Cal cleared her throat and took his hand. "From the word your family has been getting, and from the letters my parents have sent..." When she bit her lip, searching for the right words, Emry frowned. The hesitation wasn't helping his nerves.

"Cal?"

She took a breath. "There was damage from the wave, as we expected. Forests and farms lost, of course, and—thousands of people weren't able to find shelter in time, either. For those that survived, the medics are doing what they can with Cedar's method to heal them."

Emry examined the dead grass as he recalled the glowing hands striking Aspen's shield. It was too easy to extend his imagination to the bodies that must have piled up beyond the shimmering wall. "What about Senne?" he mumbled.

She rubbed her thumb against the back of his hand. "Senne did well, for such a northern city. With its proximity to the caves, and all of its stone buildings...Senne will be fine."

He nodded, trying to push away the intrusive image of his hometown as dead and blackened. They were fine, he told himself. His city was fine, his family was fine, his friends were fine.

But she hadn't told him everything yet.

"That doesn't explain why I can't leave the house." He met her gaze. "What else happened?"

She took his hand in both of hers this time, and a smile spread across her face. "The Council's plans and the spirits that Cedar spoke to saved thousands, Em. The papers keep mentioning domes and shields appearing all over Vidanya. Farms and forests, even entire villages, were saved. Not to mention the places that would have starved if their crops had died. People are..." Hesitation crept into her smile. "They're connecting all those stories to what you did in Dawnstone, and they're starting to talk. About you specifically. They want to know what you did and how you did it."

Emry swallowed. "How do they know it was me?"

"It may have been our fault," Cal said quietly. "We called out your name in the cave a few times, and—well, when your eyes glow and your entire body glows and you're protecting hundreds of people who just traveled the river system with your last name on it...some people were very vocal about connecting the dots."

They fell silent, and Emry watched a bird flit around the fountain for a while. The horrific images of the aftermath had come so easily to his mind, but the idea of people talking about him—that was more difficult to envision. "They've reached out to my family, then."

"Your family hasn't told anyone anything, and Aspen's been hiding," she reassured him. "But...there's no explaining away what you did. Some people are starting to think you created all the shields, or that you turned into a spirit."

"That's ridiculous—"

"It is, but they've got nothing else to go on. The stories will only get bigger with the less information they have."

"I'll wait it out, then." Emry ran a hand through his hair. "I'll just stay inside for a year and they'll forget all about it."

"Stay inside with your family for a year?"

He sighed. "You're right, never mind."

They both sat in the company of the birds and their tumbling thoughts for a while, until Cal smiled again.

"What? You've got something?" Emry nudged her. "Is it better than faking my death? Because I was thinking about what my cause of death would be. If we told everyone that Georgie finally snapped and killed me, I think most people in Senne would believe it."

"No, not that."

"You're right, I have to consider the how." Emry tapped his chin. "Poisoning is too subtle for her. I'm thinking a good, honest stabbing—"

Cal stood. "Ella Sorman still owes you a favor, right?"

Emry looked up at her. "I suppose so."

"Then write to her," she said. "She knows how to handle this sort of fame. Perhaps she can write a song to deflect the attention, or explain what really happened."

"And people would listen to that?"

"Well, people are out there now listening to rumors about how you're Hara's son, so I'd say yes, they'll listen to Ella's song." She took his hand. "Come on, let's go write the letter."

He stayed put on the bench. "One kiss before we go in? You're so overwhelmingly pretty when you're helping me avoid faking my own death."

She rolled her eyes, sat down next to him, and obliged. "Is that all, Mr. Karic?" Her eyes lingered on his lips. He grinned at her.

"Absolutely not, Ms. Breslin."

Eventually, the letter did get written, and several days later, Cal ran out of excuses not to return to her parents in Etris.

"But you'll return in a month, won't you?" Aspen begged at the front door as she prepared to leave. They had returned to their terrier form, though it was rather small. "You'll be back for my birthday?"

"Yes, Aspen." Cal bit back a smile. "I'll return for your birthday, I promise."

As soon as Aspen realized that people visited others for such events, they had insisted that they, too, had something called a birth-day, and it conveniently landed right on the next opportune time for Cal to visit.

But the month without Cal still dragged. With no access to a functioning lute, the only entertainment—or stressor—Emry had while he convalesced were the stories that came in about him, and his ensuing attempts to leak out a more modest truth.

"This is Mrs. Castaic coming along the path now," Tessa whispered to him as she reached for the front door. "You remember her—she used to give you marzipan when you were little?"

"I remember. Terrible gossip?"

"The worst."

"Excellent. And what does she think of all this?"

"She thinks you wrestled the wave with your bare hands."

Emry rolled his eyes. "Oh, please, anyone who's seen me cannot possibly think that—"

But his mother was already opening the door with a warm smile. "Mrs. Castaic, you are so kind to drop by!"

"Of course, of course!" The old woman shuffled in, a box of marzipan sweets in her hand. Marley graciously scurried off with it, while Emry leaned on the cane that Nana had left at the house. Mrs. Castaic's eyes practically glittered when she spotted the man of the hour. "How are you feeling, my dear boy?" She looked him up and down, as if she expected him to still be glowing. "I have heard the strangest things..."

If she had entered thinking that he had gotten into fisticuffs with a natural disaster, she left with a slightly more boring, if more truthful, story to tell—though Aspen had certainly charmed her in their fluffy terrier form, as a sort of consolation prize.

"I don't mind this." Aspen transformed back into their human form as the door closed behind the gossiping woman. "I'm meeting a lot of people this way. Do those marzipan things taste any good?"

"Doesn't matter, Marley's eaten them all by now," Emry said. "Mum, do you think anyone will be visiting tomorrow?"

"Of course, dear. My money's on Ms. Larga visiting again."

He groaned. "But I told her all about Cal last time she visited, specifically to dissuade her."

"In her eyes, if Ms. Breslin doesn't have a ring yet, that means you're still ripe for the taking—"

"Mum, *please.*"

Tessa grinned. "Northern women are insistent! How do you think I landed your father?"

"Hara take me—"

Marley swung into the hall, licking the last of the sugar off her hands. "Emry, I need to go into town. Would you like to come with me?"

"Yes, please!" Aspen was already out the door and running down the path. "You keep talking about the city, but you haven't let me see it yet!"

In some ways, walking about in broad daylight was easier than entertaining guests in Senne. One could say all they liked behind closed doors and in their teahouse huddles, but Hara forbid one say anything directly to the man in question while he was running his errands.

"This is nice," Emry said, breathing in the winter flurries that were melting over the cream-colored canals. The white sky and light stone of the city made the day feel as bright as springtime, while retaining the chill he had missed so much. "So, what are we shopping for today?"

"Nothing." Marley shrugged and brushed a few snowflakes off her gloves. "I just thought you'd like the walk."

"That's kind of you, Mar."

The corner of her mouth twitched upward. "But there is a new chocolatier around the corner..."

"I knew it."

All was still going well when they entered the shop—and that's precisely when his luck ended.

"Could you please explain to me what all of these taste like?" Aspen was immediately on their tiptoes at the counter, trying to peer over the glass at the little squares on the other side. "I'm a spirit, you see, and I can't eat food. But you've decorated these things so nicely—"

That was all the shop needed. There were certainly rules against bothering humans, but the book about bothering spirits had yet to be written.

"Could I get your opinion on this type of mint I've been growing?" One of the chocolatiers held up a finger and rushed out to the back of the shop. As he ran, a young boy leaned over to ogle at Aspen's lute, which was now bound together with a mix of vines and wood glue.

"Do you really live in there?" the boy asked.

"Yes, I do," Aspen said. "Here, would you like a flower?"

A bloom unfurled out of the lute's rose, and Aspen handed it to the child, whose eyes grew wide. But before he could ask any more questions, a young woman sipping drinking chocolate at a table leaned in. "Can spirits make people fall in love?"

Aspen snorted. "I wish. You should've seen the trouble I ran into trying to get Emry and Cal back together."

The woman's eyes flicked to Emry, who immediately tried to hide behind Marley. "Mar, how badly do you want this chocolate?" he whispered. She waved him off.

"Just let them enjoy themself and help me pick which caramel to get."

But the shop kept filling up with newcomers and questions.

"So, is there really a spirit at the fane up on the hill?" one man asked. "Because I've been offering fruit there for weeks now and my garden still won't grow. Do you think they hate me?"

"They don't hate you, but they can't grow your garden for you. It's probably too far away—"

"Was it actually you that put up the shield in Dawnstone?"

"How many other spirits do you know?"

"Is Hara real? Do you talk to her often?"

Marley shoved a cup of chocolate into Emry's hand and dragged him over to the table in the corner to observe Aspen, who was now sitting on the counter dispensing advice, handing out flowers, and growing the chocolatier's mint plant until it spilled over onto the floor. Emry sighed and sipped the chocolate. "What am I going to do with them?"

"Let them figure it out themselves." Marley popped a caramel into her mouth. "This is their new life, after all."

FORTY-EIGHT

When Cal finally graced the Karics' doorstep again, no response had arrived from Ella Sorman—but Cal clutched a letter of her own as she ran through the dusting of snowflakes toward their front door.

"Gods, finally!" Emry threw open the door as soon as she appeared. "Someone *sane* will finally enter this house—"

"Cal's here!" Marley shouted up the stairs behind him. As she turned, a blur of gray fur shot out of the entryway.

"Cal!" Aspen's wolf form almost bowled over the newcomer. "I've missed you so much!"

Cal grinned and scratched their ears. "Happy birthday, Aspen. I missed you, too."

"Cal, how was the—" Emry started out into the snow, but Marley shoved past him, followed by Tessa.

"I'll help get your luggage!" Marley called.

Tessa examined Cal's thin sleeve. "Dear, is that the only coat you've got? I must find you something proper, otherwise Senne is going to freeze you solid."

Georgie wandered up next to Emry. "Cal's here already? Damn, I should've told Dad to come back an hour ago." She checked her pocket watch and started outside, but Emry blocked her.

"Excuse me, I refuse to be last in greeting her—"

But he had just made the mistake of making it a competition, one that he promptly lost when Georgie hip-checked him into the snow and gave Cal a victorious hug. "You didn't get stuck in the mud outside of Briar, did you?"

"No, thank Hara." Cal tilted her head down at Emry, whose clothes were soaking in the snow. "Are you going to say hello to me, Mr. Karic?"

"Say hello?" He scrambled up to his feet and grabbed her waist. "Oh, I'll do more than that."

He dipped down and kissed her. Marley made gagging sounds off to his right, while Georgie groaned and walked away. Cal squirmed as his wet sleeve tickled her neck. "Shiro's beard, that's cold—"

"Welcome to winter in Senne!" He picked her up and carried her into the foyer, melting like the snow in her hair as she laughed into his collar.

"Tea will be out shortly!" Tessa called as he set Cal down on her feet again. The moment she had regained her balance, she dug into her pocket and shoved an envelope into Emry's hand.

"Here, read it."

He glanced at the return address—the Council building in Vornik —then took out the card and mumbled the first words aloud. "Dear Ms. Breslin, we offer our congratulations on your impending gradua- tion—wait, hold on, are you serious?"

She tapped the paper. "Keep reading."

"And we'd like to offer you a position..." He looked up. "They're offering you a job?"

"I'd be an aide. A research one, focusing on surges." She pointed to the letter. "That paragraph there is praising my work with the Alacova shelter, and that one is pretending like they already had surge research to begin with..."

"And that one there?"

"Saying I would start in a month."

He searched her glowing face. "And you're sure this is what you want to do?" He set his hands on her arms. "You don't have to, you know. You can still stay at the Academy, continue your classes…"

She nodded, unable to contain a wide smile. "I'm sure. I'd like to do this."

He shouted, dropped the letter, and lifted her up off the floor in as tight of a hug as he could give, trying to infuse it with all the pride he felt—and in return, she bubbled happily and kicked her feet. "I thought about writing to you before I got here, but I couldn't. I had to see your face when I told you!"

"I'm so glad you waited. I cannot describe how proud I am—"

"What happened?" Aspen shifted into human form to pick up the letter, and Marley read over their shoulder. Marley then squealed, which summoned the rest of the house all over again.

"How much can I change the menu for tonight?" Tessa nearly ran in circles in the foyer. "We've got to have something more celebratory—"

"Incredible, Cal, truly." Georgie grinned. Behind her, Aspen was using the news as an excuse to hug everyone in the room.

"I don't know what an aide is, but I am also very proud." Aspen looked up at Cal. "Does celebrating mean you can stay for even longer?"

"I don't know about that, but"—Cal kissed their cheek—"I also don't want to completely take away from your newly minted birthday. Would you like to open a present?"

Human form was no longer enough for Aspen, for they immediately popped into terrier form and streaked around the foyer.

"Yes! I'd love to! What'd you get me? Do I have to guess? How do presents work?"

"Is it in your luggage?" Marley was already halfway up the stairs. "I'll lead you to your room!"

Aspen settled for running in circles and leaping on all the Karics' laps in the drawing room until Cal came back down the stairs, having shed her coat and retrieved a very lute-shaped case.

"You didn't." Aspen froze. "You didn't!"

They immediately burst into owl form, flapped halfway through the foyer, descended as a wolf, and came sprinting back as a dog.

"Aspen, you haven't even opened it yet!" Cal dodged them on her way into the room. "Come on, sit and let me give it to you."

"Did you know about this?" Aspen fell into human form in a chair next to Emry's, breathing heavily. Emry laughed and nodded.

"It was my idea."

"You'll really teach me how to play?"

"That's the whole point. Go on, open the case."

As the spirit carefully lifted the lute out of the case and babbled about all the songs they were going to learn, another knock sounded in the foyer.

"Your father?" Cal glanced over, then turned her attention back to Aspen.

"No, he never knocks." Georgie leaned to look out the window. "Weir's eyes, that's a large coach."

Tessa opened the door to allow a woman inside, her impossibly bright colors and stately posture a stark contrast to the watercolor sky behind her.

Everyone in the drawing room leapt to their feet at once, except for Aspen, who remained sitting and swinging their feet. When they saw the newcomer, they held up their new lute.

"Hello, Ms. Sorman!" they said. "Look at what I got for my birthday!"

SEVERAL MINUTES and nervous introductions later, Emry sat alone in the drawing room with Vidanya's most prominent musician, the shuffling of his family's feet behind the door betraying their poorly hidden attempt to eavesdrop.

"May I offer you any tea?" he started.

"No, thank you, I'll only be a moment." She waved her hand. "You seem to be fully recovered from your time in Dawnstone."

"Yes, thank you."

"And Aspen as well," she said, her eyes glittering in amusement. Emry gave her a nervous smile.

"Yes—they bounced back rather quickly, as you can imagine."

"I can."

Emry tried not to fidget. "Ella, about that letter I sent, I hope it wasn't an impertinence—"

"Ah yes, the new yoke of fame." Ella reached into a large bag at her side. "You know, Vornik still thinks you summoned all the spirit shields yourself."

"I can assure you that's not—"

"I know." She handed him a stack of sheet music. "Here."

He scanned the music and the lyrics written below it. Hummed a few of the bars under his shaky breath. "You...really wrote a song about me?"

"If I read your letter correctly, the lyrics should be a more...accurate depiction than what's currently circulating." She tilted her head side to side. "Though I admit I embellished slightly for impact."

"I..." His cheeks grew hot. "I can't thank you enough, Ella. This is more than I ever expected."

"I never said this would come for free." She took the sheet music from him and dropped a small velvet bag into his hand instead. He overturned it, and a simple golden circle on a pin fell into his palm.

He nearly dropped it out of shock.

"But—I thought..." Was he still breathing? Unclear. "I thought I had completely ruined my standing by—"

"You only ruin your standing if I say so, Mr. Karic." Her eyes flashed. "And what I have in mind for you is more than you may think."

He tore his gaze away from the pin, hardly able to think straight. "I'm sorry?"

"There is a need to bring the Guild back to its roots. What it used to do before the Thalis councils found peace."

"And what is that, exactly?"

Ella stood. "Visit me when you're next in Vornik and we'll discuss. Oh, and"—she reached back into her pocket and procured another velvet bag—"I am extending the invitation to Aspen as well. If they aren't returning to their grove in Tazlo, that is."

"I'm not!" Aspen's voice echoed through the door, followed by several panicked hushes. Ella inclined her head to the door, holding back a smile.

"Until we meet again, Mr. Karic."

Once she retreated back into the flurries outside, the parlor door flew open.

"Emry?" Cal managed to throw one arm out and block the family from stampeding in, but she couldn't wipe the smile from her face. "Em, what was that?"

He held up the pin with an unsteady hand and a shaky grin. "Cal...can I come with you to Vornik?"

WANT MORE?

Did you enjoy *The Stray Spirit*?

Leave a review and spread the word!

~

Want bonus scenes?

Sign up for my newsletter to get three bonus scenes:

https://rkashwick.com/newsletter/

~

THE LUTESONG SERIES

The Stray Spirit

The Spirit Well

The Spirit's Curse

THE SIDE QUEST ROW SERIES

A Rival Most Vial

A Captured Cauldron

A Draught for a Dragon

ACKNOWLEDGMENTS

This truly took a village, and I could write a whole second book filled only with thanks.

First and foremost, to my husband Joe: your patience is everlasting, your feedback is immaculate, your face is handsome. This book would not have existed without your support.

I'd also like to thank those who who turned this into a readable book. Starting with my beta readers and sensitivity readers—Emma, Mel, Nik, Creed, Zani, Eve, Milo, and Beau—all of whom lent their time and knowledge to improving this story. Then my editor, Kim Halstead, who swooped in with near-psychic insights that added a level of depth I didn't realize I was missing. And a final thanks to my proofreader, Stephanie Slagle, who saved me from my gross misuse of the word *towards*.

Let's not forget my cover designer, Andrew Davis, and my illustrator, Lucia Vázquez de Prada. It was an utter privilege to work with you both. Thank you so much for your time and talents.

And finally, to my family, teachers, and friends who have supported me throughout my journey, even when I was a child writing horrendous mystery novellas and unfinished epic fantasies: thank you, thank you, thank you.

ABOUT THE AUTHOR

By day, R.K. Ashwick herds cats in the animation industry. By night, she writes, bakes, and herds her literal cat around the living room. She lives with her husband (and said cat) in California.

The Stray Spirit is her debut fantasy novel—but don't worry, she hasn't learned her lesson, and will write again.

For more information, visit rkashwick.com.